END OF LIES

A POLITICAL THRILLER

COUNTLESS LIES SERIES

BRADLEY WEST

COPYRIGHT AND DISCLAIMER

Bradley West
www.bradleywest.net

Published in 2019 by Bradley Alan West
Cover art, layout and design: Aneirin Flynn
Editing: Geoff Smith
Proofreading: Sèphera Giron

Disclaimer: *End of Lies* addresses many real-life topics, starting with Russia's interference in the 2016 US elections, but the characters and events depicted are fictitious and the reader should draw no factual inferences from the story that follows.

End of Lies / Bradley West – 1st ed. March 2019
ISBN: 978-981-11-8388-1 (paperback)
ISBN: 978-981-11-8387-4 (eBook)

TABLE OF CONTENTS

CAST OF CHARACTERS IN ORDER OF APPEARANCE

ROBERT "BOB" NOLAN: former CIA codebreaker, hero of MH370 hijacking plot, project Abyss operations head, outside Ft. Irwin, California.

TRAVIS RYDER: former SEAL, retired head of South and Southeast Asia Security, DEA Rangoon; gun shop owner, Nacogdoches, Texas.

ALI HANIF: Co-Head of Enforcement & Operations, Anti-Narcotics Force ("ANF"), Karachi, Pakistan.

YU KAILI: personal envoy of president Liu Zhenchang to North Korea, former head of the Foreign Affairs Bureau (CIA-equivalent), Ministry of State Security, China.

JOANIE LAM SHAO YIN: Estranged Mrs. Bob Nolan, Singapore.

MAJOR GENERAL (RET.) NEIL PAYNE: Special Presidential Envoy on national security matters, head of project Abyss, Washington, D.C.

ANATOLY CHUMAKOV: head of the Farewell Group, political lobbyists, Washington, D.C. Former Director of Surveillance, Federal Security Services ("FSB," domestic successor to the KGB), Moscow.

ANDREI PORTNIKOV: head of the Federal Security Services ("FSB"), Moscow.

MISTER LOVE: pseudonym of the leader of Higher Love, a right-wing US organization plotting to overthrow the Constitution and install a military dictatorship.

MEI LING NOLAN: real estate investment banker and Brazilian ju-jitsu student, Novato, California.

BERT NOLAN: fresh graduate of Tulane University, New Orleans. Former Singapore Army Commando and amateur mixed martial arts fighter.

FRANK COULTER: former senior CIA clandestine operations officer held under house arrest in Northern California.

SAM HECKER: Deputy Director, Office of Investigative Intelligence, Drug Enforcement Administration ("DEA"), Washington, D.C. Former head of the DEA South and Southeast Asia.

PAOLO AND JAVIER DOZIER: Sons of Minnie Dozier, head of the Medellín Cartel, and nephews of Randy Dozier, Washington, D.C.

VLADIMIR AUTUROVICH GREGORIEV: second-in-command of Russia's Foreign Intelligence Service ("SVR," the successor organization to the KGB's First Chief Directorate), Washington, D.C.

DON RANDY DOZIER: Head of the Medellín Cartel US operations, Washington, D.C.

COLONEL RICHARD ("DICK") BURGE: Commander of Camp Stanley, San Antonio, Texas. Former US Special Forces (a.k.a. Green Beret) senior officer.

TONY JOHNSON: former US Army Ranger and CIA interrogator, former contract employee of Black Ice (Afghanistan), freelance military operator, Houston.

DAVE MARMOT: former vice president of the United States.

END OF LIES

BRADLEY WEST

CHAPTER ONE

ANOTHER TRIP TO THE ATM

MONDAY MORNING, JULY 14, 2014: SHARJAH, UNITED ARAB EMIRATES

Retired CIA officer Bob Nolan had declined the White House's entreaties to head a new, ultra-secret project and instead decided to reconcile with his estranged wife and children. The next day Nolan departed D.C. for his home in Singapore, with a week's detour in the United Arab Emirates on personal business. In the three months he'd been away, he'd realized that a life in perfect isolation was much less desirable than an imperfect marriage. Now it was a matter of how to handle that fraught conversation with his wife, Joanie.

At the moment, Nolan sat in a sweltering surveillance van with two Drug Enforcement Administration moonlighters. His hired hand was in the lobby of the Sharjah Bank branch that serviced the surrounding industrial zone. At the appropriate time, the man posing as the account holder would power up a clone of a dead hacker's phone, retrieve the confirmatory PIN, and provide the bank with the six digits required to complete the two-factor identification process. What the stand-in didn't know was the US's all-seeing National Security Agency would flag the clone as soon as it connected to a cellular network. Within a half-hour, the bank would be abuzz with armed men.

By Nolan's calculations, collecting the four fifty-five-pound suitcases was a twenty-five-minute event, from front door to loading dock. His man had been in Sharjah Bank for twenty-six minutes. More importantly, thirteen minutes had passed since he'd activated the cloned phone. The operator seated next to him monitored the video feeds while the headset-wearing driver scanned the conversations captured from the mikes they'd placed inside the bank earlier in the week. One of Nolan's burners buzzed. "Yes?"

"Better late than never. Our van just pulled out," said Travis Ryder, the DEA's head of South and Southeast Asia security. The former SEAL fidgeted in an office that faced the bank's parking garage entrance and exit. He'd collected a through-and-through in his right hip saving Nolan's ass in Pakistan. Ryder was a fan of the former Agency codebreaker, more recently recast in the roles of vigilante and unwilling media darling, but he didn't want to be Bob's bullet catcher again.

"About time. One of your men on it?"

"Yeah, the motorcyclist. Your squirter won't be able to give my man the slip even if he's Langley-trained."

"Hold on. Let me confirm the money's on the move." Nolan checked the adjacent screens. "Probably a decoy. None of the suitcases left the bank. I didn't tell Mustafa to switch cases, and he wouldn't have been able to swap contents in the fourteen minutes he's been AWOL."

"Here we go!" Ryder said. "Silver Cadillac Escalade, black windows, drove into the parking lot eight minutes ago and exited at speed in the opposite direction to our van. What do the beacons say?"

Nolan examined the screen and saw the flashing dots separate from the bank branch. "Money's on the move. Put your tails on the Caddy, and I'll swing around and pick you up in three."

"Aye, aye. Downstairs in two." Ryder winced as he stood up. He wiped his prints, limped out of the empty office, and took the service elevator. The DEA van pulled up. Nolan told the driver to hang back and look for anyone following the two DEA vehicles up ahead. This was Quantico Counter Surveillance 101, a course that Nolan had completed the prior month as part of a sixty-day crash course on field craft, compliments of the FBI.

Ryder answered his buzzing cell and put it on speaker. The motorcyclist's voice crackled. "I followed the lorry to a turnoff and have it in my binos. It drove across vacant land to a warehouse one hundred meters from the main road. It's nowhere near the handover point. From the map, there's no other way out. Advise."

"Observe, but don't interfere," Ryder said as he eased into the last captain's chair. "Let us know if you see anything else and follow it if it moves."

Nolan watched the progress of the Cadillac, splitting his attention between the radar scope and a large-scale map. It had left the surface streets and was on a freeway headed east, farther into the parched wasteland.

"OK, that's good enough. Let it go. Head to the Hilton on Corniche Street. Take your time and make certain we aren't followed." Their driver swung his head around in surprise but turned off Sheik Zayed Street and slowed.

"What are you doing?" Ryder asked. "The Hilton? Why the hell are we headed to the *Hilton*?"

"To safeguard our op, I arranged for the real pickup at Sharjah Bank's main office in a half-hour. Yesterday, I left four red suitcases at the branch office loaded with twenty-five kilograms each of photocopy paper. Then I asked the manager to safeguard the bags and, for a healthy bribe, persuaded him to release the luggage to anyone purporting to be Mr. Fareed Diyafah. We have to collect the person I recruited to impersonate Diyafah for the real handover."

"We're clean," the driver called out without taking his eyes off the rearview mirror. He was careful not to tip off possible pursuers, going so far as to brake before a fresh yellow light to give the impression of not being in a hurry.

"Goddammit, why didn't I know about this? If you didn't trust me, why fly me down here and hire me to pull together this team? I should have played golf."

"Your hip's bad and your knees are shot. You'd be lucky if you could drive the cart," Nolan retorted.

"Well, I could be sitting in the Snake Pit lounge nursing a bourbon."

"I'm certain you don't want to see any of the women in there in full daylight. Look, this is basic OPSEC. How was I to know if your crew was clean?"

"Fair enough," Ryder conceded, "but who's your second Diyafah? If he runs, we're stuffed."

"It's your old friend Ali Hanif."

"Ali Hanif? He's a Pakistani for Christ's sake!"

"His Arabic is perfect thanks to King Saud University. He's planning a big night out, so I hope you packed decent clothes," Nolan said. "Take a right here. We'll pick up our friend around the side."

"What about that oxygen thief you dropped on us?" Ryder sputtered. "Didn't you already front him twenty-five grand? He's gonna come looking for you once he realizes there's been a switch."

"That's another reason why you assembled this team. Your man on the Kawasaki has the van. If the driver's still alive, he's corrupt and the DEA can deal with him. As for the Escalade, you have two vehicles following it. Tell your men to round them up at their leisure. If you catch our stand-in and he tells you where he hid the twenty-five thousand I fronted, your crew can keep it, or give it to charity. You dispose of the hijacker and his crew any way you like."

"Your party, your rules. Let's do it."

Nolan said, "Let's focus on the next hour. We're ten minutes away from Ali. I'll give him the passport and the proper cloned phone. We'll load the cash into this vehicle and Ali will make his own way to the Sharjah Grand. As per the original plan, I'll still need you and your team to ride shotgun the rest of the day while I repack the cash and drop it off at the freight forwarders. After expenses and an honorarium to Ali, the leftover one point three mill is for you to divide among your crew. I will fly out tonight before State Security or US intel figure out what happened. I suggest that Ali and you get out of town tomorrow morning. If you'll excuse me, I need to channel my inner oilfield supplies shipping manager." Nolan removed his heavy black eyeglasses and blinked contacts into place. Then he changed clothes and readied his toiletries bag: there was a new Braun shaver to handle his mustache when this was over.

Ryder shook his head. "A lot of retirement plans depend on this Chinese puzzle box in your head, but remember, not a word to Hecker."

Nolan couldn't hide his surprise. "You think Sam's so straight he'll turn us in?"

"I used to. Now I wonder if he wouldn't bust us just so he could keep it all."

* * * * *

COOZ BAR, GRAND HYATT, DUBAI

Ali Hanif splashed eighteen-year-old Bowmore into his tumbler, then spilled some in the direction of Ryder's glass. It was late and the jazz bar was only one-third full. Ryder liked Cooz because he could always get a seat, the bartenders were good, and if he needed to leave in a hurry the hotel's main entrance was just outside.

"You might want to slow down," Ryder said. "We had two bottles of wine at dinner, and that half bottle of scotch is mostly you."

"It's my first night out since they murdered Lael," Hanif said. As the Co-Head of Enforcement & Operations, Anti-Narcotics Force Karachi, he collected enemies like Imran Khan attracted blondes. Hanif's Anglo-Pakistani wife had died when a stray round severed her femoral artery during a drive-by assassination attempt with Ryder aboard. Vengeance and mourning had been Hanif's sole companions until Nolan's offer induced him to accept this assignment.

"I know it's been three months," Ryder said, "but it seems like just last week."

Hanif looked deep into his drink and then threw the whiskey down, slamming the tumbler on the stone table and shattering the glass. A waiter hustled over muttering apologies. Ryder had already tipped a C-note when he'd bought the bottle, so there wouldn't be any fuss. They still had to fly incognito out of DXB early the next morning. Ryder's brain switched to damage control mode.

A self-confident olive-complexioned man in a suit entered the bar trailed by three heavies. He looked the patrons over before heading straight toward their table in the far corner.

"Ali, trouble brewing. Four on your six, a leader plus three trailers packing."

Hanif didn't change his body language but signaled with his eyes that he'd heard. He pulled the last sliver out of his palm and looked up.

Their uninvited guest sat down, his body men adopting the executive fig leaf posture with hands clasped across their groins as they formed a cordon behind their boss.

"Welcome to Dubai, Mr. Ryder," the man said. "We've been looking all night, and here you are hiding in plain sight." He turned to Hanif. "I'm pleased to make your acquaintance, Mr.—?"

"Fareed Diyafah," Ali said in a Saudi-inflected accent.

"Oh, still in character, are we? I'll make it easy for you. You two and your people took ten million dollars that didn't belong to you. We want the money, and we want the full story of what happened to the rightful owner."

Ryder suppressed a grimace. They were unarmed, half in the bag, and off the books—not exactly the winning hand. He looked at Hanif and recognized unabated fury. He'd seen that look before on raids when Hanif's men collared traffickers who dealt to children.

Ryder broke eye contact with his friend and scrutinized their antagonist. The man's English accent wasn't right, and his worn suit was out of fashion by ten years. This fellow wasn't an Emirati from the National Electronic Security Authority complaining about a blown sting, or even a mid-level State Security officer looking for a big score. He was an out-of-towner.

"I've got a limp thanks to your man Mazdaki," Ryder said. "He shot me on Lala Air Force Base three months ago. The base commander killed him in a fair gunfight. The money was stolen out of bin Laden's Swiss bank account. You VAJA assholes have nothing to complain about and are owed zero."

Only the headman startled at the sound of the acronym for Iran's intelligence service. Ryder intuited that his companions were local hires with lower training and commitment levels.

The Iranian stood up. "You will come with us, or my men will shoot you where you sit."

Feigning inebriation—and sobering up by the breath—Ryder lurched to his feet, peeled another hundred off his bankroll and fluttered it onto the tabletop. The former SEAL quickly doubled over, hands on knees as if he was about to vomit. "I'm going to be sick," Ryder groaned. "I need air."

The four smiled and one chuckled. Hanif held back, concurring with his friend's implicit choice. Rather than leave a bloody mess in public and possibly end up in jail, they'd take the fight elsewhere. The problem was that the four assailants might have vehicles outside with more men which could tip the odds impossibly against them. Hanif didn't care, but Ryder was taking a big risk.

Bismarck once said that God looks after fools, drunks and the United States. With good reason, the father of Germany had omitted third-rate hoodlums and freelancing intelligence officers. The Man in Charge and Thug 1 led the way downstairs via the back stairway to the basement parking lot followed by Hanif, Ryder and Thugs 2 and 3. Ryder started the night's anaerobic exercise class with a vicious back fist to the center of Thug 2's face. The man's hands flew to his crushed nose, and Ryder pushed him down the steps as Thug 3 fumbled with his pistol.

Hanif dropped Thug 1 with a punch to the base of the skull, then stomped on the back of the fallen man's head.

Ryder used his left hand to impede Thug 3's draw, then thrust his right hand into the assailant's groin. The Marquis of Queensberry would have disapproved, but Ryder squeezed the gunman's balls with strength normally reserved for stubborn pickle jars. Thug 3 wrenched his right arm free and both hands flew to his assaulted crotch. Left arm unemployed, Ryder delivered a quick and powerful uppercut to the throat, crushing the man's larynx and disabling him.

Hanif leaped down the remaining stairs and caught the boss man in-between the shoulder blades, knocking the Iranian into the steel exit door. Hanif found his feet first and delivered a left-right combination to the Iranian's kidneys. Boss Man sank to his knees as Hanif seized his head with both hands and slammed his face into the unyielding door. The Iranian collapsed, unconscious.

Ryder saw Thug 2 had just cleared his weapon. The former SEAL used his elevation advantage to good effect by swinging a roundhouse left cowboy boot into the side of the man's head. The rag doll tumbled down the concrete steps, his pistol clattering along beside him.

Hanif's bottled-up rage found expression through his feet. He only regained control after a heel strike crushed the Iranian's temple with the sound of a dropped carton of eggs.

Ryder collected phones and weapons, then pushed his friend out the door before he killed anyone else. "Let's get out of here. Hotel security will be on us in a minute." Their clothes were blood-spattered, but otherwise, they'd suffered only contusions to their hands. It always helped to have a SEAL on your side . . . as well as a homicidal maniac.

CHAPTER TWO

TROUBLE AT HOME

TUESDAY, JULY 15: BEIJING

"I apologize for bringing the Foreign Affairs Bureau into disrepute and hereby present my letter of resignation from the Ministry of State Security. I further apologize for the embarrassment that my precipitate actions caused you." Yu Kaili's eyes stared straight ahead as she set the envelope on the edge of the president's desk and retreated three steps.

Liu Zhenchang, general secretary of the Communist Party and President of China, nodded, his features downcast. "I am left with no choice in this matter," he said, which was true. The disastrous spy swap had been her idea, but what had hardened both the Politburo and senior MSS officials irrevocably against her was the scandal associated with her rumored pregnancy. "I'm afraid your position has become untenable."

"I have no wish to burden you further. I shall return to Suzhou and have the child."

"Are you certain becoming a single mother at forty-four is what you want?" he asked.

"My career as an intelligence officer is over. A child will provide focus and restore meaning." Kaili hadn't harbored maternal feelings since miscarrying years ago, but perhaps a child would preserve her sanity now that she was a pariah.

"My information suggests the father is the architect of your humiliation. Yet you wish to bear his child?"

Kaili's eyes flashed. "I have no interest whatsoever in Bob Nolan. My son will be mine alone."

"A *son*? Congratulations. But as the product of a liaison between an unmarried woman and a military man, I have one piece of advice. A boy should meet his father at least once. My father had no intention of recognizing his bastard, but my mother arranged a chance encounter. The man saw his likeness in me, and subsequently supported my mother and educated me."

"I need nothing from Nolan."

"I understand, but your unborn child may feel differently." Liu was uncomfortable in this avuncular role and reverted to form. "I have a proposition that will punish America for goading my predecessor into that foolish and ruinous war. The assignment will take you to North Korea, perhaps for many years. If you wish, have your baby in Pyongyang and keep him out of view. You will report only to me. The work will be challenging and perhaps dangerous. I can think of no one more qualified than you."

Kaili slowly lowered her eyes to meet his gaze. "Please tell me what I'm to do."

* * * * *

EMIRATES FLIGHT 352 DXB-SIN

The Emirates stewardess awakened Nolan to announce they were twenty-five minutes from touchdown. The flat business class bed made all the difference, and Nolan felt like every cent of his eight and one half million bucks from the score, enough to live out his days in comfort with funds safely beyond the clutches of the divorce lawyers. A flood of memories reminding him how he'd failed wife and children in times past spoiled the mood.

Going to jail was an ever-present threat, even with a presidential pardon for all acts committed prior to March 15. That was four months ago, and Nolan had lost track of the number of crimes he could be charged with in Pakistan, Sri Lanka and as of yesterday, the United Arab Emirates. In his favor was the lack of an extradition treaty between Singapore and the UAE, plus the DEA's local UAE connections. Last evening Ryder had reported that Emirati police officers were buying drinks for his team in thanks for breaking a drug ring and recovering almost five hundred grams of methamphetamine and twenty-five thousand dollars from the leader, a criminal mastermind named Mustafa.

Jerry Flynn was the second item on Nolan's checklist, followed by Millie Mukherjee. The former was his wife's new live-in boyfriend and a former colleague in Singapore station. The latter was twenty-seven-year old trainee from Rangoon station with whom he'd enjoyed a short, torrid relationship back in March. In April, Millie had conducted off-the-books research showing that Jerry Flynn was a likely junior member of the rogue element within the CIA behind the hijacking. In thanks, Nolan had helped arrange her transfer to the DEA and relocation to Singapore.

Nolan cleared immigration as Mr. James Stewart, passport compliments of General Neil Payne's contacts in the State Department. Nolan's plans for the two-day visit didn't leave a lot of room for chats with the Internal Security Department or his former intelligence community colleagues. He pulled his bag off the conveyor and wheeled it through customs without incident. That was a good thing as he would have found it difficult to explain why he was carrying an undeclared US one-hundred-thousand in rubber-banded stacks of hundred-dollar bills.

Nolan's host, the DEA country head, had invited him back to use the same spare bedroom that Nolan had briefly occupied in April before he'd flown to Pakistan. That was four months and three lifetimes ago. He arrived to discover that his left-behind belongings had been professionally searched twice-over, a reminder that his former lover and Ministry of State Security senior operative Yu Kaili possessed an unnatural interest in, and access to, all things pertaining to him.

A quick shave, shower and change of clothes and he was in a cab. Though Joanie wasn't expecting him, she should be home now that she'd quit her job and returned to life as a *tai-tai*, a society woman of lunches, leisure and shopping. He debated whether he should call ahead but thought better of it on two counts. First, her phones were tapped by every alphabet agency on the planet. Second, she might decline to meet.

His key worked on the front gate, but his nerve failed him on his own threshold. He heard the deadbolt unlocking twice—good girl: never can be too safe—and the door opened to reveal a Caucasian of Nolan's mid-fifties vintage in a singlet, boxer shorts and the Singapore *Business Times* in hand. *Why wasn't Jerry Flynn at work on a Tuesday morning at ten a.m.?*

"Can I help you?" Flynn asked.

"Yes, you can get out of my home." Nolan tried to step inside, but Flynn put a hand on his shoulder and flexed his gym muscles. Nolan thought of the ways that his Quantico instructors had taught him to drop this sack of dung in two swift movements. He resisted temptation and called out, "Joanie! It's Bob! I'd like to talk. I have good news."

Flynn stared at him with new intensity. "Bob, I didn't even recognize you, old man!" He nodded at Nolan's nearly shaved scalp. You look like Yule Brynner in *Westworld*."

And you look like a sponge. His wife came downstairs and approached the front door, mindful to keep Flynn between her and her estranged husband. "May I come in?" Nolan asked.

Joanie nodded and Flynn stepped aside. Nolan shed his shoes and walked into what had been the family home for almost five years. Despite no change to the furnishings, it felt different, alien. It didn't smell right: different foods and strange odors. Maybe it was pheromones, or maybe Flynn had pissed in the corners. He sat uneasily in the indicated armchair.

Their Filipina helper Juanilla emerged from the kitchen and beamed in recognition. "Hello, sir," she chirped in the characteristic singsong English of her homeland. "Would you like coffee?"

"No thanks."

"No, he won't be staying long," Flynn proclaimed. "Now run inside the kitchen and make my breakfast—the usual, and don't over-butter the toast."

Joanie and Flynn stood side by side while Nolan contemplated crushing the man's instep as a prelude to shredding his knee. After a lifetime riding a desk and assaulting keyboards, physical fitness and adolescent fantasies of kicking asses had come to him forty years later than in most men. But however much he wanted to stomp Flynn into the ground, he knew it wouldn't win his wife's affections.

"Joanie, I'm back and want to be with you. I turned myself around: no more women, no more booze. I even turned down a job working for Obama because I wanted to be here with you."

"Bob, you signed the separation papers three months ago. It's over."

"I only signed those papers to mollify you. I'd screwed up and all our money was lost, our children were under threat from that gangster Chumakov, and I was struggling to understand how our government could be behind something as terrible as the MH370 hijack."

"Struggling? You left your wife in a Guangzhou jail, fucked your way across Asia, blew the family retirement funds, and turned your CIA colleagues against you," Flynn said.

Nolan gripped the armrests so tightly his hands ached, but he spoke in a deadpan. "Your man is a fraud. The only thing true about him is that he occupies at a dead-end Agency job. He's probably a traitor. I haven't figured out who he works for, but it was his boss who told him to cozy up to you to keep tabs on me."

"I'm not the fraud, Bob. *You're the failure.* Everything you touch turns to shit, tainted by your ego, sexual perversions and recklessness. You're hollow, a little man who puffs himself up to try to compensate for his inadequacies."

"You're describing yourself." Nolan rose as Flynn took a large step back. "You don't know anything about what I've done since MH370 disappeared. I found that plane not once, but twice. I'm free and have the full confidence of the president. Don't talk to me about failure. Instead, look in the mirror and decide if your hair weaves, Botox, bleached teeth and phony muscles make up for treason."

"That's twice you've called me a traitor. You do it a third time and I'll break your hands and you can code with your nose."

Joanie stepped between the two men and faced Nolan. "What about the Russians who threatened my children and me?"

"One's dead and the other is back in Moscow, either dead or in prison. I took care of that in April before I left for Pakistan. That other killer, Coulter, is confined to his mountaintop home and can't hurt you. Besides, we agreed to a hands-off on each other's families."

"And what about the China spy-whore?" Joanie asked. "Didn't I read in *People* that you were with her in Sri Lanka in the penthouse on top of that airport? That article said you might be a double agent."

Nolan snorted. "You're too smart to believe anything you read in a gossip magazine. I was Yu Kaili's prisoner. I escaped and took Coulter and her hostage, then—"

"That's bullshit," Flynn interrupted. "I've read a classified report listing your Bob as a suspected car bomber, murderer of innocent civilians, and complicit in the targeted assassinations of CIA operatives. He's also to co-star of the wildest fuck sessions ever recorded on audio."

"Bob?"

"Those are lies, Joanie," he said through clenched teeth. "*Most* of them are lies. It's complicated. That was months ago, and things are different now. I've changed for starters. I put country before family and paid the price. I don't expect you to take me back, not right away. I want to spend time with you, share my ideas for our future together. I'm sorry I was away when your mother passed, but I was in D.C.—"

"—Spare me the false sympathy," Joanie snapped. "Where can I reach you when the divorce finalizes?"

"Yes, you have every right to divorce me, but tell this man that you don't want to marry him. He's a phony and if he's not spying on you under orders, then he's after your money."

"*Money?* I had to work as a receptionist to get by after you bankrupted us! If it hadn't been for Jerry, the Singapore authorities wouldn't have released the funds to repay the second mortgage and I'd have lost my home. He's the most generous man I ever met. I have a million dollars in the bank thanks to him."

"*Him?*" Nolan exclaimed over Flynn's attempt to interject. "He told you that? I explained everything in my emails."

"Bob, you haven't sent me an email in three months."

"What do you mean?" Nolan turned on Flynn. "You son of a bitch! You intercepted my emails and made it look like you were behind everything good that's happened to my family's finances."

"That's preposterous! How could Jerry do something like that?"

"The CIA built its own version of the NSA while no one was watching after Mark Watermen stole those NSA files back in 2013. There are programs that he can use to screen your email. I wondered why I never heard back from you but didn't want to push it because of all the senseless things I'd done. But I was surprised you didn't even acknowledge the US million dollars I wired to your account."

"You need to leave and not come back," Flynn said.

"Let me give you another scenario. I'll go find a computer. Within two hours, I'll know exactly what's happened to my wife's email. I'll come back here to show her what you did, starting with deleting my emails and committing fraud."

"Jerry?" Joanie asked, eyes wide.

"Don't believe him. Don't believe anything he says. In two hours, he can create a false trail—"

"—Joanie, if you let me use the computer upstairs, you can watch everything I do."

"I . . . I don't know," she stammered.

"No!" Flynn shouted. "He fooled the Iranians, the Chinese, the Sri Lankans and even his own people. He's an arch manipulator. Don't let his lies convince—"

"—You win, Jerry." Nolan held up his hands. "I'll produce proof of origin for all the funds transferred to my wife's accounts. And I'll have Obama sign off on a letter confirming that the restoration of my pension was his idea. Just for kicks, I'll also prove that you've read my wife's email for a long time, well before you two started dating. Maybe you can explain that one away and she'll marry you anyway. At this stage, I don't care." Nolan stood up and left the silent room. Once in the street and out of sight, tears of frustration and regret flowed. How could he have been such an idiot? He had to leave Singapore. There was nothing for him here.

He flagged a cab on the main road and in twelve minutes he'd cleared out of the flat and was headed back to the airport with his toupee in place to match Jimmy Stewart's passport photo. Running through the earliest departures, the best match was the Garuda flight departing for Jakarta in two hours, and then nonstop to Amsterdam. Indonesia was one of the few countries in Asia that didn't have an arrest warrant on him, and extradition treaties were either non-existent or unenforced. In Amsterdam, he'd gather his thoughts and perhaps move funds around to diversify geographic risk. He'd also spend a few hours skewering Flynn and passing the evidence to Joanie in case she was interested in the truth.

* * * * *

Joanie sat in front of her computer, the screen full of celebrity malfeasances, paparazzi snaps and tattle. She'd had a feeling about Jerry for the last six weeks, ever since he proposed. The man in person was kind enough, but he didn't exhibit anywhere near Bob's intelligence or commitment to a cause, any cause. Yet he was the most generous man she'd ever met, showering her with gifts culminating with what he claimed was one million dollars in inherited funds from a despised uncle. Jerry had said that he couldn't accept the funds in good conscience, so he'd decided to donate them to charity, his favorite cause being Joanie. She tried to refuse, but he insisted. She hadn't touched it—there was no need after the previously sequestered monies were released back into her accounts and Bob's pension was restored. She also harbored doubts as to its provenance.

Where Jerry shone was in his empathy, his understanding of her needs, her moods, her desires. Bob was miserable in all those categories, a passive personality given to long hours at work, long hours at the computer and long trips abroad. This past March and April, Bob had disappointed, infuriated and amazed her at every turn. The hero of the MH370 investigation, recipient of the CIA's highest medal and a presidential pardon. Then other close calls in the Pakistan desert and Sri Lanka that ended in his disappearing for three months only to show up an hour ago. Bob wasn't above lying—his pathetic attempts at covering up his dalliances with bar girls spoke to that—but she was sure that what he'd just said about Jerry was genuine. That he'd spent the last ten weeks working for the president told her he retained credibility in the places that mattered. And if Jerry was reading her emails—and presumably everything else in her computer and phone—then that explained his emotional clairvoyance.

What she wanted now more than anything was to sit down with Bob one-on-one and talk everything through. But how to reach him without tipping off her live-in boyfriend? Her sibling Rikki lived a ten-minute drive away. She could drop by and send an email from an unmonitored account to set something up for later today or this evening. If Jerry had to dine alone, so be it.

CHAPTER THREE

CRIME OF THE CENTURY, PART II

THURSDAY, JULY 17: AMSTERDAM SCHIPHOL AIRPORT

In Changi Airport Nolan read Joanie's email asking for a meeting, and he replied that he had to leave Singapore or face arrest. Could she come to Jakarta for a day? If so, he'd defer his onward flight. But he heard nothing before Garuda closed the door, and again nothing on arrival in Amsterdam last evening.

James Stewart's room in the four-star Sheraton Amsterdam Airport didn't disappoint, and neither did the gym. Cutting out the booze and eating better had had more of an effect on how Nolan looked and felt than did exercise, but in combination it was unbeatable. His current existence lacked flair, but at this rate the actuarial tables would add a decade to a life expectancy recently measured in hours or minutes. He'd already seen the world through the bottom of a whiskey glass, and the results were mixed . . . no, make that fuzzy.

Nolan was surprised to see a fresh message on the dark web from Obama himself instead of his cut-out General Payne. He read with trepidation, anger and then resignation. After months of resistance, the Malaysians had agreed to permit the FBI to discreetly investigate the Director Central Intelligence Perkins' murder on April 22 in Putrajaya. The list of people to be interviewed totaled a half-dozen. As Nolan was already next door in Singapore, would he mind hopping up to Kuala Lumpur for a day-and-a-night to join the interrogation team? The president would very much appreciate the old spy's take, particularly in light of Coulter's testimony that then-Malaysia PM Izran Rahim had ordered his bodyguards to shoot Admiral Perkins for reasons unknown. Rahim had even offered to host a meal for the hero of MH370 before the inquiry kicked off. Could he be in Malaysia in time for Friday lunch at the former PM's home?

Three minutes online confirmed that Malaysia Airlines flight 17 left just after noon Amsterdam time and landed in Kuala Lumpur Friday morning at 6:10. That would give Nolan time to clean up and buy decent clothes before the midday photo op. He sure as hell wasn't eating or drinking in Rahim's presence, not after Coulter's admission that he'd left a vial of ricin with the PM. Nolan already held Rahim culpable in the hijack of MH370 and wouldn't be surprised if Rahim pinned the blame on a convenient foreigner, followed by a quick trial and a short drop on a long rope. The problem with egomaniacal politicians was that they stayed in power too long. Even as a retired PM, Rahim would operate beyond the reach of the law so long as his handpicked successor remained in power.

Nolan replied that he'd arrived in Amsterdam earlier that morning but would board the next plane back and participate as requested. He'd write his eyes-only report for Obama on the return trip. He pulled on his crumpled travel clothes, packed a meager carry-on with eight thousand in cash secreted under the false bottom and placed the remaining ninety-two thousand in his suitcase. Then he had second thoughts. Instead he stood on a chair, unscrewed the cover of the HVAC vent and slid inside the bags containing the surplus cash. Then he replaced the screws, careful not to nick the paint.

At checkout, Nolan again reserved Room 812 for Sunday night. The woman at the desk with the green-tinted blond hair and Central Europe accent pointed out the only sights from that vantage were of the access roads, terminal buildings and the odd landing or takeoff. Nolan smiled and said he'd always been a bit of a plane spotter. At that, she suggested that he instead consider either Room 801 or 802, as they were at the other end of the floor and afforded superior vantage points from which to observe Piers D and E. He insisted on 812 anyway. To save time at either end, he also left his large suitcase with the concierge, pressing a twenty-Euro note into the man's hungry palm.

Nolan skipped the lounge and instead used the forty minutes before boarding to flex his new tradecraft. He started by picking out airport security cameras, rent-a-cops, store CCTVs and entrances and exits. He walked and timed several routes, being careful not to heat up an area by appearing too often. The techniques that FBI trainees used these days were a far cry from what he'd learned as a CIA fledgling on the Farm back in the early Eighties. Nolan was surprised when he spotted a man surreptitiously taking photos of him. Another up-and-back saunter detected two more loiterers taking an unnatural interest. Six months ago, Nolan would have been oblivious to anyone out of uniform, but circumstances had forced the former desk man to recast himself as a trainee field operative.

He decided that the best way to shake the tails was to walk through an intrusion point to force the hands of the surveillants. In his nervous excitement, Nolan chose poorly as the laptop and peripherals shop he walked into had only a single entrance. He was trapped at the back and stood next to the register with two goons out front and a third moving in. In the background, a recorded voice in English announced last call for MH17. If these three were from the Netherland's Domestic Security Service, he had nothing to worry about. If they were from another outfit—and the busiest international airports were full of competitors—he was in trouble. The man on the shop register looked like he hailed from the Indonesia archipelago.

"*Teman*," Nolan said in Bahasa Indonesian, "*Saya dalam masalah.*"

The shopkeeper looked at him in shock. "Trouble?" he replied in English. "What sort of trouble?"

"Terrorists. If you have a silent alarm, trigger it. Otherwise, signal distress to the nearest CCTV camera. We don't have time."

The merchant reached under the till, then straightened and stared at the camera while tugging on his right earlobe. An announcement in urgent Dutch came over the loudspeaker and one of the men on the entrance barked an instruction at his advancing companion. The man turned and exited the store, following his two compatriots. Less than twenty seconds later, two putative tourists, a man and a woman, came running into the shop with weapons drawn. A woman outside Nolan's peripheral vision screamed. An older man, also dressed in mufti, trotted in and made a beeline for the back. Nolan knew the drill and put his hands on his head and sank to his knees, grateful for Dutch efficiency. Two armed security agents ensured that the other shop patrons didn't make any sudden movements and kept their hands within sight.

"Are you DSS?" Nolan asked.

"Airport police. Please stay still," said Gray-hair. He turned and spoke rapidly in Dutch to the diminutive merchant who pointed at Nolan with a quavering arm.

"Let me explain," Nolan began. "I'm a former State Department employee working as a consultant in national security. I have credentials in my wallet. There were three men in this shop less than one minute ago. They were photographing and following me. They've run off, but they must still be in the terminal. If you check the video footage, you'll see who I mean. They may be SVR, as I heard one of them speak in a Slavic language.

"I need to board Malaysia Airlines flight 17 for Kuala Lumpur and the doors are shutting. My wife is already aboard. I didn't know what those three men were planning, so I asked storekeeper to sound the alarm."

Gray-hair pulled a phone out of his pocket. "Look at the camera over your shoulder, and take off your hat," he said to Nolan. "Give me your passport, security ID and boarding pass. Is your wife seated next to you? We're taking her off the plane. Do you have any checked luggage?"

Nolan smiled for the camera, wondered if his expensive toupee passed muster, and re-thought his tactics. "My wife has several pieces of hand luggage. She also panics easily, and it would be easier if I went on the plane to escort her off. We also have checked luggage."

"We'll go to her, but don't attempt to flee or you will go to prison." The two men set out at a trot for the gate. Two Malaysia Airlines employees stood at the empty gantry as they approached. Gray-hair showed his identification and they stood aside. As they raced down the aerobridge, Gray-hair's phone rang. He slowed to answer and listened, then stopped, replied in Dutch and hung up. From the look he gave Nolan, the former spy knew the game was up. "There's no one related to James Stewart on the flight, and you checked no luggage. What did you hope to accomplish by boarding the plane?"

"I planned to call the president's national security consultant and have him speak to you."

"That is not permitted. Come with me and walk slowly, very slowly. We have all the time in the world." Three minutes later, Gray-hair and a bearded agent with a ponytail faced Nolan with their backs against the door of a small interview room behind the public areas.

At their insistence, Nolan had taken a seat at a tiny table. "You need to detain the three men who followed me. That could have been a hit squad for all we know."

Ponytail ignored Nolan's protest and emptied his carry-on contents onto the tabletop. After minimal rummaging, four thousand dollars and change appeared. The rest of the meager contents merited scant attention, save for the toiletry bag that the agent set aside for further inspection. Next up was the laptop case. "Boot this computer."

"You're making a big mistake," Nolan said as he complied. "Please call the tower and hold the plane, and call General Neil Payne to confirm my—"

"The security of Schiphol Airport and its passengers is my only concern. Until you convince me you are not a threat, you'll speak to no one but Agent Lurvink and me. What are your plans in Kuala Lumpur?" asked Gray-hair.

"To interview government officials about the circumstances surrounding the April 22 murder of Director of Central Intelligence Admiral William Perkins."

"Perkins wasn't murdered. He died in a climbing accident in Borneo."

"Are you that gullible? He was shot four times and buried in a closed casket. Now can you please call the tower and tell them to hold the plane? Then call the acting Director of Central Intelligence Stuart Johnson and tell him you have Bob Nolan in detention, and he will miss his flight unless he intervenes."

"Bob Nolan? *Wat een klerezooi*," said the hirsute Lurvink.

"What a mess, indeed," echoed Gray-hair.

* * * * *

THURSDAY, JULY 17: RUSSIA-OCCUPIED EASTERN UKRAINE, NEAR PERVOMAIS'K

Following Anatoly Chumakov's deportation from Singapore in mid-April, his prospects had risen from death row to respected FSB henchman bouncing around the Muslim republics and restive provinces. Now it was early July and he found himself in the company of unwashed drunken swine. How in God's name had he come to be based in Russia-occupied Ukraine organizing the security for the 53rd anti-aircraft missile brigade out of Kursk? Apart from the men who managed the Buk 9K-37 TELAR mobile missile launch vehicle, Chumakov's security detail was deplorable.

The Tatar stopped this line of self-inquiry lest he forget how the good far outweighed the bad. He was back on a payroll and, miracle of miracles, his Moscow flat with its modest furnishings and immodest collection of couture clothing had been returned to him unscathed. He was doubly fortunate that Vladimir Putin and Federal Security Services head Andrei Portnikov thought well of him. FSB strongman Portnikov forwarded Putin's orders to Chumakov when Russia's leader had a job that was too sensitive to stay within formal channels. One downside of being the fixer of choice was Chumakov didn't know where he'd be from week-to-week.

Those were quibbles compared to his major gripe. In return for successfully scraping the MH370 airframe for surveillance devices, Portnikov had promised Chumakov "Bob Nolan on a platter." That was a direct quote, uttered months ago. The Museum of Crimes Against Humanity had opened at Moscow's Domodedovo Airport with the first exhibit on display being that ill-fated Malaysia airline. Transit passengers could walk through the plane and read the placards in Russian, French or English describing in florid terms the CIA's hijacking and murder of 238 souls. Meanwhile, Nolan was in Washington, D.C. where he cozied up to Obama and testified before closed-door committees. All this while Chumakov coped with an acrylic left eye, shrapnel in his brain and a missing half a kidney thanks to a Nolan-thrown hand grenade.

The satphone buzzed in Chumakov's breast pocket. It was Portnikov. Putting on his loyal lieutenant voice, Chumakov answered. "Director General, how may I serve you?"

"Maybe God exists after all and he is a Tatar. Malaysia Airlines flight 17 from Amsterdam to Kuala Lumpur takes off just after noon Amsterdam time with a cruising altitude of thirty-three thousand feet. I can instruct air traffic control to vector it to waypoint RND. It will be the only aircraft at that location and altitude, and as re-routed will pass within three kilometers of your current location. Bob Nolan will be on board. I have a green light should you wish to proceed, but you will owe President Putin another large debt of gratitude. Me, I like my tribute in dollars, vodka and big-titted whores."

"Nolan? Are you certain?"

"Yes. His alias passport came up on our system two hours ago, and our men at Schiphol saw him board the plane before they left the terminal. He's yours for the taking, but you need to decide."

"I want him dead today."

"I'll notify the military. Stand by. In two hours, there will be a fireworks display even a one-eyed man can appreciate."

"Thank you, sir!" Chumakov turned off the satphone. *Nolan!*

* * * * *

Chumakov looked at his watch: it was 13:21 and sections of aircraft were tumbling from the sky, trailing smoke with this happy scene spread over many kilometers. A proximity fuse in the nose of an a 9N-314M surface-to-air missile packed with eight-hundred bowtie-shaped iron fragments had detonated next to the cockpit. Somewhere up there was Bob Nolan, or parts of him. Chumakov hoped he was alive all the way to ground, screaming in terror. This was a day to savor, a day to remember. Chumakov's body trembled with a feeling akin to orgasm.

* * * * *

WASHINGTON, D.C. AND SCHIPHOL AIRPORT

Acting Director of Central Intelligence Stu Johnson waited while minions patched him through. "Bob, you all right?"

"I'm fine. I was angry about being held in solitary until they told me that two hundred and ninety-eight people died on that flight. That it's another Malaysia Airline's plane has me perplexed. Can you have me released so I can catch a later flight to Kuala Lumpur?"

"I spoke with the president a short while ago and debriefed him on intelligence just in from Kuala Lumpur. There's a credible report that former PM Rahim has ordered your death. There are also wire service reports out of Russia claiming that Bob Nolan was on board MH17."

"Oh, hell."

"The safest place for you is in US protective custody. On POTUS's authority, I've dispatched a private jet to pick you up at Volkel Air Base outside Amsterdam. Our Dutch friends will ensure that you make that plane. On your flight to Andrews, think hard about how you wish to proceed. The president said his offer is still open to lead the Abyss investigation, and to remind you that your country needs you more than ever. I don't know what that specifically refers to, but having our enemies think you're inoperative provides an advantage. Please consider all your options before answering."

"I'll do that, sir. Thank you for the assistance." Nolan stared at the mute phone. *Dead again.*

CHAPTER FOUR

THE TORMENTED

TWO YEARS LATER

MONDAY, AUGUST 15, 2016: PYONGYANG, NORTH KOREA

Yu Kaili, intelligence liaison from the People's Republic of China to the Democratic People's Republic of Korea, sat in stunned silence. Last month, after two years of negotiations, flattery, stealth and seduction, North Korea had handed over a nuclear electromagnetic pulse device, an NEMP. Ostensibly, China's nuclear weapons scientists would review and suggest design modifications to enhance its yield. In fact, on President Liu's orders the bomb had gone to a terrorist group that pledged to detonate it over the Eastern Seaboard of the United States. Chaos would result as E1, E2 and E3 energy surges destroyed power transmission and distribution networks. Liu had seen more than enough of America's democracy in his seventy-five years. The world's largest countries would be better off governed by military men committed to peace and security rooted in acceptance of geographic spheres of influence.

Her mission in North Korea complete, she was to depart with her little boy on the next available flight, disguising her absence as a short holiday so as to not arouse suspicions, then drop the child in China and acquire commercial cover ahead of the United States visit. The president wanted Kaili as his emissary to the conspirators running the government-in-waiting and determine whether China could do business with Mr. Love and his organization.

* * * * *

TUESDAY, AUGUST 16, 2016: OUTSIDE CAMP IRWIN, CALIFORNIA

MH370 SLEUTH DIES IN MH17 EXPLOSION

The two-year-old press clipping hung from the bulletin board over his desk. How true, how true. Bob Nolan, the most decorated CIA officer in Agency history, was alive in this tin can and dead everywhere else. Deceased in name and memorialized with a white grave marker in Arlington National Cemetery. Dead to his family who thought he'd boarded Malaysia Airlines flight 17. And he would have died, at least in spirit, if he hadn't come to believe in a higher cause: Operation Abyss.

Eat, sleep, exercise, shoot and Abyss defined a hermetic existence in the high desert off the highway from Los Angeles to Las Vegas. Not that it mattered where Nolan physically existed, as he seldom ventured from his parcel of sand and rock. Once a week, someone from the Q-Group delivered provisions and picked up his shopping list. As a defunct person, he received no mail or emails in his real name. Nolan had memorized everything on Arch Stanton's false IDs in his wallet but had never had to produce one for a bank teller, traffic cop or airline employee. Uncle Sam paid all of Mr. Stanton's bills and kept his name off the grid.

Nolan was a lord of the dark web, master of the crevices where treason hid its stench among the perverts, the dealers and the shadow people. Here and there he found a crumb: a morsel of code, or a repeated alias or phrase in an obscure place. Something that set him off in a frenzy for the next twenty-four or forty-eight hours to find the connecting thread ahead of time decay and security sweepers. Nolan didn't even know how many people worked for Operation Abyss, but it numbered in the dozens. No one knew anything about him other than his project handle, Reese. The closer the Abyss team came to unraveling the labyrinthine structure of Higher Love, the faster everything blew apart and recombined in a new tangle of obfuscation, and the Sisyphean labors started anew.

Only General Payne, Abyss's patron and POTUS's confidant via the nebulous title of "Special Presidential Envoy", had the full organization chart. Everyone else knew only their proximate contacts so they couldn't betray the entire group. Nolan had cautioned Payne to keep this information on paper only, for nothing in a computer was secure. He smiled at the irony of being one of the world's top cryptanalysts, yet his doublewide trailer held more safes than it did computers. Electronic storage media, air-gapped or otherwise, couldn't be trusted.

Nolan was close to identifying Higher Love's leader. Only through interrogation of the top man would Payne's team learn the names of the multiple layers of traitors dedicated to the overthrow of America's republic and the establishment of an imperial regime. To that end, Abyss's staff had assiduously ignored the smaller fry to focus on the man referred to in his own organization as Mr. Love.

The MH370 hijacking planning, execution and coverup had sent the president's mind down a dark path that walked the line between messianic quest and obsession. There was persuasive circumstantial evidence of a deep state, an organization of government insiders past and present dedicated to the usurpation of United States foreign policy. From the Oval Office, POTUS could do little on his own, particularly as he could trust so few. Retired Special Forces Major General Neil Payne was one of a handful. Payne in turn had his own reasons to rely exclusively on the FBI's Associate Directorate for Security and Counterintelligence—"Q-Group" for short, and "the American Stasi" to civil libertarians. Q-Group was the body charged with policing the NSA's analysts and programmers. It maintained a loose cordon around Arch Stanton on Payne's orders. All the FBI minders knew about their subject was that he had enough computers to control a manned mission to Mars, enough safes to back up Fort Knox, ran five miles a day and shot a carton of two hundred hollow points every weekend.

The ex-senator from Illinois and his consigliere from Macon, Georgia, took comfort from the satisfaction that most military and intelligence types expressed whenever Nolan's death came up. Nolan's skillset included the creation and deciphering of codes, high-level programing, electronic surveillance and hacking. He was creative, and since the moving to Camp Irwin's environs two years prior, obsessive.

Then in May everything went to hell. Abyss had progressed to the point that Mr. Love's opaque form began to take shape: a mature ex-politician personally known to few, revered by most and feared by all. So confident was the president of Abyss's inevitable success that he added a second objective to the team's brief over Payne's objections. As of May 21, Reese and his people were also to review the evidence of Russia's tampering with the upcoming 2016 presidential election. Nolan hadn't been happy to learn about the additional goal, but Payne explained this wasn't an Athenian democracy and he needed to fall in line.

Nolan knew far too well the dangers of mission creep, but he accepted the additional work with a shrug. After all, just how crazy would Putin have to be to yank the tail of the world's largest cyber power? Russia's hacking into the private email server of the Democrats' nominee when she had been secretary of state was fair game but stealing the contents of the Democratic National Committee's computers and dumping them onto WikiLeaks was beyond the pale. But what POTUS didn't appreciate, and Nolan feared, were the unintended consequences of comingling targets. Abyss's hunt could inadvertently push the quarries—the Russians and Higher Love—into overlapping orbits with unpredictable results.

* * * * *

WASHINGTON, D.C.

Anatoly Chumakov, head of the Farewell Group's D.C. office, understood why JFK had changed shirts twice daily during the summer. The capital's humidity bonded grit and pollen to the skin, and the high heat turned it into a slurry. He finished tucking in his last fresh shirt, a two hundred-count Egyptian cotton Turnbull & Asser that felt like silk as long as he stayed indoors. He finished trimming an errant cuticle as the receptionist signaled that his three o'clock had arrived.

"Peter, Peter, welcome!" Chumakov effused. Peter Mandrake was one of Republican presidential candidate Douglas Ginger's new men, ostensibly in charge of campaign strategy.

"Do you have any more material for us?"

"Our friends at WikiLeaks are highly confident there will be additional disclosures," Chumakov said, luxuriating in his role as a registered lobbyist representing the Russian Federation. He cracked his knuckles and snuck another look at the new Vacheron Constantin watch adorning his wrist, a present from Portnikov.

"That's great," Mandrake said, "though with twenty thousand DNC emails already out there, Crandall's mighty fucked as it stands."

"I smile every time I log on the *Washington Post's* website and read the Politics section. The unofficial slogan of *Pravda* used to be, 'If you tell us what to write, we'll publish it.' I'm pushing the *Post* to adopt it as their masthead, but in the meantime my expense account looks like your country's national debt."

"Precisely! Those liberal hacks spend their time claiming Ginger is a fool, but they're too stupid to understand what's happening until it's too late."

Chumakov grimaced and gestured toward the ceiling in an appeal for discretion. "I have good news on other fronts. I can confirm your client paid your firm's most recent invoice."

"When did this happen?" Mandrake asked.

"Earlier today. Here, this is your copy." Chumakov handed over a scan acknowledging receipt of three million dollars from Ukraine's Party of Plenty to the go-between's political image consulting firm, Davis Mandrake. The signature was that of the officer manager in the Kiev office.

"Thanks. Let me see how long it takes Boyko to notify me. He's been slack on that count of late. I think he's banking the interest on the float."

Chumakov winced at the sound of the Ukrainian surname. The receptionist rang and said he had an urgent call, prompting the Tatar to extend his hand in farewell. "Busy as Stalin launching a pogrom. You keep me posted on developments, and let's get together with Junior or Gerard this coming week."

"Absolutely, Anatoly. I'll be certain to rope in—"

"I'm sure it will be an impressive list. Now you'll have to excuse me." Chumakov prodded the smaller man out of his office before he could utter anything else that the FBI would find of interest.

After the elevator doors cut off Mandrake's drivel, Chumakov sighed as he strode back into the reception area. He spoke in Russian to the athletic woman behind the front desk. "Valeyriya, who's on the phone?"

"He couldn't wait and hung up." She gestured him over and revealed a name on a yellow sticky.

"I'm going downstairs for a cigarette. Please take a message should anyone ring."

And just when everything was on track. Something must be very wrong as Tim Weill didn't rattle easily. In the lobby, Chumakov pulled out his cellphone and sent two secure text messages, then walked out the door onto M Street into another filthy D.C. steam room. So much for the razor-sharp creases in his shirt. He took ten minutes to reach the Four Seasons Hotel and waited less than fifteen seconds for his pickup. Then it was a short surveillance detection route circling northwest D.C. until he was certain they were clean. The off-duty embassy driver, an ex-Special Forces man he used from time to time, dropped him in a parking lot behind a liquor store fronting Wisconsin Avenue in swish Georgetown.

Chumakov entered Peterson's Liquor from the parking lot, found the right key on his copious ring and opened a metal door to reveal an ill-lit set of stairs blocked by another metal door. Behind that heavy barrier, the lighting improved and the temperature dropped ten degrees.

Tim Weill was the Farewell Group's principal asset, an ex-NSA project leader with divorce expenses and a hatred for the intel establishment. The man was usually the epitome of cool, yet here he was with hand tremors. "I chased a ghost all weekend," he said. "He escaped and we have a major problem. Obama has had a team working undercover the past two years, so deep even I can't penetrate the security. They're looking for someone called Mr. Love who heads Higher Love. I called for a face-to-face to see if you can make sense of any of it."

"Higher Love donated funds to Wiki-whatever to encourage them to release more DNC and Crandall emails," Chumakov said. "I don't know anything about them other than that, and I don't care. It's probably the pseudonym for a three hundred-pound Republican billionaire sitting in bed. I'm hot and tired, so get on with it."

"I haven't slept in two nights," Weill said. "The NSA transmissions I've stumbled across include wide-ranging compartmented top-secret intel, so much so that the president or his gorilla Payne are the only ones with the clearance to read it all. This Abyss group has made rapid progress on the DNC hacks and they're too close for comfort. They're directed by someone who's smarter than I am, and from the speed they're moving, they have greater resources than the official FBI task force. Abyss's already tied me to the theft of the twenty thousand DNC emails, and it may even know I work for Farewell Group. We need to get them off our backs. Fortunately, I planned for this day. With your approval, I'll dump most of the NSA's hacking tools on the dark web. That will buy us the time we need to cover our tracks."

"Tell me, who is the mastermind you so fear? Can we turn him?"

"I doubt it. He's relentless, patriotic and devious. He's also supposed to be dead, killed two years ago in the crash—"

"Of MH17." Chumakov finished Weill's sentence. "Bob Nolan is back from the grave?"

"How do you know Nolan?"

"He and I have a blood feud. That's all you need to know."

"I can pinpoint where he's located," Weill said. "It will take less than two hours once I'm back online. But he'll be well-protected. I doubt you'll be able to get near him."

"You have no idea how many people will want Nolan dead once you prove he's alive," Chumakov said. "They will do our jobs for free. If the Kennedy assassinations taught us anything, it's that everyone can be gotten to."

Weill left Chumakov sitting in the basement. In the last five minutes Chumakov's mood had changed from deep satisfaction to a building rage that the cornerstone of his well-being—Bob Nolan's death high above those Ukraine fields—was a fraud. Nolan had fooled him yet another time. He clenched his fists until his dead eye socket ached.

Portnikov and Putin would tell him that there wasn't time for personal vengeance, that the bumbling Ginger campaign and its bagmen, tricksters, cronies and blowhards required his full attention if their bombastic candidate was to win the election. Putin wanted so very much to have his own marionette in the White House, even one who didn't yet know that he was on the end of the strings.

Chumakov needed a drink—no, several drinks—to work out his master plan. Inside the unlocked basement cage sat a carton of Khortytsa in liter bottles. Given what the D.C. *rezidentura* paid each month to the shop's owner, Peterson's Liquor could consider it a donation to their benefactors.

* * * * *

ROCKVILLE, MARYLAND

Weill settled into the desk chair in his attic home office. The exposed pink fiberglass insulation under the eaves irritated his skin and lungs, air purifier notwithstanding. Before climbing the rickety staircase, he'd ditched his contacts for glasses, and used eyedrops to start fresh. Old posters from James Cameron movies illustrated the otherwise barren walls. Arnold glowered at him with red eyes with Sarah Connor running away from a burning semi in an enlarged studio promo shot.

He'd had no idea how Chumakov knew Nolan, but since he did, the Russian must have been present for the Sri Lanka beach massacre back in 2014—and also a part of the handover team escorting Watermen to the tracks where a PLA sniper put a bullet into the NSA consultant's head. *SLAUGHTER IN SRI LANKA* was one tabloid headline. Two weeks later, Obama hung a medal around Nolan's neck, and Chumakov was in intensive care recuperating from near-fatal shrapnel wounds. Yep, that would leave a grudge.

Weill didn't know what to make of Chumakov other than his polished manner and hard-to-place urbane English accent cloaked an obscure background that invalidated the international public relations pedigree he'd laid claim to. With a swarthy complexion and muscled physique, he looked like an ex-soldier from the Middle East, but he dressed like a Saks Fifth Avenue window display with enough bling to make an Israeli millionaire blush. Chumakov's panache hid a filthy temper too.

Swift keystrokes and hard labor left the former NSA program director sweat-soaked and frustrated with streaming eyes. Where in the hell was Nolan? Earlier today, he'd had a bead on his location somewhere out west, possibly inside a military installation. He'd held off digging deeper, knowing that this might alert his quarry. Now with his client urging him on, Weill had retraced his steps and there was nothing. No traceable IP addresses, no chained server locations, not even the identity of the overseas servers Tor used to chop up messages within the dark web. Apparently, Nolan had detected his presence and then eradicated all traces. But how was that possible? Weill was using the NSA's best software. The answer had to be Nolan had access to the same toolbox and had been faster to take defensive measures.

Chumakov wouldn't be happy, but he'd become enraged if Weill delayed alerting him.

* * * * *

WASHINGTON, D.C.

Chumakov sleepwalked through the return trip to the office. After he locked up, he drove to his plush townhouse rental in North Alexandria and took a short, infuriating phone call from Weill. The bottle went straight into the freezer. He stood in the shower a long time. Bob Nolan's death on MH17 two-plus years ago had catalyzed his rebirth as a trusted senior man in the Federal Security Services, the FSB. President Putin hadn't ordered the murder of two hundred and ninety-eight airline passengers to appease him. He'd later said to Chumakov that Nolan's death "was a down payment on five billion rubles' worth of equipment and six lives in Pakistan." Former KGB head Putin operated like a Mafia don: he did favors and collected obligations. Every time Putin gave Chumakov a new task, the mission was ever riskier and more grandiose. Chumakov had accepted every one of them and boasted a perfect track record to date. Riches, prestige and authority followed, and today Chumakov earned an unimaginably large salary to lead the most audacious espionage program in Russia's history.

Bank account overflowing, physical vitality restored, Chumakov of late courted the rich women he formerly only dreamed of. Anatoly Chumakov was someone, a player, and he had the car, clothes and accoutrements to prove it. At forty-eight, he could bench-press one hundred kilos and run ten kilometers in under forty-four minutes. He'd even become used to missing an eye and half a kidney, permanent reminders of Nolan. His implacable hatred had rescued him from an invalid's fate, and the bliss derived from knowing that his enemy was dead cushioned his every waking minute.

That Bob Nolan still breathed sent that hard-won self-esteem into the gutter and filled him with rage. Nolan was the architect of his disfigurement, the cause of the psychological and physical pain he'd suffered to compress six months' rehabilitation into six weeks. Back in April 2014, a barely ambulatory Chumakov and his body man Ustinov had sprung a trap, but Nolan had triumphed instead. Singapore's security services deported Chumakov to Russia to face capital punishment on corruption charges. The former head of the FSB's Surveillance Directorate saved himself through a mixture of luck and meticulous management of an electronic surveillance sweep of the Boeing 777 known as MH370. Thus began the road to a spectacular career resurrection. On a July afternoon in Ukraine, a lifetime's worth of insults, discrimination and disrespect melted away, anchored in the certain knowledge that he'd proved himself the better man as bits of Nolan and airplane rained down.

Shower ended, Chumakov wrapped a towel and dripped downstairs for a glass of Khortytsa. The first two slugs went down without touching the sides. He pounded the glass on the countertop and poured a third measure. How could this happen to him? Nolan had outsmarted him again. That old American was laughing at him—no, he was stalking him, ready to tear down a world he'd spent the last two years constructing.

Chumakov felt himself hyperventilating. That vodka on an empty stomach left him nauseous. He wasn't the drinker he once was, not with his lacerated viscera. The barrel-chested Tatar forced himself to breathe deeply and steady his heartbeat. All he had to do was wait until Weill found his error and found Nolan. Chumakov would then notify Portnikov and let the FSB hand the assignment over to their overseas counterparts in the SVR.

Chumakov left the vodka on the counter and placed a gourmet bachelor meal in the microwave. Returning to the bedroom, he dressed in silk and linen blends, Armani and Zegna accentuating his musculature. He combed his hair and looked in the mirror for reassurance. See, nothing had changed. An instant later, he backhanded every skin cream, exfoliant, conditioner and scent bottle off the marble counter, breaking glass and spraying contents across the tiled walls and floor. *I'm fucking far from all right.* Only one thing can make things better: Nolan's head in a sack.

Medieval kings solicited heads on lances, but no longer. No one took unnecessary chances as the stakes were too high in a post-9/11 surveillance-crazy United States. There wouldn't be a scrap of Nolan's DNA anywhere on the hit team, much less a positive identifier like a severed thumb. But Chumakov would never be whole again unless he saw Nolan's body firsthand.

All well and good, but Portnikov and Putin wouldn't let their senior liaison and D.C. office head take a week, much less a month, to assemble a team, track down his foe, plan and execute the hit, and exfiltrate. Every day presented new challenges and opportunities to leak information damaging to Democratic nominee Crandall to the Ginger campaign and the press. No one save Chumakov had the complete matrix of contacts and connections stored in his head. If he abandoned D.C. without permission, his career and maybe his life would be forfeit, irrespective of whatever happened to Nolan. He had to think this through, find a way to bring Nolan to him.

The microwave's chime signaled that dinner was ready. He looked at the mess that littered the vanity in his bathroom. He hadn't had a fit of rage in years.

An idea struck him, and he grabbed his encrypted phone and dialed Weill. "Listen carefully. Dump all the NSA tools onto Tor and affix the blame on a new organization. Just make up a name. Tie it Nolan to in some obscure way. We put him on the defensive and leave Abyss leaderless. Let Obama's hounds find our rabbit. I will then take the necessary action."

"Are you certain you want me to dump all the tools? We spent millions acquiring them."

"Give a few away to excite the hackers, then put the rest up for sale. We'll recoup our costs, and criminals will show the West what the NSA has been doing in secret the past decade."

"Nolan is hard to catch and even more difficult to hold onto," Weill said. "I doubt the Feds can keep him all the way to D.C."

"If he evades their grasp, I will bait a trap even clever Nolan won't avoid. I will tear his world apart before I kill him."

"Whatever you say." Weill disconnected and stared at the handset, half expecting the earpiece to glow red.

The sound of a key in the front latch startled Chumakov. The door opened and a footfall sounded in the marble foyer. "Anatoly, it's me!" a familiar voice rang out. "I was shopping in Old Town and thought I'd surprise you. Why don't you take me to dinner tonight? I spoke with a woman at the salon, and she raved about the new chef at the 1789 Restaurant."

"Honey, I've just pulled dinner out of the microwave. I had a long day and would like to stay in. I've had a few drinks already as well."

"Oh, you naughty man! Drinking without *moi*? You're dressed fine as usual. Throw on some shoes. I'll drive. We have a booking for eight o'clock."

Here he was orchestrating the takeover of the American government and the death of his archenemy, and his girlfriend of one-month's standing was leading him around by the nose. He was appreciating more and more that money alone wasn't enough to keep a society woman, particularly an oligarch's adulterous ex-wife left penniless post-divorce. Ludmilla should come with "Fragile" stickers pasted on her handbags. But she did dine at every Western embassy and chichi new restaurant, so on balance he was grateful to Portnikov for the introduction. He reached the front door, kissed the proffered cheek and spied his dark green patent leather Gucci's by the wall. "Yes, dear, but let's make an early night of it. I'm too tired to go clubbing."

Ludmilla switched to Russian. "After a romantic dinner, bring me back here and I'll see if I can raise the dead." She smiled and led him by his hand out the door, microwaved casserole forgotten.

CHAPTER FIVE

RECRUITING

TUESDAY, AUGUST 16: FORT MEADE, MARYLAND

Director of the National Security Agency Madeline Sturridge sat dumbfounded. An unknown group calling itself the Shadow Brokers had hacked into the holiest of the holies, Tailored Access Operations, which was charged with surveilling friend and foe alike. Someone had stolen three of what the NSA euphemistically referred to as the "ops disks" that contained the millions of lines of code that allowed the NSA to log every phone call and email in the world, irrespective of Silicon Valley's encryption efforts. Now all of the TAO's crown jewels developed before mid-2013 either were available for free, or up for sale on the dark web. The release of the ops disks contents into the wild meant every targeted organization had the means to detect and block the NSA. Hundreds of millions of conversations and billions of emails a day would disappear. How was the NSA to do its job? This was the Watermen scandal times ten and that fiasco had cost her predecessor her job.

She keyed the intercom with sweaty fingertips. "Tell the president's chief of staff that I must meet POTUS today at his earliest convenience." She hung up and stared at her desktop. With gallows humor, she remembered the old saw about the resigning CEO handing her successor two envelopes, the one on top labeled, "In case of emergency, open first." Inside was the message, "Blame me." The second envelope contained the advice, "Fill out two envelopes." She wondered if a hearty mea culpa would be enough to keep the second envelope in the drawer.

Over in Langley, the Center for Cyber Intelligence staff would be licking their chops. With conscious effort, Sturridge rejected the urge to ascribe every NSA setback to CIA chicanery. After a period of forced reflection, the only plausible villains were Russia or China. Russia already vied with the US to employ the world's most gifted IT mercenaries. All it would take is a single mole and Russia or its proxies would be inside the NSA's firewalls. The world's best cyber offense hadn't deserved the same accolade on the other side of the ball for years now.

The director emerged from her funk with a start. Mr. Love would be furious, more so even than the president. Without programs like PRISM, Upstream, BLARNEY, MonsterMind, MAINWAY, MARINA, Presenter and XKeyscore, that was the end of Higher Love's real-time feeds from the military, law enforcement and intelligence services. Tracking and preempting the bureaucrats before they could subvert Higher Love's foreign policy objectives had gone from routine to impossible.

She punched up the intercom again. "While we're waiting on POTUS, get Andrew Jordan over here on the double." General Jordan was an NSA director and commander of the NSA's smaller military analog, the US Cyber Command. Unlike the CIA, Jordan and his people were bureaucratic allies. She had to act fast, but first she needed a scapegoat.

* * * * *

THE WHITE HOUSE

Sturridge and Jordan stood in the Oval Office while the president reviewed the NSA's findings and recommendations following the massive theft. "I don't care what your team found," Obama said. "I assure you that Bob Nolan—if he is even alive—did not steal the ops disks. Back in 2014, I spent several hours with him. His testimony differed from many others', yet the facts bore him out. I can't conceive of Nolan being behind the so-called Shadow Brokers. He's been framed."

"With respect, sir," Jordan began, "I believe you may have been mistaken in 2014, and only now are Nolan's true colors showing."

"General, we purged fifty-two senior intelligence officers and blacklisted a greater number of contractors. Since then the Agency's covert operations have functioned smoothly. Are you telling me that Nolan gave false evidence that implicated more than one hundred innocent men and women, yet our clandestine branches run better because of it?"

"Sir, you were fed a mixture of misinformation and lies, with a sprinkling of truth to convince you of the veracity of the remainder. You've eaten fruit from a poisoned tree and—"

"Spare me the mixed metaphors," Obama snapped. "Nolan nailed the right people, and enough of them turned on one another to generate thousands of pages of corroborating testimony and more than thirty successful prosecutions."

"Let's focus on the present, sir," Sturridge said. "Nolan is clever. We don't even know where he is, but he must be operating under government cover to have the above-top-secret access that this theft required. That, plus the residual suspicions the general alluded to, suggests we should confirm whether or not Nolan is alive. If so, we must interview him to see what he knows."

"I know where Nolan is," Obama said. "He works for General Payne and me on a special assignment. I will order him to D.C. to hear his side. Once you've listened to him, you'll concur that America has no greater patriot."

"Mr. President, I must insist that Nolan be detained without prior warning," Sturridge said. "Only then can the FBI can ascertain whether he is in possession of stolen NSA property, or has connections to the Shadow Brokers."

"Easily done, Madeline—the FBI provides his security. Now if you'll excuse me, I have to talk Netanyahu out of invading Syria."

In the hallway, the two NSA directors spoke softly as they walked. "What if Nolan isn't behind the Shadow Brokers?" Jordan asked.

"It doesn't matter," Sturridge said. "If you can't create enough evidence to convict Nolan, you really shouldn't be running Cyber Command. Besides, it'll never come to trial. Nolan has many enemies. I doubt there's a safe place for him anywhere in federal custody. General, have your people keep an eye on whomever POTUS sends to fetch Nolan, and make certain we don't have to rely on speculation. Think Waco."

"Ah, Waco." *Burn, baby, burn.* As they parted, Jordan still couldn't ascertain why the NSA director was so keen to see Nolan dead. After all, he was the CIA's problem, wasn't he?

* * * * *

AIR CHINA FLIGHT 990 PEK–JFK

Her hair shorn, Yu Kaili's bare neck felt chilly as the flight took off into the post-midnight sky. She already missed Ying Sheng, but the little fellow's grandparents had taken a surprising shine to the *guizi*— white devil—and she knew he was in safe hands. That's more than she could say for herself, with nothing to rely on but a Four Seasons Hotel booking under her cover identity and instructions to await contact.

This was to have been purely a business trip. But president Liu's personal message just before takeoff told her that Bob Nolan was alive and keenly sought by Higher Love, so she had a personal agenda as well.

* * * * *

OUTSIDE CAMP IRWIN, CALIFORNIA

The fox had turned on the hounds. Nolan and the Abyss team had spent two years hunting for clues proving the existence of a deep state and eventually identified both the organization and the leader's pseudonym. Three months into the parallel search for connections between Russia and Ginger's presidential campaign, it became clear that a cyberespionage antagonist was hunting Abyss's principals.

Never a believer in coincidence, Nolan had spent the last three hours searching the archives until Chumakov's name jumped off a page. The former head of the FSB's Surveillance Directorate lived in D.C., hiding in plain sight as the executive director of the Farewell Group, a Russia-affiliated lobbyist. How Nolan had missed him once he'd tied Tim Weill to Farewell was an uncharacteristic lapse.

The NSA fired Weill in 2014 after China fed Weill's Project Acapulco false intel. Ostracized by the defense establishment as a possible mole, Weill sought both payback and lucre by working for the Farewell Group. Until recently, his job was to disguise the origin of how the DNC and its candidate's emails were hacked. With Nolan and Abyss on his trail, he stole the ops disks to shift the heat. Weill created the false trail that hinted the CIA in Asia under the guise of the Shadow Brokers had sabotaged the NSA, its institutional rival. Weill and Nolan both knew that the CIA would be only too willing to blame a pariah.

The false attribution of the NSA worms and viruses theft to Singapore station meant that Weill knew Nolan was alive—and Chumakov would be coming for him. Even worse, the former FSB director could target Nolan's family. His first instinct was to call General Payne and get another dozen Q-Group men assigned to his hideout. However, the release of the ops disks onto the dark web and the insinuations that someone on the inside from Asia was behind the theft created problems. At a minimum, he'd have to travel to D.C. to clear his name. At worst, he'd end up dead or in jail. Neither of those two options was as bad as the certainty that, once he was off the scene, Chumakov would kill his loved ones. Nolan would have to solve his problems alone at least until the family was safe. And if he was going on the run, he couldn't leave anything behind because there was no telling who would be the next person through the front door. He'd bring the originals out in a format only Payne could read and destroy the rest.

Nolan had mentally rehearsed a rapid retreat, but it still pained him to set the plastic explosive charges on hundreds of thousand dollars' worth of computer and communications equipment. He'd previously microfilmed every original document pulled from the safes; sometimes the old ways were still the best ways. It took two hours to shred the printouts and dissolve the paper swarf in pails set outside, filled with diluted hydrochloric acid. The memory sticks, USB drives and MicroSD cards he retained were protected in ways that would take the NSA or CIA months to decipher without the decryption instructions he'd uploaded to Payne via Tox, a chat application within Tor. But as Nolan knew too well, ever-stronger computing power pushed the frontiers of codebreaking further by the day. Nothing would stay safe if quantum computing became feasible somewhere down the road. For now, that wasn't a proximate concern.

Nolan had two important phone calls to make before Reese composed his last message and the Abyss team went dark. He tracked the charter pilot to his base in Dallas, confirmed availability and outlined the mission. The next task required more finesse. He stared at the number before him, wondering what gave him the right to ask so much from someone who had already put his life on the line for him many times.

* * * * *

NOVATO, CALIFORNIA, AND SINGAPORE

"Mom, it's me," Mei Ling said. "I hope I didn't wake you."

"Honey, I've been awake for more than an hour," Joanie said. "I haven't slept well ever since your father died."

"I miss Dad too, even if he was a cheating asshole. But I have something important to tell you. You may want to sit down, but don't worry, it's good news."

"OK, OK, I'm seated. Are you engaged?"

"Even better. I'm pregnant!"

"Pregnant? I didn't even know you were dating someone. Who's the father? Are you getting married? You know I was in my second trimester when your father and I—"

"Mom, Mom, let me speak. For the past four months, I've been seeing someone from work. We moved in together two months ago, and I'm six weeks along."

"My goodness! What will you do?" Joanie asked.

"I'm keeping it."

"You'll have to quit kickboxing and that Brazilian juju."

"*Jujitsu*, Mom. Yes, I know. I was training hard but cut back a month ago when I started feeling off. No more fights or even sparring until after the baby. I wanted to speak with you about the father."

"It's a married man, isn't it?"

"Mom, we're living together. He'll be divorced soon. You know him."

"Know him? I don't think I've met one of your boyfriends since the volleyball player your sophomore year."

"It's Bruce," Mei Ling said. "Bruce Goodhill."

"What? Bruce Goodhill is my age! And what about his wife? They are good friends with your father and me."

"Last year Bruce started training at the same gym I belong to, and things just happened … I know he's my boss, but it wasn't like he forced his attentions on me. We travel a lot, and after a few years of business dinners, awful airports and fourteen-hour days you get to know one another. I've never been happier. Lena knows about us. For what it's worth, she blames Bruce rather than me. She seems glad to be rid of him and plans to travel once her settlement comes through. Her brothers aren't happy, but that's for Bruce to sort out."

"I certainly don't see the attraction," Joanie said. "You're a beautiful and successful young woman. You realize that when you're forty-five, he'll be over seventy."

"I can do the math," Mei Ling said. "He's got a great sense of humor, he's in better shape than Dad ever was and he's way more interesting than the other men I dated. I need to go. I have a presentation tomorrow."

"Have you considered that maybe you're compensating because your father's not around?"

"Mom, don't get all Freudian on me. My shrink and I went through that. I've been off my meds since Bruce and I started living together. If I need to de-stress, I do it with a glass of wine. Oh, and as of last Thursday I'm off my psychologist too."

"Well, you know I only want the best for you," Joanie said. "Tell Bruce I said hello, and let's speak again soon. I love you."

"Love you too, Mom." Mei Ling hung up. The conversation had been less awful than she'd feared. From the other room she heard Bruce yukking it up on the phone with a client. She poured a big glass of pinot for Bruce and a small one for herself. Three ounces of wine a day was fine, right?

Eight thousand and five hundred miles away in Singapore, Joanie Nolan sat in a stupor with a cordless telephone in her hand. Her daughter was pregnant? Depressed, careerist Mei Ling without a mothering instinct in her body, given over to fighting, fitness and work, had paired up with fifty-something Bruce Goodhill? This was the man who had weaned Mei Ling off Prozac and into a life of maternal happiness and domestic bliss?

She booted up her PC and headed straight to the Singapore Airlines website.

* * * * *

OUTSIDE CAMP IRWIN AND NACOGDOCHES, TEXAS

"Is this Travis Ryder?"

"Maybe," Ryder said. "Who's calling?"

"Travis, it's Bob Nolan. I don't have much time and I need your help. I can pay you and will explain more when we next speak."

Ryder thought he recognized the accent, but he was half-cut. "Congratulations, you're the fourth Bob Nolan to call in the last year. Leave me be."

"I'm the only Bob Nolan who passed a gym bag containing one point five mill across in Sharjah two years ago just before MH17 flew into a missile."

"Well, that's a new one. What did I say when you came back from your visit to the rice farmer in the Irrawaddy Delta after the house incinerated?"

"You told me not to be stressed out because 'shit happens,' which I recall as the most callous thing I've ever heard out of a friend's mouth."

"And what made our companion laugh?" Ryder asked.

"Oh, you and Sam calling the corpses 'Bob's barbecue.'"

"Sunofabitch! I always wondered if you were on that plane, but they pulled your DNA out of the wreck, so I figured your luck had run out. I made the trip to Arlington. You didn't have many mourners, but I did meet your wife and kids. You've got a nice gravesite, by the way."

"I watched the surveillance tape and saw you hit on my daughter," Nolan said. "But that's not the reason for the call. I'm working for the government under deep cover. Only three people in the US knew I was alive until yesterday. Chumakov is in D.C. and now he knows too. He'll go after my family to draw me into the open. I need you to protect them until I take him out for good. I reckon we have less than forty-eight hours before he kidnaps either Bert or Mei Ling."

Ryder put down his empty glass and contemplated a refill. It wasn't even four o'clock and he was half a bottle of Dickel to the worse. And he'd started before lunch with a six-pack of Lone Star. Or was that half a rack? He shook his head. "Bob, slow down. Why not ask the FBI to arrest Chumakov? Seems simple enough."

"Because arresting him isn't straightforward, much less a conviction and a long sentence. What I really need is Chumakov taken out. Authorizing the murder of a foreign intelligence officer on US soil isn't a decision the president would take lightly. This is my problem to sort out. Right now, I need someone to protect my family. If you could dedicate the next two weeks, I'd be pleased to pay you one hundred thousand dollars, plus expenses."

Ryder laughed. "I don't want any more money from you. The IRS prosecuted me for tax fraud because I didn't declare that million dollars from the bounty on Mazdaki, or the half a mill from the Emirates bank job."

"How on earth did the Feds find out about either of those?" Nolan asked.

"Seems I'm shit at money laundering. I bought the biggest gun shop in Nacogdoches and paid cash. Paid cash for my fifteen-acre horse farm outside of town. Paid off Pa's mortgage on his farm, then picked up a big funeral bill when he passed. Sally lives at Ma and Pa's old place with the kids and a helper. The IRS seized the shop and the horse farm against back taxes. I lost the rest of it speculating in commodities futures, plus I've got lawyer bills out the ass and—"

"You're babbling. Will you do this for me or should I call Hecker?"

"Hell, no!" Ryder said. "Hecker's in the pocket of one cartel or another. He's the real reason why I quit the DEA. Of course I'll help you. If it wasn't for all the wounds from our time together, I wouldn't have been able to retire on full disability."

"You'll need to move fast. First stop is New Orleans to pick up Bert, then on to Houston where you should be clean to fly commercially under your own names. Take the 8:30 a.m. Southwest Airlines direct to Oakland. Rent a car and drive to Marin County to my daughter's house. Mei Ling will be a tougher sell, but between Bert and you she'll relent. Once you have her, you'll need to hide out. Bert did his Singapore military service in the Commandos and received jungle survival training from the SAS so find a place in the woods. Put a proper perimeter in place and don't skimp. I'll wire you cash for upfront expenses."

"You want me to show up and tell them their dead father says, 'hi' and there's a Russian madman on the prowl?" Ryder asked.

"No, don't tell them I'm alive. Tell them I left instructions with you in the UAE in July 2014 about what you were to do if Chumakov, Yu Kaili or anyone else ever came after them and I wasn't there. I'll write a script for you when I have time, but I need you to go to the Angelina County Airport first. There's a plane and a pilot waiting. His name is Pasan. The charter is in the name of Underhill. I paid in advance, no names and no questions. Pasan will wait for you in the airport café. When you identify yourself, he'll show you a blank piece of paper with a purple pinwheel on it and nothing more. Anything else is an abort signal. After this call, download a secure messaging app called Signal to your phone. I'll text you with my burner numbers, Bert's cell and Mei Ling's home address. Once you've dug them in, leave Bert and her with a week's worth of food, water, weapons and ammo. Then we're on for Phase II."

"I'm afraid to ask but tell me anyway."

"We'll meet in four days in a certain city where I believe I'll be able to identify a person I've been tracing for two years," Nolan said. "The man I gave up my family and friends for. The biggest enemy of the United States."

"What, that little North Korean fat boy?"

"It doesn't matter. Use Signal and we'll take it from there. I don't know how I can thank you for this."

"Well, don't go all teary-eyed," Ryder said. "I've been living inside a bottle these past six months. I'm not the man you knew in Burma and Pakistan. I'm out of shape, separated, broke and—"

"You're underemployed, that's all. Stop feeling sorry for yourself, sober up and put your SEAL game face on. Goodbye, and thanks."

Ryder stared at his empty glass. In a life full of weird exchanges, that conversation might have topped the bill. Bob Nolan, the ultimate survivor, was back. How had he ever doubted that the old codebreaker was indestructible? Now to pack a few clothes and see if he could scrape together enough cash to pay the fare on a thirty-five-mile cab ride. But first he'd have another four fingers of Dickel over ice to help him collect his thoughts.

CHAPTER SIX

THE FUGITIVE

WEDNESDAY, AUGUST 17: OUTSIDE CAMP IRWIN

Nolan knew that Ryder was right. He should be on the phone asking Payne to convince the president to act, but there were complicating factors. First, it wasn't good enough for Chumakov to be deported or even locked up. The man had threatened to kill his children on camera and make his wife watch the recording before he killed her, too. Second, everyone but Payne—who didn't even have an official role in the administration—would blame Nolan for the theft of the NSA malware tools. Knowing how cautious POTUS was, at a minimum Obama would summon him in D.C. to answer questions. If Nolan refused, that would put him under even greater suspicion, and make it even less likely that the executive branch would negate Chumakov's threat.

Earlier today, Nolan had put Abyss on ice and alerted his direct reports to notify their people they were all on stand down until they heard from Silberman, Payne's *nom de guerre*. Based on what Payne/Silberman learned in the coming days, the president could pass judgment on Nolan and determine whether to restart one or both lines of inquiry. In the meantime, if General Payne or the president received reports that Nolan had died, don't give them much credence.

Nolan concluded his email by saying that he would go dark until he cleared his name of the Shadow Broker link and determined the identity of Higher Love's leader. To that end, his research today had unearthed the suggestion that on August 21 Mr. Love would be at a certain time and place. Nolan aimed to be there too. Once he'd fingered their top man, he'd contact Payne to take him off to a black site for interrogation.

A soft beeping from the security console alerted Nolan to an anomaly outside. A flurry of keystrokes later, he had three bogeys on the radarscope. He shouldered the power supply rucksack borrowed from Ghostbusters and hefted the Battelle Drone Defender. Several rapid trigger pulls sent jamming radio waves to force the drones out of the late afternoon sky. He ducked back inside ahead of a potential sniper's bullet and shed the pack. A glance confirmed that the bogeys no longer appeared on scope.

He sat down and drained the last of his protein shake. Then the main power failed, and the backup generator sputtered to life. A new, higher-pitched tone signaled that someone had crossed the ring of motion detectors poking out of the sand four hundred meters out. He wasn't spooked: he could still escape short of fast-ropers clattering onto the doublewide's roof.

Plan A called for Nolan to depart on foot and travel fifteen to twenty-five kilometers a night and lay up in the daytime at preselected and preprovisioned safe areas unknown to his FBI minders. Three nights' worth of journeys would put him outside the search grid. Unfortunately, Plan A was a nonstarter. Gunshots sounded, first sporadic and then punctuated by automatic bursts. Nolan scurried from one C4 charge to the next, setting the timers for three minutes. The large cork bulletin board covered in photos, pushpins and colored yarn with an empty spot at the top reserved for Mr. Love's photo received a rinse of gasoline slopped from the red plastic canister under his desk. There was no time to pack. Monitors beeped their alerts until the second backup generator cut out. Rounds ripped through the trailer's aluminum walls and dropped Nolan to the floor in a gas puddle. From that vantage, he saw the red LEDs blinking their countdowns with the wires feeding into those innocuous chunks of PE. This was no Payne-ordered roundup: it was a straight hit.

Plan B might work yet. General Payne had instructed the FBI to construct a vertical shaft and escape tunnel in late 2014. Under the kitchen sink above the trapdoor sat a firefighter's breathing apparatus and oxygen tank. Nolan turned on the feed, donned the gear and balanced on the ladder leading down. Another burst of waist-high automatic fire was his final signal to descend. The trapdoor closed flush and he latched it tight from underneath. Down the ladder Nolan half-climbed, half-fell. At the bottom of the shaft, he stood up and disengaged the hook holding the blast lid, then crouched as he lowered the asbestos-lined steel cover. He would be safe short of a grenade dumped down his rabbit hole.

The first explosions echoed dully overhead and continued for twenty seconds. He counted five primaries and two secondaries: the charges had ignited the gasoline vapor. From the racks lining the tunnel, he collected his bugout bag and confirmed there was a laptop inside. Into the rucksack went the microfilm and various tiny disks and drives, followed by emergency rations, a gallon of water, a sidearm and spare magazines. He stripped and put on clean clothes, leaving the gasoline-impregnated garments on the floor.

If the hit team knew about the spider hole and tunnel, they would kill him as he emerged from the other end. Setting that unpleasant scenario aside, who were they? Weill wasn't good enough to find him so fast, and even if he had, mobilizing a team and flying it to Las Vegas or LA would have added another day to the timeline. Someone other than Chumakov wanted him dead, and the shortlist had three names on it: Higher Love, Frank Coulter, and Yu Kaili. Kaili had gone missing and Nolan flattered himself to think, if she were somehow in authority, that she wouldn't want to see him dead. It equally was beyond Nolan how a seventy-eight-year-old Coulter could organize a hit team while under house arrest in Northern California. Besides, Coulter and Nolan had a 'no families' clause in their blood feud that Coulter had honored to date. Meanwhile, Higher Love had insinuated itself into every arm of the federal government, and that made HL the leading suspect.

Nolan could only wait. He had to time his flight to follow the departure of the shooters up top yet precede the arrival of the investigating authorities. He'd have a fifteen-minute window sometime in the next half-hour.

* * * * *

THE WHITE HOUSE

As the president's go-to man inside the Beltway, retired general Neil Payne seldom had to apply force to his oratory. This was one of the exceptions. "This is unacceptable. I need to know what happened, not conjecture. Arch Stanton worked directly for me. He was a desk man, so it's inconceivable that he killed the two FBI agents guarding him, shot down three other men serving the arrest warrant, and left a wounded NSA attorney as the sole survivor. I want you to direct the Air Force to put up a drone and track everything with a heat signature within thirty miles of Stanton's trailer. Make certain the attorney general signs off on the order and keep the president out of it in case it all goes south. Am I making myself understood?"

"Yes, General," said General Stevens Sharkey, head of the Joint Chiefs of Staff. Putting a Predator loaded with surveillance equipment up above California in an election year would give the Pentagon's Judge Advocate General's Corps a case of the kittens. The AG's team wouldn't act any faster either. The drone preppers at Creech Air Force Base would be sitting on their hands for hours to come.

* * * * *

THE SOUTHWEST AND NEW YORK CITY

"She's in her hotel room," Kleinwort said. "I see no reason to meet here. Simply sequester her and issue the ultimatum."

"We've been over this before. I will not raise the alarm prematurely," Love said. "Despite her unofficial status, she remains a favorite of her president. I don't want the Ministry of State Security involved until a time of my choosing. In your long career as a diplomat, surely you have conducted more challenging deceptions than what I require of you tomorrow?"

"I'm an old man. I was younger then, sparring with Zhou Enlai and his ilk. The stakes were lower. You do realize that Liu will reveal our plan to Obama in return for a concession elsewhere, most probably US acquiescence to China's annexation of the South China Sea?"

"That won't happen. Yes, Liu will be furious when we detain Yu in Texas, but if he tells the Americans that a North Korea nuclear device has been smuggled into the US then China loses control of the situation. A weak leader like Obama might lash out with tactical nukes and decapitate North Korea's regime or otherwise botch an intervention a la Libya and Qaddafi. Furthermore, once Kim knows that the Americans are onto the NEMP, he'll realize he's a dead man walking. Then the risk is that Kim bombs Seoul and China finds itself once again at war with the US."

"I say again that you've miscalculated this situation. We should not kidnap Liu's darling to extort the arming codes off the Chinese. It's needlessly provocative."

"Enough! I will further sweeten the deal. Once we receive the codes, not only will I release Yu but also I'll give Liu what you so fear he'll seek from Obama. I will concede China's military control of the South China Sea and the annexation of parts of Burma, Laos and Pakistan. I will acknowledge China's claim of hegemony over the Western Pacific. Should Taiwan resist, we will allow China to invade without fear of US intervention. Do you still think Liu will betray us to America's last president?"

Kleinwort paused in horror before replying. "That's seventy years of Asia foreign policy down the toilet in one afternoon. Surely you are not serious?"

"When the Unity Party is in charge, agreements will be subject to reinterpretation at my convenience. In the short term, China can have its vassals and we'll annex Latin and South America as quid pro quos. If Europe's slow on the uptake, Africa will be for the taking. Putin will reestablish the Soviet Union. Managed trade, fixed FX rates and high tariffs will protect jobs and ensure social harmony. As for the subject peoples, they never counted anyway."

Kleinwort abandoned his failed defense and shifted tacks. "So then why allow the discovery of the nuclear EMP weapon on US soil? Should we save it in case our coup doesn't proceed as planned?"

"Until very recently, Doctor Kleinwort, I respected your intellect. Now I wonder if I've been paying too much attention to the musings of a senile university professor. The measures already in place will allow for Ginger to defeat Crandall in November, but the election is still too close to call comfortably. Therefore, we need to release concrete evidence of Obama's incompetence in national security matters to destroy what remains of his ill-deserved reputation, and discredit candidate Crandall. A once close election becomes a rout. Subsequently, evidence of Russia's control over the funding of Ginger's real estate businesses, plus blackmail by Putin, will lead to the Republicans' obliteration in the 2018 midterms. Out of the ashes will rise the Unity Party, funded and staffed by our own. Chaos and violent confrontations follow, and from there, it is but a short step to military intervention to restore public order."

Kleinwort sighed. That was the problem with putting ideas into the head of an iron-willed ideologue: once in place, there was no displacing them. "I have one final question. Why do you take such an interest in the reappearance of Bob Nolan?"

"After he faked his death, he was the impetus behind the intelligence services purges. And now he's after me."

"Ah, yes, I see why he should be killed."

"We tried and may have failed. It's too early to say," Love said. "However, I've reconsidered our position, and gave instructions to take Nolan's family hostage rather than pursue him further should he have survived today's attempt. Focus on your meeting with Yu and leave operational matters to the experts."

* * * * *

NEAR CAMP IRWIN

Nolan emerged behind the generator shed forty meters from the smoking remains of the doublewide. Night-vision googles in place, he surveyed the grounds and saw nothing. His hearing, heightened by twenty minutes in sensory deprivation mode, detected not even the faint buzz of a quadcopter. But in the next ten minutes, a convoy of black ops and Q-Group agents would charge up the road or descend from the sky.

He scuffed the dirt fifteen meters from the opening of the tunnel's exit hatch until the outline of the camouflage netting revealed itself. Nolan pulled the cover aside and spotted the small loops of parachute cord. Lying beneath the root cellar doors and wrapped in heavy plastic sheeting was a SilentHawk stealth electric dirt bike.

It would be morning before the searchers worked out that he wasn't on foot. Helmet and NVGs in place, he walked the bike over stony ground for another thirty meters before starting it on full silent electric mode. His first course was due south in a feint. The order of operations was clear in his mind. First Chumakov, second Ryder/kids/wife, and then Mr. Love.

*　*　*　*　*

ANGELINA COUNTY AIRPORT, TEXAS

"I'm Underhill. Do you have something for me?" Ryder asked.

A middle-aged brown man in an aqua blue boiler suit with JEEVAN AIRWAYS on the left breast pushed a slip of paper across the top of the coffeeshop counter. Ryder unfolded it and confirmed that it contained a solitary purple whorl. He nodded. "What next?"

"I'm Pasan Wanigasekara, your pilot for the next twelve hours. You want to use the toilet and tidy up before we fly?" The Sinhalese gestured to the signs and gave him a smile of encouragement.

Ryder knew that he wasn't dressed for success, but what stared back in the men's room mirror was a shocker. He hadn't shaved in four days and his oily hair reached almost to his shoulders, reminding him of a Lynyrd Skynyrd band photo circa 1973. Unfocused, bloodshot eyes didn't disguise he'd missed a button on his checkered short-sleeved shirt, the better to show his protruding gut and a tuft of navel hair. His faded jeans featured fashionable mustard stains and orange Cheeto dust, and a shirttail peeked out of his fly. The room rippled when he looked down to rebutton his shirt. For support he clutched the sink with both hands.

This was pathetic. He was pathetic. From decorated SEAL sniper in Iraq and Afghanistan, to kick-ass DEA security head across Asia's two heroin centers—the Golden Triangle and Golden Crescent—to unwashed buffoon. He stumbled into the stall and put a pair of grimy fingers down his throat. Twenty seconds later, a gallon of bourbon-infused beer had vacated his stomach. Ryder's tongue tasted like battery acid, but as he wiped away the last of the dribble he already felt better. After rinsing, he washed his face and policed his appearance. Next stop: New Orleans and Bert Nolan.

*　*　*　*　*

OUTSIDE CAMP IRWIN

Nolan made good time on the motorcycle despite falling off once on a rocky descent. He stayed in the shadows under the nearly full moon until he was out of the foothills and into the desert scrub parallel to Interstate 15. Heavy wire cutters made short work of the Bureau of Land Management fences he encountered. In little more than an hour, he intersected Death Valley Road just north of Baker, switched on the headlights and turned on his GPS to locate a waypoint. He parked the bike and hiked the last quarter-mile over broken ground. Into the cache under a flat rock went a Ziploc bag containing the microfilm and most of the storage media. For the D.C. end, he'd only need a couple of IDs, cash, his weapon, burner phones, the ops disks and the shockproof laptop. The rest of the paraphernalia and booty would have to await his return, if ever.

Nolan rode the SilentHawk in hybrid mode, pushing the bike to its limits as his invisibility window diminished by the breath. Shoshone was less than twenty miles to the north. There he'd leave the bike before drones with infrared sought him out. If he couldn't hitch a ride, he'd steal a car. Airport security would be on alert, but he could hide among six hundred thousand people spread over the one hundred fifty square miles that comprised greater Las Vegas.

＊ ＊ ＊ ＊ ＊

WASHINGTON, D.C.

Even after Nolan's purported death, Chumakov had still kept tabs on his wife and children. From time to time he'd contemplated making good on his promises to kill the three of them but had done nothing. Taking revenge against a dead enemy's family was the coward's way. His moral calculus had changed now that he knew Nolan was alive. His wife was in Singapore where ex-SVR and FSB assassins were thin on the ground, and his son's whereabouts in New Orleans seemed to change by the week as he flitted from one sublet to another. The easiest one to kidnap would his daughter, who was cohabitating in Northern California with her boss, a middle-aged man of slender build who posed no physical threat.

The next step was to find trustworthy and capable men on short notice. There were ample current and former Russia intelligence officers in the US, but most of them were retired analysts and not field men. The various Russia mobs supplied violence at a price, but from prior professional observation Chumakov wasn't impressed. Anything more complicated than a straight murder was beyond their ken. Then an idea struck him. He summoned embassy driver and ex-Spetsnaz ground forces Corporal Egorov to meet in Rock Creek Park. The fifty-year-old former tanker listened while the Tatar outlined his requirements, the need for immediacy and a two-hundred-thousand-dollar fee payable half in advance and half upon completion. Egorov promised to revert within the next twenty-four hours. When Egorov's men had Nolan in custody, Chumakov would fly out to administer the last rites. He could do the turnaround in a day: he wouldn't be missed by either the maddening Americans in Ginger's employ, or the madmen to whom he reported.

* * * * *

WASHINGTON, D.C.

Payne had General Sharkey on the line. "It's been two hours and the drone still isn't airborne. It's unacceptable."

"I didn't expect the JAG to take so long," Sharkey protested. "Not when you were behind the order. With respect, sir, I have no control over the Attorney General. In parallel, I ordered night-vision-equipped helicopters out of Miramar. Loadout and pre-flight briefings should be done within ninety minutes. The helos will be in the sky in ninety minutes provided the AG signs off."

"Miramar? That's in San Diego. What about Edwards? It's just down the road."

"Edwards is fixed-wing only, sir. Budget cutbacks led to the relocation of the squadron to San Diego years ago. And we've also dispatched a forensics team to search for whatever's left of Stanton's body."

"He's alive," Payne said. "History has shown that this man is resilient. I have to go, General, but I want you to call me as soon as the drone and helicopters are aloft. We need Stanton alive and unharmed, do you understand?"

"Yes, General." Sharkey waited for a dial tone and put down his handset. He wondered why the president of the US felt so little confidence in his professional military that he relied on the retired founder of Delta Force for advice on military and intelligence matters. It was an insult to serving professionals over and beyond the indignity of a retiree of inferior rank ordering around the Joint Chief. And why did POTUS have people living in the desert undertaking top-secret assignments for his eyes only? The *Post* would be most interested to learn about this, not to mention Fox News.

Payne switched to line two where FBI Director Frank Salmick had been on hold. "Now that there are agents on site, do you have a better understanding of what happened? How did a desk man know that the team was coming and kill five of six men, wound the last one, and escape without leaving a trail?"

"I don't have a satisfactory answer for you, sir."

"And I have a report from Quantico in front of me that this man was a barely range-certified marksman just two years ago."

"Are you saying Arch Stanton is or was with the bureau?" Salmick asked.

"Not under that name, but yes, Stanton underwent field training," Payne said. "I want to know everything about the two NSA lawyers who joined the warrant servers. And I want the wounded man's hospital room guarded by FBI or local police—not NSA personnel. And I must find out who in the NSA assigned those two men to the detail, and who in the FBI agreed to this. Report your findings to my ears only. Any final questions?"

"No, sir, only that Q-Group detected several current and former NSA staff who likely spy for Russia. We have tracked them for more than three months, hoping to follow the chain to their handlers, either within the embassy or under commercial cover. We've made progress, but the investigations are ongoing."

"Send the files to me and I'll decide what changes, if any, to recommend to the president. Joint Task Force Ares may be able to subsume your investigations if you're moving on parallel paths. But for now, assume the Stanton situation stands apart from the ongoing Q-Group investigations. Keep quiet about this conversation, Director. I know how keen the bureau is to enjoy good press relations, but now is not the time for leaks."

"Yes, sir. Understood."

Payne pressed the heels of his hands into his forehead. At a minimum, the NSA and FBI were compromised. He hoped that Nolan was safely away—he couldn't lay on any more delays without attracting suspicion.

CHAPTER SEVEN

FLIGHT OR FIGHT

WEDNESDAY, AUGUST 17: LAKEFRONT AIRPORT, OUTSIDE NEW ORLEANS

Bert Nolan didn't know, and didn't much care to know, Travis Ryder. Bert's late father had mentioned that Ryder had saved his life several times in Burma and Pakistan. But in the end Ryder's heroics hadn't helped much, as Dad still died just months later. Such was his father's notoriety after MH370 vanished and the MH17 crash, Bert transferred from University of Washington to Tulane. He changed his last name from Nolan to Janus, hoping that the Roman god of entrances and exits would offer him a fresh start and a modicum of privacy. It had, and as of May 2016 Bert Janus owned a bachelor's degree in business and a taste for life in the French Quarter.

He had nothing planned for the night, so he'd borrowed a friend's car and driven the eight miles out to the municipal airport at Lake Charles. He should have been watching an old UFC rerun, but curiosity and Ryder's insistence had induced him to venture out. It was late and the airport was empty. However, the main terminal was still open, and one of the runways was lit. He'd give it a half-hour.

The Ryder at Nolan's funeral in early August 2014 had cut a striking figure in his white sailor's cap, blue uniform with the SEAL Trident above the campaign ribbons, silver star and purple hearts. Though not a big man, he had oozed physicality even with a pronounced limp. Ryder had removed his coveted Trident and slammed the Budweiser in his balled fist into the lid of Bob Nolan's ceremonial coffin. He saluted with a bloody hand and turned to face the mourners, saying "Damn few." Bert had been struck by the depth of the man's affection and respect. But that was long ago, and it was late on this insufferably muggy night.

"Bert, that you?"

Bert looked up to see an unshaven, greasy-haired homeless person trailing an odor of stale beer. "Who are you?"

"We spoke earlier," the man said. "Our plane's refueling. It's ninety minutes to Houston. We'll sleep in the terminal and fly to Oakland tomorrow morning."

"Let me see an ID."

"Look, we need to reach your sister's place as soon as we can. You're both in danger."

"For all I know, you're the danger." Bert stood up, accentuating his five-inch height advantage. An accomplished Muay Thai and amateur MMA fighter, he was used to throwing his weight around. Bert edged closer and curled his lip.

Ryder was having none of it and closed the gap to inches. "I spent the last week in a brewery, but I'll put you down in ten seconds." Ryder was surprised to hear himself say these words with conviction. He doubted he could wrestle open a bag of Fritos.

Bert took a step back and reconsidered. The flash in the green eyes reminded him of Ryder's face at the memorial service. This drunkard was serious, and with Bert's next fight in three weeks, he didn't need to break a hand on the former tough guy's forehead. "Just tell me again where we're going and why."

"We're headed to your sister's in Novato. Once we collect her, we'll seek out a safe spot until I can neutralize the threat."

"What threat?"

"Anatoly Chumakov," Ryder said. "I can explain more on the plane, but this airport closes at midnight and we're cutting it close."

"You have me until Houston, but I'll need a lot more detail if you want me to fly to California."

"Fair enough. I'm jogging. Try to keep up."

* * * * *

SHOSHONE, CALIFORNIA

It was after ten o'clock local time, and both the bike and Nolan were beat. He left the SilentHawk behind the Chevron station with the key in the ignition and helmet on the seat after wiping his prints from both. With any luck, someone would take it for a joyride and distract his pursuers.

Nolan shouldered the bugout backpack across the street to the Crowbar Café. Encouragingly, he saw two big rigs parked nearby. He ordered a draft, but the highly carbonated domestic beer tasted terrible and he abandoned it. A crumpled Las Vegas *Sun* sat on the counter, headlines indicating a possible connection between Putin and the Dems' hacked emails. *Indeed.*

The fellow closest to Nolan fit the spec: sweat-stained straw Stetson, the crows' feet of a highwayman or ranch foreman, a double helping of chicken-fried steak and crinkle-cut fries, and half a pot of coffee.

"Pardon me, I'm looking for a ride and am willing to pay for the privilege."

Stetson stroked his chin. "Whereabouts you headed?"

"I'm flexible," Nolan said, "but I'd like to leave inside the next thirty minutes."

"I'm not looking for that type of travel companion."

"You haven't heard what I'll pay."

"No, and I don't want to. But I'll offer you some free advice. See the feller at the corner table in the green shirt looking over? The chief of police ain't no friend of mine, but most everyone in here knows him, so you'd best be careful who you approach next."

"Thanks for the tip. Anyone you recommend I have a word with?"

"Well, let me take a look." Stetson stood and placed his hat on the counter before he ambled to the men's room. Nolan gave it a ten count and followed him in. The bathroom was spotless despite thirty-year-old wall tiles and cracked, yellowed linoleum peeling off the floor.

Stetson spoke over the sound of running water and lathering hands. He looked at Nolan in the tarnished mirror and said, "Kid at four o'clock by himself seems nervous. Don't know how keen you are to wrap his troubles around your own, but he's not from these parts."

"I owe you."

"If you feel strongly about it, I'll send my supper check your way."

"Safe travels," Nolan said, turning to leave.

"One last thing. You'll need new clothes if you're gonna stay outta custody."

Nolan looked down at his tattered shirt with a bloodstained right forearm and road dirt forming a dark brown ring above his collar. His trousers were brown, no longer blue. The door swung shut behind him as Stetson made his way back to the dinner counter.

Nolan scrubbed his face and neck and cleaned his cuts. His clothes still looked like hell, but at least he'd made an effort, and that alone might signal that he wasn't an outlaw.

Twenty minutes later, Nolan and his new BFF, "Bud, call me Greaser Bud," departed the Crowbar Café and made their way around the side out of the glare of the front window. A pickup truck sat parked against the wall with a full load secured by a tarp. The price was five hundred and the location was anywhere in Vegas, but they had to make one stop along the way. Oh, and was the old timer handy with a gun?

Nolan considered his options and decided that driving around the desert at night to make a delivery with Greaser Bud was a less-bad option than turning himself in or waiting until daylight when the Highway Patrol would recognize his face from the overnight BOLOs.

Nolan reassembled his burner and dialed Ryder's mobile, but no joy. He called Joanie in Singapore and found the answering machine. He was pleased that she'd thrown Jerry Flynn out after their last face-to-face meeting two years ago but wondered if that creep still tapped her phone and emails. He hung up rather than leave a message. Phone powered down, off went the back cover and out came the battery and SIM card. Everything went into a sandwich baggie, and from there into the bugout bag. Greaser Bud returned from rinsing the wall and unlocked the rig.

The chief of police from the café stepped out of the shadows. "Step away from the vehicle and keep your hands in view. You're both under arrest."

"On what charge?" Greaser Bud asked.

"Urinating in public for you, and suspicion of homicide for your friend. Now both of you place your hands on the hood and spread your legs out good and wide."

"Who are you, and who do you think I am?" Nolan asked, trying to buy a little time.

"I'm Chief Furness and you're Arch Stanton, wanted in the murder of five federal agents. Now turn around and lean on the vehicle, palms flat and legs spread."

The sheriff was in his late fifties and twenty-five pounds past his prime. He needed to take this small-town cop before backup arrived. Nolan whirled around and snapped a kick at the outside of the sheriff's left knee. Well-executed, the move shredded the anterior cruciate ligament. Poorly delivered, it left a bruise on the lower thigh. Sheriff Furness cursed, took a step back and swung a fist at Nolan's head. Nolan blocked the blow with a raised forearm and launched a left-footed kick at the sheriff's groin. This, too, missed its mark and Furness took another two steps back and clawed at his holster. Nolan now appreciated the difference between sparring with a live person and going through the motions in front of YouTube videos.

Greaser Bud flew around the front grill and tackled the sheriff before he could clear his sidearm. Nolan pounced on the lawman and used two hands to wrench the pistol free. The pickup truck driver landed two fists to the sheriff's face and applied a chokehold.

"Stop resisting or you'll be number six on the day," Nolan said, raising the sheriff's Glock. Furness and Greaser Bud disengaged, and the younger man moved out of the line of fire. A minute later, the sheriff was handcuffed, phoneless, gagged and locked in the back of his civilian vehicle, now stripped of its emergency repair box.

Fortuitously, none of the café's diners or staff had wandered around to the side to check out the commotion.

"Thanks for taking him down back there," Nolan said. "He might have shot me."

"He might have shot us both," Greaser Bud replied. "The meet is in an hour and forty miles away on bad roads. We gotta roll."

"Try to keep it under the limit. You don't want to get pulled over. By the way, I didn't kill anyone today."

"The ride to Vegas is up to a thousand and I want to see the cash."

"Depends. What's under the tarp?"

"Four-dozen peyote cactuses."

* * * * *

BEECHCRAFT BARON N168TT OUTBOUND ICAO-HOU

"I'm supposed to believe that you somehow spotted my father's mortal enemy Chumakov in Washington earlier today?" Bert asked.

"I didn't say I saw him," Ryder replied. "One of my network spotted him on the street."

"Show me a picture. My father must have left you a photo along with his instructions. Let me see the letter too."

"I don't have either with me. I came here in a hurry. As you can see from my appearance, I'm not at my best."

"Not at your best?" Bert repeated. "You look like a Bourbon Street drunk. How do we pay for the tickets to Oakland?"

"I was hoping you could put them on your card. I will pay you back in a few days."

"Pay me back? With what? Empty beer cans? You're wasting my time. We're turning this plane around. Pilot—"

As Bert tapped Pasan on the shoulder, Ryder pulled him back into his seat. Bert's reaction was instantaneous. "Take your hands off me! The next time you touch me, I'll break your fucking arm."

Ryder closed his eyes, curbing his urge to incapacitate the brat. "OK, I'll level with you. Your dad is alive and he's going after Chumakov himself. He works for the president on an off-the-books project. He didn't want me to tell you to keep the information tight."

"Dad's alive? Do you have any proof?" Bert wanted to believe—and had often imagined having Dad walk through the door—but they'd found his DNA on what was left of a seatbelt.

"He said he'd call after we landed in Houston."

"Holy shit. Do Mei Ling or Mom know?"

"I don't think so."

* * * * *

NOVATO, CALIFORNIA

Mei Ling gasped, then fell onto her side. When her shudders of ecstasy subsided, she took the glass off the nightstand and drank her last mouthful of pinot.

"You know what the only downside is to making love to a pregnant woman?" Goodhill asked.

"She's super horny?"

"No, the two tiny hands grabbing onto the end of your penis."

Mei Ling threw a pillow at Goodhill as he scrambled out of the bedroom, tight buns and slim, muscular legs on display.

From the staircase he called out in his characteristic tenor. "I'll pull the plates out of the dishwasher."

"And throw out that gun! I don't want it in the house."

"That's just not possible. When I told Lena our marriage was over, her brothers went crazy. Thomas is a felon, and Robin has eyes that look like those on TV in the serial killer crime shows."

"Fine," Mei Ling said. "Just keep it locked up, OK?"

"I'd rather keep it in the bedside drawer," Goodhill said. "The man in the gun shop said that gunowners who died in home invasions did so because they didn't have ready access. What's the use of locking it in a safe if someone's coming through the window?"

* * * * *

WASHINGTON, D.C.

"I have two men for your job," Egorov said over the scrambled embassy line.

"That's excellent news," Chumakov said. "I'm surprised by the speed."

"They're in the Bay Area taking their children on college tours. They can spare you two days away from their families to perform your mission."

"Tell me a little more about them."

"Mid-forties, former Spetsnaz ground forces. Fought mostly in Chechnya. Co-own a firm that supplies security services to businessmen in Saint Petersburg."

"Friendly to Putin or not?" Chumakov asked.

"Friendly, friendly. No conflicts."

"Excellent. I've prepared a briefing document with a house floorplan and several temporary storage facilities to hold our product. Send me the two men's contact details, and I'll pass the information along."

"The men require half the payment be in their account before they begin," Egorov said. "I have all the bank details. They borrowed their work names from Chekov, so you'll be dealing with Trofimov and Borisovich."

"Fine. I'll wire the funds overnight."

* * * * *

NORTH OF SHOSHONE

"Yeah, I'm good with a 9-mil," Nolan said.

"Ever shoot anyone, Arch?" Greaser Bud had the disconcerting habit of turning his head completely when addressing his passenger. They were doing eighty-five on secondary roads, veering from shoulder to shoulder. Nolan would have preferred Stevie Wonder behind the wheel.

"No one today." Nolan wondered if this sallow, acne-scarred youth was a laid-back stoner with an aggressive streak, or a Manson family grandkid trying to fake that he was mellow.

Two tires left the road and hit the dirt. Bud jerked the wheel and they were back on the other shoulder. A small animal fled, eyes glowing red in the headlights.

"Either slow down or stop looking at me when you talk. You'll get us both killed."

"Hah! That's the weak-ass shit Terry used to say," Bud said. "He never had the balls for the business."

"Bud, what is your business if you don't mind my asking?"

"You promise you won't go into competition?"

"I promise. I'm a fugitive, so I'm busy just now."

"What is it you do, Arch?" Bud fished a large joint out of his front shirt pocket and tried to light it. His BIC lighter scorched his thumb and he dropped it to the floor mat with a curse.

Nolan picked up the lighter and ignited Bud's joint, the biggest one he'd seen since high school in Ohio back in the 1970s. "You tell me first, then I'll tell you."

Bud took a deep drag. "Tell you what? Oh, what I do. Got it. I'm a middleman. I drive down to the Mexico border mostly in Arizona, but sometimes all the way to Texas. I meet sellers, but instead of drugs I buy peyote cactuses after the Indians have harvested the buttons. That way I get 'em cheap and legal. The cacti come off Indian reservations south of the border around Real de Catorce. I pay a few dollars a plant, then drive 'em to my customers who run the nurseries up here. Next year, there'll be peyote to harvest and everyone will be happy playing pinball with the stars."

"Huh. Peyote cactus nurseries?"

"Sure. People all over the world buy cactuses from Cali nurseries. Got forty-eight plants in the back. Sell the big peyote plants for a hundred bucks and the small ones for fifty."

Hardly worth the trouble, Nolan thought. "I guess it's a living if you don't have to split with a partner."

"Terry? You talking about Terry Henderson?"

"I guess so," Nolan said.

"Terry hasn't worked for me in over a year. First, he had a woman in Old Mexico, and then he got himself a king-hell H habit. Before this run, I did him a solid and promised to drop his ass at his folk's place around Needles. I didn't realize he was holding until the fucker pulled his works out while I was motoring up I-95. Next thing I know, he's passed out with a syringe hanging off his arm. I took the next exit, found a vacant lot and dumped him."

"Was he still alive?"

Bud ashed his joint into the Mountain Dew bottle in his cupholder. "As of, I dunno, eight hours ago I guess he was breathing. Right now? I ain't got no fucking clue, but if he wakes up, I guess he's hitchin' to Needles 'cause it's too fuckin' far to walk. You want a hit? This is some fine Sinaloa MJ."

Nolan waved off the offer. The pickup shuddered as they struck what might have been a skunk. Bud reestablished control with one hand and took another toke.

"Where we headed?" Nolan asked.

"Just past Death Valley Junction and before Ryan there's a side road. Up in the hills there's an old Mormon who grows and sells the buttons over the internet. He's good for about fifty plants twice a year. We should be there in thirty. Do our business in another thirty, and I'll have you in Vegas before sunup. I still need to see that thou first, though. 'Ass, cash or gas, no one rides for free,' and all that jazz."

"I'll pull your money out in a moment. Why did you ask if I was good with a gun?" Sneaking in under the pot smoke, Nolan's nose picked up a long-forgotten odor: they'd hit Pepé le Pew's nephew.

"Jonah said he thought the DEA had him staked out," Bud said. "He was going to try to lose them before our little rendezvous. But you best be ready if the bullets start flying."

"I don't need to go to Vegas tonight," Nolan said. "Drop me in Death Valley Junction, and I'll pay you the grand anyway."

"What, are you a narc? Sunofabitch!" Quick as a flash Bud pointed a small automatic at Nolan's midriff. "You think I'm dumb? Put your hands on the dash, bitch."

Nolan declined to reply. The smoke from Bud's joint had the sharp tint of a permanent marker, suggesting it was laced with PCP. The pickup was all over the road just like Bud's paranoid mind.

Five minutes later, the Death Valley California Junction had come and gone. There was a single dark strip mall, certainly no place to find a ride in the middle of the night. Bud took a hard left onto California 190, and fifteen minutes later pulled off onto a dirt track and downshifted. The automatic was still in his right hand, speaking volumes in the silence.

The pickup slowed as they came over a rise. Below in a shallow wash was another pickup silhouetted in the moonlight.

"Get out and walk out around front," Bud said as he cut the engine. His nickel-plated ladies' automatic was up and aimed at Nolan's forehead.

This would be too easy. Bud must have forgotten that he still had the cop's Glock in his waistband. Nolan opened the door, stepped down and had the weapon up and leveled over the hood before Bud could stumble from the driver's seat and remember to keep his gun pointed at his captive.

CHAPTER EIGHT

JUST DESERT

WEDNESDAY, AUGUST 17: NORTH OF SHOSHONE

"Drop it!"

Halogen spotlights lit the desert floor from three directions. "DEA! Everyone drop their weapons and down on the ground!"

Nolan complied, but Bud had other ideas and fired once. Three gunshots replied. Nolan still had his face buried in the dirt when practiced hands cuffed his wrists behind his back.

On the other side of the Ford, the agents checked Bud's vitals. "He's gone," said a voice. "Took two in the legs and one in the head. That must have been you, Larry. Ever since you came back from Asia, you can't shoot to wound worth a damn."

Asia? Nolan saw his salvation. "Larry, do you know Sam Hecker, former head of the DEA in South and Southeast Asia?"

"Shut up unless you're spoken to," Cuffs said as he shined a penlight in Nolan's eyes.

"Who said that?" Larry asked as he walked around to the other side of the Ford. The third agent loosened cargo straps while a fourth emerged from the night with a gagged and cuffed man scuffling in front of him, no doubt Jonah.

"I did," Nolan said. "I worked undercover for the DEA in Pakistan in 2014. I'm undercover now, but it's not a DEA assignment. Wake Hecker up in D.C. and I'll straighten this out in two minutes."

"Hecker has nothing to do with undercover operations. For all I know, you pulled his name off the website."

"His wife's Sophie and they have a son who must be about three or four named C. J. Hecker's the number two in the OII, the Office of Investigative—"

"Intelligence," Larry finished. "I know where he works. Who should I say is calling?"

"Call his personal cell, 202-689-4521. I'll give you a name in a second." Nolan was on his knees and could see that Larry was in his early thirties with a body language that broadcast alpha status. Nolan wondered which of his many aliases Hecker would remember.

"Let's book these two," Cuffs said as he jerked Nolan the rest of his way to his feet. "They can make their phone calls after processing."

"It's a matter of national security," Nolan said. "You tell him Derrick Larson from Rangoon missed MH17. He'll take the call."

"MH17? Wasn't that the Malaysian plane the Russians shot down over Ukraine?"

"Yes, July 17, 2014 with the loss of two hundred ninety-eight passengers and crew. I was listed as a passenger and have been undercover ever since."

"And Hecker knows about this?" Cuffs asked.

"No, only a few people do."

"So why aren't we calling one of them?"

"Because the DCI can't order the DEA in California to put me on a plane to Washington tonight."

"And Hecker will?"

"It's ringing," Larry said. "I'll put him on speaker."

After four interminably long trills, a sleepy voice answered. "Hecker."

"Deputy Director, sorry to disturb you. This is Larry Bird with the Los Angeles Division. I'm in Death Valley where we've made a bust of suspected Sinaloa heroin. We have one perp dead at the scene and two in custody. One of them had your phone number and wants to speak with you."

"A member of the fucking Sinaloa Cartel has my cell number and wants to speak with me? What exactly do you think he'll say, Agent Bird?"

"Tell him I'm not in the Cartel," Nolan said. "I was a hostage and my name is Derrick Larson and we worked together in Rangoon in 2014."

Agent Bird relayed Nolan's message and received an earful in reply. "I don't know any Derrick Larson from Rangoon. Can't this wait until morning?"

Bird looked accusatorially at Nolan. "Sorry to disturb you, sir. I very much apologize, but I believed the man to be credible."

"Tell him it's Nolan. Tell him Karachi Bob Nolan didn't board MH17."

All four DEA officers and Jonah stared at Nolan. Bird cleared his throat and spoke in a barely audible voice. "Sir, are you still there?"

"I'm taking a piss, and then I'm hanging up. What is it?"

"He says he's Bob Nolan and he didn't get on MH17."

"Mother of Jesus! Describe him for me."

"Six-foot-plus, one hundred seventy pounds, graying black crewcut, clean shaven, black horned-rim glasses, good physical condition, fiftyish."

"Tell him Chumakov is alive and in D.C.," Nolan said, "and that I have to stop him before he kills my family."

Bird held the phone to Nolan's ear. "Tell him yourself."

* * * * *

THURSDAY, AUGUST 18: MCCARRAN INTERNATIONAL AIRPORT, LAS VEGAS

Nolan's DEA escorts walked him to the gate and left him with three hours to kill before the United flight to Dulles departed. It had been an eventful four hours, the first and best part being the verbal reunion with the profane and enthusiastic Nolan loyalist Sam Hecker. Then came the awkward three hours entailing three more phone calls to Hecker, and multiple calls between the DEA men on the ground, the Shoshone Sheriff's department and the FBI's regional office in Las Vegas. Arch Stanton remained wanted for murder, but he was Robert Nolan as evidenced by his fingerprints. With no warrants to his name, the authorities finally saw fit to release him unconditionally with bugout bag intact. Hecker unhelpfully quipped that, if everyone could wait until lunch, matters could soon change.

Vegas Airport buzzed even at five o'clock in the morning. Nolan refreshed his wardrobe at a souvenir shop. Players pressed buttons on slots and quaffed drinks, outbound passengers still looking for their pots-o'-gold in the desert. Nolan nursed a margarita but didn't like the taste much more than the truck stop beer. At least his beef chimichanga hit the spot.

He had three priorities. Ryder didn't answer, so that meant he was still in the air—Pasan would have alerted him if Ryder hadn't taken off from New Orleans. Nolan transferred ten thousand dollars to the former SEAL via PayPal, grimacing at the three percent transaction fee. The US needed a cheaper *hawala* system.

Next on the list was the murder of Anatoly Chumakov. Nolan had spent thirty-three years at the CIA formulating and breaking codes. Along the way, he received practical training in electronic surveillance techniques and learned enough programming that he was able to conceptualize the world's first cyberweapon of mass destruction, Stuxnet. People died as a consequence of his work, but he'd made it three-plus decades in the Agency without personally killing anyone. Then on March 8, 2014, MH370 disappeared and his world inverted. Before two weeks were out, Nolan had hired a sniper who killed intelligence operatives from Russia and China, thrown the grenade that wounded Chumakov and civilians, and witnessed people murdered. Not a month later in Pakistan, he stabbed one man and shot three others. He rationalized that he'd killed only two of the four, but this personalized violence, plus the MH370 and MH17 episodes, had hardened his worldview.

Not that any of the preceding mattered one bit. Chumakov had threatened his family in the most explicit and obscene fashion. Thousands of rounds fired in the desert had honed Nolan's shooting skills. Every pistol shot taken had been aimed at Chumakov. Having mentally rehearsed his enemy's death so often, Nolan had no doubt that he was up to the task. But unless the gas chamber was to be his end, he couldn't just walk up and shoot the Tatar. To start, he had the Farewell Group's office address on M Street. Shooting the man behind his desk, or even in the office building's basement parking area, sounded like the recipe for a bad personal outcome. His target was a surveillance expert so that further complicated matters. The solution presented itself in Tim Weill, the Farewell Group's rent-a-spook.

Hecker had said that he'd send a car to Dulles. Nolan already knew where Weill lived. With luck he'd take him captive there and dictate what he would say in a call to Chumakov. The rest would be straightforward but not necessarily easy.

The third step was the one with the greatest uncertainty. Even with General Payne behind the scenes deploying substantial resources, efforts to break Higher Love's 256-bit encryption had met with limited success. On rare occasions, someone had become careless and used a short password before filling in the gaps with a repeated letter or character. That's how the organization's name and the pseudonym of its leader came to light. Brute force codebreaking wasn't Abyss's forte, but they'd made several breakthroughs using known weaknesses in the A5/1 algorithm used to encode one of European standard GSM mobile phone networks' seven frequencies. The US employed predominately CDMA technology, limiting Abyss's ability to eavesdrop. But one Higher Love mid-level operative subscribed to German-owned T-Mobile USA, and a recording of a snatch of conversation revealed that the main man could be expected on August 21. The correspondent included two snippets of interest: "A pickup at King John's" and "*Viva la revolución.*"

Nolan listened to the exchange five times before he deciphered it. The best clue was the slogan exhorting Che and his minions to rise up. This might not be a reference to a communist/nihilist/terrorist organization, but instead a place where revolutions happened ... or started. He went online and confirmed that Camp Stanley was indeed situated outside San Antonio. Furthermore, it was adjacent to Lackland Air Force Base, and "John Lackland" was the nickname that the father of the future King John I had given to his son years before the latter was forced to sign the Magna Carta by his rebellious barons.

Camp Stanley had a single claim to fame, that being its strong desire to remain unnoticed. The veil of anonymity had slipped, and a few ex-analysts and investigative reporters believed that the infamous Midwest Depot was housed within. Over the years the inquisitive had asked where the arms came from to support US proxies abroad as they fought their wars of liberation. There was a reason why the CBS Evening News never showed a film clip of a towel-headed man shaking an M16 over his head, irrespective of his political leanings. The automatic weapon of insurrection was the AK-47 and it fired a 7.62mm round. For every tactical rifle and banana clip magazine supplied by Russia or China, the US needed a match it if it wanted its flavor of freedom fighters to prevail.

Two tables away, a couple erupted in argument, chairs knocked over as the pair leapt to their feet after the woman slapped her companion. A waiter and a waitress restrained the pugilists but not before the tiny table upended, flinging beans, rice and tortillas to the floor amid broken dishes. Nolan left the sweaty margarita and a big tip. He needed to find a quiet place to sleep two hours somewhere away from the frenzied humanity of Las Vegas.

* * * * *

WILLIAM P. HOBBY AIRPORT, HOUSTON

"I'm showing a missed call," Ryder said. "It must have been your father—no one else calls at five in the morning. But he didn't answer when I called back."

"I knew it," Bert said. "You're full of shit! My father's dead and I'm in Houston with a broke scam artist."

"Give it an hour and we'll call him back again. First, we'll wait until the Southwest counter opens, then buy our tickets and grab a bite."

"How about you fuck off before I choke you out?"

Ryder and Bert were in a cab on its way to the terminal housing Southwest Airlines. Their driver was a Vietnamese man who looked about fourteen years old. He pulled to the side of the road. "I don't want ya'll fighting in ma' cab. Get out," he said with an accent signaling that he was a local.

"No, turn around and take me back," Bert said. "I'm not walking."

"You're making a huge mistake," Ryder said. "If your sister gets hurt, you'll never forgive yourself."

"Get the fuck out of this cab!" Bert shouted.

Ryder again had two choices and picked Gandhi's path. He stepped out of the taxi and watched it make a U-turn and peel back the way they'd come. He could see the passenger terminal maybe half a mile away and walked toward the lights. Checking his phone, he saw an email detailing Adam Birch's deposit of ten thousand dollars into his PayPal account. The move would be enough to prove to Bert that Ryder wasn't lying about his father, but he'd be damned if he would call and beg that prick to come back.

Funds for his ticket taken care of, Ryder had to figure out how to obtain a weapon on short notice upon his arrival in Cali. He searched Google and saw that the state had a ten-day waiting period to buy rifles or handguns.

* * * * *

MANHATTAN

Kleinwort didn't mind security measures provided he wasn't the one who was inconvenienced. This place would do nicely for their discussion, and it wasn't far from his home. At ninety years of age, the former secretary of state found increasing comfort in routine. His breakfast guest arrived on time, though she showed signs of hurry with no makeup and yesterday's hair. They shook hands, and the secretary's bodyguard left them in the nook abutting the main dining room in the Central Park West co-op selected to host.

"Madam, you have traveled a long way," Kleinwort said. "I understand that your job is to interview Mr. Love and me prior to authorizing the release of the arming sequence. I too have questions."

"Mr. Secretary," Kaili began, "first let me say I am here as a private citizen and—"

"Madam, my group possesses its own intelligence capabilities. I am aware that you report to President Liu and are a liaison between China and North Korea in the areas of espionage and strategic weapons development. If that is not the case, I accepted this meeting in error."

"I see you are a blunt man, so I shall be direct. My president has information leading him to doubt that your group intends to make good on its promise to detonate the nuclear electromagnetic pulse bomb we supplied. Should Higher Love fail to deploy the weapon, our only conclusion is that your organization wishes to use the North Korea origin of the device for propaganda purposes inimical to China. I should also mention that China retains the ability to remotely detonate this device at any time. President Liu is most interested in your response to these concerns."

"This is spectacular fantasy with no basis in fact. Please share the details behind these allegations." The secretary's voice was calm, but his eyes were nervous behind his thick lenses.

"There are two sources," Kaili said, "but the main question is whether you have a delivery vehicle for the NEMP. Do you have a plane and a crew, or access to a missile able to reach the upper atmosphere at a minimum? If so, please share the details."

"If Liu Zhenchang was not confident that Higher Love possessed an adequate delivery method to ensure the weapon achieves maximum destructive potential, you wouldn't be here today."

"Humor me, Dr. Kleinwort."

"Higher Love's goal is the overthrow of the US political system, hastened by the high-altitude detonation of a low-yield nuclear device producing multi-layered electromagnetic pulses which in turn destroy the US power transmission and distribution grid from the Mid-Atlantic to Boston. Once we assume power my organization is willing to withdraw US military forces from the Western Pacific and recognize China's hegemony over all territories within the 9-Dash Line."

"These matters formed the substance of the negotiations that led to the transfer of funds and the loading of the device in Shanghai earlier this month. Your ongoing obfuscations lead me to conclude that you have not secured a means of delivery yet."

"Madam, you forget who you're speaking to," Kleinwort said. "I was negotiating with Mao and Le Duc Tho before you were born."

"My instructions from Liu are explicit. I cannot recommend the release of the arming codes until I understand the details of the proposed delivery."

"I'm merely a mouthpiece for our leadership. I do not seek to involve myself in—nor should I be involved in—tactical military matters. However, I may be able to arrange a meeting where Mr. Love will supply the details you require. Before I attempt to do so, I wish to understand how much you know about the origins of our organization and the fifty-year quest that we stand on the threshold of fulfilling. Perhaps then you will be more tolerant and trusting in our intent."

"If I had known there would be a test, I would have studied."

"Humor me, Madam Yu. For both of our sakes, you need to understand the capabilities of the people with whom you hope to deal."

"Fine. In 1959, Vice President Nixon formed Operation 40. The leader was a clandestine CIA senior officer, Ted Shackley. The group's remit was to undertake operations too secret—and too illegal—to exist inside the CIA and the intelligence oversight framework. Shackley would soon become infamous for his role in planning the Bay of Pigs invasion. It is unclear whether Operation 40 played the lead or merely a faciliatory role in the assassination of John F. Kennedy and the subsequent coverup punctuated by Oswald's murder and the farcical Warren Commission.

"In the mid-1960s, Operation 40's locus moved to Indochina where a combination of illicit wars, narcotics trading and rogue operators led to unwanted notoriety around what was rebranded as the 'Secret Team,' though still led by Shackley and other Operation 40 alumni such as Edwin Wilson, Thomas Clines and Rafael Quintero. Based out of Thailand, the Secret Team stockpiled millions in dirty money and untraceable arms. By the 1970s, Vietnam was a lost cause and the operational HQ had shifted to Tehran. You became aware of the group at this time and helped pilot its long-term strategy. Nixon resigned in August 1974 but you remained inside the Ford Administration until Carter took office.

"The 1976 election is where matters went awry—in 1977 Carter appointed Stansfield Turner head of the CIA, and Turner fired Shackley. Even though the Blond Ghost was officially off the scene, Shackley's people propped up the shah until he was ousted by Khomeini in 1979. The CIA handed the 1980 presidential election to Ronald Reagan in July when former DCI William Casey met the Iranians in Tehran. In return for military spares otherwise embargoed, the mullahs agreed to delay the release of the embassy hostages until after November, thereby forestalling an 'October Surprise' that could have swung the election back to Carter. For reasons I do not understand, Shackley and other Secret Team principals opposed Casey's move. Perhaps it was because you felt a Carter reelection might make the country ripe for the coup you still plan forty years later.

"Shackley's Secret Team was reborn in early 1981 as Higher Love. Through a mixture of covert operations and deep penetration agents, Higher Love tracks information flows that bear on all US foreign policy matters. For thirty-five years, your group has run parallel State and Defense Departments with objectives often in conflict with official government policies. You have tired of life in the shadows and have seized upon Russia's blackmail and control of Republican Party candidate Douglas Ginger as the tipping point for a constitutional crisis that which will see the military emerge as the only sensible leadership alternative. This is a view President Liu conditionally also shares."

"You have an impressive grasp of late twentieth century intelligence matters, as befitting the former head—however briefly—of China's international spy agency."

"Yet there are gaps in my understanding that you might remedy," Kaili said.

"I make no promises," Kleinwort said, "but ask away."

"9/11 was Higher Love's idea as were the ensuing Iraq and Afghanistan invasions. The required military buildup meshed with your organization's longer-term objectives irrespective of short-term waste and distraction. At several junctures, the pending defeat of al Qaeda and Taliban forces left your group in a quandary. With al Qaeda's senior leaders bought off, Higher Love's solution was to covertly back the rise of al Qaeda in Mesopotamia, which metastasized into the Islamic State, Daesh."

"Another conjecture that William of Ockham would have enjoyed."

"Presumably Higher Love uses the same NSA spy tools against the US government that the NSA deploys around the world against enemies and friends. Therefore, Higher Love didn't steal the three ops disks last week since these leaks indirectly resulted in the shutoff of vital information flows from the US government."

"No comment."

"The staged MH370 hijacking was not in Higher Love's interest either," Kaili continued, "because your group knew the US was paying off al Qaeda's senior leaders to keep the war out of the US heartland. That provided the leverage you used to good effect against DCI Perkins and his predecessor. Higher Love's people infiltrated the hijack team and paid one or both pilots to suffocate the passengers. You wanted to maintain the status quo."

"An interesting line of reasoning, but not as nuanced as I might have hoped."

"The reason I bring this otherwise trivial matter up is our two groups share a common enemy in Bob Nolan."

"Ah, Nolan. I believe you bore his child, did you not? How is young Ying Sheng these days?"

Kaili flushed.

"I've embarrassed you," Kleinwort said. "I apologize. Maybe you'll appreciate that Higher Love's intelligence capabilities start with what the nineteen official US agencies gather. Then we add everything that the government's black ops produce before overlaying our proprietary data and analyses, with analytical tools sourced from our own portfolio of Silicon Valley software companies and the NSA. Higher Love first and foremost is the world's finest intelligence analysis organization.

"President Liu and you must understand that our reach is vast, and our information sources are unrivaled. There's a fundamental, irreversible information asymmetry embedded in this truism. If China and my group are to harmoniously coexist, each must accept its partner's and its own strengths and weaknesses."

"So, you will not mind sharing Higher Love's weaknesses, Doctor?" Kaili asked.

"We're wealthy in knowledge, but our financial assets remain stretched. Historically, we funded operations through a bureaucratic construct called the Bishop's Fund. This military slush pile captured the spread between the price the US government paid to third parties to obtain petroleum products and what DOD billed its in-house customers. Since 2010, Higher Love has siphoned twenty-three billion dollars out of the Bishop's Fund. I'm afraid as aspirations climb ever higher, so too do funding requirements."

"What do you need?"

"Five billion dollars per annum to start," Kleinwort said. "Consider this a down payment for all the East Asian military bases that China will occupy after US forces withdraw from the Western Pacific."

"I'll need to consult with President Liu. I would wish to do so only after meeting your leader, should you be able to arrange it."

"Yes, I will see what I can do on that front. If I am able to do so, my people will provide you with discreet transportation. Until then, you will have a day or two on your own. Is this your first visit to New York City?"

"Yes."

"Then you'll have plenty to keep you busy. Leave Robert Nolan off your sightseeing itinerary. He's not important to our plans, and the Ministry of State Security may take comfort in knowing that we will neutralize any threat he may represent."

Kleinwort rose unsteadily to his feet and extended a hand. Kaili took it and was surprised to find the palm clammy and the grip effete. She said farewell and collected her phone and handbag in the kitchen. The service elevator doors opened and the bodyguard within beckoned her to enter. She shook her head. Kleinwort was one of the toughest diplomats alive. What had discombobulated him in the last half hour?

CHAPTER NINE

COLLATERAL

THURSDAY, AUGUST 18: WASHINGTON, D.C.

It was a well-paid and prestigious post to be certain, but the fools he had to suffer. The latest in a litany of incompetent actions—these from Moscow—had arrived minutes ago from the embassy, inner envelope addressed in Portnikov's own hand. Rather than the commendation he craved, Chumakov instead stared at the description of a colossal misadventure. It seemed that the military intelligence–sponsored hackers from the GRU had of their own volition lifted the Democratic National Committee's research file on candidate Ginger. Though Chumakov concurred that this was great material for the vodka bar, the intruders had been detected by the FBI, which dubbed it the work of "Fancy Bear." The bureau's further enquiries turned up a second breach, this one the FSB's invasion of candidate Crandall's personal email server, all the unencrypted White House and State emails and the crème de le crème, the twenty thousand-plus delicious DNC emails they'd whisked away in June to be released to the public via DCLeaks.

The GRU's ham-fisted Fancy Bear penetration efforts would bring the clamps down on the FSB's Cozy Bear operation as well. Portnikov wanted a full damage report and loss mitigation strategy in the next twenty-four hours. The timing couldn't be worse—the two Chekhovs would abduct Nolan's daughter this evening. Once she was secreted away, Chumakov would use Weill to alert Nolan to the exchange. That would take another day to arrange, then Chumakov would fly overnight to San Francisco to apply the coup de grâce.

But Chumakov didn't have the luxury of fuming. His eleven o'clock had arrived. He locked the folder in a desk drawer.

Valeyriya ushered Helmut Krenn into Chumakov's office. Krenn was an Austrian hacker of renown, and the liaison between Alfonse Salti at WikiLeaks and Guccifer 2.0, a fictitious hacker personality created by the FSB. This was their first face-to-face meeting, but Chumakov had authorized payments to Krenn totaling one hundred-thirty-thousand dollars in small sums that ducked under the US Treasury Department's reporting rules.

"It's a pleasure to meet a consummate professional," Chumakov said, concealing his surprise at Krenn's appearance. Before him was a sixty-year-old with an upper body that rivaled Chumakov's own toned physique. A heavily weathered face spoke of much time outdoors, and Krenn brandished a grip that a blacksmith might envy. The Austrian sported a Saville Row suit in medium charcoal chalk stripe. Disconcertingly, his heavy eyelids and full mustache made his visitor look like Joseph Stalin before the war. The combination of good dressing and veiled malice was a style Chumakov appreciated.

"I understand you are in Washington on other business and this is a social call, but is there anything the Farewell Group can do?"

Krenn drained his espresso and placed it in the center of its saucer. For a man who looked like a well-clothed peasant, he had a deft touch. "I don't do social calls. I came to alert you in person that your operation was compromised, but not by DCLeaks or WikiLeaks. For mutual protection, you must cease operations. I will provide details later through the usual confidential channels, but US intelligence operatives found—"

"It was the FBI, Mr. Krenn, and it was another party with similar goals but different patronage that was detected. Regrettably, that exposure led to renewed scrutiny of our targets, and I concur with your prescription. But tell me, this appointment went into my calendar Monday. It's now Thursday. Did you learn of this three days ago and not inform me?"

Krenn stared hard. "I needed to know where the breach was. I didn't want to compound the folly. Your team is competent, so here I am. I must go, however, as my cover appointment in this building is for 12:15. You'll find there's a gap in your security video footage between 11:58 and—" here the big Austrian stopped to look at a large-dialed Ulysse Nardin watch— "12:06. The audio recording devices in this room will be restored shortly. One piece of advice. It wasn't the FBI who found you through the GRU. That's a cover story. Another intelligence operation with much higher skill levels detected us. This unknown group tipped the FBI." Krenn stood up.

Chumakov arose a little too quickly, face flushed. "How do I reach you?"

"I've been paid in full. I ask you not contact me. Perhaps in the future, we may work together. *Da svidania.*"

"*Da svidania.*" Chumakov followed Krenn into reception, but the Austrian left without a glance back. He turned to Valeyriya and said, "Clear my diary this afternoon and no calls." Back in his office with the door shut, Chumakov had his first anxiety attack since moving to the US. Why, oh why did this happen with Nolan was within striking distance? Am I always to be haunted by this man? Did Nolan tip the FBI? He found his antacid tablets and swallowed four.

* * * * *

DULLES INTERNATIONAL AIRPORT, VIRGINIA

Nolan checked his burner and saw three missed calls. Ryder's Signal texts filled in the barebones: the former SEAL was en route to Oakland and on to Marin, and Bert had bolted from Houston back to New Orleans. Nolan would call his son as soon as he found a taxi: he needed him on site in California to free up Ryder to take down Love.

What on earth? It was Sam Hecker in the flesh hanging in baggage claim with a hand-lettered sign reading DERRICK LARSON.

"Mr. Larson? Do you have any bags, sir?" Hecker grinned, then steered Nolan toward an escalator. "Sorry I missed your funeral a couple years back."

"I'd love to hear how the anti-narco czar of South and Southeast Asia came to be a bureaucrat in D.C., but it'll have to wait."

"Nice clothes," Hecker snorted, nodding at Nolan's I ♥ LAS VEGAS sweatshirt and gray sweatpants. You look like you just spent a weekend getting cleaned out by the penny slots."

"I bought this designer outfit at the airport," Nolan said. "I was wearing rags by the time I got there."

"You never were much on style." Hecker hit the remote and the lights flashed on a fire-apple red Porsche Panamera. Nolan chucked his ruck in the back and slid into the passenger's seat.

"In the glove compartment you'll find a Glock 17, two full mags, a mag pouch and two burners. Try not to put a hole in my car—I owe six more years in payments. Where're we headed?"

Nolan dropped the mag, ejected the chambered round, confirmed that the magazines were fully loaded, worked the slide and sighted down the barrel: all good. On closer inspection, the weapon lacked a serial number. "This isn't DEA issue."

"No, this is one of those you find on a bad guy and save for a rainy day. Your life is one long rainy day as far as I can tell."

"I need a vehicle and a GPS," Nolan said. "I'll use one of Chumakov's men to find him. You need to stay far away from me. This could go wrong." This was Nolan's first time riding with Hecker behind the wheel. He drove the Porsche like the accelerator was stuck to the floor. "Maybe drop me at a rental lot and I'll try to catch up with you later tonight or tomorrow."

"I have a better idea," Hecker said. "I meet confidential informants at various levels. I called in favors and you have a wet lease on Paolo and Javi, Colombian tough guys whose instructions are to do more or less whatever you say for as long as you need them. They don't know my name or yours beyond 'Adam Birch.' I'm dropping you off at Tyson's Corner in Garage A. Turn on the blue burner and reply to the text message to arrange a pickup. They understand English, but I don't know how well they speak it. We'll be there in twenty, traffic gods willing."

"Thanks. I have to call Bert, who refuses to believe I'm alive."

"Refuses or prefers you dead?"

"You're thinking of Joanie."

* * * * *

NOVATO, CALIFORNIA

The former Soviet commandos had been busy. A month's rent in advance and another month's security deposit gave them the use of a small storage locker less than nine kilometers from their target's address. An émigré in Berkeley provided their weapons. They'd wanted MP445 Varjag pistols in forty caliber but settled for Beretta 9mm's. They procured rope, duct tape, cable ties, rags, a box of latex gloves, two ghoulish party masks and a pair of pillowcases. The younger of the two, Trofimov, insisted on a floor fan, a bottle of Stoli, two boxes of Cliff's Bars, two battery-operated lanterns, three sleeping bags and a pair of action novels. Borisovich thought him soft but didn't argue. They had an expense account and time was tight.

They parked the silver Chrysler minivan one house down from the target's driveway. The location was poor with Montego Key being a dead-end road. The houses on the more expensive side faced an artificial harbor with small boats bobbing at anchor. Nolan daughter's place was on the other side with a salt creek akin to a ditch running behind it. A barren park abutted the west side of the property, making it easier to surveil, but also increasing the likelihood of someone spotting them. They'd agreed to make the kidnap attempt only if conditions were perfect. If not, they'd keep the advance and tell Egorov to send their apologies to his client. They waited in the moderate heat, windows cracked.

Less than thirty minutes later, a sedan pulled up and an Asian woman in her late forties exited, grabbed a bag of groceries and pulled a suitcase out of the trunk.

"It still has the luggage tags on it," Trofimov said.

"Who in the hell could it be?" Borisovich asked. "There's just supposed to be the two of them."

The men watched in silence as the woman rang the doorbell, knocked on the door and finally let herself in with a key she found left hidden in an ornamental wreath hanging by the door.

"Probably the mother coming for a visit," Trofimov said.

"Let me call Egorov and see if the client has an opinion on this. I'm thinking we leave."

"What, we're letting a Chinese woman scare us off?"

"A deal's a deal," Borisovich said. "Our contract calls for minimal use of force to effect one kidnapping, then supervise a one-for-one swap. She's not on the list, and I didn't sign on for murder. Let me make the call."

At the same time that Borisovich dialed D.C., Joanie Nolan used the cordless handset in the kitchen to call Mei Ling's cell and let her know about the surprise visit. She left a message on voicemail, shelved groceries and unpacked her suitcase. A shower would feel good after two flights and nearly twenty-two hours airport-to-airport.

* * * * *

DULLES, VIRGINIA, TO NEW ORLEANS

"Bert, it's Dad," Nolan said. "Ryder told me you refused to fly to Oakland. I need you to look after your sister for up to a week. I'll transfer funds if you need money."

"It was shitty to fake your death. After everything else, it put Mom through hell. You know she doesn't sleep anymore? Her health is bad because of you. Mei Ling is right—"

"Son, I deserve all that and more. But listen, the Russian knows I'm alive and he's—"

"Yeah, yeah," Bert said. "Spare me. I heard all about it from your drunk buddy, the SEAL hero."

"This isn't for me, it's for your sister. Will you do it?"

"I'll be there by tomorrow morning. I have Ryder's phone number."

"Use Signal from here on out and buy a burner."

* * * * *

OAKLAND INTERNATIONAL AIRPORT, CALIFORNIA

Ryder still had the sweats and the shakes to go with a killer headache that four Advil hadn't dented. He withdrew a grand from a cash dispenser in the concourse. In the old days, he'd never thought of dying in a gunfight. Back then he'd been surrounded by the best warfighters in the world, his knees were intact and his instincts honed to a keen edge. Today he was a separated man with a drinking problem who didn't know whether he'd see his little boys again. He felt the fever coming back, and looked at the beer taps on display in the airport bars as he walked past. Just a quick one to calm his nerves, right? He shook his head. He had to bring himself into the here and now or he'd be dead. He called Nolan.

"I'm in Oakland walking out of the terminal. I'll take a shuttle to a rental car lot. Where are you and how are you?"

"I'm with two friends of our mutual friend, and we're headed to the home of the go-between."

"Hecker?" Ryder asked. "I told you not to trust him. The man changed before my eyes, from gung-ho to sitting on his ass all day, ignoring tips and missing busts. Meanwhile, he started collecting toys. What's he driving?"

"A Porsche," Nolan said.

"Not something you buy on a government salary."

"He's paying for it over six years on installments. I'll keep my eyes open, but I need the extra firepower. Speaking of which, I spoke with Bert and he'll join up with you by tomorrow morning. Expect a text on your cell from his new phone. I'm switching phones as well. I'll SMS you my two new numbers."

"Buy your phones from Target," Ryder said. "Don't use any devices Hecker provides. I'm telling you, he's tied to one of the cartels. The people he supplied, they're Mexicans, right?"

"Near enough," Nolan said. "We're at the address. I'll call you after I tell Mei Ling you're on the way. Keep me informed."

Forty minutes later Ryder walked out of the A-OK Pawnshop on Telegraph, weapon and box of shells in a brown paper bag. The cash economy was alive and well.

* * * * *

ROCKVILLE, MARYLAND

Nolan motioned for Paolo to stop down the block and out of range of the CCTV cameras that Weill would have in place. The old cryptanalyst had spent much of the cross-country flight from Las Vegas working out the best way to take the rogue NSA program director hostage before he triggered alarms, destroyed evidence or fled.

Since identifying Weill one month ago, Nolan had delved into the man's habits and peccadillos. Recently divorced, Weill had taken to frequenting online dating sites. Nolan had catfished Weill using the persona of Melanie Cartwright, a thirtysomething divorcee. Nolan-as-

Cartwright messaged Timmy the great news: she was in the Hard Times Café behind Woodley Gardens Park unwinding after a long day on a short-notice business trip. She was staying at the Best Western just across I-270. Could he join her for drinks and dinner, and maybe a nightcap? He could, indeed, and would be there in fifteen minutes.

Less than thirty seconds later, Weill came hurtling out his front door, not even stopping to lock it, and ran to the curb staring at his phone. Excellent, he was looking for an internet cab. No one ever paid attention to vehicle type so long as it came in a hurry, and the driver knew your name. Javi opened the passenger door and waved the randy hacker in. Weill didn't take his eyes off the oversized Desert Eagle fifty-caliber pistol as he did so, and Nolan removed his phone from his limp hand.

"Hi, Timmy. It's Melanie," Nolan said.

Weill's facial expression was a mixture of self-loathing and pure hatred. The SUV took a left at the corner, passing a white Prius headed in the other direction.

"Nolan. You fucker. I found you. I had you."

"That's right, you had. Now the shoe's on the other foot. Listen up. If you want to live beyond tonight, you'll give me Chumakov's cell number. Then you'll arrange a crash meeting at the usual place and authenticate the appointment. Either our mutual friend Anatoly shows up alone at the stated time, or he doesn't. Either way, we're leaving a body behind. *Capisce?*"

"Hand me my phone so I can unlock it," Weill said. "Here. Dial 202-788-2304."

* * * * *

ROCKVILLE TO WASHINGTON, D.C.

"I've linked Nolan's group to a shell computer security company called Safeworks," Weill said. "It knows that Farewell Group is behind DCLeaks, and the WikiLeaks feeds can't be far behind. I'm headed to Mexico until this blows over."

Nolan leaned around Javi to seize the phone, but Weill fended him off and lurched hard against the door as he absorbed a verbal tirade from Chumakov.

"I don't care if you pay me for August or not. It's too dangerous in D.C. I need to work on my Spanish anyway ... You should think about leaving unless you have diplomatic immunity. Last time I checked, you hadn't even bothered to register Farewell Group as foreign agents. Oh, you did? Well good for you, Anatoly ... I don't see any purpose to a meeting ... OK, OK, stop shouting ... Don't threaten me. I'll button everything down tight. Nothing but pulled plugs and scorched earth ... OK, OK, I'll meet you in sixty minutes at the usual."

Weill disconnected the call, the phone hummed and he entered a series of numbers before looking up at Nolan. "We're on despite your best efforts to fuck it up. Head to Wisconsin Avenue in Georgetown. You'll want to arrive early to disconnect the CCTV cameras."

"If this is a trick," Nolan said, "my two friends will give you a Mexican necktie instead of a trip to Cancun."

Javi leaned over and leered at Weill. "We'll fuck you up real good, *hermano.*"

Nolan hoped these two were only practicing their lines. "Paolo, pull over here," he said in his normal deadpan voice. "I need to make a call. Shouldn't take more than five minutes."

* * * * *

ROCKVILLE, MARYLAND

Nolan stood halfway up someone's lawn and used his second burner to call Mei Ling's cell. His body flooded with relief at the sound of her voice. "Are you driving?"

"Who is this?" she asked, not believing her ears.

"If you're driving, pull over. It's Dad. I have important news."

"Dad? My dad's been dead two years. I'm hanging up, and if you call this number again, I'll report you to the police."

"Don't hang up! Pull over somewhere safe."

"Bruce is driving," Mei Ling said.

"Anatoly Chumakov is the Russian I almost killed in Sri Lanka. He's in the US and knows I'm alive. He will come to either kidnap or kill you. Go home, pack a bag and wait for Travis Ryder to arrive. He's the former SEAL who attended my memorial service."

"I remember him. The man in uniform who bloodied his hand hammering a badge into your coffin and then propositioned me."

"That's the one," Nolan said. "Travis will take you somewhere safe. I spoke to Bert earlier. He's flying overnight and arrives tomorrow to watch over you. I'll make Chumakov disappear. When that's done, we'll give it a few days to make certain he didn't send anybody before I got to him. With any luck, it will be over in under a week."

"This is unbelievable! You don't contact anyone for years and you pop up out of nowhere to tell me someone is trying to kill me. Why don't you call the police?"

"It's complicated. I owe you a lot of explaining, but I don't have time. Please fill in Bruce, but don't tell him where you're headed."

"I'm not leaving our house without Bruce," Mei Ling said. "I'm pregnant and he's the father. Oh, and Mom just showed up out of the blue for a visit and she's at home waiting for me. Like you said, we have a lot to talk about." Mei Ling hung up.

Numb, Nolan walked back to the big SUV.

CHAPTER TEN

BARTERED

THURSDAY, AUGUST 18: THE WHITE HOUSE

Ginger's stump speech included the crowd pleaser that once he became president, he would drain the swamp in D.C. Elsewhere, the man who had occupied the Oval office for almost eight years smiled through tight lips as he thought of the shock whoever succeeded him would feel when their own appointees revealed themselves disloyal. On the television, the noble anchorman led with the leak that the president had sanctioned a desert secret hideout where a lone wolf accessed computer systems connected to the nation's most sensitive databases. This man, known only as Arch Stanton (an alias taken from a Clint Eastwood Western), had blown up a state-of-the-art communications outpost after murdering five agents and wounding a sixth. "Was this treason on the part of the president?" the talking head asked.

Obama swore that General Sharkey would be jobless come sunrise, and despaired that Abyss might yet miss Mr. Love. It all came down to whether Nolan was alive or dead, and, if alive, free or under interrogation. The president regained his composure and contrasted what they knew with what he feared. General Payne's report made clear that there wasn't even a composite artist's sketch of Arch Stanton, much less a photograph. The helicopter and drone searches had come up empty. The only lead was a Special Forces stealth motorcycle found abandoned behind a Chevron station in the one-horse town of Shoshone. The local police hadn't even reported the find, stating that their department was "in the process of returning it to the DEA."

Payne had signed the order that shipped the bike to Nolan under the noses of the Q-Group. The Delta founder observed that the top-secret motorcycle morphing into DEA property smelled of classic Nolan. Payne would bet the president that the old code breaker had made it to Shoshone and disappeared. Being dead once more hadn't made Nolan any less cautious.

Payne usefully included an annotated map in his brief. Area 51 was only sixty miles to the north of Shoshone over the Nevada state line. It would be fitting that the strangest duck serving the executive branch ended up taking shelter among the nuthatches in that alleged UFO sanctuary.

As for the identity of the two so-called NSA lawyers, they were both employees of Black Ice Security and ex-SEAL Team 6. At present it wasn't clear whether the FBI, the NSA or a third party had assigned them to the Q-Group's arrest team, but gunshot residue tests confirmed that both the living and the dead phony lawyers had fired weapons. Abyss had been compromised, and everyone assigned needed to lie low. Task Force Ares' existence had trickled out, so let it muddle along with its investigation of Russia's election subversion. Nolan was safer on his own than in so-called protective custody. Just where he was and what he was doing was another riddle altogether. Obama shook his head in awe at Neil Payne's laser logic and told him to keep him apprised, but otherwise run with the situation.

* * * * *

WASHINGTON, D.C.

"Sorry to disturb you sir, but I received a call from Team Chekhov requesting clarification."

"What is it?" Chumakov asked.

"They observed an Asian woman in her late forties enter the subject's house. They believe it could be the target's mother and want you to advise next steps."

"Once they have collected the subject, confirm the identification of this woman. If it's Joanie Nolan from Singapore, take her as well."

"The team is too small to host three guests."

"Leave the man behind," Chumakov said, "but let them know there's another fifty for them if you can get both the mother and daughter alive."

"Understood, sir. I will convey your instructions."

The light changed and Chumakov turned and headed north on Wisconsin Avenue. Simply sort out Weill, that nervous Nellie, and everything would be manageable. He'd drop by early and pull another few bottles of Khortytsa out of the basement. There would be a major celebration once this business concluded.

* * * * *

NOVATO, CALIFORNIA

Borisovich hung up after a brief conversation. "There's another fifty thousand for us if we take both women, so long as the older one's her mother."

"Fifty each, or fifty total?" Trofimov asked.

"I didn't ask."

A Tesla pulled into the driveway and a couple climbed out. They turned and noticed the two men seated in the minivan, which prompted them to hurry up the pathway. Both men exited and trotted toward the house, hands inside jackets. Mei Ling looked at them with wide eyes as she slammed the door. Trofimov angled around to the side while Borisovich dispensed with subtlety and put his boot through a living room window. Inside a woman screamed and a younger woman's voice shouted, "Call 911!"

Borisovich used his sleeved arm to clear the bigger shards out of the frame and climbed through, leading with a drawn weapon. He heard a door open in the back and shouted in Russian. Trofimov tore around the corner at the rear of the house. In short order the two women were back inside the kitchen, hugging one another as Trofimov slammed the door behind him. Borisovich cleared the dining and living rooms. Finding nothing, he catfooted upstairs.

Bruce Goodhill had time to dial 911 and say, "Come now!" before he dropped the receiver on the bed. His Smith and Wesson .38 was in hand when the kidnapper ducked in and out of the master bedroom doorway. Goodhill fired once through the open door, the gun's louder-than-expected report and kick disorienting him. Borisovich reached around the jamb from ground level and shot Goodhill twice in the chest. Goodhill dropped to his knees and pitched forward, firing a single shot at a downward angle as he fell.

In the bedroom, the police dispatcher shouted through the abandoned handset: "Shots fired! Shots fired! All units to 1415 Montego Key! Shots fired!"

In the kitchen, Mei Ling's damsel in distress act ended when Trofimov took a first step toward the sound of the gunshots from upstairs. Breaking free from Joanie's grip, Mei Ling swung a roundhouse kick into his jaw. The blow would have dropped most men, but Trofimov had survived a year in Grozny fighting Chechen terrorists, a good number of them hand-to-hand. He staggered back as a second kicked whistled past his chin. "*Hvatit!*" he shouted, raising his Beretta. Mei Ling put her hands in the air.

Behind him, Trofimov heard Borisovich say in Russian, "Shoot the young one if she's too much. We only need one. I'm hit and the police are coming."

Trofimov shrugged. "As you wish." He lowered his aim so as to not to mar that beautiful, frightened face. Mei Ling crumpled, clutching her left thigh. Joanie threw herself down next to her stricken daughter only for Trofimov to grab a handful of hair and yank her back to her feet. Trofimov stuck the Beretta into Joanie's ribs and said in English, "Shut up. Move or die."

Borisovich knew his wound was serious, but he willed himself to keep moving. Across the street, a sprinkling of neighbors stood on their lawns to investigate the source of those bangs. Two quick shots into the air drove the rubberneckers back indoors.

Joanie's legs gave out and Trofimov half-dragged, half-carried her to the van. Borisovich slid the side door open. "Restrain her and I'll drive," said the wounded man. They were underway within twenty seconds. The smaller man tie-tied, gagged and blindfolded Joanie and shoved her to the floor.

Inside the house, an unconscious Bruce Goodhill bled on an antique Qom Persian rug while in the kitchen a faint-headed Mei Ling used Bruce's chef's apron to tie a tourniquet above the entry wound, and a wooden salad spoon to torque it tight. Waves of nausea pulsed through her as fears for the safety of her lover, her mother and her unborn child cycled at a manic rate.

Her handbag lay on the floor near the kitchen door. Her phone rang. She crawled on her elbows, groaning from the pain. She clawed the iPhone from the bag, and she saw it was an unknown number. Not Bruce, oh no. She hit reply and speaker, and managed to say, "Yes" before another wave of pain overwhelmed her.

"My name is Travis Ryder. I was sent by your father to take you to safety. I'm near your house and want you to come to—"

"They've taken my mother. They shot me. And Bruce too, I think. Find my mother. Silver minivan, two men."

"I'm coming to you. I'll find your mother later."

"Police are coming now. Find—"

"Silver minivan? I just passed it."

"Follow it. Follow it!"

"I will, I will. Don't hang up. Talk to me about your wound." Ryder executed a tight U-turn that had the tires squealing. He squeezed the steering wheel to control the shakes, but his head throbbed. The only comfort was the 1911 Colt on the seat next to him. He could shoot a .45 automatic while seeing double if need be.

Three police cars and an ambulance hurtled past the van and his SUV, lights flashing and sirens wailing as they headed to the source of the 911 calls. Mei Ling's phone went silent.

* * * * *

GEORGETOWN

While the Humvee headed south into the District of Columbia, Nolan had Weill talk them through the floor and security layouts of Peterson's Liquor Store. Javi handed a black hood to Nolan that smelled like its last user had been a farm animal. The white rings around the eye and mouth holes reminded Nolan of the mask worn by the Scorpio Killer in *Dirty Harry*. That fellow didn't strike Nolan as being very hygienic either. Maybe dirty laundry came with the serial killer turf.

At Calvert NW and Wisconsin Avenue, Weill ordered a right turn and a quick left down 37th Street NW to the parking lot in the rear. After a brief exchange in Spanish, Javi exited the SUV and headed back to Wisconsin Avenue to inspect the liquor store from the front, inserting a Bluetooth earpiece as he walked.

As their vehicle turned into a half-full parking lot with eight spaces, Weill let out a gasp. "That's his car! Chumakov's early."

"Which one?" Paolo asked.

"Midnight blue classic Mercedes 450SLC."

Paolo spoke in rapid fire Colombian-inflected Spanish and clicked off.

Nolan drew on his stale Quantico training and ventured, "Why don't we park and watch for a while? See if he's with anyone."

Paolo nodded in acknowledgement and reversed back into the street. By a miracle, a resident pulled away from the curb, leaving an empty space. 37th Street was populated with large houses gone to seed thanks to the combination of slumlord owners and college student tenants. There were mildewed couches on sagging front stoops that spoke of hungover weekend naps. No one was around, but the beer cans and junk food wrappers in bursting black plastic trash bags by the curb spoke to the timeless dietary preferences of college students.

Nolan turned to Weill and showed him his weapon. "If you run, I'll shoot you. If you alert Chumakov, I'll shoot you."

"And after you kill Chumakov, then what? Your Latino gunmen and you will let me walk when I'm a witness to murder?"

Weill had a point: Nolan hadn't thought that far ahead. This was akin to asking Erwin Rommel in 1944 what the conspirators would do after they'd assassinated Hitler.

Paolo finished an assembly project up front and waggled his Desert Eagle, a twin to Javi's with the exception of a six-inch suppressor screwed onto the end. "Dumdum subsonic rounds," he said, leering at Weill. Paolo smiled, oiled glossy black ringlets reminding Nolan of Kenny G.

Nolan decided that a tough love pep-talk was called for. "You set up Chumakov and you walk free, but you leave town and never come back. Remember, I've tracked you for seven months and know your every online move. One email and the Q-Group arrests you for stealing the NSA hacking tools for Russia. Don't even fantasize about witness protection and a clean start at a Best Buy in North Dakota, not for treason."

Weill slumped and closed his eyes.

"Someone's left the liquor store." Nolan said.

Weill looked up. "That's him. That's Chumakov."

From fifty meters away, Nolan wasn't positive. For starters, the black eyepatch was missing. And sending a double to flush him out would be just like Chumakov. But on closer inspection, the confident rolling gait and the same steroid-enhanced build with swarthy features looked right. Chumakov opened the Benz's trunk, dropped a bulging bag inside and shut the lid, turned and walked back through the metal door.

"That door leads down to the cellar?" Nolan asked.

"I told you that already," Weill said. "There's an AV room with the CCTV monitors and server. Next to it is a locked door leading downstairs to a cage filled with liquor crates, plus the anteroom where we meet."

"Take him now!" Nolan said.

"*¡Disparale!*" Paolo commanded.

Nolan's burner rang.

"They have your wife!" Ryder said.

"We need Chumakov alive!" Nolan shouted. "Don't shoot!"

"*¡Detener!*" Paolo said. "*¡No dispararle! Lo necesitamos vivo.*" He started the Humvee and it surged into the parking lot and screeched to a stop short of the door. A yellow Lamborghini followed them in and pulled up on the left. Nolan and Paolo jumped out, brandishing their pistols. The supercar reversed at speed, executed a deft one-eighty and roared away.

The back door opened and out walked Chumakov with Javi's arm around his throat and a large pistol poking the back of the Russian's neck.

Nolan turned to Weill. "Go. Don't look back and I never want to see you again." Weill nodded, opened the rear passenger door and was halfway out when Paolo shot him in the base of the neck. Weill tumbled forward without a sound, body sprawled in the fading light. The suppressed Desert Eagle still made enough noise that Nolan wondered if the neighbors would come out to check. He looked around, but no passersby were in sight.

"Get back in the car," Paolo said.

Nolan did as he was told, with Javi following Chumakov into the back seat.

"Cover me while Javi cuffs and hoods him," Paolo said. Nolan obliged. Paolo backed up and pulled out onto 37th Street.

Chumakov grinned at Nolan despite the Glock pointed at his face. It took self-control for Nolan not to convert that smirk into a half-dozen bloody holes. Javi took a filthy ski mask, flipped it backward, and slid it over Chumakov's head. Nolan hoped he gagged on it.

Javi confiscated Chumakov's cell phone and let out an expletive. "This *hijo de puta* hit some kind of panic button."

"He messaged the Russia embassy. It's only a quarter-mile up the road—they'll be coming fast. Hand the phone over."

Javi passed it up front and put his weapon on Chumakov. Nolan used both hands to disassemble the device and disable its GPS-tracker.

Paolo and Javi spoke in rapid-fire Spanish while Paolo drove at high speed down dark residential streets. Nolan redialed Ryder, who picked up right away. "We have Chumakov. What's the situation?"

"I've got eyes on Joanie and two men, ex-military and maybe SF. One of them is hit bad. The other dragged your wife into a self-storage unit and shut the door. I think there's only one way out, and they know I'm here. If they have backup, I'm toast. You want me to call the cops?"

Paolo drove up a dead-end street, turned the Humvee around and cut the engine. Nolan watched as the Colombian opened the back and pulled out two sniper rifles fitted with night-vision scopes. He propped one against the front seat next to Nolan and shouldered the other. Paolo sprinted up the block to set up a firing position. The evening air was humid and insects hummed. A malfunctioning street lamp hissed, randomly putting them in either dim light or darkness.

"There's no way Chumakov arranged a team and a backup unit on one day's notice," Nolan said. "Besides, we're looking to do a swap in the next fifteen minutes, or not at all. Hold the line." Nolan pulled the phone from his ear. "One of your men is wounded," he said to Chumakov. "The other has my wife. You order them to release her and stay where they are until my friend drives off. Then they're free to go. When my friend knows he's not being followed, I'll free you."

"Fuck off," Chumakov said. "I saw what happened to Weill. How about I trade you a clean kill in each direction? My men don't rape or mutilate your wife, just shoot her. You agree to shoot me. That's my best offer."

"What, you want to die?"

"I know I'm dead. I'm negotiating means."

Chumakov didn't sound like a dead man walking. *He had a GPS beacon on him.* "Javi! Tell Paolo we have to leave. We're about to be hit. Take off Chumakov's clothes starting with his shoes, belt and watch. Throw them out the window as you go."

"*¡Cógeme!*" Javi went to work stripping Chumakov, summoning Paolo in a torrent of Spanish.

Ryder was still on the phone. "Did you hear that?" Nolan asked.

"Most of it. Looks like your man doesn't want a trade. I have CS gas and flash bangs, plus NVGs. A couple through the door and I'll have Joanie safe and out of there in no time. Just give me the word."

"If you don't hear back from me within fifteen minutes, it's a go."

"Aye." Ryder wondered if Nolan had picked up on his bluff. He had a solitary sidearm, one magazine of ancient .45 ammo and a right hand that as of two minutes ago was shaking involuntarily. His tongue stuck to the roof of his mouth, his face burned and his blood pounded so hard he could hear it coursing through his ear canals. He needed a drink to settle his nerves.

Paolo came back at the double and climbed in. "If anyone shoots at us, kill that piece of shit."

"Agreed," Nolan said.

Twenty minutes passed in silence as Paolo drove out of Georgetown, across the Key Bridge and onto the George Washington Parkway. Ryder texted Nolan the actual situation, including his unfitness for combat. Nolan considered the options and favored none of them

At last Paolo decreed that their tail was clean and pulled off the parkway onto an unlit road leading to Fort Marcy Park. They continued down the road until they reached the end of a large empty parking lot. Paolo retraced their route until they were next to the start of a footpath. There he cut the engine and lights. The two Colombians held an animated discussion in Spanish, one too long to talk about emasculating a naked spy and choking him to death with his genitalia, but perhaps long enough to debate whether Nolan would be digging one grave or two.

"Chumakov," Nolan said, "even if you have a subcutaneous chip, your friends won't be here in enough time to save you. What will it be?"

"Bob Nolan, family man, I give you a chance to show how much you love your wife. You drive off and leave me with my phone. If I'm alive in fifteen minutes and you're at least ten kilometers away, I'll call my men and they'll release your wife. And I promise not to pursue your family in future."

"You promise to release my wife? You promise not to attack my family? Why should I believe you?"

"Because if your man was any good, he'd have already have freed your wife. Because my backup team will be here any minute. Because there's zero chance you can take me to California in time for an in-person swap. Because if you let me go and I kill your wife, I know you will kill me slowly should you ever recapture me."

"And if you let her go, do you expect me to stop looking for you?"

"No, I expect you to look after your family better than you have these past two years, and I'll be somewhere you'll never find me until one day I kill you. The game ends only when one of us is dead. No more deals."

"I have another plan," Paolo said. "We shoot this fuck and in one hour my uncle's men in Cali kill this *malparido's* people and recover your wife."

"Wait. We can do the exchange right here," Chumakov said.

"I'm listening, but not for long," Nolan said. He watched Paolo scroll through the contacts on his cell. "When Paolo finds the phone number, time's up."

"Give me my phone back. You call your friend and I call my men. You let me walk ten meters, then your wife steps ten meters from the door. Your friend starts out fifty meters away from your wife. Ten meters at a time we step. Then at fifty meters, your wife gets in your friend's car and they drive. For me, I will run into the woods and call my people for pickup."

"That might work," Nolan said.

"One more thing. These two stay inside while you and I walk up the trail and around the corner. I don't want Pablo Escobar junior or his brother putting the crosshairs on my neck. Plus, that way they can't shoot you either."

"I have a number in Marin," Paolo said. "I need an address. What's your decision?"

"Javi and you hang here and shoot anything coming down the slip road," Nolan said. "I'll be back in fifteen minutes. If you hear gunshots, head down the trail and shoot Chumakov."

"If you're not back in twenty, we leave," Paolo said.

CHAPTER ELEVEN

RABBIT

*THURSDAY, AUGUST 18: U-STORE-IT COMPLEX, NOVATO, CALIFORNIA;
AND FORT MARCY PARK, NORTHERN VIRGINIA*

"I'm fifty meters from the storage unit," Ryder said. "You're on speaker and my weapon is next to me, but if they have night-vision and a long gun, I'm dead."

"Chumakov's in a worse position," Nolan said. "He's naked, cuffed and standing next to me."

"The mosquitoes are out and we've walked far enough," Chumakov said. "Are you ready?"

"Travis, tell me when Joanie's ten meters outside."

"Release the woman," Chumakov said into his phone.

* * * * *

After an eternity, the storage unit door swung open and out walked a person. At that distance, Ryder wasn't certain what he was seeing.

"There's someone out there," Ryder said, "but I can't ID her as your wife."

"Call to her."

"Joanie Nolan, is that you?"

"Yes!" The figure broke and took two quick steps until a yell in Russian stopped her.

"Don't run! Just walk!" Ryder shouted.

* * * * *

Nolan told Chumakov to count out ten paces, nice and slow. Chumakov mumbled in Russian into his phone.

"English only!" Nolan barked. "Speak Russian again and you're done."

Joanie limped another ten meters. She was in bare feet and moved slowly over the graveled lot.

Ryder gave Nolan the go-ahead, and Chumakov counted out fifteen steps until Nolan ordered him to halt.

Joanie was less than thirty meters away. The sight of the helpless woman picking her way among the sharp stones sent a surge of anger through Ryder. His hands stopped shaking. Time slowed and his senses sharpened. The door Joanie had exited was twenty-plus meters from the end of the building, three lockers down. He saw movement behind the building and to the side, then nothing. One of those kidnappers was on the move. The wounded assailant had to be lying prone inside the doorway. His job would be to take Joanie out and go for Ryder next. The unwounded rat on the prowl would try to flank Ryder from the left once he'd cleared the row of storage garages that formed the short end of an "L" with a gap between the two buildings. Ryder's Ford Explorer rental sat in the center of the shared parking lot in the heart of the kill zone. Ryder casually picked the automatic off the trunk and walked around to the front of the vehicle. Joanie remained still, awaiting instructions.

The former SEAL put the phone to his ear. "I'm being stalked. I have Joanie in sight. Take care of your end. Out."

* * * * *

Back up the road behind them, Nolan heard four shots, a pause and then a string of fireworks detonate. Chumakov's embassy team had arrived, drawn by the reactivation of his cell phone.

Chumakov was twenty-five meters away and spoke rapidly in Russian into his phone. The naked man made a break for heavy brush five meters off the trail, juking as he ran.

Nolan fired once and Chumakov tumbled ass-over-elbow off the footpath and into the thicket. Nolan walked to where his adversary lay partially obscured and raised his gun to administer the kill shot when the roar of a vehicle coming down the road forced his eyes away.

* * * * *

U-STORE-IT COMPLEX, NOVATO, CALIFORNIA

"Joanie!" Ryder yelled. "Get down! Lie flat!" The former SEAL flopped on his stomach and let loose two pairs of shots aimed through the open doorway a foot off the ground. Bullet impacts sounded on his eight o'clock and he rolled right. *Stick and move, stick and move.* More bullets cracked past or skipped off the gravel. *That's a 9mm, not a tactical rifle, and the shooter's rusty. That makes two of us.*

"Joanie, crawl to the truck. The keys are in it. Drive off with lights off and don't stop until you find the police. Do you hear?"

"Yes, yes." Joanie squirmed forward on elbows and knees. The pause in the rat's firing signaled a reload. Ryder was up and running straight, eating gravel as the next shots whipped past. Everything hurt, but he wasn't hit. Now he was even with the end of the second set of storage units. The kidnapper had fired from the manzanita scrub behind the building. Ryder had to keep him there until Joanie drove off. He rolled left and bounced up, ran four steps and hit the ground as another trio of bullets missed.

Joanie had closed half the distance to the Ford. To his horror, Ryder saw a second form dragging himself outside the storage facility's doorway. The creeper inched along in the dim light. *Sunofabitch!*

Ryder had started with eight rounds and he'd fired four: two shots left for each. One last mad dash took him into the scrub. "Joanie! Joanie! There's someone after you. Run a zigzag and go around to the driver's side."

He couldn't see her, but from the muzzle flashes, she'd drawn fire. Ryder put a pair onto the rat-bastard's muzzle flashes and heard a body crash into the brush.

A vehicle door opened and shut, then a single gunshot rang out before the engine started. The shot was from behind: the creeper. Ryder's brain screamed for Joanie to move, but the Explorer sat silent. *Shit, shit, shit! She's hit!* He fought through the thorn bushes and ran for the Ford. The creeper had been invisible in the shadows, but there was a glint as sparse light reflected off metal. Ryder dropped to one knee, fired his remaining two rounds and saw the gunman collapse to his elbows, his weapon dropping with a clunk.

The SUV roared to life and took off, but in the wrong direction. *What the hell?* Tires spinning, Joanie took a tight right turn and ran over the motionless body, skidding to a stop. In a second flourish, she reversed over the Russian before swinging around to face the exit. Ryder reached the vehicle breathless, happier than at any time since the birth of his twins.

"Get in," Joanie said.

"I can't yet. I wounded one and he's still in the bushes." Ryder ran to the corpse, bent down over a bundle of mashed bones and came up empty on a pulse. Borisovich's Beretta lay nearby. Ryder swapped in the spare mag he found in the dead man's coat and grabbed the small flashlight.

"Drive up to the front gate but leave your lights off and look in the rearview mirror. When I come up the road, at forty meters I'll give you two short flashes and one long one. If you see another vehicle or person, or any other signal, drive like hell until you find an open store. Go in and have them call 911."

"Mei Ling?" Joanie asked.

"I don't know, but she sounded good on the phone," Ryder said. "We'll find out soon."

Five minutes later Ryder blinked and flashed his light as he approached the Explorer. He opened the driver's door. "Found him. Lucky headshot: he's dead. I needed a few minutes to collect my casings." In his post-drunken haze, he'd loaded his pistol without using gloves. He'd found six casings, but not the two in the manzanita scrub. He wondered when and if the police would find them and match his prints but shook it off. No time to worry about details. His hands were back to trembling uncontrollably. "Move over. I'll d-d-drive."

Joanie appraised the battered, disheveled former SEAL and shook her head. "I'll drop you off at a hospital."

Ryder said nothing as he didn't trust his voice. He climbed into the passenger seat and started picking thorns out of his hands and forearms. A shattered cell phone came out of his front pocket: not much good now.

"Why is this happening?" Joanie asked.

"Bob's alive. It's complicated."

* * * * *

FORT MARCY PARK, NORTHERN VIRGINIA

A spotlight isolated Nolan and a vehicle roared up the road. He bolted into the thicket alongside the path. Rounds snapped past him as he stumbled down the wooded hillside. He tripped and fell into the brush, losing his weapon. He took off again at a reduced pace, and another forty meters found him at the bottom of a ravine covered in downed trees along a dried creek bed.

In less than a minute, his pursuers could be picking their way down the hill to where he lay. Anyone with a night-vision capability would find him if he moved. If they had infrared he was just as dead. He got up and scrambled over and under fallen trees and through the undergrowth. Road noises increased and then he could see the reflections of the headlights on George Washington Parkway. His breath came in ragged gasps and he paused to catch his wind.

His phone buzzed, startling him. On instinct Nolan answered as he started clawing up the embankment toward the freeway.

"What in the hell's going on?" Hecker asked.

"Russia embassy security behind me. I shot Chumakov. I'm next to the GWP near Fort Marcy and—"

"I live nearby. I'll be there in ten and call when I'm close." Hecker hung up.

Ten minutes might as well be an hour with two shooters in pursuit fewer than one hundred meters behind. Their flashlights played among the foliage at the bottom of the ravine. Nolan realized he'd caught a break—if they'd had NVGs, they wouldn't be using lights. Nolan came up to the road and saw there was a break in the two-way traffic. Hecker lived in Virginia, so he'd come from the north. Nolan dashed across the freeway and jumped down the slope on the other side. A burst of traffic passed in either direction. He crawled another five meters and hid in the thickest cover he could find.

* * * * *

NOVATO, CALIFORNIA

Ryder related Bob's back-from-the-dead story.

"I never did submit the divorce papers," she said after a long pause.

Ryder changed topics. "I don't need a hospital," Ryder insisted. "And if you drop me there, I'll end up in a jail cell. Pull over at that drugstore and park around back."

Ryder emerged in ten minutes with meds and two burners, one of which he gave to Joanie. "Drive south on 101 and take the second exit. We'll stop a block short so this rig doesn't come up on CCTV and you can walk to the police station. They'll take you to Mei Ling. Insist that they put two policemen on the door. I'll find you tomorrow, and Bert and I will take you both somewhere safe until this is settled."

"What do I tell the police?"

"Mostly the truth but leave Bob and me out of it. Kidnappers shot your daughter and took you hostage. There was a gunfight at the storage complex, and you escaped but your unknown rescuer was left behind. You ran to the road and hitched a ride with a nice Hispanic man who spoke no English. They won't believe you, but if you keep it simple and don't change the story, they'll have to accept it."

"I'm worried sick about Mei Ling. Her leg bled a lot and she's pregnant."

"Pregnant? I had no idea." Ryder couldn't help but think of the unfortunate Lael Hanif, shot through the femoral artery by a stray round in Karachi two years ago. "I'm sure she'll be fine. I was on the phone with her when an ambulance passed less than a half-mile from her house. Now slow down and stay in the right lane or you might kill us both, which would stress her out even more."

Joanie slowed from eighty and hit the exit ramp at sixty-five, braking enough to keep the Explorer upright.

"Bert flies here overnight to guard Mei Ling and you. If you give me your phone, I'll call Bob and find out what happened to Chumakov."

"My cell doesn't have international roaming," Joanie said.

"That's fine. I bought you a burner and I'll call Bob later. In the meantime, keep Mei Ling's phone on you. Even if Chumakov's dead, we'll need to find a safe place to lay up for a few days."

"What if he's not dead?"

"Then Bob and I will take him out. In the meantime, you three lay low."

* * * * *

OFF THE GEORGE WASHINGTON PARKWAY NEAR FORT MACY PARK

Every time there was a lull in the traffic, Nolan expected black-clad ninjas to cross the road and shoot him where he lay. He burrowed into the dead leaves and smeared mud on his face and forearms. He'd hit Chumakov in the middle of the back, but that didn't mean he was dead. The phone's buzz shook him out of his reverie.

"Where are you?" Hecker asked.

"Off the GWP southbound side lying in the woods. I'm below road level. There are two shooters across the freeway. How will we do this?"

"I'm almost there. Stay on the line. You come up the hill and I'll flash the high beams. Don't waste time getting in."

"I'm moving up to the road and will lie behind a low stone wall that's less than two feet high. I'll look for you and jump up."

Hecker's Porsche rolled into view in the HOV lane. The red sports car stopped and within seconds Nolan was inside. A single bullet entered the left rear passenger's window and buried itself into the front of the passenger front door. Nolan didn't hear a report, just shattering glass and massive acceleration as the Panamera surged away southbound.

"Thanks for the pickup. That was close."

"Yeah, I'll send you the repair bill. Where to?"

"Take the first exit and turn around. We have to go back to Fort Marcy."

"Won't it be full of Russians?" Hecker asked.

"Maybe. But I need my bugout bag and my files." Nolan called Ryder and received an out-of-service message. Then he called Mei Ling's home phone and a police officer picked up. He hung up and tried her cell. He reached voicemail: zero for three.

"Don't you think the Ruskies will have the vehicle by now?" Hecker asked.

"Maybe, maybe not. They had a shootout with maybe twenty shots exchanged, then sped down the road toward Chumakov and me. I ran off and their men followed. The two shooters you just drove away from will be the ones cleaning up the scene while the others take Chumakov to the hospital. If the SUV's still drivable, they may take the bodies and make everything disappear."

"Or they're sitting in ambush waiting for you to come back," Hecker said as he signaled right to take the Fort Marcy exit.

"Pull over early and park. Let's go in on foot and take a look. I dropped my weapon when I fell in the woods. Do you have a spare?"

"You had the Glock all of five hours and lost it already, and you want another one? What, do I look like the D.C. Armory?" Hecker reached into the glove box. "Sorry, nothing extra. I did bring my Glock and a spare mag."

"Let me have them both, please. We can scavenge weapons from the vehicle."

"Bob Nolan, CIA Asia code warrior, goes full John McClane." Hecker handed his weapon over and again noted Nolan's fluency with the Glock platform as he racked the slide back and forth and cocked the trigger to ensure everything was smooth.

The two men jogged up the side of the slip road. In the faint moonlight they saw the SUV sitting with the front doors open. Nolan felt a glimmer of hope: his bugout bag had been in the back. Twenty-five meters away he saw a body on its back, arms and legs impossibly bent. Hecker rushed up and felt for a pulse. Coming up cold, he frisked the corpse and pulled out a phone. A giant pistol lay by the dead man's side. "Fucking Desert Eagle. Can't even grip it properly. If Javi had packed a nine, he'd still be alive."

Nolan shushed his overeager friend and looked inside the vehicle. He wasn't surprised to find Paolo dead behind the wheel, a handful of tightly patterned bullet holes in the windshield explaining the gaping chest wounds. Nolan claimed the man's cell, ignored the suppressed pistol used to kill Weill and grabbed the sniper rifle with the Starlight scope. The backseat was empty. *Damnit.* Where could that bag be?

"Bob!" Hecker hissed. "I hear voices. Let's get the fuck out of here."

Nolan pulled his head out of the back seat and attuned his ears to the night. Off the path where Chumakov and he had walked came the faint sound of footsteps and snippets of a Slavic language.

Hecker double-timed it up the road. Nolan passed him without breathing hard and stopped at the open gate. He knelt and used the metal rail as a rest, pointing the rifle back down the road.

"Are you out of your mind? You shoot one of the embassy guards and we'll have hell to—"

Nolan fired once and three seconds later fired again. He stood up and said, "Let's go."

Hecker turned and sprinted the rest of the way to the Porsche while Nolan jogged. The long gun went far into the roadside weeds, and Nolan eased into the leather bucket seat up front.

"What are you doing sniping at Russian embassy staff?" Hecker asked as he floored his Porsche. "You'll start WWIII!"

"I shot out the front tires to keep them from following us. You can slow down."

"Doesn't look like you have your bag."

"No, the Russians have it. I'll get it back one way or the other."

"If it's all the same to you, let's wait until we've had a couple of scotches before you tell me what the fuck happened today."

"Sounds good," is what Nolan said, but his thoughts were across the continent.

* * * * *

KEHLSTEINHAUS, TRINITY ALPS, OUTSIDE WEAVERVILLE, CALIFORNIA

For the first time in two years, Frank Coulter would be free. He saw it for what it was, the president allowing him out to curry favor with the South Florida Cuban-American community. That might pay dividends for the Dems in the fall, but in the near term it gave Coulter a chance to sniff fresh air and drink a few glasses of corn squeezings with damned fine men.

The former senior CIA clandestine operations officer switched off the television set and pulled his geriatric frame upright as a preamble to freshening his bourbon. No-good cheatin' wife version 2.0 Donna poked her head into the living room. "If you pull out the clothes you want for the ceremony, I'll pack them for you."

"I don't fly until Saturday," Coulter said, "so there's still time."

"Don't forget to take photos of you with little Frank," Donna said.

The mention of his son Frank IV brought an instant smile to his craggy face. Hell, the initial reason for petitioning so hard to attend the ceremony was the chance that Four Sticks could attend and watch his old man collect an award for kicking Che Guevara's ass. But these news bulletins put a different twist on matters. That shootout and fire at a secret communications enclave outside Camp Irwin had all the signs of a presidential skunkworks. The only person Coulter knew who POTUS trusted enough to sift through data on his own was supposed to be dead. Now, maybe not. This was important because Bob Nolan was someone who needed a killing in the worst fashion.

CHAPTER TWELVE

SELF-MEDICATED

FRIDAY, AUGUST 18: GEORGETOWN UNIVERSITY HOSPITAL

Vladimir Auturovich Gregoriev, formerly the SVR's Sri Lanka *rezident*, waited in the visitors' area for two hours outside the Concentrated Care Center. A doctor still in scrubs conferred in whispers with a nurse who pointed through the window where the intelligence officer paced behind the glass.

Dr. Marcelino walked through the swinging doors and broadcast a glum demeanor. "Mr. Gregoriev, I understand you are Mr. Chumakov's next of kin in the US?"

"Anatoly and I worked together overseas," Gregoriev said. "I don't believe he has any relatives here. Tell me, how is he?"

"Not well, I'm afraid. That bullet struck between the L4 and L5 vertebrae and injured his spinal column. He lost a foot of his small intestine too. He faces a long rehabilitation process."

"Will he walk again?"

"I'm not a neurologist, but from the damage I'm not optimistic," Marcelino said. "Some day he should be able to pull himself into and out of a wheelchair. That's all one can reasonably hope for."

"Thank you, doctor. May I see him?"

"He's conscious but groggy, and is aware he has no feeling in his lower extremities. I haven't yet shared my diagnosis or prognosis. He's angry and curses in Russian. The only word I understand is 'Nolan.' Does that name mean anything?"

"No," Gregoriev lied.

"At the request of your ambassador, we haven't allowed the police into Mr. Chumakov's room. But since he doesn't have diplomatic immunity, we cannot prevent law enforcement from entering once you see him."

"The Russian Federation would be grateful if you permitted me fifteen minutes by my friend's bedside before the police speak with him."

"As you wish, Mr. Gregoriev."

* * * * *

MCLEAN, VIRGINIA

A nurse answered Mei Ling's cell on Nolan's third try. She informed him that the patient was out of surgery, stable and sleeping. As per hospital rules, she was unable to divulge more over the phone. Perhaps he could try the next of kin for more details?

"I'm her father. Her mother was with her and was abducted. Is she a patient as well?"

"I'll transfer you to the switchboard. Please hold." The call dropped.

Nolan slammed the dashboard with both fists as Hecker tucked the Panamera into his garage.

"Bad news?"

"Mei Ling's had surgery and is in the hospital. No word on Joanie or Ryder."

"Let's go to the man cave. C. J. and Sophie are asleep, so we'll keep it down. You mix the drinks while I call D.C. Metro and have them check the hospitals and morgues for your pal."

A large whiskey apiece later and the story was out. Nolan had the presence of mind to substitute Bert for Ryder in the evening's festivities, knowing how Hecker's former righthand man felt and suspecting that the sentiment might be mutual.

"I don't think you appreciate just how much shit we're in," Hecker said.

"My wife's missing, my daughter's wounded, and I can't reach my son. Tonight I shot, but maybe didn't kill, a man who's sworn to torture and kill my children and wife. I'm wanted in California for a quintuple homicide I didn't commit. I've been framed in the theft of the NSA's most valuable spyware, which the Russians presumably have due to my carelessness. Did I leave anything out?"

"You can manage. I've seen you do it at least twice before. The real problem lies with the Colombians. I borrowed two Medellín Cartel up-and-comers to help, and they're both dead. I have no idea who they spoke to, or what record there is of what happened."

"You're the DEA, for Chrissakes," Nolan said. "The traffickers should be afraid of you, not the other way around. Two dead hit men are nothing to these guys. You owe them a pitcher of mojitos and a few favors, right?"

Hecker poured another liberal measure of Lagavulin 18. "You've been dead too long. Drug enforcement these days is a cooperative undertaking between the DEA and the cartels. Both sides know we lost the war, but as long as we know our place, we can record busts, lock up the odd top bad guy someone wants to be rid of, and keep the enforcement charade intact for electoral purposes. Meanwhile, the Colombians move tons of product a week into this country, and they crush everyone who inconveniences them. The people we're up against have more money, guns and lawyers than our side. If you think the Russians are scary, I assure you they're nothing compared to *los Sudamericanos.* I broke all the rules in asking a big boss for a favor, and I'm exposed just when I'm sneaking up on twenty and a pension."

"That's depressing to hear from someone who kept the generals in Burma and Pakistan in check for four years."

"They don't kill us because it's bad for foreign aid, military assistance and college visas for their kids. The Colombians and Mexicans fear nothing other than their own kind. The last thing either of us wants is to be interrogated by El Patron or one of his people. I've seen the results. We have an hour to tighten up our story before someone calls. You'll be right behind me on their list."

"Why not tell them the truth?" Nolan asked. "The Russians killed Paolo and Javi."

"The way you told it sounds far-fetched. Worse, it means we understated the risks: I didn't mention that a half-dozen military men in an embassy rapid reaction force might be coming after you. Don Randy was their uncle, and their mother heads the revived Medellín Cartel."

Nolan topped up his glass.

"Leave the liquor store out," Hecker said. "Too close to the embassy and their reaction squad. You dumped Weill's body there after finding out where Chumakov was. You grabbed Chumakov somewhere near Fort Marcy, learned your wife was alive and switched the mission from assassination to a swap. Chumakov somehow signaled to the embassy Russians despite you taking the precaution of stripping him naked and disabling his phone. The Russians weren't expected, and Paolo and Javi died covering your ass. You shot Chumakov and ran for your life. I came by and picked you up. We saw the brothers' bodies, disabled the vehicle, and as we drove off one of the Russians hit my car with a stray shot. How does that sound?"

"If they ask Chumakov, he'll tell another version."

"Fuck! I hadn't thought about that. It all hinges on whether that bastard survived."

Nolan stared into his glass. "What happens if Randy decides I'm to blame for the deaths of his nephews?"

"They'll duct tape us to chairs, skin us alive with razor blades and blowtorch what's left." Hecker's phone hummed. He looked down and shook his head. "Chumakov's warded at Georgetown University

Hospital. A bullet severed his spine and fragmented into his guts. He won't do you any favors."

"We have to kill him tonight."

Hecker's phone hummed again, and he blanched as he saw the screen. "It's El Patron. I need to take this."

* * * * *

GEORGETOWN UNIVERSITY HOSPITAL

Gregoriev stood over Chumakov's bed. The last time he'd seen Chumakov was the night before Nolan's grenade attack In Sri Lanka. Two-plus years later, it was Nolan's bullet that had robbed the Tatar of his legs and maybe his cock.

At the touch of Gregoriev's hand on shoulder, Chumakov opened his eyes and spoke with difficulty. "Embassy. Find Egorov. Tell him to find the Chekhovs. Tell me what happened with the Chekhovs and Nolan's wife."

"Easy, easy. I'll handle it."

"Nolan?"

"Escaped into a car driven by his DEA friend Hecker. They returned to the park a short while later and searched the vehicle and his two dead bodyguards. Don't worry. We have what Nolan wants: three thumb drives. I'll forward them to Moscow tomorrow via diplomatic bag. They'll break the encryption at head office."

Chumakov nodded. "My legs?"

"The bullet hit your spinal cord. The doctor says you may not walk again, but most doctors don't know beets from bell peppers. You lost thirty centimeters out of your small gut as well. Nolan makes a meal of you a piece at a time."

Chumakov slumped back against the pillow.

"I'll contact Egorov and report back," Gregoriev. "The police are waiting outside. You need to decide how much to tell them about Nolan."

"Nothing. Leave Nolan for me. Find Egorov and find out about Nolan's wife and daughter. Tell Egorov that the Chekhovs are to kill them both."

* * * * *

MCLEAN, VIRGINIA

Hecker concluded his fairytale. "Don Randy, *lo siento muchísimo* for your loss. There was no way for us to foresee a team of Russian soldiers—maybe Special Operations men, who knows?—would murder your nephews without provocation. Like I said, Nolan survived by chance because he was in the woods."

"Why was Nolan so far from my nephews?" Randy asked.

"The exchange was Chumakov for his wife in California. She was kidnapped by two Russians, Chumakov's people. The swap fell apart, Nolan shot Chumakov and the embassy team killed Paolo on the spot. Javier fought bravely, but there were too many."

"And why didn't Nolan return to help my nephews?"

"Your boys were dead within the first few seconds," Hecker said. "Nolan was too far away and outnumbered. He ran to save himself and enact our revenge."

"And what happened to his wife?"

"We don't know. We lost contact with California and have heard nothing."

"I want a phone number for Nolan's wife, now!"

Hecker walked back into the bar area. "Randy wants Joanie's phone number. Here." He handed over the hot potato.

"Don Randy, it's Bob Nolan. My wife's cell is a Singapore number that doesn't work in the US. My daughter was shot in a failed kidnapping. Let me give you her cell, and either my wife Joanie or Mei Ling will tell you what happened."

"If you are a praying man, kneel! Hold the line." A torrent of Spanish ensued as Nolan put the angry man on speaker.

Three minutes later, the don was back online. "Your wife doesn't know shit, but she saved your lives because her fucked-up story was so confused it could only come from a woman who wasn't rehearsed. And she said she'd thought you were dead for the last two years. You faked your death in a plane crash and abandoned your family? What kind of man does this?"

"A man who has enemies sworn to kill his family, sir. If you'll allow me, I'll kill Chumakov as a partial repayment for your loss." Nolan took the phone off speaker and handed it to Hecker.

"Where is this Chumakov?" Randy asked.

"Nolan put a bullet in his spine," Hecker said. "He's paralyzed and under police guard at Georgetown University Hospital."

"Find out where they have him."

"He's in the Concentrated Care Center, room nine. We're headed there now."

"I have a man in the hospital and will make a call. Answer this phone the next time it rings. I have to go to the morgue to identify my nephews, then call my sister-in-law in Bogota. After I speak to their mother, I may want to talk with Chumakov. If your story doesn't check out, I'll feed Nolan and you to my fighting dogs, starting with your balls."

"Yes, sir. Don—" Hecker held the dead phone and eyed the screen.

Nolan looked at his friend. "Ideas?"

"Drive to the hospital ASAP. Hope to Christ that Don Randy's insider can give us Chumakov. We'll take the wife's Lexus. My car's too hot for the road."

* * * * *

SAN RAFAEL, CALIFORNIA

Ryder closed the door to his motel room and dumped the bag on the table. The new burner was charging on the bedside table where he'd left it before heading out for late-night food and drink. The pair of burritos went into the microwave and the six-pack of Ballast Point Grapefruit Sculpin IPA went into the freezer.

He headed to the bathroom and in the mirror saw a Lynyrd Skynyrd band member after the fatal plane crash. Both arms were covered in bloody scratches. Dirt streaks and crimson smears stained his checked shirt. His favorite jeans were torn and bloody at the knees. The toes of his Ariat boots looked like shit. His beard and hair had leaves and twigs in them. He hurt all over. Yet it had been a great day: Joanie Nolan was alive because of him, and he still had his SEAL mojo. *Well, some of it.*

The microwave signaled that it was chow time. He decided to leave the food be while he unwound in the tub and let the shower pour over him. The hot water felt good, but he scarcely had the strength to use his knife to lever out gravel and excise thorns. The scar tissue on both knees and shins glistened beneath fresh cuts and bruises. His pelt wouldn't fetch much at auction, that was for sure.

He did the best he could with the new scissors to hack off his beard. Tomorrow he'd go for a proper haircut. If he lived long enough, Sally would be happy while Les and Paul might recognize him. Newfound resolve in place, he pulled the beers out of the freezer and dropped the full carton straight into the trashcan. He'd always told himself he didn't have a drinking problem. Now was a good time to walk the talk. Still, sixteen bucks a six-pack and letting it all go to waste? He fished a single bottle out of the trash. Off came the top and he chugged a third of it to capture the foam as it bubbled off. Damn, that beer was good.

The burritos were still cold in the middle, but another minute on high brought them up to spec. His choice in tee shirts had been limited, with a "Jack Links Beef Jerky" in black being the best he could manage. It was loose everywhere save his gut. He drank three glasses of tap water out of those tiny plastic cups that motels put in their bathrooms. That last eight hundred milligrams of Ibuprofen stuck halfway down his throat. He knew too well that SEAL candy was eating his stomach lining, but that didn't feature high on his list of personal concerns. Two swigs finished off the beer and left him wanting more. What was the old saying, "One is too many and all of them never enough?" AA had been thinking of him when they coined the phrase.

It was two in the morning on the East Coast, and Bob would just be getting started on the evening's next round of adventures. He dialed Nolan's burner and someone picked up, but nothing came out of Ryder's end. "Bob, it's me, the Lala cowboy."

"New phone," Nolan answered. "How are you?"

"I'm fine. I dropped Joanie off at the Novato police—"

"Joanie's with Mei Ling in the hospital. She's fine. I don't know about Mei Ling."

"My cell died in the fight," Ryder said. "I nixed Chumakov's men. Did you kill him?"

"Halfway. Shot in the back and paralyzed from the waist down. We're on the way to finish the job."

"I hope you're not with Hecker or anyone he introduced you to. I'm telling you, he's dirty—"

"I heard you the first time."

"Text my number to Bert and his number to this phone," Ryder said. "Bert and I need to link up in a few hours. If Chumakov's alive, he'll send more people. Bert won't be enough, but I think I can bring Zaw up from Southern California."

"Zaw?" Nolan asked. "The police major from Burma?"

"The very one. The DEA sponsored green cards for his family and him. He's been Stateside the last eighteen months working in private security. It's a six-hour drive from LA, and he'll have weapons too."

"Get him if you can and take some rest—you sound like hell. And thanks for saving my girls. I never had any doubts."

"Well, that makes one of us." Ryder sat and watched his right hand shake like a tambourine in a Dylan song. Maybe a nightcap would do the trick.

* * * * *

SAN RAFAEL AND ANAHEIM, CALIFORNIA

Ten minutes later, Ryder had Zaw on the line. The legendary antinarcotics officer from Shan State had defied the generals and received internal exile as his punishment. Zaw had befriended the DEA and vice versa, but the resulting second go-round with the people who run Burma left him friendless. Ever pragmatic, he took his family and emigrated to Disneyland, though life in Orange County wasn't the lark it had seemed from afar. Zaw was underutilized. In return for an adventure and a fistful of Ben Franklins, he was up for a drive. Give him seven hours, give or take, and he'd be on the scene.

Ryder finished the second burrito. His head barely made the pillow before he was asleep, a loaded Berretta and Colt .45 on either night table next to empty bottles.

* * * * *

NOVATO COMMUNITY HOSPITAL, CALIFORNIA

Joanie gripped Mei Ling's hand so hard her daughter opened her eyes and jerked her arm backward.

"Where's Bruce?"

"He's critical," Joanie said. "He was shot twice in the chest, through both lungs. Lena stopped by fifteen minutes ago while you were asleep to check on you. She filled me in on the details. You have other things to concern yourself with."

"What other things? Bruce is my life."

"Your baby for one thing. The hospital will do another scan tomorrow, but they found a heartbeat." Joanie wiped away the tears running down Mei Ling's cheeks, then dabbed her own. "The wound in your leg missed the bone and major blood vessels. It went straight through and took a lot of muscle out the back. You will need additional surgery and a graft, but rest for the time being."

"Dad?"

"Someone angry with a Spanish accent called your phone an hour ago and asked me a lot of questions," Joanie said. "There were more shootings in Washington, but your father's all right. The two men who shot you and Bruce ... well, they're dead. Bert's on his way and Dad's friend Travis will be back tomorrow morning."

"When can I see Bruce?"

"Let's wait until tomorrow. I'm sure you'll be able to see Bruce then."

Mei Ling lay her head back and shut her eyes. Within seconds her even breathing signaled sleep. Joanie returned to her solitary bedside vigil, her concern for her daughter equally balanced with her anger at her husband. For just once, couldn't he just stay dead?

CHAPTER THIRTEEN

STRANGE BEDFELLOWS

FRIDAY, AUGUST 19: GEORGETOWN UNIVERSITY HOSPITAL

"Stay in the car," Nolan said, his voice quiet and insistent. "I'll call if I need you. No reason for two of us to get jailed for a one-man job."

"Trust me, if Metro PD picks you up, I'll be next," Hecker said. "We're both up to our necks in this, and there's no fucking way I'm waiting in the car."

Dr. Oscar Marcelino met them with a broad brown face and a big smile just inside the emergency room entrance. Nolan looked at the array of drunken or stoned college kids, accident victims and homeless people. Those with phones and able to use them tapped away.

In Marcelino's wake, Hecker and Nolan waltzed past the reception desk and into the ER treatment area. Curtains separated patients and beds. The doctor pressed a finger to his lips and pointed to two sets of green scrubs. Hecker and Nolan donned them in silence, stashing their street clothes in a cupboard. On went two surgical masks and caps. Nolan recalled the last time he'd worn scrubs, his godson's brains spattered across them compliments of a PLA sniper. Marcelino produced two ID cards on lanyards. Nolan wished he had surgical gloves, but they weren't part of an orderly's attire. He'd watch what he touched.

The physician led them through swinging doors and into an abandoned staff break area. "There are cameras in two corners but no audio. Don't look up. Your target is in Room Nine of the Concentrated Care Center on the fourth floor. I need one of you to accompany me. I'll inspect his chart and X-rays and order him prepped for emergency surgery. The second one of you waits here at the bottom of the elevator bank. Through this door to my left is a hallway connecting the CCC to the Surgery Center. I'll bring the patient and one of you to pre-op, then I'll leave to scrub up. The corridor should be empty this late. There are no cameras in there, so you do what you have to do, and reverse your paths."

Nolan experienced a surge of hope: they might pull this off.

Hecker thought along different lines. "If you're the surgeon, can't he die on the table the second time?"

"Don Randy's father lent me the funds for medical school in the US. I worked off my debt as the doctor in a jungle cocaine lab. The family sponsored me into the US, and I do favors from time to time. But I'm a thoracic surgeon, not a butcher."

"Fair enough," Hecker said. The elevator descended, floor by painstaking floor.

"Besides, another surgeon and nurses will be in the OR with me. There's no certain way to make it look like an accident and kill a man undergoing surgery for a perforated bowel."

A ding signaled the opening of the twin doors. The elevator was mercifully empty. Nolan stayed below while Hecker and Marcelino got in. Nolan retraced in his mind the short walk back to the staff break room and into the ER treatment cubicles. Following the directions on the wall, he stepped into the adjacent corridor and could see an illuminated sign for the Surgery Center. Someone at the far end of the corridor gestured at him. Nolan retreated, found the men's room and took a seat while he composed his thoughts. How would he kill Chumakov so it didn't look like murder? He needed a vial of an instantaneously lethal liquid, but cyanide and strychnine were hard to come by even in a hospital.

Upstairs, Marcelino led the way. Hecker's spirits crashed when he saw a blue uniform seated outside Chumakov's room. The cop didn't even glance up as the two men entered the room. There sat the second shocker, a dolled-up fortysomething Eastern European bottle blond in a chair by the head of the bed. Chumakov was asleep. Marcelino pulled the patient's clipboard and a large brown envelope off the hook at the foot.

Chumakov's visitor spoke like Zsa Zsa Gabor. "Doctor, vhat vill become of my Anatoly?"

"Madam, he suffered a single gunshot wound to the lumbar region. The bullet partially severed his spinal cord. It's too early to say whether he'll walk again—that will be for our neurologists and rehabilitation experts to determine. Unfortunately, the bullet fragmented and perforated Mr. Chumakov's small intestine. Earlier tonight I removed a section. My next step is to see if he's stable enough to go back into surgery to remove the remaining fragments and make certain there's no internal bleeding."

The doctor pulled out an X-ray and clipped it to the light wall. Chumakov's better half joined the scrutiny. She passed Hecker smelling like a walking distillery.

Hecker put on a priggish voice. "Ma'am, it's after visiting hours. I'm afraid you'll need to leave. You can come back after nine o'clock tomorrow morning."

"Vat are you talking about? The nurse said she'd bring a bed. I stay next to my Anatoly."

Marcelino examined the surgical incisions on Chumakov's zippered and discolored torso. "He is bleeding internally. We need to take him back into surgery. Madam, I don't care if you stay here, but you can't accompany your friend." The doctor pulled a phone out of his white coat and used the walkie-talkie feature. "It's Dr. Marcelino in the CCC. I need an operating room readied for immediate use. I have an orderly with me and will accompany the patient to the prep area myself. Yes, it's that urgent. Get moving!"

"Oh, no! I must be vith him. Let me be by his side! Anatoly, Anatoly! Can you hear me?" The man in the bed stirred at the sound of Ludmilla Popova's voice.

In five steps Hecker was at the door and leaned out. "Officer, please remove this woman. She's hysterical and we have to take her husband into emergency surgery."

The old-timer in uniform jerked awake. As Hecker had hoped, Ludmilla took the intervention badly. For a society dame, she packed a good right hand and landed two blows before the policeman managed to cuff her.

"Go up front and the nurse will have a gurney," Marcelino said to Hecker. "Let the staff load the patient, and the two of us will take him downstairs to the Surgery Center."

Nolan was still downstairs and wondering where everyone was. An elevator finally lit up and crept to the CCC on level four before making a straight drop to the ground floor. This was his big chance to end his nemesis. His palms were sweaty as he thought about what this man had done to Mei Ling and Joanie. The door opened and out stepped a policeman dragging a woman by one elbow, hands cuffed behind her. *What the hell?*

As the woman thrashed back and forth, the cop dropped her fancy leather bag and all manner of sundries rolled free. Nolan bent down to pick them up while the woman cursed her captor in Russian.

"It's hard enough when you're married to one," the cop said, "much less when you have to bring in a drunk whose boyfriend's been shot." Nolan dumped a double handful of skin creams, combs, contact lens cases, brushes, lipsticks and keys into the cavernous bag. "Thanks," the policeman said with a tight smile as he strong-armed his unwilling companion through the ER staff room exit.

Nolan looked at the box in his palm. Ludmilla Popova had a Fentanyl prescription with two blister packs of four pills, each two micrograms. Nolan didn't know his narcotics well, but this was the most powerful opioid around. The second elevator opened behind and Nolan turned with a start. Out walked Marcelino carrying the patient's records and wheeling a metal rack with two IV bags swaying, one red and one clear. Alongside him was a gurney pushed unsteadily by Hecker. The doctor led them down the next hallway to the entrance to the surgery center. "You have ten minutes," Marcelino said to Nolan.

"I'll grab our clothes and bring the car to the main doors," Hecker said. "Call me when you're done or if there's trouble. Good luck."

How to kill Chumakov undetected? From TV dramas, Nolan knew that a syringe full of air injected into a vein could cause an embolism and induce a heart attack. Nolan grabbed the tube feeding the clear drip and yanked it free, tape and all. Chumakov groaned. Inspiration joined desperation. Nolan shut off the feed valve under the clear IV and pulled the needle free. Then he tucked the tube under Chumakov's blanket. The liquid drained out of sight into the mattress. Nolan seized the tube leading from the blood IV and jabbed the liberated needle into the plastic tube filled with transfusing blood. He took a deep breath, bent over and blew as hard as he could into the needle's nozzle. At first, he tasted blood. He suppressed a gag reflex and kept blowing until he thought his eyes would burst. Out of breath, he removed the needle from the tube. Uncrimping the line, the flow was restored but with a difference: there were six inches of air in the blood tube jammed into the vein on the inside of Chumakov's elbow. Nolan reattached the clear plastic tubing to the needle and reinserted it into the same spot he'd pulled it from a minute ago, then restarted the IV feed. Nolan watched the red blood march inexorably downhill, with the giant air bubble inching toward Chumakov's arm. Everything would look normal when and if he managed to make the bubble disappear.

"Nolan!" growled the man on the gurney.

He turned around and clamped his hand over Chumakov's mouth.

The Tatar shook his head with surprising vigor and twisted his mouth free of Nolan's grip. He managed, "Trade you my life for Higher Love," before Nolan silenced him.

"What did you say to me about no more deals?"

Nolan relaxed his hands enough to allow Chumakov to speak in a whisper. "I know Mr. Love. I will tell everything." Chumakov fell back with the effort and appeared unconscious.

Nolan grabbed the blood drip tube and pinched it hard just above where the blood met the air. He dragged his fingers down the tube until the three inches of blood pushed the entire bubble into Chumakov's arm. The Russian went into convulsions and Nolan once again pressed his palms over the former FSB director's mouth as he fought for air. Seconds later, Chumakov stopped thrashing.

"The game ends only when one of us is dead," Nolan recited as he restored the flattened tubing to its original shape.

The OR prep room remained empty. Nolan exited, his eyes aimed at the floor and heartbeat up to one sixty-five. He fished for his cell and saw Hecker was out front. Nolan followed the exit signs out of the surgery center and into the night air. A pair of headlights flashed, and he pulled off his facial mask and hair net as he approached the car.

His DEA driver lowered the passenger's-side window. "Get in the back."

Nolan complied. "That's the most relieved I've felt in years," Nolan said. "He wasn't dead when I left, but he will be soon."

"I'm happy for you, buddy," Hecker said. "That'll save our asses from El Patron's pit bulls. But I have some bad news as well. My friends on the force tell me there's an APB out on you. I don't understand why, and you can't afford to find out."

"I'm not leaving town until I know he's dead."

"I'll call Marcelino in twenty minutes. But if you missed Chumakov, you'll never come close again."

"Don't be so certain," Nolan said. "It will look like a heart attack. Except Chumakov woke up and tried to cut a deal. Was there a blond hanging around his room?"

"Yeah, a drunk girlfriend," Hecker said. "I had the cop on the door throw her out."

"Find an address for her."

"You think she's of value?"

"Let's see who pays her a visit once word gets around about her boyfriend."

* * * * *

WASHINGTON, D.C.

Hecker put a call into Metro PD and determined that Ludmilla Popova was in custody. They parked across from the Idaho Avenue NW police station entrance and waited. Nolan went online and discovered that her home address was on 20th Street NW in Dupont Circle, only ten minutes away.

"Staying here is a bad idea on at least two counts," Nolan said. "She could drive off and we'd never see her. Second, we're double-parked. Let's drive to her home and wait outside. She'll show eventually."

"Agreed." Hecker started the engine but was interrupted by his phone's buzz. "Damnit, you're not the coldblooded murderer I thought. Chumakov's alive, but in a coma with an uncertain prognosis. They revived him after he suffered a massive heart attack. They postponed surgery and he's back in intensive care. Marcelino says there are two men on his door, these ones in plainclothes."

"Damn."

"I'm a fair judge of character. I guess either Madam Popova or Dr. Marcelino would want to earn extra cash provided Chumakov never wakes up."

"I have access to a million points of persuasion," Nolan said. "Make a call."

"Normally, I'd agree. But we already owe the cartel big time. Let's put our cocks out on the table and bail out the drunken junkie blond. Find out how much in love she really is."

"You walk in there with me, they'll be hunting the two us once they review the CCTV footage."

"Life behind a desk never did suit me," Hecker said. "As long as your sponsors look after me as well, I'm up for it."

"In that case, pull into the lot and park in the corner farthest away. I realize it's an unusual question, but do you have a syringe in the vehicle? I thought I saw one when I put our weapons in the glove compartment."

"Those are Sophie's. She's developed diabetes. Why?"

"Just   mulling   over   a   couple   of   ideas."

CHAPTER FOURTEEN

DEAD IN BED

FRIDAY, AUGUST 19: RUSSIA EMBASSY

Egorov departed Gregoriev's office, leaving the senior SVR officer to process what he'd learned. Chumakov had used Egorov's Spetsnaz ground forces alumni network to retain two middle-aged vacationers willing to kidnap Nolan's daughter for tuition money. These men were pushing fifty, and a dozen years beyond active duty. They had been with their wives and high school–aged children on a tour of prospective US universities. The kidnapping went south, at least two civilians were shot, and the two retired soldiers were killed by a person or persons unknown. The expected press coverage would be voluminous and unfavorable, two things the embassy was keen to avoid in this election year.

Tomorrow morning his first call would be to FBI Director Salmick to make certain that he knew Chumakov acted alone, for as certain as morning follows night the bureau would link Chumakov to Egorov to the two moonlighters. Connecting the dots ahead of time would earn the SVR slack in the brouhaha to follow. Second, Gregoriev would tap the SVR's blackmail trove to clamp a lid on the network news and print coverage. Such a waste of painstakingly assembled influence.

Then there was Chumakov. He wanted Nolan dead as never before, and damn the consequences. Gregoriev considered pulling out a bottle of vodka but feared he might not stop once he'd started. Instead he massaged his temples and stared at the keyboard. Being the second in command of SVR's visible US presence was a plum assignment. Most of the time, all he had to do was manage the infighting and run the odd spy ring. Tonight? Well, tonight was a career-ender played out in real time in multiple dimensions.

His cell trilled from an unknown caller and he answered without speaking.

"This is Yaroslav. Call me when you are in the Iron Maiden."

"I'm in the office, sir. I will ring you back in five minutes."

The caller disconnected, leaving Gregoriev to look up "Yaroslav," which turned out to be the codename for Federal Security Services Director Portnikov. *Just wonderful.* In theory, Gregoriev's reporting lines within the Foreign Intelligence Services were independent of the

FSB and Portnikov. In reality, Portnikov was Putin's righthand man and that fact trumped any organization chart. Gregoriev wondered if the next ten minutes would be his last in his role of US deputy chief. Was it too much to hope his next post would be back to Sri Lanka where the food was good, the people friendly, and the Americans and Chinese easier to manage than his own side?

Gregoriev's phone rang again. What was it this time? He answered without breaking stride. "This is Nurse Rachet from Georgetown University Hospital's Concentrated Care Center. I'm afraid your friend suffered a severe myocardial infarction—a heart attack—at 2:05 this morning that left him in a coma. To your knowledge, does Mr. Chumakov have any end-of-life instructions on file, a do-not-resuscitate order or similar?"

"None that I'm aware of. I'm in the middle of something. I will return to the hospital within the hour." He hung up. *A heart attack?* Chumakov was as strong as a bull. How would a bullet to the back precipitate a heart attack? He smelled a hospital screwup or foul play.

Gregoriev passed through two security checkpoints and a body search before gaining admittance to the Iron Maiden, the embassy's permanent Secure Compartmented Information Facility. The Americans monitored every scrap of bandwidth emanating from 2650 Wisconsin Avenue NW, but past experience suggested that conversations within this isolated and insulated cube stayed confidential. The secure line to Moscow, well, that was another matter. He dialed Portnikov and waited for the explosion.

"Vladimir Auturovich Gregoriev, I congratulate you on a spotless career. Seeing as how your superior chose to holiday in the Hamptons with the Jews of New York for the next two weeks, I present you with the opportunity for further personal achievement. You are the senior SVR officer present in Washington, no?"

"Yes, Comrade Director," Gregoriev said.

"And why are you in the office at three o'clock in the morning?"

"There's been an incident, sir, involving the shooting of one of our nationals."

"Is it Chumakov to whom you allude?"

"Yes."

"Protect him with your life! He is a national treasure! President Putin wants him medevacked to Moscow today. After this phone call, I will instruct the ambassador to provide whatever manpower and resources you require. You must not permit the Americans to question Chumakov, much less detain him. We cannot allow any chance of his talking while unconscious or under anesthesia. If there is any possibility that Chumakov has already talked, exercise your professional powers to prevent this from occurring again."

"I'm unclear as to what you expect of me, Comrade Director," Gregoriev said.

"President Putin expects you to serve your country even if you must take life, even at the price of your own freedom. The consequences of failure are unthinkably high. Do not disappoint." The line died.

Gregoriev was too tired to decipher that Delphic doublespeak. On the walk back to his office, he accepted he was in a no-win situation. How was he to know what Chumakov had said and to whom?

But maybe there was still a way out. For one thing, the man was in a deep coma from which he might never awake. Chumakov had told Gregoriev not to mention Nolan to the police, so he would have kept quiet when they questioned him. Chumakov's girlfriend would be his next stop. He also needed to get hold of Egorov and ensure that nothing else was planned against Nolan or his family. His phone rang yet again.

"Gregoriev? It's Ludmilla. We met earlier at the hospital. I was arrested when two men posing as doctors tried to take Anatoly—"

"Where are you now?"

"I'm at the police station on Idaho Avenue. Two Americans posted my bail. I don't know who they are, but they may be plotting to kill me."

"I'll be there in less than ten minutes. Speak to no one and don't leave the station." Gregoriev broke into a run as he speed-dialed the ambassador.

* * * * *

WASHINGTON, D.C. METROPOLITAN POLICE DEPARTMENT, IDAHO AVENUE NW

Hecker's DEA credentials trumped the protestations of a half-drunk, half-sedated shouting Russian woman, and the desk sergeant helpfully held open the door as they escorted a writhing Popova down the steps and into the parking lot. The two men and their captive had just reached Hecker's Lexus when a dark sedan screeched to a halt, blocking their exit. A slender Caucasian man leapt out and started shouting.

Nolan had heard enough Russian for one night. He pulled his pistol out of his waistband, stepped out of the car and pointed the weapon at the animated man. "Shut up, calm down and speak English."

"Who are you and why are you holding a citizen of the Russian Federation against her will?"

"My name is Birch. Your friend ordered my wife and daughter kidnapped earlier tonight. You'd be dead if we weren't at a police station. So move very slowly, and keep your hands in view."

"You don't dare harm me. I have diplomatic immunity."

Hecker joined the conversation brandishing his own pistol and Popova's handbag. The woman stayed in the back seat at Hecker's order. "Bob, move this piece of shit out of our way. We need to go."

Nolan pulled open the backdoor of the Lexus and rummaged through his rucksack. Two empty water bottles, forty thousand dollars banded in hundreds, a flashlight and two energy bars later his search left him unfulfilled. "Where's the rest?" he asked.

"At the embassy waiting to go out in a diplomatic bag tomorrow to Moscow. Careless of you."

"What's your name and what do you do?" Nolan asked.

"Gregoriev. I'm number two in the SVR."

"Connection to Chumakov?"

"Met him once before in Sri Lanka where I was the Colombo *rezident* when Chumakov arrived with Watermen." In response to Nolan's unasked question, he added, "Chumakov has no family here, so he asked for me after you shot him."

"Why not his girlfriend?"

"You've met her."

Nolan decided that he had little to lose. "I suspect you want to go back to the hospital. That's where we're headed with Ludmilla. Chumakov's regained consciousness and will cooperate provided we prove his girlfriend is all right and permit her to leave the country. I'll stay out of sight, but my friend will show Ludmilla to Chumakov and she'll say goodbye. We'll take her to the airport where we'll video her getting on the first flight to Moscow. Chumakov will tell us everything he knows in return for limited political asylum."

"This is a very interesting story," Gregoriev said. "Why share it?"

"We both have strong reasons for wanting Chumakov silenced. He's sworn to kill my wife and children. If he talks, he will speak of Fancy Bear and Cozy Bear, and stolen top-secret NSA hacking tools. He's already mentioned Translator, which may mean something to you."

Gregoriev felt a wave of nausea pass through him. *Translator?* How on earth did Nolan or Chumakov know about Translator? This was the name given to a multiyear, multi-million-dollar project to infiltrate and corrupt Western social media to sow dissent and undermine democracy and social stability. It was the single-most important ongoing SVR program in the United States. Only he and his boss knew of it within the *rezidentura*, even though they didn't manage it. Chumakov must be Translator's manager in the US. No wonder Portnikov was so keen to medevac or silence him.

"I see I have your attention," Nolan said.

"What do you want?"

"I want both of us to still have our freedom come sundown tomorrow. For this to happen, Chumakov has to die. He's under guard, but there's one person who can get to his bedside."

"Ludmilla," Gregoriev said.

"Precisely. We need to send her into his hospital room and make certain that he doesn't leave it alive." Nolan reached into his pocket and pulled out a slender carton of medication. "I found these in her purse earlier tonight. Eight large doses of Fentanyl. If we grind these to powder, dissolve them in hot water and load a syringe, all Ludmilla has to do is inject him."

"Why would she do that?"

"I will deposit one million US dollars split between your bank accounts. I can demonstrate proof of funds using my phone. I'll provide full payment once Chumakov is dead, and I have the three USB drives."

"What if she's not motivated by money?"

"Just bend the truth," Nolan said. "We both know that Chumakov will be executed upon arrival in Moscow if he's not euthanized on the plane. You tell her the FBI will torture Anatoly to make him talk, and you have orders to kill him painlessly through an overdose. In thanks for her assistance, President Putin has authorized you to deposit a large sum into her bank account. Once she's injected him and escaped without detection, she is to leave the US and not return."

"It sounds weak," Gregoriev said. "I don't know if I can rely on her, or you for that matter. What if you don't pay?"

"You make a phone call. There's an APB on me in any event. You may end up with a reward. As for the woman, the SVR always applies more stick than carrot. Drop the names of her sister or her aging parents. Someone she cares about. She'll do what she's told."

Gregoriev nodded.

"You sell it to Ludmilla while I liquify the Fentanyl and fill the syringe. Then you'll drive her back to the hospital. I'll sit in the backseat and my friend will follow. You return to the embassy to retrieve my thumb drives, and I'll wire funds to whichever bank accounts you designate. I'd also appreciate it if you made certain that Chumakov doesn't have any more embassy-linked people looking to harm my family or me. That's optional."

"Why optional?"

"My family is so well protected right now a SEAL team couldn't get to them. Plus, if anything happens, I'll come for you."

"I will call off Chumakov's people," Gregoriev said.

"Thank you. You'd best do whatever you need before you wake up Goldilocks—she's passed out." Turning to Hecker, Nolan said, "I'll need the syringe plus fingernail clippers, the lid from the thermos in the center console, a lighter and water."

Gregoriev opened the back door, leaned in and gave Ludmilla two sharp slaps on the face. She stirred, rolled to her side and deposited a liter of vodka tonics on the floor of Mrs. Hecker's Lexus. Gregoriev ignored the woman's complaints and pulled out a pen and paper. He wrote swiftly and handed Nolan a business card. "Here's my account with Bank of the Bahamas. I'll cover Madam Popova's share from my end. Prepare two syringes if you have them and split the dosages. Give both to me."

Nolan looked at the writing on the back and returned the card to Gregoriev. "Got it. Give her water and walk her around while I prep."

* * * * *

EN ROUTE TO GEORGETOWN UNIVERSITY HOSPITAL

"Anatoly loves life! Even if vhat you say is true and he'll be a cripple with a broken prick, he still won't vant to die. He has me!"

Gregoriev spoke in English for Nolan's benefit. "The FBI won't let him go. They'll inject drugs to keep him awake that will destroy his nervous system, cause him tremendous pain and leave him a vegetable. But in his last hours, he'll have mental clarity and no ability to withstand their questioning. We can't allow a hero to die a traitor, even an involuntary one. You must act to rob the Americans of their unfair and cruel victory, and salvage Anatoly's reputation."

"He's right," Nolan said. "Once the FBI injects Sodium Pentothal, he'll be helpless to resist."

"You need to do this for your country and for President Putin," Gregoriev added.

Ludmilla searched her handbag with increasing intensity. "Putin? He's a gangster and a murderer. He persecuted my ex-husband because he wouldn't swear fealty and kick back even more money. If this is about making Putin happy, you kill Anatoly and leave me out of it."

"I will if I have the chance, but it's unlikely they'll let me into his room," Gregoriev said. "I will avow that you are his fiancé and next of kin. They will grant you access for a few minutes before they take him to a government facility for torture and interrogation. If Anatoly dies before sunrise, there's a quarter of a million dollars to ease your pain and cherish his memory."

"A quarter million dollars? How is that possible?"

Nolan spoke again like the chorus in a Greek tragedy—or maybe a comedy. "It's a gift from me because of the guilt I feel over having shot Anatoly earlier tonight."

Ludmilla ended her frenzied inventory of her handbag. "I need my medication. I had a prescription in here and it's missing. I need to take a pill."

Nolan leaned forward. "You need to focus. Calm down and compose yourself, or they won't let you into his hospital room. Inject this into his arm. Hide the syringe and raise the alarm when he stops breathing. Once they confirm he's gone, you ask to go to the toilet and wrap the syringe in toilet paper, step on it hard to break it into pieces, and drop it all into the bowl and flush. Answer questions from the police and they'll let you go in one or two hours. Gregoriev will pick you up, and I'll deposit the funds into your bank account."

"I vant a drink. I feel ill again." Ludmilla opened the passenger door and lurched out, dropping her handbag to the ground and once again spilling its contents in the dimly lit hospital parking lot. She cursed in Russian and fell to her knees to collect her belongings.

From the backseat, Nolan handed Gregoriev two wrapped syringes. "Be careful with those. I'll meet you at the top of the Exorcist steps at six o'clock. The fallback is the lobby of the Georgetown Inn at seven-thirty. That gives you plenty of time to retrieve my property and make certain that Chumakov didn't dispatch a backup hit team. I'll transfer the funds once I've inspected the media." He handed the Russian a slip with the number of his burner.

"Don't toy with me, Nolan. Not if you care about your family."

"Just kill Chumakov and clean up this mess. I'll see you at six." Nolan exited the car and noted that Ludmilla had decided to apply more lipstick seated in the parking lot. He walked to where Hecker sat in the idling Lexus.

"How'd it go?" Hecker asked as Nolan got in, his nose wrinkling at the smell.

"Gregoriev's on board. Ludmilla's not."

"Well, that's why we gave him two syringes. I spoke with Marcelino. Don Randy told him to stick around Chumakov until I told him he could go home. He'll smooth access. We don't have anything to worry about."

"Oh, yes we do."

* * * * *

Gregoriev was surprised to see the Latino surgeon who'd operated on Chumakov. This fellow was in his late thirties, too old to be serving a resident's indentured servitude with its insane hours.

"Mr. Gregoriev from the Russian embassy?" the doctor asked.

"Yes, I'm back with Ms. Popova, who has recovered from an imbalance in her medications that led to her outburst earlier. We'd like to see the patient."

"Mr. Chumakov hasn't regained consciousness," the head nurse said. "We'll do an EEG tomorrow and evaluate brain activity. He's able to breathe on his own and little else."

Ludmilla turned to Gregoriev. "The Americans lied," she said in Russian. "They said he was awake."

"Let's see for ourselves," Gregoriev said. Marcelino led them to Chumakov's door, which was guarded by two plainclothes officers.

"I'm here with the next of kin and a senior official from Russia's embassy," Marcelino said. "I wish to discuss Mr. Chumakov's outlook with them in private once they've viewed the patient."

"Our instructions are that no one goes into the room unaccompanied," said one of the men, standing to add weight to his argument.

"It's four in the morning. I don't care what you do," said Gregoriev to the surprise of his two companions. The four of them entered the room. Chumakov lay unconscious, hooked up to even more monitors than before. Marcelino looked at the readouts and picked up the clipboard.

"Speak to him," Gregoriev said to Ludmilla. "Sometimes the voice of a loved one in his native tongue is all that's needed to bring a patient out of a coma."

Ludmilla gave Gregoriev a blank look. He looked down at her purse. Her lips made an O of recognition and she turned to face her insensate boyfriend. She cooed to him in Russian.

"I'd like to see your identification, officer. I will be reporting back to the ambassador that US police denied a consular official private access to a citizen of the Russian Federation."

"You're playing the consular official card, are you?" the shorter man answered. "I'm Special Agent Bustin. By all means report me to Director Salmick and, for that matter, Boris Yeltsin or whoever is in charge these days of your failed country."

"You impudent swine," Gregoriev said. "I should like to have you step outside this building so I could teach you some manners."

Bustin drew himself up to his full 5'7", sneered to reveal bad teeth and took a step toward the younger and fitter SVR man.

The monitors erupted, buzzers and beepers wailed, and a red light over the bed flashed. Ludmilla let out a squeal and dropped her handbag yet again. She bent over the motionless form of her boyfriend and wailed in Russian. "Anatoly! Anatoly. Vaht have I done?"

"We have a patient in cardiac arrest!" Doctor Marcelino shouted into his phone. "We need to defibrillate!" He turned to the two men staring dumbly. "Go get help! Go to the nurses' station!" Both Bustin and Gregoriev complied, colliding with Bustin's FBI colleague, weapon in hand as he charged through the door.

"He's had another heart attack," Bustin said. "Put it away."

Ten seconds later, Popova walked out into the hallway in a daze. Gregoriev hugged her and said, "Let me take you to the toilet."

"Where in the hell are you going?" Bustin asked. "No one leaves here until I say so."

"She just watched her fiancé die," Gregoriev. "I'm taking her to the ladies so she can splash cold water on her face and use the toilet. Come along and watch if you wish."

"I think I'll do just that," Bustin said, glaring at Gregoriev.

Gregoriev turned his back on the FBI agent and led an unsteady Popova toward the women's room. He had the second syringe in his left hand inside his pants pocket.

*　*　*　*　*

THE EXORCIST STEPS, GEORGETOWN

Gregoriev's phone displayed a photo of Chumakov in a hospital bed, stone dead and surrounded by idle medical personnel. Marcelino's text to Hecker twenty minutes ago had confirmed the same. How fitting that Nolan saw the proof of his demon's demise where the young priest, possessed by his own devil, hurled himself down those steps in the cinematic classic. *The Exorcist* was one of the reasons why Nolan wasn't a horror movie fan. After seeing it at the theater, he hadn't slept well for a month. This time he imagined he'd sleep well for the rest of his life, a fair tradeoff. He could have hugged the SVR man.

Gregoriev holstered his phone and handed over a baggie with the thumb drives containing Nolan's encrypted copies of the NSA's best hacking tools. The former codebreaker retreated up the street where his laptop sat in the back of Hecker's new ride. He confirmed that the drives were originals and sampled eight files. All recorded unsuccessful copy attempts but were otherwise untouched. Nolan told Hecker it would be ten minutes more. He exited the BMW with laptop in hand and headed up the street toward Gregoriev's glowing cigarette.

"The drives are fine."

"Where's my money?" Gregoriev asked.

"Give me five minutes."

"Once you finish, stay put while I transfer the funds to another account."

Nolan juggled a combination of laptop keyboard, burner cell and security dongle. "If you have Popova's account details, I'll deposit the two-fifty direct and the balance three-quarters to you and save you twenty-five dollars."

Gregoriev snorted. "Unnecessary."

Nolan executed a handful of instructions and walked the laptop to the SVR man. Gregoriev examined the electronic trail and nodded. Nolan returned to his perch on someone's front steps while the Russian worked his cell phone.

Five minutes later, Gregoriev walked over to where Nolan sat plinking on his laptop, searching in vain for emails from family, Ryder or General Payne.

"You're free," the SVR officer said.

"This is the last time we'll see each other. I don't believe in coincidences."

"Nor do I. Stay out of my shadow and your name stays out of my world."

Nolan closed his laptop and walked down Prospect Street toward the 5-Series BMW as it pulled away from the curb and coasted up to him.

"Everything good?" Hecker asked as Nolan opened the door.

"Yes, all square. Chumakov's dead and I'd wager the blonde's gone too."

"Shame to let him walk after a double murder. Lie down flat to keep that ugly face off the street surveillance cams."

"Particularly one I paid him to commit. No, this is a situation where the fewer the people who know, the better. You said you had a way for us to travel to Texas I wouldn't like. I'm guessing a wooden box with air holes."

"Nothing that good. You'll know more when we reach Wesley Heights, just off Foxhall Road."

"Where Don Randy lives?" Nolan asked.

"Bingo."

"I need to send something to POTUS for safekeeping. You know of a courier company open this early?"

"I'm driving," Hecker said. "Look it up."

"After I do that, I'll call Ryder and then wake up the wife and tell her that Mei Ling and she are out of danger. Maybe that will rehabilitate my image on the home front."

"Don't hold your breath. Osama bin Laden has better PR than you."

"Hand me your cell. It's time you disappeared."

CHAPTER FIFTEEN

TEARS

FRIDAY, AUGUST 19: THE WHITE HOUSE

Until yesterday evening the president had been certain that Bob Nolan was Hercules standing unshakably firm with Abyss supported on his broad shoulders. But after reading Payne's brief, Obama had learned of former NSA program director Tim Weill's murder and the related deaths of two Colombian narcos. Nolan was the common link based on fingerprints found in both the vehicle and on a pistol recovered from the woods near Fort Marcy. Nolan had used that same weapon to wound a Russian lobbyist and former KGB and FSB senior officer named Chumakov, and may have been part of two follow-up efforts to murder the man. And there was either the suicide or murder of Chumakov's girlfriend, found dead of an overdose in a hospital restroom. These weren't the actions of a man dedicated to unmasking Love and unraveling Putin's involvement in the election. Obama needed Payne to sit down with Nolan and hear his side of it. There might be a logical explanation, but how?

Obama's secretary buzzed. "I realize this is quite unusual, sir, but there's a bicycle courier at the front gate with a parcel that requires your personal signature to accept. The message on the package reads EYES ONLY: ABYSS ARCHIVES. No one knows what it means."

"Detain the courier and find out who sent the package. Screen the contents ASAP and bring whatever is inside to me as soon as you confirm it's safe."

* * * * *

SAN RAFAEL EN ROUTE TO OAKLAND INTERNATIONAL AIRPORT

The DEA in Burma found that the national police force contained honest and capable senior officers, none more so than Zaw Htway. Ryder and the major had worked together in Rangoon on joint drug interdiction operations from 2012 until late in 2014. For once, Uncle Sam had rewarded a loyal supporter, and Ryder still recalled the pure joy on Zaw's face when Hecker handed over the US immigration permits and plane tickets.

That had been two years ago, and Ryder hadn't been in touch until last night. There was plenty to catch up on, but Zaw always put business first. Ryder felt fuzzy due to a few more beers than he'd intended, a poor night's sleep, Nolan's early call and a hundred cuts and punctures from last night's exertions.

They sat in the Denny's near the Oakland International Airport. Bert Nolan's flight from New Orleans would land in an hour. "Nolan says that Chumakov died without a backup team in the field," Ryder said. "That means Nolan's wife and daughter should be safe, but we're not taking any chances. Holing up off the grid for a week has the further benefit of denying the feds bargaining chips: they can't detain his family if they can't find them."

"Nolan worries too much," Zaw said from behind his trademark gold-rimmed aviator shades.

"Not necessarily. Two days ago, someone killed five FBI and NSA officers looking to take Nolan into custody near Death Valley. Whoever did it tried to shoot Nolan too. That wasn't the Russians either—it ties back to Nolan's secret work for the White House. I have no idea what it is, but you can bet it's dynamite."

"I understand. I have M249 SAW light machine gun, two M-4 carbines, ten thousand rounds of 5.56, smoke grenades, three Glock 19s and one thousand rounds of jacketed hollow point 9mm."

"Jesus," Ryder said.

Zaw smiled. "And I have two Remington Model 870 shotguns and one hundred double-aught buckshot shells, four Claymores, M4 firing wire, one pair of NVGs, three ballistic vests and four secure walkie-talkies, fully charged. I do not have a sniper rifle. I am very sorry." Zaw acted as if this last omission had invalidated the rest of his efforts.

Ryder's fork paused in mid-motion where both men could see the tremors. He set it on the plate. "Let's go back to the beginning. You have a Minimi GPMG, bipod mounted?"

"Yes. Seven hundred fifty rounds per minute fed by two hundred-round M27 metal-linked belts. I brought five belts and boxes."

"Where did you get them?"

"When I arrived two years ago, I couldn't find work," Zaw said. "My English was not good as today. I know nobody. I was janitor in fast food restaurant. Relatives of men who run Burma see me."

"You work for the junta?" Ryder asked.

"I manage security for children and relatives in California. Los Angeles and San Francisco have more Burmese than any cities in USA."

"And these weapons?"

"They belong to employer," Zaw said. "I sign out. If we don't use, we replace no problem. All weapons from Burma, but all US military."

"I'll bet. Do you have men based in Northern California?"

"Two dozen in San Jose and San Francisco, but only eight off duty a day. I cannot take on-duty people without making mad my bosses."

"Do you have a place where we can hide the two Nolan women?" Ryder asked.

"A general owns a vineyard in mountains in Sonoma. The main house is empty. I have the keys. The vines are fresh and give no cover. Two men can cover approaches to house, except from air. The SAW can shoot down helicopters."

Ryder finished his coffee and signaled for the check. "Let's talk more on the way to the airport. From the sound of it, I should be taking orders from you."

"Yes, I think so maybe," Zaw said. "You in poor physical condition."

"It's nice to see you too, after all this time."

* * * * *

WESLEY HEIGHTS, WASHINGTON, D.C.

Hecker drove in once the overhead security camera had finished its scrutiny and the iron gate swung open. Behind the three-story colonial brick mansion set fifty yards off the main road, a man with an AR-15 slung over his shoulder motioned to the space in front of an electric-blue Maserati MC12. Hecker wondered how El Patron would react if he floored it and crushed that sexy three million-dollar tribute to Italian penile envy. He put his suicidal thoughts to the side, attributing them to too much scotch and not enough sleep. In the back seat, Nolan awoke and struggled to regain his equilibrium. The sentry showed them indoors.

Don Randy Dozier, brother-in-law of the leader of the revived Medellín Cartel, sat on a barstool at the kitchen island, a blondish George Michael stubble and bathrobe half-open to display bronzed pecs replete with gold nipple rings. Nolan was surprised to see that the don was only forty or so, though he'd had work done to his face so the estimate might be a decade light. A sullen, sinewy young man ate yogurt and granola on the adjacent stool. El Patron pushed a grape between the boys' pursed lips. "*Vete*, Romero." The sulker sashayed out of the kitchen, displaying most of a full-back angry clown tattoo under his white string tank top.

Their host didn't ask them to sit. His eyes narrowed as he sucked on an uchuva.

"Thanks to you, Don Randy, everything went well," Hecker said. "Dr. Marcelino was a great help. Nolan paid the Russians to finish off two of their own, including the man who ordered your nephews killed."

"I have a driver. You'll ride in a minivan out of sight. It's a clean vehicle, unconnected with my business. What is your destination?"

"San Antonio, sir," Nolan said. "Will that be a problem?"

"When do you need to arrive?"

"Late Saturday night."

"Nothing to worry about. You even will have time to sightsee."

"We are indebted to you," Hecker said.

"Yes, you are. Some in my organization blame my nephews' deaths on you. The GPS tracks and timetable contradict your stories, as do the final movements of their cell phones. I said that Bob was tired and under stress and these demands made him forgetful. No friend of Sam's would endanger my own blood through carelessness, but my men were insistent. They want revenge on whoever caused the deaths of Paolo and Javi."

The Colombian abruptly stood and stared at them, anger hardening his features. "Who shot them?"

"As Bob said last night, it was five Russians, all military or intelligence professionals from their actions. We don't know who exactly, but we will find—"

"*Basura!* Don't tell me it was the Russians! I can't kill everyone who walks out of the embassy. I want names. Someone must pay!" He flipped over the fruit bowl on the counter. At the sound of the breaking porcelain, a Hispanic man rushed into the room, pistol at the ready. The drug lord stopped him with an upraised palm.

"There's a senior intelligence officer named Gregoriev who works in the SVR," Nolan said. "He sent the team who killed your nephews. If you take him alive, he'll provide the names."

The don gestured at a pad and pen at the end of the counter. "Write it down."

Outside once again, Hecker and Nolan eyeballed the Maserati while waiting for the van and driver.

"You think Gregoriev dispatched those shooters?" Hecker asked. "That doesn't make sense."

"We needed to give El Patron a name if we wanted to leave the kitchen alive. I hope it wasn't Gregoriev. If he says that Chumakov signaled for help from his phone four blocks from the embassy, it won't do us any favors."

"Well, Don Randy's people will pick up Gregoriev. When that happens, it's one call, the van pulls over and we end up dead in a fucking ditch. You want Chattanooga for the over/under?"

"Gregoriev is smart," Nolan said. "I doubt they'll take him alive."

"Your plan is that we hope Gregoriev dies in a shootout before we reach the Alamo?"

"I don't have a plan. Give me an hour and I'll come up with something. But whatever we decide, your wife and son need to leave town."

"I'm way ahead of you," Hecker said. "They'll be on a flight to the Czech Republic later this morning."

"That was quick work."

"I learned how to leave in a hurry from a Jedi master, and I've had two years to plan it."

Randy took two men aside and spoke rapidly in a low voice. There was little harm in questioning Gregoriev to find out what had really happened, and who pulled the triggers on his nephews. He might not want to kill Nolan and Hecker, but he couldn't speak for his sister-in-law. Minnie was a vindictive bitch and needed to be as the widow of the murdered leader of a resurgent cartel. The men nodded and headed inside to change clothes and pick up sidearms.

* * * * *

OAKLAND INTERNATIONAL AIRPORT TO MARIN COUNTY

"Thanks for rescuing my mom," Bert said from the backseat of Zaw's pickup. "I should have been there. I owe you." The MMA fighter spilled powder as he mixed a protein drink.

"I appreciate that I wasn't convincing," Ryder said. "You don't owe me anything, but you do need to persuade your mother and sister to follow our instructions until we're certain there's no danger. Your dad makes enemies faster than we can kill them."

"We're not leaving the hospital if the doctor says that Mei Ling needs to stay. Can't we guard her hospital room instead?"

"It's a piss-poor option. For one thing, I won't be able to show my face because the police may have found my fingerprints alongside the two dead kidnappers."

"That has to be justifiable homicide," Bert said.

"Probably, but I'll end up in jail and out of action until I make bail—if I make bail—so it's an unacceptable option. The more important reason is hospitals are crappy places to defend. We might not even be able to smuggle weapons inside."

* * * * *

NOVATO COMMUNITY HOSPITAL

After a round of hugs and tears, Bert made the pitch for Mei Ling and Joanie to accompany Zaw, Travis Ryder and him to the wine country for up to a week of safe convalescence.

"Mei Ling's surgeon said she would be able to go home in one or two days if she deferred a muscle graft until later," Joanie said. "If where you have in mind is close to a doctor, I'm—"

"I'm not leaving as long as Bruce is in intensive care." Mei Ling interrupted.

"Bruce? Who's Bruce?" Bert asked.

* * * * *

THE WHITE HOUSE

The message inside the envelope containing the storage media was signed by Nolan. There was also a hand-drawn map complete with an "X" and, more helpfully, GPS coordinates of the site in the California desert where microfilms, disks and drives of Nolan's two years of research lay hidden under a rock. If General Payne checked his Tor inbox, he'd find the decryption instructions.

The last sentences were what gave Payne pause. "I urge you to order the arrest of all Higher Love operatives identified in these materials, but don't act before Monday. We should roll up the rest of the organization only after I identify Love Sunday. I will advise on Saturday where we'll need the snatch team for Sunday. Any leads on who tried to kill me? Reese."

Monday was three days away, enough time for Nolan and the Higher Love leadership to be drinking martinis in Timbuktu if Nolan was rotten. Obama would play it by ear until Payne reported back on what was in Nolan's files, particularly that partial list of the Higher Love traitors. The question of who had tried to kill Nolan remained unanswered. The mercenary from Black Ice who had impersonated an NSA attorney managed to die on the operating table from an allergic reaction to the general anesthesia. An autopsy was pending, and the surgical team had been sequestered.

Payne pushed the heretical thoughts out of his mind. Even as damaged goods, Nolan still retained more credibility than ninety-nine percent of the defense and intelligence officials whose first language was doublespeak and whose sole allegiance was to themselves.

* * * * *

MANHATTAN

The Americans had invented the onion router, but no one had hacked all of Tor, so every government and intelligence agency—and criminal organization—in the world made use of it. Kaili sent President Liu her recording of the breakfast meeting and the recommendation that he assign security to her.

Kleinwort's clammy hand was next on her agenda. As of this morning, Higher Love wanted five billion dollars per year in addition to the arming codes for the nuclear electromagnetic pulse bomb. Asking for money was a masterstroke, shifting focus away from Higher Love's true intentions. Liu's initial assumption was that Higher Love wanted to detonate the North Korea NEMP weapon as a precursor to a coup. Then last week, the MSS's people inside the US military had come up empty on the delivery platform and triggered Kaili's last-minute trip.

To her eye, the most likely outcome was that the NEMP wouldn't be detonated, but instead would be "discovered" and used as propaganda against Obama, perhaps leading to more military aggression against China. She'd further mull this over before jotting down her thoughts for Liu, but if she didn't receive confirmation forthwith of a meeting with Love, then that was the only plausible conclusion.

* * * * *

WESLEY HEIGHTS

Don Randy joined Hecker and Nolan outside. "Until my investigation concludes, you remain in custody." On cue, a white van drove up the driveway. "That will be your new home."

The van wasn't something off the lot. The poor visibility through the windshield spoke to bulletproof glass. The tires were low-profile run flats. The wire screen behind the front seats confirmed Nolan's suspicion: it was a prison transport. The driver exited and slid open the side door to reveal a pile of orange jumpsuits and flipflops.

"Hand them their new clothes. Strip down to your underwear and put these on. Hand me your phones, watches and jewelry."

"You don't have to do this," Hecker said.

"I do, particularly as your wife and son are at Dulles. Sending your family overseas isn't the move of an innocent man."

"Don Randy, Sam's only mistake was vouching for me," Nolan said. "You shouldn't penalize him too."

"I know Hecker, not you. Your debts become his debts. Once you've changed, get in the back. If you reach San Antonio alive, you passed the investigation and I will not speak of it again."

"I'll do it. I'll give you the information you want," Hecker said. "Aerial surveillance, phone and wiretap transcripts, bank accounts and movements of key personnel in and around Cali and Bogotá."

"And no interference from the DEA, cops or the army when we hit them?" Randy asked.

"None."

"*Bueno.*" Turning to Nolan, Randy asked, "What's the fastest, most private way for you to journey to Texas?"

"Private plane. There's a pilot in Dallas I trust."

"Bring him up. Have him land at Freeway Airport." Turning to Hecker, Randy said, "You go to work. Stay out of custody too. I don't care what stories you tell but leave my organization and me out of it. If any of this blows back, there will be two more unsolved murders in Prague. Understand?"

"I'll drive Nolan to the airport," Hecker said. "He's more or less on my way to the office."

"You go alone before I change my mind. I require the information by Monday morning."

"Yes, Don Randy." Hecker shook Nolan's hand.

"I'm sorry I dropped you in it again," Nolan said. "Stay out of jail."

"The least of my worries. Never a dull moment with Maximum Bob." Hecker turned to face the Colombian. "Thank you for the second chance."

Don Randy ignored him and addressed Nolan instead. "Come inside and make the necessary arrangements with your pilot. If he's not available, we have people who fly charters, but they tend to be booked in advance."

"Thank you for the offer. May I have my phone back?"

* * * * *

WASHINGTON, D.C.

Portnikov had been less interested in the details of Chumakov's death than the confirmation that he hadn't spilled secrets. Next on Gregoriev's Friday morning agenda was a staff meeting where he instructed his direct reports to apply all leverage to minimize the Russia angle on the Novato kidnapping and shootings. That took two hours. No sooner was he out of the room when it was Moscow again, this time eyes-only instructions to erase the electronic and physical footprint of the Farewell Group before returning to Moscow for urgent consultations. That last instruction didn't ring true. Gregoriev certainly favored leaving the US before police or the bureau questioned him about Chumakov and Popova's deaths. His preferred destination was the Caribbean instead of Lubyanka Square. There were new friends he was keen to meet in the Caymans, a million of them. From there, who knew where next?

He sat behind Chumakov's desk with Valeyriya screeching and cutting brown tape, building cardboard boxes in between dabbing her eyes. Whether the tears were for her late boss or the end of her sinecure, Gregoriev couldn't say. There wasn't much paper in the office. Anything other than bogus marketing brochures had already been shredded or sat on the desktop waiting its turn. What had him on edge was that the Austrian IT consultant Portnikov insisted he'd use hadn't shown up yet.

Valeyriya knocked on the open door. "There are two men here to see you. They have Spanish accents. What shall I tell them?"

Before Gregoriev could formulate a reply, the first man shouldered past the startled secretary and produced a pistol while the second man grabbed her by the upper arm and walked her into Chumakov's office. Gregoriev adjudged their field to be crime and not espionage. What in the hell had Chumakov got himself into?

"I'm afraid the person you're looking for is dead. Anatoly Chumakov expired—"

"We seek Vladimir Auturovich Gregoriev, Economics and Political Affairs Department, embassy of Russia. You are him?"

What was this about? Marcelino. The Hispanic doctor was connected, which meant Nolan was behind it. "I am with the embassy of Russia. I am a diplomat and you cannot detain or question me. Surely Bob Nolan told you this." Gregoriev scanned both men's faces to see if the name had any effect.

"Bob Nolan is who we want to ask you about. Did you send men from the embassy Thursday night to rescue Chum-koff from Nolan?"

Ah, Nolan was the one in trouble. How to play it? The embassy's rapid response team of five hadn't suffered any casualties, but they had killed two Latin males ... *ah hah! This could be his head in the noose, not Nolan's.* "No, I didn't send anyone. There was a team, but they report to embassy security and not me."

"You take too long to answer. Come. The *jefe* wants to meet you."

Valeyriya let out a yelp as her abductor crumpled to the floor, head bleeding from the heavy candy dish Helmut Krenn had used to strike him. Gregoriev's inquisitor turned and took aim as Krenn dodged out of the doorway. Gregoriev moved to step around the desk, but he was too far away, and the man swung his suppressed pistol around.

Gregoriev kept coming and figured he'd die with powder burns on his chest. Valeyriya lunged and came up with the first man's weapon, then shot the gunman in the back. The wounded man's suppressed gunshot missed Gregoriev's head and buried into the bookcase behind him. Gregoriev wrested away the 9mm pistol and kept it trained on the inert body. Ten feet away, Krenn had a knee in the back of the unconscious candy dish victim.

Valeyriya disappeared and reappeared seconds later with heavy zips and tie-tied their wrists and ankles.

"Good work," Gregoriev said. "Where did you receive your training?"

"Federal Security Services," Valeyriya said. "I worked under Chumakov years ago. What do you want to do with them?"

"Gag and search them and stand guard until we finish up. Think where you'd like to move to, because we've worn out our D.C. privileges." Gregoriev picked up the phone on Chumakov's desk.

CHAPTER SIXTEEN

REVELATION

FRIDAY, AUGUST 19: WESLEY PARK AND NOVATO COMMUNITY HOSPITAL

Pasan Wanigasekara of Jeevan Airways confirmed a four-p.m. arrival at Freeway Airport with a one-hour refueling turnaround. Nolan's call to Ryder caught the former SEAL in the backseat of the pickup loading 5.56m rounds into ammo belts and folding them in the accompanying metal boxes. Ryder told Nolan that Mei Ling had refused to abandon her boyfriend despite Joanie and Bert's efforts. A downcast Nolan wanted to take up Don Randy's offer of a meal, a shower and a bed before he headed to the airport. Instead he steeled himself for one more call.

Nolan's relationship with his daughter had frayed and broken after his extramarital affairs in 2014, first with the young librarian from Rangoon station, next with China spy Yu Kaili, and finally with the daughter of a Pakistan Inter-Services Intelligence Directorate exile. The last romp would still be a secret, but the second time around with Kaili in April had queered his relationship with both Nolan women. After he'd apparently perished in the MH17 crash, they'd posthumously forgiven him. Reappearing earlier this week revoked his immunity and put him bottom of the manure pile once again. His hand was slick as he held the phone tight to his ear. Mei Ling answered on the third ring.

"Honey, it's your father. How are you feeling?"

"Like I've been shot through the left thigh and the bullet missed my femur by less than an inch. Like Bruce may still die from being shot through both lungs. Like Mom could have been killed by the same kidnappers who shot Bruce and me. Like you're to blame for all of it."

"I understand and I feel awful too. But your mother, brother and you are the only leverage these people have over me. If you stay somewhere safe this week, I'll put an end to it."

"I've heard it all before. Remember, I was the idiot who flew to China at your request. I didn't even make it through immigration before I was arrested and jailed alongside Mom."

"Chumakov died earlier today," Nolan said. "He was the former threat. The new one is an organization called Higher Love. It is ultraviolent, highly secretive and needs to silence me before I expose its leaders and plans. Higher Love's goal is the overthrow of the US government and its replacement by a military dictatorship. It's not as unlikely as it sounds given how badly the political system functions these days. Uncovering this organization on behalf of the president is what I've done night and day the last two years."

"Hire Dan Brown to write the screenplay," Mei Ling said. "Maybe you can cast Tom Hanks to play you. You'd like that."

"However it sounds, it's the truth, and for everyone's safety you must leave the hospital and hide until at least Thursday. Bruce will be safe since these men know I won't sacrifice myself to save him."

"You bastard! He's your best friend, maybe your only friend."

"Blood's the only permanent tie. If these people take any of you three, they'll offer to trade your lives for mine. I don't care about myself, but I don't trust them to let you go either. It's best you all stay out of sight."

"I have another idea. Tell them the truth: you don't give a shit about anyone except yourself. That you won't trade your ego for the safety of your family and your obsessive fucking. Maybe these days you really do want to save America's democracy, but you destroyed Mom's life ... all of our lives. Don't tell me how much you care about us. Life is about deeds and not just words."

"That's not true. Mei Ling, you have to listen to—"

"Mom wants to speak with you."

Joanie came on the line. "Your daughter used to worship you and today she can't bear to hear your voice. Do you at last understand why no one trusts you?"

"Travis Ryder, the man who saved your life last night, believed me enough to leave his wife and two little boys in Texas to fly here. If you respect his judgment, you'll do what we ask."

"Have you seen Travis these days? He looks like Nick Nolte in *Down and Out in Beverly Hills.* His hands shake and he can't make eye contact when he speaks. But you're right, he has more credibility than you."

"The alternative is I call Washington and have the FBI guard you. They'll take you to a safe house, and by tomorrow there's a fifty percent chance you'll all be dead."

"You're saying the president's part of this cult?"

"No, he's the one who is rooting it out, but we don't know who we can trust other than a retired general who oversees my area."

"The president trusts only you to find this Love?" Joanie asked.

"More than thirty people are working on the project. I'm in charge, but I only have the names of the five people who report to me.

Obama asked me to pretend to be dead after I missed the MH17 flight out of Amsterdam two years ago. I agreed since I thought you would divorce me and marry Jerry Flynn. I didn't have a lot to go home to, and that was completely my fault."

"Jerry Flynn? I threw him out three days after you came to the house, just after I learned you were dead. Don't you try to blame anything that happened on—"

"I'm not, I'm not. I'm speaking to my state of mind after Russia shot the plane down and the newspapers announced I was on board. I thought I could spare you the embarrassment of having me in your lives and do good for the US at the same time. It also kept my enemies from trying to hurt you. As usual, I was wrong. I'm really sorry for—"

Joanie sobbed softly. "You're such an asshole. You always had your family to support you. If you had so little faith in us, maybe you should have stayed dead. I shed all my tears at the first funeral. Goodbye, Bob."

Joanie hung up and saw that Mei Ling was crying too.

Nolan used a dishcloth to blot his own tears in Don Randy's kitchen. He couldn't say how many he shed out of concern for their safety, and how many from self-pity. One thing was certain: once Mr. Love was in custody, no one would ever hurt his family again.

* * * * *

MANHATTAN AND NOVATO COMMUNITY HOSPITAL

The gnawing in Kaili's stomach persisted. She paced her room and confirmed that Liu had received her transmission. She needed to see the city, but her legs wouldn't take her to the door. In desperation she sat to clear her mind. Each time she did so, the same topic crept into the frame. In Sri Lanka in 2014, Bob Nolan had bartered his own and Coulter's freedom for David Leung, the CIA's top man in Asia, but a Coulter ally and MH370 villain. Leung had died of ricin poisoning before he could be interrogated, costing Kaili the leadership of MSS's Foreign Affairs Bureau. Nolan had outsmarted her, something no other adversary had ever done. He also was the father of her son, a child she'd had in defiance of the advice from doctors, political commissars and even an MSS-appointed psychiatrist. Ying Sheng was the best thing in her life, yet every time she gazed upon him, there was young Bob Nolan staring back. She still hated Nolan, but it didn't mean that she wanted Higher Love to murder him. If anyone killed Bob, it would be her. She looked up a number and tapped the screen.

"Hello, Mei Ling's phone."

"Who am I speaking with?" Kaili asked.

"This is her mother. May I ask who's calling?"

"I have a message for your husband. Tell him that Higher Love hunts him, and he needs to take strong precautions. They will come at him through you. Also tell him that he is the father of my son, and I will need him to sign the papers to obtain US citizenship."

"Who is this?"

"My name is Kaili."

"Kaili? As in Yu Kaili? The spy-whore who ordered my daughter and me arrested in China? You and your baby can burn in hell." Joanie hung up.

Mei Ling put down the day's *Chronicle*. "Mom? Mom? Are you all right?"

Tears ran down her mother's cheeks. "That spy for China just called. She said she has your father's baby and—"

"Mom! Mom! She's a bitch. She's said it to hurt you."

"I know, I know, but the main reason she called was to warn me that a group called Higher Love aims to kill your father by kidnapping us. I believe her. We have to hide."

* * * * *

NOVATO COMMUNITY HOSPITAL PARKING LOT

Ryder worked with his head down, fingers still busy jamming cartridges into link belts. The engine ran with the AC on low while KFOG played classic rock. Another day of sobriety and its attendant horrors were upon him. Joanie tapped on the glass and Ryder started like he'd heard a backfire. He opened the door and she leaned in, catching a whiff of halitosis.

"Mei Ling and I just received a call from Yu Kaili," she said. "I need you to persuade Mei Ling to leave."

Ryder reached up front, turned off the engine and extracted the keys. "Tell Bert to find out where we can rent a wheelchair-enabled van with a spacious back cargo area. Zaw can help. I'll be with you as soon as I call Bob and make certain we're on the same page." He pushed a pamphlet into Joanie's hand. "This will explain how to operate the secure walkie-talkies Zaw brought. Read it and make certain Mei Ling and Bert do too."

* * * * *

DEA HEADQUARTERS, ARLINGTON, VIRGINIA

Hecker refused to be mollified despite the efforts of his two bosses in the Office of Investigative Intelligence. "The fucking Medellín

Cartel has a tail on my family! Randy's threatened to kill my wife and son. We need to hit them now!"

"The only way to shut them down is simultaneous raids here, Miami, LA and Medellín. If we just take out El Patron, the rest will scatter and we'll have wasted three years of undercover work. The director is aware of your sacrifices, and you'll receive a commendation once this operation concludes."

"This isn't the nineteenth-century British army. Back then they used to say, 'You can't buy a man's life, but for a bit of ribbon he'll give it to you.' That's horseshit. We agreed when I was still in Asia and the Cartel reached out that you'd protect my family first and foremost. Well, it's time to put up. I want Sophie and C. J. in the Prague embassy under guard as soon as their plane lands."

"We can't do it without alerting Randy and maybe blowing the entire operation. But we'll speak with the ambassador and ask him to put a shadow on them to be on the safe side."

"We have enough on Minnie and Randy to file federal murder charges," Hecker insisted. "The other big dicks in the cartel would each face at least twenty years. We have the locations of the top five in Medellín, plus Randy here and that muscle boy Carlos Gomez in LA. Hit all seven before Sophie's flight lands and take my wife and kid to the embassy for protection."

The second man spoke. "Uh, Sam, there's been a change of plan in the past hour. When we notified the president of Colombia that the Doziers had grabbed the bait, he instructed us to provide real and not doctored intel."

"Why in the fuck would we do—"

"We would do it because we want the Medellín Cartel to take down the Cali Cartel and save the Colombians and us *mucho* blood and *dinero*. If somehow Cali comes out on top, then we hit them. Otherwise we strike once Medellín comes up for air. Only half as many to fight, and we all end up looking good."

"How many times have we tried this approach in the past?" Hecker asked. "How many times have dozens of civilians ended up dead? How many times has this worked? *Never. Not once in my nineteen years in the DEA.* Why? Many reasons. Sometimes the plan leaks. Other times it's the law of unintended consequences. Most of the time the winners increased the payoffs to the government and the military, the news of the big operation spread, and the narcos took evasive action. Then we waited another five or ten years for governments to change or another cycle of violence as the cartels sorted out the pecking order before there was a new opening. Arrest the top seven today and you'll never regret it, even if a few medium-level operators escape."

"I'm sorry you see things through such a cynical prism."

"If you'll excuse me, I have intel to collate," Hecker said as he rose.

"We have staff sifting through the unretouched datasets and transcripts already."

"Yeah, well, seeing as how it's my family on the line, I'll doublecheck it. The last thing we want is a half-assed hit by the Medellín mob and leave Cali strong enough to strike back."

"Sam, we're truly sorry about your predicament. We understand your concern, but everyone will come out of this fine."

Hecker stomped out of the room. He still had six hours before Sophie and C. J. disembarked in Heathrow. Once they were taken care of, he would orchestrate the death of El Patron.

* * * * *

NOVATO COMMUNITY HOSPITAL

The nurses strapped a removable cast around Mei Ling's left leg. Then the orderlies set her down in a wheelchair. She rolled out of the room at speed and braked just in time to avoid running foot-first into the corridor wall.

Joanie was settling the bill downstairs. Ryder had wheedled a disposable razor from the nursing station and was shaving when Mei Ling made her break. With a curse he wiped the foam off his half-smooth face and raced after her. He slowed down when he turned the corner and saw the double doors leading to the Intensive Care Unit.

Mei Ling was in Bruce Goodhill's room, but if she had anticipated a loving reunion, she was disappointed on two counts. Bruce remained unconscious and seated around his bed were Lena and their two college-aged children, Bryan and Tabitha.

"How's Bruce?" Mei Ling asked.

"Fighting an infection," said Bryan, a six-footer with a lean surfer's build. "They're culturing it. We hope it's not MRSA."

"What happened?" Tabitha asked, wiping the tears from her cheeks. "Why did those men shoot you and kidnap Auntie Joanie?"

"It has to do with my father," Mei Ling said.

"But he's dead," Tabitha said. "Last year we all visited his grave in Arlington Cemetery."

"You need to leave," Lena said.

"Oh, Mrs. Goodhill," Mei Ling said, "I didn't mean for this to happen ... Yes, Bruce and I are in love. I've—"

"You have one and only one way to prove you love him: leave and not return until whatever your father's involved in is settled. Every second you're in this room, you're putting my children, husband and my lives at risk. Go and don't return."

Mei Ling said nothing.

"Mei Ling just came by to check on Bruce," Ryder said. "She's already checked out. We're moving to an undisclosed location. We'll all stay there until this ends. Bob can't be here because he's after those responsible. I'm in charge of family security. I believe you'll be safe here, but you may want to request the police to post a guard outside."

"I've done that," Lena said. "They can't send anyone until four o'clock this afternoon."

Ryder turned around Mei Ling's wheelchair and took a step toward the exit. "Can you handle a pistol?" he asked Bryan.

"Mostly just pellet guns and *Call of Duty* stuff."

"Then go to an outdoor store and buy several cans of bear spray. It works just as well as pepper spray but has a thirty-foot range instead of ten feet. Just point and press."

"How do we contact you if something happens?" Bryan asked.

"Buy temporary phones and only use those to call this number." Ryder wrote down his burner number. "Good luck."

* * * * *

WASHINGTON, D.C.

Valeyriya answered the insistent knocking on the front doors. The two embassy rapid reaction force members dragged in a dolly containing heavy-duty collapsed shipping boxes with a roll of thick plastic sheeting on top. She relocked the Farewell Group's entrance and shut Chumakov's office door behind the newcomers. In reception Helmut Krenn sat in a plush armchair and ran diagnostics on a cell phone connected to his laptop.

Gregoriev was relieved to see Egorov with an embassy heavy. "One dead and one knocked unconscious, but he'll come around. I need you to find out who he works for and why he came here. Then dispose of him alongside his companion. The fellow outside is hacking their phones. They weren't carrying any ID, just keys. Before we subdued these two, they asked for me by name, and asked whether the embassy sent a team last night to rescue Chumakov from Nolan."

Two firm slaps on the face had the slender Latino's eyelids fluttering. Egorov and his fellow ex-soldier pulled the man up and sat him in Chumakov's chair. "What is your name, and who do you work for?"

Their subject winced as his eyes adjusted to the light. "*Agua.*"

Egorov took a half-cup of stale coffee off Chumakov's desk and threw it across the man's face. "Answer the questions and I'll give you water."

"*Chupame la pinga, puto.*"

"The walls aren't soundproof," Gregoriev said. "We'll have to do this elsewhere. Gag him." Egorov's companion complied.

Their captive's hateful eyes recorded their faces. "This one will tell us nothing," Egorov said. "We may as well kill him here. That way we can fit both bodies into a single box and save a carton."

Valeyriya opened the office door and stuck her head in. "Mr. Krenn would like a word."

Gregoriev stepped into reception. The Austrian studied his laptop. "They're narcos from Colombia," Krenn said. "The most common names in their communications are Randy, Paolo and Javi. I don't read Spanish, but I can pass the longer emails through Google if you want a crude translation."

"The two we killed last night in the park were Paolo and Javier Dozier," Egorov said.

"*Ty che, blyad!*" Gregoriev cursed. "Find out their residential addresses."

Egorov pulled out his phone and dialed as he walked to the other side of reception.

Gregoriev walked back into Chumakov's office. Egorov's sidekick had wrapped plastic sheeting around the dead Colombian. The Russian approached the live prisoner waving a box cutter. The prisoner's eyes grew wide.

"Listen up. There is only one way you leave this room alive. You write down the addresses where the Doziers live: Don Randy, Paolo and Javi. If it doesn't match what we have, you die. Once we finish our business with them, you have to disappear because the Cartel will think you informed on them. If we ever see you again after today, my people will either kill you or hand you over in Medellín with a ribbon tied around your cock. Understand?"

The man nodded.

Egorov walked back into Chumakov's office. Gregoriev pulled the gag out of the prisoner's mouth. "Where does Don Randy live?"

"*Dos mil doscientos tres calle* Garfield."

Gregoriev looked at Egorov. "I think he means 2230 Garfield Street."

"Wrong answer," Egorov said, raising his suppressed weapon.

"No, no, I said two thousand two hundred and three Garfield Street."

Egorov lowered his arm. "Better. Speak English next time."

Gregoriev reinserted the gag into the man's mouth. "Keep him alive until we hit the house. Milk him for entrances/exits, layout, staffing and armaments."

"Are you sure about this?" Egorov asked. "I thought these two were after Nolan?"

"They could be working for Nolan for all we know," Gregoriev said. "Last night your team shot the sons of the Medellín Cartel's leader. Regardless of their interest in Nolan, when they find out who pulled the triggers, they'll murder us. They may even kill your people's families to send a message."

* * * * *

MANHATTAN

"Pack an overnight bag," Kleinwort said. "Don't contact anyone. At seven o'clock a driver will meet you in the lobby. Your meeting is later today. Should you wish to return to New York City, we will fly you back later on Sunday. Have a safe flight."

Kaili notified President Liu via Tor that she would meet Mr. Love Saturday p.m. at an undisclosed location. She hastened to pack, dress and wipe down anything she'd touched since the night before.

CHAPTER SEVENTEEN

UNHAPPY CHANCE

FRIDAY, AUGUST 19: NOVATO TO NORTHERN SONOMA COUNTY

"Two vehicles on surface roads headed north toward the US 101 onramp one hundred meters ahead. We remain unobserved."

"Excellent work, Anaconda Red Six. Please advise numbers and disposition of targets."

"Lead vehicle is a late-model black Toyota Tundra driven by an Asian male, age fifty, and accompanied by Bert Nolan, age twenty-four. Second vehicle is a white panel van with handicapped license plates driven by a Caucasian male, late thirties, unidentified. Passengers include Nolan's wife and daughter."

"Be discreet, do not engage. We will have a drone overhead within fifteen minutes. If they divert to remote roads, we will interdict the rear vehicle if feasible. Otherwise we will evaluate options and advise once we determine their destination."

"Roger that."

* * * * *

"Tonight there's likely to be shooting," Ryder said, "so keep those vests on at all times. But they'll try to capture you, not kill you. That makes a huge difference. Stick together, stay behind cover whenever possible and separate yourselves from the rest of us if the firing is intense. You won't be targeted, but a stray bullet kills you just as dead. If we go down or you're alone, surrender. If we're still in the fight, take the safety off your shotgun, aim at the man's chest and press the trigger. At less than fifty meters a twelve-gauge shotgun is a deadly weapon and doesn't require precise aim. After you fire, pump it once like this to put a new round in the chamber. You have eight shots before you must reload."

"I already told you, I won't fire a gun," Mei Ling said. "Not after what happened to Bruce and me. And I'm in a lot of pain. May I have another pill, please?"

"You can save your mother's life and your own if you follow my instructions. And no more pain meds until this is over."

Ryder turned to Joanie. "You sure you're OK to drive?"

"We went over this at the hospital. I'll be fine."

"The switch will be tricky, but it helps that you're so thin. I'll recline the seat all the way, you ease onto my lap and take the wheel, and I'll slide out from under. Don't take your eyes off the road."

"Are you sure it's necessary?" Joanie asked.

"I hope not, but we were followed out of the hospital and I need to set up a machine gun and point it out the back. If the shit hits the fan, we'll have seven hundred-fifty rounds a minute to keep the flies off."

"I'll call Bert and Zaw so they can watch you two play Twister," Mei Ling said.

"Use the walkie-talkie. Tell them to have weapons up—the silver SUV with dark windows behind us is a tail. There may be others."

* * * * *

WASHINGTON, D.C.

Helmut Krenn finished his IT hygiene routine and left with their thanks. Gregoriev gestured for Valeyriya to sit. She had an attractive face with classic Slav features and a cascade of dark hair. Her physique was athletic, perhaps a swimmer or water polo player with broad shoulders, muscled thighs and defined biceps. The only thing wrong with her was she was at least four centimeters taller than Gregoriev, but as a wise man once observed, people making love were always the same height. The last two hours had proven her resourcefulness—Chumakov had chosen well.

"After we're done speaking, call the Metro PD and report shots fired at 2203 Garfield Street NW. I will call the FBI and alert them that the Medellín Cartel and Bob Nolan are holed up at the same address. Once the police knock on the door, violence likely follows. That will be my signal to flee. I suggest you do so too, since the police, the traffickers, the FBI and perhaps our own people will be after us."

"Is it so bad?" Valeyriya asked.

"Chumakov's death, the deaths of two Cartel family members last night, this situation here today, and the raid on the Dozier family home will stir the hive. The best thing for you would be to disappear."

"I am an FAA-certified private pilot for twin-engine aircraft. If you have the funds, we can rent a plane this afternoon."

"Excellent. I will cover the cost. Do you have your passport?"

"Yes, I brought it this morning to the office after I learned of Anatoly's death. I also withdrew two thousand dollars from a series of ATMs."

Gregoriev smiled and nodded in approval. He patted his left breast pocket of his suit jacket. "I, too, arrived prepared. File a flight plan for

Miami. We'll refuel there and head out to sea under the radar if you can manage it."

"I have the skills to fly fifteen meters above the waves."

"If you fly us to Cuba, I'll pay you one hundred thousand dollars."

Valeyriya returned his smile. "If you give me one hundred thousand dollars, you'll have a new girlfriend."

* * * * *

THE WHITE HOUSE

You'd think, as leader of the free world, the president could spend more than four consecutive hours of his day without Bob Nolan's name surfacing, but here it was just after lunch and his secretary was rushing in with another eyes-only brief. With trepidation Obama read that the FBI's IT forensics team had worked overnight on the computers found in the attic office of former NSA program director Timothy Weill. Last night Weill had been found dead of a gunshot wound to the base of the neck behind a liquor store in Georgetown. A search of the single man's home turned up a trove of classified information. Metro PD called in the bureau, and the FBI's cyber experts compiled a preliminary report. FBI Director Salmick's one-page summary was a showstopper that the president forwarded to Payne for his feedback.

Weill was one of the principals involved in the dissemination of the hacked Democratic Party and candidate Crandall's emails. He also appeared to be the thief who lifted the three ops disks containing the NSA's most powerful surveillance programs. Finally, in the past two days Weill had devoted inordinate time seeking the physical location of Bob Nolan, though he appeared to have failed to do so. What he had done instead was pin the NSA theft on the "Shadow Brokers" from Asia and suggest that Nolan was behind the moniker.

Weill had a client list of just one name—the Farewell Group. The bureau would visit the Farewell Group's offices this afternoon and detain all persons and records found within. The small lobbying organization listed its leader in the Foreign Agent Registration Act filing as Anatoly Alkaevovitch Chumakov. In the past sixteen hours, Mr. Chumakov had been shot, suffered a heart attack, and died in hospital of a suspected opioid overdose. Chumakov's lady friend Ludmilla Popova, ex-wife of an ostracized Putin oligarch, had also died of an overdose—accidental or otherwise—as well.

Robert Nolan's fingerprints and Weill's were found in the vehicle shot up outside Fort Marcy Park, Virginia, late last night. Inside and next to the black SUV were two murdered scions of the Dozier crime family, leading lights of the resurrected Medellín Cartel. Nolan was sought for questioning in respect of all five deaths.

What did the president advise with regard to the degree of focus placed by the bureau on apprehending Bob Nolan? Obama put down his reading glasses and punched the intercom. "Ferial, get me Director Salmick on the phone." While Obama waited for Salmick, he wondered when he'd have the list of Higher Love members identified by Nolan. Right now, he could use a scorecard to tell the good guys from the bad.

* * * * *

WESLEY HEIGHTS

Three years ago, a good month was a top line of forty or fifty million for east of the Mississippi. This year the Cartel was on track to do three billion in sales in the eastern US, even after incurring the distribution levies imposed by the Mexicans. Product costs, domestic transport and warehousing, money laundering fees, bribes, staff salaries and benefits, pensions for incarcerated members, lump sums for murdered employees' families and legal expenses ate into those revenues, but in most months El Patron's enterprise churned out one hundred million dollars in free cash. Added to the sixty or so contributed from lazy fucker Carlos Gomez for the western US, Don Randy had an investable surplus of two billion dollars per year.

Ever since his brother Freddie's assassination—a murder avenged many times over by his widow—El Patron had taken on additional responsibilities that had yielded an ulcer. The drug business ran itself provided you had the right people. That was the *Colombiano* skillset, and the Medellín Cartel offered good career progression for middle managers who stayed alive, unaddicted and loyal.

On the other hand, with regard to finance, his homeland contributed nothing but technocrats and second-rate money managers. El Patron had done his best starting from a low knowledge base. Today the Dozier family's collection of high-end residential properties, modest office buildings, fine art, jewelry, precious metals, cut gems, yachts and collectibles rivaled that of any robber baron from Leland Stanford's era to the present.

Keeping track of what they owned and how it could be accessed occupied another twelve people based on a floor in a suburban Maryland office block. Recently, El Patron's IT people had detected outsiders probing their firewalls. When he'd learned of it, he realized that a clever thief could wipe out their cash reserves. He hadn't slept well since.

Yet here in his own home was Bob Nolan, the superspy who'd found MH370 twice over, was awarded a medal and received a full pardon from Obama. Fuck the medal, but the pardon was something that Don Randy appreciated. He had already bought two from prior presidents of Colombia. The Cartel needed a full IT and security audit and upgrade. Rather than defrocked consulting partners of dubious merit, why not hire the real deal in Nolan? That would buy peace of mind, and there the man was, six meters away taking a nap.

His cell rang—it was an encrypted call from Minnie. He pushed the sequence of buttons and braced himself. "Hello. I wasn't expecting to speak with you again so soon," he offered.

"I've sent the jet to collect the bodies. See they're on board no later than Monday."

"Monday will be the earliest that the coroner will release them. More likely, it will be Tuesday or Wednesday."

"What's the point of being billionaires if we can't do what we want? I want to see my sons and you not later than sundown on Tuesday. Do I have to come north myself?"

"Minnie, you're wanted in the US and eleven other countries. You're not going anywhere. I understand your pain and frustration. Yes, of course I'll accompany Paolo and Javier home, but I can't leave until Hecker supplies the intel."

"Did you avenge my sons yet?"

"Bob Nolan gave us a name and I sent Dante and Nacho," Randy said. "I haven't heard from them. I'll let you know."

"And what does Nolan know?"

"He gave us the name of the Russian at the embassy. Nolan didn't do anything wrong. We need to focus on eliminating every one of those Cali nosepickers once we have their locations."

"Let me handle military tactics," Minnie said. "Do me one last favor."

"Anything."

"Once Hecker supplies the intel, kill him. He's outlived his usefulness.'"

"Minnie, this makes no sense—"

But the line was dead. Randy shook his head in dismay. Why on earth did Freddie marry such a *loca*?

The staff break room door opened and out walked a bleary-eyed Nolan. "Hello, Don Randy. Thanks for taking such good care of me." The Anglo walked over to where his phone was recharging and scrolled through his messages.

"I need a favor," Randy said. "When you finish whatever it is you're doing, I want you to conduct an IT security review of our entire business process. I fear we've become vulnerable to hackers and possibly law enforcement. I will pay you whatever you ask, but the job is a large one so please budget one month."

Nolan looked up from his phone. "I'll do it for free, but I need my own favor right away, that is, if it's not too much trouble."

"What is it?"

"Last night, Paolo offered to send men to where kidnappers held my wife. In the end, my man freed her and killed both kidnappers, but now there's another armed group that wants to capture my wife, son and daughter. I have two men with them, but it may not be enough."

"Where are they?" Randy asked.

"Headed north out of Marin Country into Sonoma. They'll be staying in the hills at a private winery. I can find the address."

"I will have six men assembled in three hours, and on site in another two-to-three."

"That should work." Nolan scribbled on a pad. "I've left the phone numbers of my two burners, plus one for Travis Ryder, the senior man on the ground in California. If you could put your men under Ryder's control, he's a former SEAL and will deploy them to best effect."

"My people are security experts. They will do what is necessary, and they report only to this family. Tell Ryder that Felipe will call him for the brief. If it's amateurish, they'll leave. I won't waste valuable men."

"Yes, of course. I didn't mean to give offense."

Randy smiled. "I'm a bit oversensitive because my sister-in-law just spoke to me as if I was a servant. Your driver is out back waiting. Go to the airport and let me make my calls."

Nolan shook the don's hand. "I'll be free in September. Just let me know what you'd like me to look at, and I'd be pleased to help." Nolan walked out in better spirits and with a clearer head. Owing favors to narcos was bad for your actuarial tables, but that was the price you paid for muscle on short notice.

* * * * *

Romero came downstairs and brushed past Randy without speaking. Randy shook his head. If he'd wanted a bitch for a partner, he'd have stayed married. No, not really. Screwing a woman felt like wiggling his finger in a bucket of worms.

He called San Francisco and passed along Ryder's contact details and outlined the mission. The head of Northern California wasn't happy about having his weekend spoiled.

"Did you clear this with Don Carlos?"

"Fuck Carlos!" Randy shouted. "You cleared it with me. Contact this man Ryder, gather five men, issue weapons and get your asses out to Sonoma. The man I'm helping is assisting me on a very important matter. Carlos doesn't need to know. Get moving."

Insubordinate prick. Who was this punk to imply he took orders from Carlos? If he wasn't Minnie's little brother, El Patron would have had him beaten to death outside one of those shitty Venice Beach steroid gyms he habituated.

There was a knock at the front door. *Where the hell was his security? Oh right, collecting a Russian spy or driving Nolan to the airport.* Out sashayed Romero through the swinging door, past him again with no acknowledgement, and through the living room. The front door opened. There was a murmur of voices, and a boost in volume as Romero switched from English to Spanish. The conversation ended with traded shouts and a slammed door.

Randy dialed Dante and once again received an out of service message. His follow-up call to Nacho generated an identical outcome. Something was wrong, very wrong. He needed to stop standing around scratching his ass and locate his two men and this spy Gregoriev.

Romero stalked past. El Patron had to physically block his path before the pouty young man deigned to look at his benefactor. "Who was that?"

"The police. Said there was a report of gunshots at this address and asked if they could walk around the back of the house. I told them they were crazy and to fuck off if they didn't have a warrant. They said they'd be back."

Randy slapped the young man's face. "Are you out of your mind? Do you realize how much I pay every month to ensure that no police ever have a reason to obtain a warrant for my home?"

"There aren't any drugs here," Romero said.

"No, not unless we count the MDA, poppers, pot and coke in our bedroom. Plus the unlicensed firearms and millions of dollars in cash. Pack a bag. We need to leave now. You idiot!"

* * * * *

FREEWAY AIRPORT, BOWIE, MARYLAND

Valeyriya was flustered. The flight school where she knew the owners was closed. The man handling aircraft rentals in an unaffiliated company wanted nine thousand dollars in advance for a thirty-six-hour charter of a Piper Seminole. She conferred with

Gregoriev in Russian, adding to the unease of the man handling the paperwork.

"How much cash do you have?" Gregoriev asked.

"About two thousand two hundred," she replied. "What about you?"

"Far less. Reduce the charter to eight hours and pay cash."

"That will be impossible. I told him we're flying to Miami for my goddaughter's baptism tomorrow morning. It's a six-hour flight each way."

"We must be airborne soon. The embassy is searching for me. The police may find those two bodies Egorov disposed of. The Dozier family will hunt for their men. We need to find seven thousand dollars in a hurry."

Gregoriev looked up from the counter and surveyed the modest terminal. The place was empty save for a skinny Indian man dressed in a pilot's boiler suit. "Wait here. Let me see if this fellow can fly us for a big payout at the other end."

Gregoriev approached the man and, as he came near, Pasan Wanigasekara stood up, tongue-tied. When Gregoriev stopped in front of him, Pasan's mind went blank. "Are you two with Bob Nolan?"

Gregoriev's eyes widened. "Yes, yes we are. We're waiting for Bob. What's our destination today?"

"You'll need to discuss it with him, but I only packed food for two. You'll want to grab sandwiches and drinks. I have a cooler on board."

"Excellent suggestion. When do you expect Bob?"

"At any time. I have a scheduled five o'clock departure."

"Let me inform my girlfriend."

As Gregoriev grumbled at the thirty-dollar bill for a pair of sandwiches, chips and drinks, Bob Nolan walked into the terminal. The two men sized one another up. Nolan turned and dashed out even as he dropped a strap on his rucksack and swung the pack around to his chest. Gregoriev shouted for Valeyriya, who followed him outside.

Nolan had Hecker's Glock in his right hand buried in the knapsack containing forty thousand in cash, a water bottle and a spare magazine. He stopped and whirled about, expecting to see an armed adversary. Gregoriev halted ten feet away and held his hands in full view at shoulder height. A Russian looker descended from strong farming stock was right behind her countryman. She stopped as well.

"We are unarmed," Gregoriev said. "We can help one another."

"This morning you said you didn't believe in coincidences. I don't either. I should shoot you where you stand."

"I went to Chumakov's office later to clean up our mess. Two Colombian hitmen showed up and asked for me by name. They also mentioned you. You sold me out."

Nolan raised his hand inside the knapsack to shoulder height and pointed the hidden pistol at the center of Gregoriev's chest. "If you had any sense, you would have been on a plane to Moscow by the time they showed up. Last night your embassy's rapid response team tried to rescue Chumakov. Instead, they killed the two sons of the woman who runs the Medellín Cartel. Her brother-in-law lives in D.C. and he's hellbent on revenge."

"And you threw him my name?" Gregoriev asked.

"You're the only Russian I know at the embassy. It wasn't personal."

"I'm prepared to overlook this as part of our deal."

"Our deal? There is no deal. You need to reread your Chairman Mao: I'm the one with the loaded gun."

"If you wish to fly with Pasan at five o'clock, you can't pull the trigger. Your arm must be tired. Please lower it—people are staring."

How on earth would he know that? Pasan told him, the blabbermouth. Nolan lowered the bag, but kept the weapon pointed from waist height. "What do you want?"

"We wish to fly with you, then be left to make our own arrangements with Pasan. My friend is a licensed pilot. With the million dollars you gave me we'll be able to come to an arrangement where Pasan benefits and we anonymously leave this country."

"Fine," Nolan said. "Once this is over, make it a point to never let me see me again."

"While you two have a hug," Valeyriya said, "I'll pick up our food before someone gives it away." She walked out of sight around the corner.

"She's a feisty one," Nolan offered.

Gregoriev smiled through pursed lips. "I'm looking forward to finding out."

CHAPTER EIGHTEEN

STREET SURVIVORS

FRIDAY, AUGUST 19: ZAX PEAK ROAD, SONOMA COUNTY

Zaw took a right at the Desperado Resort and Spa onto Zax Peak Road. They were only ten miles from their destination, but the road was in poor repair. In compensation there was no other traffic. The acidic sand was baked into hardpan that supported clumps of manzanita, coyote bush and California sagebrush. They left the desert and entered foothills with a smattering of vineyards. Overhead, a hawk rode a thermal. Heat shimmered off the blacktop: the midday sun was relentless. They drove three miles and the road began to climb. The vegetation shifted to California live oaks and madroño. A jackrabbit zigzagged across the road.

Ryder's burner signaled an unknown caller. He put it on speaker. "Hello."

"This is Felipe," he said with a heavy Hispanic accent. "I have five men. We will be with you within three hours. Where will you be?"

Ryder frowned. More of Hecker's shady friends. "This is an open line. I can't tell you where to go until we have encryption. Get on Signal and I'll text you the address."

"I will do so."

"Pack for trouble. Thank you for the help, Felipe."

* * * * *

"Anaconda Red Six, this is Anaconda. Do you copy?"

"Anaconda, I copy."

"Our drone intercepted a call to one of Nolan's men. He has six reinforcements arriving within three hours. Act now if able. Anaconda Blue Six is in place approximately one point five clicks north of target vehicles. Anaconda Blue Six, do you copy?"

"Roger that, Anaconda."

"This is Anaconda Red Six. We are a go."

* * * * *

Ryder pulled out the walkie-talkie and keyed it to attract Zaw's attention. "I just saw the silver SUV three hundred meters back. Around the next bend, find a place to pull over where we'll be out of sight. If he passes us, we'll double back. We also have a friend supplying six more armed men, but they won't arrive for three hours."

Before Zaw could acknowledge Ryder's message, a red pickup truck roared out of a hidden driveway and clipped the rear of the Tundra, sending it into a spiral and then a dusty, noisy halt. Zaw's black pickup sat slewed across the road with a hill on one side and a drop into the scrub forest on the other. The red pickup blocked both lanes in front of them.

"Brake hard!" Ryder said to Joanie. "Keep straight. Good. That's it. Now use the side mirrors and back up as fast as you can until I tell you to stop. Ignore everything else."

Gunshots sounded ahead as the occupants of the two pickups opened fire barely twenty meters apart. Zaw unclipped Bert's seatbelt and shouted, "Out, out, out!" Young Nolan exited as the first bullets hit the windows. He landed hard on the ground and took aim with the M-4. One assailant was out of the pickup, his ankles visible under the Tundra through the dust. With economy of fire, Bert shattered his left ankle with two shots, waited until the man fell gripping his leg, and finished him with a headshot.

Zaw clambered out wounded and unarmed, flopping beside Bert. Their adversaries still directed fire at the truck. From their voices, at least two were still in the fight.

"Where are you hit?" Bert asked.

"Shoulder. Left side. I can shoot. Get me a weapon."

Bert handed the wiry man his carbine. Zaw crawled and took up a position shielded by the engine block as he crouched behind the right front tire. Zaw's return fire forced heads down on the other side. Bert used the lull to swiftly extract the second M-4 and the bag containing the spare magazines, pulled out two mags and flipped the sack to Zaw. One of their adversaries had moved away from the pickup and over the edge of the road. With a shout at Zaw to give him cover fire, Bert leaped off the road, chased by a burst from an M16. Zaw had expended his mag supporting Bert and swapped out for a fresh one. His left hand barely functioned.

One hundred meters downhill from the wrecked pickups, Ryder ordered Joanie to halt. The silver SUV was within view at the bottom along this straight stretch. Mei Ling handed her mother one of the Remingtons and picked up the second pump-action shotgun.

"Look in front and to the sides," Ryder said. "Mei Ling, I'll slide the door open so you'll have a wider field of fire. Joanie, you take the passenger's seat and cover the other side. If you see someone you don't know, hold the stock tight to your shoulder and pull the trigger.

Pump the foregrip hard like I showed you to eject the casing and load another shell. You have eight shells but reload every time there's a break in the firing."

Behind Ryder's van, automatic weapons crackled up the road. Zaw and Bert would have to handle that end. Ryder prepped the SAW and threw open the rear doors before lying down behind the bipod-mounted weapon. One hundred fifty meters down the hill, their foes were slow to react. Both side doors had opened, but as yet no one had fired. Ryder squeezed off a burst that put dozens of bullets into the engine block, through the opened doors, the windshield and into the brush on either side of the road. Gunsmoke filled the van. Ryder paused to allow the barrel to cool, confident that the rear threat had succumbed to the SEAL's deadly combination of surprise, speed and violence of action. Then a bullet tore past his head and punched a hole in the left side of the van as it exited.

"Sniper!" Ryder shouted to Mei Ling. "I'll lead him away. Stay here and fight. He's not aiming at you." Ryder dropped down flat in the back, hot shell casings burning his already scabbed body. A second shot went over his head by centimeters and crashed into the dashboard's center console.

Mei Ling screamed, but he heard Joanie say, "We're all right. We're all right."

Fuck, fuck, fuck. "I'll take him from the woods. If the shooting up the road stops and the red pickup moves, drive past it and kill everyone you don't recognize. Pick up Zaw and Bert and go hard until you see an occupied building. Drive up and call the police. Take your chances with them. I'll be fine out here." He squeezed by Mei Ling's wheelchair, flopped through the open side door and crawled under the van.

Ryder squirmed on his flabby gut and wriggled out from under the front grill. There wasn't an Olympic event called the six-meter dash, but combat soldiers knew that only two prizes were ever awarded, life and death. Ryder made a running, rolling, scrambling sprint off the shoulder and into the scrub, a third bullet snapping past his body. The report sounded like a Barrett, the military sniper rifle that was lethal from over a mile away. Ryder surmised the operator wasn't Spec Ops–caliber, or else he'd have sprung leaks. The former SEAL made haste down the slope, ignoring the need for quiet in the cover afforded by the brittle vegetation. The sniper was off the road, yet still able to put rounds into the van. That meant he had to be either very close or on high ground. Ryder would circle in a broad arc to put himself behind the shooter, come up from the rear, and finish him.

The shrubs and trees thinned out enough to allow him to move quietly once he'd made it some distance inland.

What Ryder didn't know was one of the men from the red pickup was less than fifty meters away and working down the side of the hill through the scrub toward the van. Bert tracked the tracker, applying his faded-but-not-forgotten stalking skills. Bert was slowed by pain in his right ribcage under his right armpit where he'd been shot. He touched his ballistic vest, and sure enough there was a hole. Whether or not it had made it all the way into his flesh was neither here nor there, but his finger came back dry, so he took that as a plus.

Up on the road, Zaw felt his concentration slip due to blood loss. A single gunman remained, shielded behind his vehicle, as was Zaw. His adversary was more mobile and tried to flank him multiple times. Each time Zaw moved to counter the feint, he bled more. If he passed out, he'd die and so would Nolan's women. He wanted to see his little girls and wife and take them to Disneyland one more time before school started, but he suspected it wasn't to be. His left arm no longer functioned, and his peripheral vision narrowed. He extracted two smoke grenades from his web gear.

Joanie and Mei Ling sat exposed in the van, gun noises absent after a cacophonous five minutes. Up ahead they saw green smoke engulf the red pickup truck. A gunman emerged from the cloud and backpedaled down in the middle of the road. He was fifty meters away from the pickup when a hunched-over Zaw came into view. Zaw looked into and around the pickup but didn't see the man in the black jumpsuit raise his M16.

"Zaw!" Joanie yelled. "Zaw! Watch out!" Zaw heard her, but too late as the man in black aimed and fired. Zaw staggered backward into the smoke. The assailant turned to face Joanie in time to absorb the blast from the Remington pump. At fifty meters, a twelve-gauge shotgun sends nine lead pellets at thirteen hundred feet per second with a dispersal diameter of five feet. Zaw's murderer was dead before the spent shell casing hit the road.

From down the hill came two shots from the scrub. Behind Joanie, Mei Ling fired once. Joanie dropped flat but maintained a stranglehold on the shotgun as she racked it again like they did on TV cop shows, and was surprised when a live shell ejected. Mei Ling's target lay at the edge of the road twenty meters away, weapon in hand but unmoving. Joanie raised herself to one knee and lifted the Remington. Two more shots from nearby sounded, and the man shuddered at the impact. Joanie and Mei Ling looked at one another: neither had fired.

Bert ended their befuddlement by creeping into view. The former Singapore commando scanned up and down the road to check for other threats. To the north one hundred meters beyond Zaw's truck an unknown vehicle stopped, executed a three-point turn and retreated at speed. Bert confirmed that the gunman on the shoulder was dead and stripped him of his weapon, ammunition, phone and wallet.

Joanie rushed to his side. "What's wrong? Are you injured?"

"I took one in the side, but I think the vest stopped it. I'll be all right. We need to check on Zaw and move those vehicles. You two have to go. Where's Ryder?"

"He went into the woods after a sniper from the SUV."

Bert looked at the destroyed SUV in the late afternoon sunlight, radiator steam hissing, windshield shot out and two bodies visible. "I'm amazed anyone survived. I bet they dropped the sniper off down the road and he hiked up. Look! There's Ryder."

Out of breath, dirtier and more banged up than ever, Ryder dragged his prizes onto the road—the sniper's Barrett M107 with another ten rounds in the accompanying ammo box. Then he pulled everything still functioning out of the SUV. It was a short list: fifty zippy rounds of 5.56 bouncing around chewed up a lot of cargo. Gore from three bodies turned the salvage task into spaghetti and meatballs without cutlery. Ryder was crimson up to his elbows.

From the van, Mei Ling covered mother and brother up the road. The gunfight felt like it had lasted an hour, but fewer than ten minutes had passed. The smoke thinned out. Hearing returned bit by bit.

Joanie hustled to Zaw's side and knelt over him. "He's dead. Oh, this is all because of me." She wiped her tears and dropped her shotgun. "What have I done? This can't be happening."

Bert ignored his mother as he jogged past, weapon up, and inspected the red pickup. Nothing save for two corpses. He removed whatever weapons, ammunition and other materiel he could find. "Mom! I need you to stack these things all in one place where we can drive up and throw it into the back. Pull it together!"

Mei Ling asked what was happening from her obscured vantage point behind the driver's side of the van. Joanie turned to the sound of her daughter's voice and stepped toward the vehicle.

"Mom!" Bart snapped. "This isn't the place. We need to go!"

Joanie complied in a daze and built two piles of contraband that would arm and equip a half-dozen men. What was it about Bob that made these people crazy? A squirrel scampered down the hillside and ran across the road, skirting the substantial blood puddles surrounding Zaw and his faceless killer.

Ryder, out of breath, was at the van. "Nice work up here," he said to Mei Ling. "Everyone OK?"

"Zaw's dead. Mom killed the man who shot him, and the other two are also dead. The bodies are on the road. Bert was shot in the vest. He's moving, but it could be the adrenaline. Can you check him out?"

"If he's well enough to walk and shoot, he can hang on until we reach the house. Zaw gave me the address—it's another five miles up this road. We're all targets. I'll drive us down to the SUV and load what I've salvaged, then we head up the hill before the police arrive."

Ryder was on autopilot as he shuttled the van and Mei Ling down the hill and back up to the two wrecked pickups. Bert and he pushed the vehicles to the shoulder, then loaded Zaw's body into the back of the van. Joanie took advantage of the pause in the action to drink a liter of water in one go and vomit it out. What she had done was unthinkable. Mei Ling cried softly, tears of pain mixed with remorse. So much death and all of it because of her father, one way or another. What of Bruce and their baby? What hope was there in the world when people did these things to one another?

A buzz sounded and Ryder pulled a phone out of his pocket. "Zaw's," he said.

"We are Zaw's men down road to south next to silver vehicle. Do you see us?"

Ryder stepped out of the van and looked downhill. Next to the shot-up SUV was a green roller skate and a man waving at him.

"I see you. How do I know you work with Zaw?"

Bert followed Ryder's cue and shouldered his M-4, dropping to one knee.

"Check caller ID. My name is Arkar."

The caller ID on Zaw's phone displayed squiggles ဝက္ကာ. "What town did Zaw live in?" Ryder asked in broken Burmese.

"Zaw born in Lashio in Shan State, but moved to Irrawaddy province, Einme town," the man replied in English.

"Come on up and we'll follow you to the house," Ryder said. "Your boss is dead."

Bert lowered his tactical rifle. They loaded the last of the materiel as an old Toyota Echo chugged up and slowed to a stop. The passenger rolled down his window and looked shocked at the bodies and blood in the road. "Zaw kill many men before he die?"

Ryder could see a pair of M-4s angled across a back seat littered with more weaponry and ammunition. "Yes, your friend saved our lives. His body is in our van. Please lead us to the house. Don't stop for anyone, even the police, unless I flash my lights. If you have to, shoot. We don't know how many other enemies are on this road, or even if they're fake cops."

* * * * *

NOVATO AND PHOENIX

"This is Anaconda. Anaconda Red and Blue teams all KIA in one interdiction. Enemy casualties confirmed at one KIA. One vehicle containing two echoes has reinforced Nolan's security team, bringing their strength to four."

"How on earth did the cast from *The Wizard of Oz* kill our men?"

"I monitored the action via drone video feed. The enemy used the terrain of the battlefield to their full advantage, and they outshot us, sir. The drone is still airborne, and it will track them to their destination."

"God in heaven. How long will it take to insert a replacement team?"

"At least six hours, sir. I made the call to activate our tier-three Spec Ops and local law enforcement sleepers. I will lead the next assault myself. There's additional bad news, sir."

"Spit it out."

"The unidentified man is a former SEAL operator named Ryder. He was a sniper until leg wounds ended his service in 2010. He took possession of a Barrett, spotting optics and NVGs. As long as he's in the fight, we'll have our hands full. Requesting permission to use RPGs against his position once identified."

"Denied. Our mission is to capture Nolan's family alive and uninjured. You have your own snipers with NVGs. Take him out before he takes you out, soldier."

"Yes, sir."

* * * * *

ZAX PEAK ROAD

Ryder flashed the brights and pulled off to the side where there was a modicum of shade. The engine made grinding noises. A sniper round had destroyed the air conditioning and God only knew what else under the hood. Even with the windows down it was in the nineties and everyone poured sweat. Ryder's head pounded. Zaw's two men stayed with their vehicle just up ahead, one facing up the hill and one where they'd just come from, M-4s at the ready.

Traveling three clicks from the battle zone had given Ryder a chance to take stock of his mental state. With every passing minute he became angrier and angrier over Zaw's death. According to Bert, the rest of their party had only survived because of Zaw's suppressing fire, even though badly wounded. Why was it that the best men were the first to fall? Because they put everything on the line to protect their brothers.

"All right everyone," Ryder said. "It's a three-minute stop to pee, drink some water and make certain that all your moving parts are attached and still work."

"I'll wait," Mei Ling said. "There's no way I'm going to pee from a wheelchair by the side of the road."

"I want to look at Bert's chest," Joanie said.

A text from Nolan appeared on Ryder's screen. *Everyone all right?*

Family and I fine. Zaw dead. Ambushed on road three km back. Killed all seven. Bert hit in vest, but OK.

"It's a miracle," Joanie said. "The bullet didn't break the skin."

"It's not a miracle, Mom," Bert said. "It's called Kevlar."

Ryder's attention went back to Nolan. Felipe confirmed *6 shooters inbound. I texted address and coming in 3 hours. Don't know how they got in front and set up ambush. Spooked.*

Nolan's reply was instantaneous. *Drone tracking. You either destroy it or surrender at police station. If you do, I'll call Obama's man and arrange best security possible. Assume all voice comms monitored. Will be in air and be offline for at least five hours.*

Got you. Speak later.

Ryder looked skyward. "Listen up! We have a drone tracking us. We'll get only one chance to shoot it down. If everyone's quiet, maybe we can hear it and spot it. I want the two shotguns loaded and laid just inside the van's sliding door. Bert, move closer. On my signal grab one and open up. I'll walk over next to you and we'll have a conversation. Joanie, kneel next to the door and I'll drop down as well. Bert, try to spot it without being too obvious."

Ryder picked up a twig and traced a fake map on the ground. "If there's a drone up there, maybe they'll send it down for a closer look."

Joanie put her shotgun into the van and did as Ryder suggested. Ryder scratched elaborate random lines in the dust.

A minute passed in silence. Far down the valley, a siren sounded. "I see it," Bert said. "Maybe one hundred feet up on your seven o'clock, three hundred feet behind us and a big sucker. More or less stationary—it's one of those quadcopter models."

"Joanie, don't look up but move closer toward me," Ryder said. "We'll make the window smaller and maybe lure it in. Bert, shift closer to the van. When you have a chance, give it a pair of double-aughts."

Ten seconds passed. "It's much closer," Bert said. "I can take it down."

"Do it."

Bert stepped to the van and surprised Ryder by turning and sitting in the open doorway. Never taking his eyes off the sky, he snatched a shotgun, brought it to his shoulder, aimed and fired in one motion. Ryder lunged for the second weapon as Bert pumped and fired second, third and fourth shots. Ryder turned and swung his weapon up as Bert ceased firing. Joanie had run ten meters away and had her hands over her ears, but eyes to the sky. Mei Ling sat frozen in her wheelchair.

Bert said, "I hit it with the third shot. I saw it disintegrate."

"Are you certain?"

"I saw something fall out of the sky and into the bushes!" Joanie shouted.

"Great work!" Ryder said. "Let's move." Looking up the road at the perplexed Burmese on sentry duty, Ryder made the roundup sign and they climbed into the green Toyota. Ryder was behind the wheel and they were underway as soon as Bert slid the door shut.

Ryder handed his phone back to Bert. "Check my messages and look for the four-one-five area code. That'll be Felipe. Text that we'll have a location for him within an hour. He should assume he'll be followed, and he can lead them right into an ambush. Ask him for descriptions of his vehicles and an ETA. If you three can hang on for another ten minutes, I'll drop you off at the house. Zaw's people and I will find a place nearby where we'll arrange a welcome party."

CHAPTER NINETEEN

SHAKEN

FRIDAY, AUGUST 19: ARLINGTON

Hecker had worked fast. United Airlines would pass his message along to Sophie as she stepped off the plane. He'd left a voicemail, email and text message saying the same thing: disappear in London for the next three days. Don't contact friends, much less the embassy or anyone in the DEA. Rent something online off Airbnb or similar under an assumed name and pay cash. Order food in, remain indoors, and stay off your phone and the internet except to check your secure email account.

Next on the agenda was the FBI. Hecker knew a few people in the bureau, some relationships dating back to when he had been a Capitol police officer twenty years ago. Mick Lonergan was a taciturn man who didn't question his source or motive. The message was simple: a big-time cartel boss named Randall Dozier had kidnapped Robert Nolan—wanted in conjunction with multiple homicides in the District and Virginia—and had him under wraps in a Wesley Park mansion. Dozier would be on the move soon, the Metro PD couldn't be trusted, and if the G-Men wanted to kick the Medellín Cartel in the balls, there was no better way than hanging a kidnapping charge on the top dog. The DEA might be compromised, so Hecker had done the prudent thing and directed this one their way. Make the source a concerned member of the public.

"Got it," was all the big Irishman had said before hanging up.

Next Hecker had to make a show of vetting intelligence photos and intercepts featuring Cali Cartel luminaries, even though he knew they'd never be delivered.

* * * * *

FREEWAY AIRPORT, BOWIE, MARYLAND

Nolan finished his text to Don Randy and scrutinized his unexpected travel companions. They all wore headsets featuring a comms channel separate from the pilot's. "You don't know what Chumakov did at the Farewell Group, do you?"

"No, but how would you know that?" Gregoriev asked.

"Because you were willing to let him die rather than be questioned," Nolan said. "If you were privy to the same information, you wouldn't have acted in that manner unless you disliked him. On the contrary, you would have run sooner. Do you want to know what he was up to?"

"It's a long flight and I don't have a book, so tell me a story."

Pasan came onto their channel and reported they were third for takeoff and should be airborne within five minutes.

"Chumakov was the D.C. end of a plot called Translator which aimed to destabilize the US political system," Nolan said. "What's in the public eye is the smokescreen: hack and release waves of emails damaging to the DNC and their candidate. The FSS was behind Cozy Bear, which in turn created a false hacker persona, Guccifer 2.0, who claimed credit for the security breaches. Your government supported Ginger and his family with loan guarantees from Putin's cronies, whose support kept Ginger and his son-in-law solvent. Last month, you saw the results at the Republican convention when the party's position on Ukraine shifted to favor Russia. Whether or not Putin has bothered to tell Ginger that he works for the Kremlin, I don't know. What is your reaction?"

"I have nothing to say in response to speculation," Gregoriev said.

"The second thread concerns the theft of the NSA's best hacking software tools, and dumping them the next day on the Onion Router. The US was further discredited in the eyes of its allies, and rogue actors around the world won twice over—now they can protect their own operations from scrutiny and attack fat commercial targets. As the number two SVR man in America, you must be aware of the *maskirovka* and *kompromat* operations aimed at the US. Share what you know and buy you and your lady friend a free ride out of the country."

Pasan taxied into the late afternoon breeze and the Baron leaped into the sky, bound for Alabama.

"You and I already have an arrangement," Gregoriev said. "We share this journey to your destination. Then Valeyriya and I will make our own deal with the pilot. You and I stay away from one another after tomorrow."

"As long as I'm free, the one million dollars I wired this morning will never come to light," Nolan said. "Mention me and you'll lose those funds. At a minimum, you'll never enjoy the freedom to spend the money with your latest find, or whoever comes after her."

Valeyriya gave Nolan a withering look.

"I see your point," Gregoriev said. "Even Bob Nolan wouldn't want murder for hire added to his already impressive list of charges. You want me to betray my country for what?"

"A flight out of the US in a private jet to wherever in the Caribbean you wish. If you think you can hire Pasan to duck under the radar directly to Cuba, or maybe divert to Mexico en route to Cuba, he may not make it. He's a bus driver, not a narcotics runner. You also need to consider the tax imposed by those governments on black flights. It could cost you a hundred thousand every time your wheels meet or leave the tarmac. And then you'd have Pasan's fee, or maybe he sells you the plane and washes his hands of you both. What can two former intel officers on the run do with just a few hundred thousand each? That's not enough for a clean start in a decent country. Tell me what you know, and I'll work your deal directly with Obama's right-hand man."

"How can I tell if you even know Obama?"

"I can request a live call. Most of the time I email him through the dark web, and he checks that daily. If what you say is actionable, he'll issue a safe conduct letter over the presidential seal."

"Give me a moment." Gregoriev and Valeyriya engaged in animated Russian. Nolan pulled off the headset to give his pinched ears a break.

Gregoriev signaled and Nolan put back on the headphones. "We'll need new identities before we leave," said the SVR senior man.

"You don't have the time to wait for new passports, plus the delay leaves you vulnerable to a leak on this side—if not now, then in the future. You're better off arranging your own at your next destination. Tell you what—if you answer another question, I'll sweeten the deal by wiring another million dollars."

Gregoriev and Valeyriya looked at one another and shrugged. "Ask, but I may not or cannot answer," Gregoriev said.

"What do you know about an organization called Higher Love?"

Gregoriev gave him a blank look while Valeyriya's eyes widened.

Nolan turned and stared at the young woman. "I think I just negotiated a deal with the wrong person."

* * * * *

WESLEY PARK

Don Randy spoke rapidly in Spanish on his cell. "There's been a fuckup. Police came to my door and one of my people was rude and sent them away. Those officers will seek a warrant. Can you delay them until Monday?"

"I can check. The FBI is here waiting for one more man. It's a short-notice operation, and they're talking about using a shotgun to breach a door. No names mentioned, but this could be your house."

Don Randy hung up. He saw there was a message from Nolan and forwarded it to Felipe in San Francisco without reading it. "Be thorough," he yelled after Romero, who was trudging up the stairs. "Leave nothing behind. Wipe every surface and flush all your chemicals. We leave in five."

Bernardo came into the dining room from the kitchen. "I dropped Nolan off at the airport. Light traffic the way back."

"Bring a large duffel bag upstairs. We're leaving, but first we empty the safe. After you fill the bag, gather your documents, weapons and ammo and ready the van."

* * * * *

Bernardo slowed as the former prisoner transportation vehicle reached the end of the driveway. Randy considered the remote control in his hands. Eight million to buy and furnish Garfield Street including original art, three million for the Maserati, another million they couldn't fit into the bag ... *fuck it.* He toggled four switches in sequence. Vibrations pulsed through the air and the van trembled. Flames shot out of the master bedroom window on the second floor and glass fragments clattered on the bricks below. "Let's go. Pronto."

Romero looked over his shoulder as more flames and smoke appeared around his home for these past six months. "My brother-in-law is a general contractor. We can use him to rebuild."

Randy ignored him. "Bernardo, head to the safe house on Grant Road. We have to find Dante and Nacho, learn whether they made contact with the Russian, and I'll speak to my lawyer. What I learn decides our next move."

* * * * *

ARLINGTON, VIRGINIA

News of the FBI's raid on Dozier's Wesley Park mansion had reached Hecker's boss's ears. "What do we do? The FBI has torpedoed *el presidente's* plan to let the Medellín and Cali Cartels fight it out before we clean up the leftovers. All those years of my work—our work—ruined. You know people in the bureau—call someone."

It took all Hecker's self-control to keep from breaking into a smile. "I'll see what I can do. Does this mean I can stop sorting and redacting transcripts for the intel handover?"

A flustered Chicken Little didn't bother to reply; he just turned and scurried away in search of the next person who might help cover his ass.

Thanks to a just-ended call, Hecker knew the information that his incompetent boss sought—the FBI team was outside Don Randy's house and the D.C. fire department had brought the blaze under control too late to save anything of consequence. They'd roped off the scene, but there wasn't a hope in Hades that the ashes would cool enough to allow a proper search before tomorrow morning. Whether or not Randall Dozier and Robert Nolan's bodies were in the charred remains, he couldn't say.

Sam Hecker had two reasons to leave the office. Eventually the Metro PD would find his prints at Georgetown University Hospital and wonder why he had pushed Chumakov's gurney. His second motive was even more compelling. During his boss's meltdown, it had dawned on him that he knew where El Patron would hide.

He locked his office and hit redial, hoping Mick was still at the fire. It was only two miles to Grant Road where Hecker and the don had held many a clandestine meeting.

* * * * *

DRIVING NORTH ON ZAX PEAK ROAD

Bert sorted through the wallets of their seven slain foes. "Looks like a bunch of phony-baloney IDs ... driver's licenses and nothing else except small amounts of cash. No credit cards, no corporate IDs. Look at these names—'Lucius Cipher' is one of them, another is 'Johnny Favorite.' "

"Use my phone to take a photo and forward it to your father," Ryder said. "I've already sent him their license plates. Big Bob may be able to find something useful."

"I can't believe how you admire my father," Mei Ling said. "You were shot because of him. I've been shot because of him. His best friend's been shot because of him. Do you see a pattern? And where is he? How do we know he's not fucking that Chinese spy, and she's the one trying to kill us?"

"Honey, we've all just been through something terrible," Joanie said. "Drink some water. Travis, can she take a painkiller?"

The SEAL fantasized about popping one himself and backed away from his earlier declaration. "One now, but no more until tomorrow. She has to be able to wake up to take second shift sentry duty."

Up ahead the green Toyota turned left, and Ryder followed it under the arch announcing Mandalay Winery and down the long driveway of a Burmese general's California getaway. He supposed with enough water you could grow grapes this high, but they sure as hell were a long way from anywhere.

The winery was decent-sized by Sonoma standards, more than one hundred acres of recently cleared land. Both vehicles fit under the open-sided carport. They laid poor Zaw's body—aviator Ray-Bans still in place—on a worktable under the corrugated iron roof. Depending on how things turned out, he might end up buried here. The decision would have to wait until tomorrow, high heat notwithstanding. Ryder glanced at his phone and confirmed they were out of cell range.

As described, the vines were fresh cuttings: too small to conceal a man unless he infiltrated in camouflage. Though Ryder didn't put it past their opponents, beating off an attack wasn't his principal preoccupation. He aimed to win via deceit, not outlast them in a siege.

Their group was shattered physically and mentally. They needed a hot meal and rest. They would be lucky to get a snack. Ryder asked Joanie to check the cupboards for canned goods and see if she could jumpstart the LPG stove.

Ryder ordered Bert to make a security sweep of the main house while he walked the property with Zaw's men. The former SEAL almost had forgotten how nice the Burmese were, always smiling even in adversity. Both of Zaw's colleagues were former commandos, with the younger Maung benefiting from a further two years of tutelage under an ex-Ranger. Robin Teller had been the implementer of the Burma end of the MH370 hijacking and a ruthless killer. He had also selected and trained his men to US Army Ranger standards.

Maung teamed up with Bert to build makeshift early warning devices that would ignite smoke grenades once tripped. Ryder and Arkar deployed four Claymores close to the entry points, expertly concealing both the antipersonnel mines and firing wire. Bert would have the master M57 firing device within easy reach from his seat next to the front door. With an M-4 and four magazines, once Bert had detonated the Claymores, he would still be a formidable obstacle to anyone set on abducting the Nolan women. Bert was tempted to ask his conscientious-objector sister for her shotgun but bit his tongue.

After a meal of canned chili over boiled pasta, Ryder and Bert carried a drowsy Mei Ling down the steps of the wine cellar forty meters away from the main house. Arkar and Maung followed with her wheelchair. The cavernous cellar was nearly empty save for metal racks, a long table and a handful of chairs. Solar panels on the roof provided the power for lights and plumbing. From the chart on the whiteboard hanging inside the doorway, the first grapes weren't due to be harvested for another two years.

Joanie joined them a few minutes later after washing the dishes. She carried three paperbacks, plus sheets and pillows. A test of their walkie-talkies generated a fair connection to Bert in the living room. Ryder asked Bert to join them in the cellar, and once he arrived, sent Arkar out to take the first shift on sentry duty near the main entrance.

The cellar was cool enough that they didn't suffer even in the afternoon heat despite their ballistics vests. Ryder confirmed that there was only one way in, and he had Arkar and Maung rearrange everything that wasn't bolted down to provide them with the maximum cover and concealment while retaining a clear sightline on the steps leading down.

Ryder wasn't one for speeches. He tucked in his ragged shirt, ran his hands over his jagged hair and drew himself to his full 5'9". He looked like a ditch digger who had fallen asleep in the back of a pickup truck only to be bounced out onto the road. "If everything goes according to plan," he said, "we'll be back before first light. Arkar, Maung and I will set up an ambush nearby, ideally somewhere with cell coverage. We expect another six men from Bob's contacts back east. If they're good, we should hold our own. If you hear gunfire in the distance, stay inside and stick with the plan.

"If you aren't attacked, and we don't come back, remain indoors and out of sight for the next three days and four nights. We'll stock enough canned food from the pantry down here to feed you, plus jugs of bottled water. If you make it until Tuesday and no one's come for you, Bert, you hike out until you can raise Bob or me on the phone.

"As for the worst case, if we don't come and you're attacked, follow Bert's lead. If he doesn't answer his walkie-talkie, or he tells you he's wounded or captured, stop resisting. This isn't the Custer's Last Stand. These people want to take you unharmed, so you don't have to die resisting them.

"Bert, if you see any vehicles approaching, even ours, treat them as hostile if you don't see two long and two short high beam flashes. Stay indoors and close to the walls—they'll have night-vision optics and probably infrared. Track their infiltration routes using the smoke but try not to draw or return fire until you detonate the Claymores. Remember, if it's hopeless, it's better to surrender. Any questions? No? Good."

"You're lying," Mei Ling said. "You know this will be over by midnight. Either we kill them all, or they take us."

Ryder shrugged. The longest speech of his life over, the former SEAL needed a drink. He drained a bottle of water and set it down on the tabletop next to the two loaded shotguns and eighty-odd shells.

"Bert, find a broom. Once we drive off the property, erase the tire tracks behind us."

Bert nodded without enthusiasm. He had his shirt off, and his mother was taping a semi-frozen gel pack to his sore ribs. Once Joanie was done with her ministrations, Bert followed Ryder and Maung up the stairs.

The three men blinked as they stepped into the brilliant sunshine. Ryder told Arkar to join them, and the four met at the carport. They looked at Zaw's shattered body, flies buzzing and discoloration setting in as a rancid smell assailed their noses.

"We can't leave him to rot out here," Ryder said. "Bert, after we're gone, see if you can find a tarp and cover him up. Seal it with duct tape and maybe the flies will leave him alone. We'll figure something out tomorrow."

Bert reacted with a sullen look.

To the two Burmese, Ryder said, "We'll take both vehicles." Ryder said to Arkar and Maung, "We need to find a spot where we're shielded from the sky and can ambush Higher Love from cover."

"I helped clear land and plant vines last winter," Maung said. "I know best spot, big forest only five kilometers away."

CHAPTER TWENTY

TURNCOATS

FRIDAY, AUGUST 19: TENLEY TOWN, WASHINGTON, D.C.

Bernardo backed the prison van up the driveway of the Grant Road hideaway and into the garage. The automatic door lowered behind them. Romero knew the place well, having lived there for the three months it had taken to displace his predecessor, a gringo bull fruit.

Don Randy received an encrypted text from one of his few men left in D.C. His foot soldier had located Dante and Nacho's car parked off M Street in the basement of a swank office building. No sign of either man and nothing to report about the Farewell Group's office upstairs other than it was empty. No one looked to be coming back, either: boxes overflowed with rubbish and cartons littered the floor. What did El Patron want him to do?

For starters, move his ass over to Grant Road to beef up security. Pull men off narcotics distribution in Baltimore and order them to the District ASAP. Make certain that Grant Road wasn't under surveillance before approaching.

El Patron called his inside man at the Metro PD and was told that the bureau had watched the fire consume his home and had lit out ten minutes ago for an unknown destination. The don told the officer that he was missing two men, and the Farewell Group's office was likely the last place they visited. He needed the CCTV footage of basement level two, all common areas and, in particular, the eleventh-floor elevator bank. Call him back when the recordings were available for collection and he'd send a man. It was urgent.

On to the last call. "It's me."

"Don Randy, how may I assist?" his criminal attorney answered.

"Yesterday, employees of Russia's embassy murdered my two nephews. I don't have the killers' identities, but once I do, I may need your assistance in ensuring that they cannot plead diplomatic immunity and evade justice."

"Your justice or the police department's?"

"Either," Randy said. "If they take refuge in the embassy, I'll want the police to handle it. If I find them first, they'll wish they were never born."

"I'll check, but until I have names it will be hypothetical."

"My home on Garfield Street burned down an hour ago. Arson is suspected. Depending on the skill of the investigators, they may find traces of remote charges and accelerants. What are the civil and criminal implications for me given that I left only minutes before the fires broke out?"

"With imagination and money, nothing we can't handle," the lawyer said. "Where are you now?"

"I'd prefer not to say." Randy's phone buzzed to indicate another call. "I have to run." The don hung up.

It was his field man. "I'm down the block. There are three vehicles and seven men, six of them wearing FBI jackets. They're gearing up to raid the house."

"When we come out, ram their vehicle. Claim it was an accident and don't resist. I'll look after your family for as long as you go away."

"*Muchísimas gracias*, Don Randy."

Don Randy hung up and shouted, "*¡Vamos, muchachos!* The FBI is outside. We leave now."

* * * * *

Sam Hecker, last to arrive, confirmed that the half-stucco two-story with the large magnolia tree in the front yard was the right one. He'd declined the flak jacket—they'd already wasted enough time. They had to hit the house while El Patron was inside. The man had a temper and with luck, they'd goad him into starting a gunfight.

Special Agent in Charge Lonergan confirmed his assignments. Two men peeled off to drive around the block and position themselves to cover the back.

"The garage door's coming up!" Hecker said. "Shit, he's on the move!" The black-jacketed agents stood in the street fifty meters away, too far away to discharge their weapons. They turned as one and ran for the bureau's unmarked van.

Don Randy's prison vehicle displayed the powerful acceleration befitting the installation of a non-stock three-liter engine. As the FBI agents piled into their vehicle to give chase down Grant Road, a yellow Dodge Viper sped down the street in the opposite direction, then veered and struck the bureau's van head-on.

Hecker was the only one still in the game. He fired up his rental BMW and left the bureau's men to deal with the numbnuts or saboteur bleeding behind a starred windshield. He didn't know where Don Randy was headed, had no FBI or DEA backup, and he fielded a single sidearm against the unknown weaponry and manpower of the Medellín Cartel's East Coast headquarters contingent. Regaining his senses, Hecker pulled over and reconsidered his options. Don Randy was on the run for real. This gave Hecker time to disappear. But where? San Antonio and Bob Nolan looked like the top choice unless he wanted to endanger his parents or disappear off the grid. Once he confirmed that Sophie and C. J. were safely to ground in London, he'd get himself down to Texas ahead of the big rodeo on Sunday. Nolan could help him later hunt down El Patron. Otherwise, for the rest of his life Hecker would jump every time he heard a key in a lock or a footfall in an empty hallway. He needed to hit the road with a new ride: San Antonio was twenty-four hours away, plus or minus.

Two miles away, the converted prison van pulled into repair shop run by the Cartel's mechanics. As they shuttered the door behind the van, Randy was already on the phone. "Felipe? Where are you?"

"We're on the road and will arrive in two hours. We're disguised as landscapers and gardeners."

"Good. Listen carefully. I have been betrayed."

* * * * *

OFF ZAX PEAK ROAD

True to his word, Maung had a dandy spot in mind. An unpaved forest service road led three hundred meters down a winding trace skirted by manzanita and madroño before a NO ACCESS sign and a single-bar iron gate blocked their progress. Ten seconds with the bolt cutters and they were through. The grade moderated and the vegetation morphed into large oaks and foothill pines. A condemned bridge across a deep gulch validated the sign. Ryder parked and picked his way across, stopping every ten meters to lie flat and lean out to eyeball the trusses below. There was plenty to be wary of. He motioned for Maung and Arkar to stay back as he crept across in the van, dodging the holes in the rotten planks. The Toyota followed without mishap.

The forest thickened. Mature live oaks ten meters tall lined both sides of the road. They proceeded another kilometer, each man surveilling the landscape and making mental note of its defensive attributes. The road ended in a vast semicircle of campsites and fire pits. The men held a quick war council.

Maung and Arkar transferred arms and materiel from the Honda to the back of the van. They concealed the Honda at the last campsite, careful to leave enough of it visible that aerial scrutiny would reveal its presence.

Zaw's C-4, plus detonators, detcord and timers took pride of place. It took two hours to situate and wire up the two IEDs. The lead one was a shaped charge designed to destroy the first vehicle. Ryder placed the rear one under the roots of an enormous dying oak that could be counted on to block their retreat. Maung and Arkar dug shell scrapes amid the forest floor detritus. Ryder busied himself constructing a hide for the SAW to cover the kill box. Maung would work the GPMG with murderous effect once the downed tree trapped Higher Love's gunmen. Ryder would be on higher ground still, NVGs and Barrett at the ready.

Ryder tapped out their locale and detailed directions to Felipe. Then he picked up his men and drove the van to just across the bridge. The cell failed to reach Bert, which wasn't a surprise. Ryder edged back out to the center span where there was a faint cell signal and sent the encrypted text. For good measure, he forwarded it to Bert and Bob, though one was out of range and the other on a plane. If nothing else, they'd know where to find their bodies.

The three men concealed the van under oaks and behind a stand of manzanita. Ryder hid the key in a nearby stump. Maung rigged one and one-half kilos of C-4 under the bridge and set the timer at six hours. Ryder marveled at the man's dexterity and courage as he slipped under the span and wedged the plastique against a beam. Anyone on the far side of the gulch at midnight would be stuck there.

Maung stood watch up the hill where he had a view of the road approach on either side of the arroyo. Unless their pursuers were reckless, they'd check the bridge before they drove across. Possibly, they'd continue on foot. Either way, Maung would be able to alert Arkar and Ryder of their enemies' advance by clicking twice on the walkie-talkie. The older men walked back along the road, grateful for the shade. They drank water, cut a little brush to provide unobstructed fields of fire and fiddled with the camouflage around their positions.

Nacogdoches, Les and Paul all seemed a long way away. Two great little boys, running on unsteady legs and babbling their first happy words. *Sally.* Ryder had never really known her, certainly not well enough to marry her, and it seemed unlikely he ever would. He never planned ahead, never invested money or time. He lived in the moment, and he'd lived large on the battlefield and in the bars. But he'd never sunk roots until a crazy-assed idea two years ago when he decided to marry his high school best friend's ex. How stupid was that? Convalescing from a shot-up hip, he launched an all-out courtship of a woman he pursued on Facebook at the urging of his hometown buddies. Sally had been so keen to marry a SEAL—even a half-crippled former operator—that she'd dumped her daughter from her failed first marriage on her parents despite Ryder's protests. She didn't want anything to interfere with their budding relationship. With Ryder's ill-gotten gains, they'd lived it up like Saturday night in Abilene. Fast-forward two years and here he was making believe he was in the Afghanistan mountains above Tarinkot setting an ambush with two of his green brothers. But 2010 was a half-dozen years behind him, and his skills had rusted. He'd been lucky last night and today not to have been slotted twice over. He smeared antibiotic cream on his deeper gashes and punctures, pulled his flop hat down and tuned out with only the Barrett in his arms, full mag of five rounds locked and loaded.

* * * * *

ZAX PEAK ROAD

"Anaconda, this is Anaconda Red Three. Target vehicles have turned off onto a side road approximately five kilometers north of the interdiction site. Maps show a forest service road leading to campsites with no other exits. We will await reinforcements and before nightfall will be in a position to launch camera and IR drones. For now, I am the sole observer."

"Anaconda Red Three, be advised new intel received. Telephone intercepts confirm the occupants of the two vehicles are drug traffickers whose new orders are to kill the Nolan party. Also, Nolan family members are in hiding at an undisclosed property in the vicinity. Ignore the two vehicles. Once drones are on site, use them to inspect every building within ten clicks of the turnoff, and recce every inhabited space. The women will be lightly guarded or unguarded, so apply minimal force. We need at least one of the three alive."

"What about the narcos and Nolan's guard detail?"

"Ignore for now, but if time and circumstances permit return to the side road and ambush anyone driving out. If we don't exterminate the cockroaches today, tomorrow they'll be all over the kitchen."

"Roger, Anaconda."

* * * * *

OFF ZAX PEAK ROAD

Ryder awoke with a dry mouth and an appreciation of the futility of their defensive position. Earlier in the day, they'd killed seven adversaries against only one death on their side. Whoever came next wouldn't take them lightly. That meant the assault would occur after sundown when the disparity in night-vision and infrared capabilities, plus superior numbers, could be telling even before considering the possibility that Higher Love had access to black ops birds. The temperature differential of their vehicles' engines would stand out like a dog's nuts, and hiding under reflective blankets wouldn't disguise their heat signatures enough to avoid a sniper's round. They needed an offensive game plan to stand a chance.

Ryder stood and hustled down the hill. There might still be time to collect Arkar and reconfigure the battlefield. He'd leave Maung on sentry duty while the two of them rewired the bridge to allow them to manually blow it. They'd reposition the GPMG closer to the gulch, too.

Ryder found Arkar and they hot-footed it up the road. Their walkie-talkies clicked twice, and the two men ducked into the scrub two hundred meters shy of the bridge. "What do you see?" Ryder hissed over his handset.

"Two flatbeds," Maung answered. "They stop short of bridge. Six men climb on back."

"Could be a repair crew."

"No, I have binos. Digging dirt and cutting bags open. Pull out plastic packages. M16s and magazines."

So, Nolan's narcos. Two-plus years with the DEA in South and Southeast Asia hadn't imbued Ryder with much trust of his fellow man, especially narcotics purveyors. They were lying scum, every one of them. And Hecker, their undoubted source, had morphed from a mentor, best friend and boss into someone Ryder didn't trust at all. Too many big fish had slipped away in 2015 before Hecker transferred Stateside.

"What are they doing?" he asked Maung.

"One man left at trucks. Five men cross bridge. One hundred meters away. Fast come."

"Retreat without them seeing you. Wait at the GPMG. If they fire on me, open up."

"Yes, sir."

Ryder raised a hand. "Arkar, leave the road on this side and find a hide. If Maung fires his GPMG or they fire on you, kill them."

"Yes, sir."

Ryder reversed up the road. He wanted to be roughly parallel with Maung and the GPMG, and close to something solid. A jumble of logs fit the bill and he stopped nearby. He needed to make a dozen feet to shelter.

Two minutes later, Ryder spotted one, then a second and finally a third man in the dappled light. Latino machismo being what it was, odds were Felipe would be in front. He waved his left arm and kept one hand on his slung M-4. The lead man turned and said something indistinct to his comrades. They separated and slowed down. Ryder stood his ground, straining to divine friend from foe. The man was close enough for Ryder to see that his hands were empty. Was he sandbagging?

"Felipe?" Ryder waved with just the one hand.

"Yes, who is this?"

"Bob Nolan's friend, Ryder." Ryder took two large steps angled toward the roadside fallen timber.

"I have a message from Don Randy for Bob Nolan's wife and children. Where are they?"

"They're somewhere safe. Your men and I will fight the kidnappers. It will be dark in two hours. Let me show you what I've set up."

Felipe moved fast, drawing from an inside-the-waistband rear holster. "Tell me where Nolan's family is. I won't ask again." The two men tracking Felipe stepped off the road into the woods, one on either side.

Ryder's brain clicked into survival mode and he juked as Felipe fired from ten meters away.

Maung's burst was high, missing Felipe's torso but hitting him once and leaving pulped watermelon where the side of his head had been.

Ryder scrambled until he was behind the logs. The Barrett and NVGs were where he'd left them covered in leaves. He put the spare rounds in his front pockets, concealed the M-4 and checked the Oakland pawnshop Colt 1911 automatic was still in place next to the Russian's Beretta. One down, five to go, and at least two of them in the woods nearby.

Down the road, a weapon fired on semiautomatic, two to three rounds coming in syncopated bursts. Closer by, Maung fired twenty rounds or more on full auto and mowed through a thicket barely forty meters away. Ryder watched as a man crawled out of the brush flat on his stomach, dragging a shattered lower leg. He wore a Hawaiian shirt, poor camouflage even in wine country. Ryder took aim and missed. The man looked at him and tried to bring up his rifle. Ryder put his next shot through his eye. The Barrett was awkward at a short distance, but with its stopping power at least there was no such thing as a flesh wound. Two down and four to go.

"Maung, two dead echoes here. I'm after the one on the south side of the road. Help Arkar."

Ryder's walkie-talkie clicked as Arkar said something in Burmese and switched to English. "Two dead echoes, copy. I kill two more."

"Very good! One more up here to go. You two kill the sentry, then come back and help me with the last one."

Ryder hunted the missing gunman in the brush. After fifteen minutes of scant movement and listening hard, there was nothing to indicate nearby prey.

Short bursts in the direction of the gulch were followed by a fusillade, a pause and one final shot. Ryder crept through the intermittent undergrowth in parallel to the road for about one hundred meters. His thighs screamed at the unaccustomed strain, and his free hand danced again to its own drumbeat. Anyone lying in ambush was likely behind him and the light had faded. He made his way to the road and jogged another one hundred meters before he turned on his walkie-talkie. "This is Ryder. Give me a sitrep." He slowed to catch his breath.

"Maung here. Sentry dead. We see you from other side."

Ryder started jogging again, relief flooding through him. At first glance, the demise of Felipe and four of his five cohorts didn't alter much. On reflection, it changed everything. Provided they could position the dead men and their weapons in defensive displays, their still-warm bodies would deceive both infrared drones and NVGs for the next several hours. They needed to leave one man behind to blow the bridge when Higher Love's people crossed over. Lying under one of those flatbeds would shield Maung or Arkar from the eyes in the sky. Once they'd set off the charge, the former commandos would alert Ryder—*Shit! I have to warn Nolan*. Ryder stopped and hastily composed a text to Bert and his father warning of Don Randy's treachery. His battery was down to three percent once he'd squeezed out the transmission.

Ryder called to Zaw's invisible men in a soft voice. They turned out to be under the far side of the bridge, clinging to the buttresses. Maung had disabled the timer and Arkar had connected detcord to a prodigious lump of plastic explosive. Once the men were back on top of the span, they concealed the wire and finished it with an electric trigger placed under the lead vehicle. Ryder hadn't said a word: these two were in their element.

"If their drones aren't up already, they will be soon," Ryder said. "I'll take first shift under the truck. Anyone driving down this road will be on a one-way trip. If it's a single vehicle, I'll blow the bridge when they're on it. If it's multiple vehicles, I'll detonate under the last one. Anyone who stops on this side, I'll handle. Anyone who makes it across, kill them. And you still have one more gunman. Where's the sentry's body?"

"Threw him there," Maung said, pointing at the ravine.

Ryder winced, but it couldn't be helped. "You both need to double-time back to the two bodies on the road. Put one in each shell scrape, along with their weapons. Half cover them with the space blankets I gave you. If you can find the third body, prop it seated against a tree at least twenty meters from the SAW. Anyone using NVGs should shoot it up. If they have tracers, you'll have a clean return shot. Shoot only if you're trapped. Otherwise, come back across the gulch as soon as you're done. One of you will stay and hide under the truck. The other comes with me on foot. We'll return to the winery to guard the women. If there's no action overnight, I'll be back at first light walking down the road. For Christ's sake, don't shoot me."

The two little men laughed with schoolboy glee at this unthinkable incompetence. Ryder shook their hands. "If you're trapped on the other side, don't fight if you can escape. Stay away from the winery. Just try to make it home and wait for someone to contact you. If no attackers come here overnight, get out of here and get rid of the weapons. Avoid the police."

Ryder was trying to be encouraging, but he wondered if they realized they faced long prison terms as matters stood. Maung and Arkar turned and jogged across the bridge. It was so dark, Ryder lost sight of them before they reached the other side. He wriggled under the lead truck, careful not to touch the detcord or trigger, and mindful to keep the Barrett and NVGs within reach.

CHAPTER TWENTY-ONE

RUN OR GUN

FRIDAY, AUGUST 19: HUNTSVILLE ALABAMA INTERNATIONAL AIRPORT

Huntsville International Airport was home to several multinational cargo haulers and a two-mile-long runway, but what was most surprising was a quality hotel onsite. Nolan paid cash for a suite and a single and left Pasan to fend for himself. The former cryptanalyst examined the hotel menu alongside his Russian cohabitants. While they waited for their food, each of them went online to use their own tricks and tweaks to obscure their location.

Nolan's inbox made for discomfiting reading. General Payne suggested that he turn himself in, but should he choose not to, advised that Nolan must realize there was zero chance of Obama's issuing a second pardon. *Fair enough. This time around, he was guilty of most of the crimes anyway.*

Hecker wrote to report that an FBI raid on Randy Dozier had failed, sending the man into flight. Consider him an adversary. That was a mixed blessing at best. Nolan didn't want to help the Cartel beef up its operational and IT security, but six men who could have protected his family were now likely out for blood.

Bert forwarded photographs of seven drivers' licenses. Nolan passed them on to Payne with the comment that his guards had killed these men while thwarting a kidnapping attempt on his family. Assume that every one of them was a Higher Love member and find their cohorts. Confine all California and Nevada military personnel to base, cancel all leave and suspend training operations in Sonoma and Napa counties. Anyone who failed to comply was prima facie HL.

Ryder's terse inbound text noted Zaw's death, the hideout at Mandalay Winery and his diversion and ambush plan that should succeed with the assistance of Don Randy's six shooters acting as decoys. He would be uncontactable until the showdown was over, so reach out to Bert for the latest news. Don Randy's men would either be no-shows—in which case Ryder's ambush would be a waste of time—or come in blazing. Ryder was one of the best, but naturally gung-ho. Only his distrust of Hecker might save him unless Nolan's warning reached him first. Nolan hurriedly tapped out a warning.

"Bob? Bob? Are you with us? There's someone at the door."

Nolan looked up at Gregoriev and Valeyriya. He jumped to his feet, opened the door, tipped the waiter and balanced the tray with one hand as he shut the door with a knee.

"I didn't realize we were your prisoners," Gregoriev said. "Could you at least hold your weapon so we feel threatened?"

Nolan had been so absorbed in his messages and blocking the door that he'd left his backpack next to the ottoman. Nolan's Glock sat on the cushion next to Gregoriev. He placed the tray on the coffee table. "At this point, the pistol's safer in your hands than mine," Nolan said. "Who wants a glass of water?"

The three ate in silence. Nolan's steak sandwich hit the spot. He finished his fries and probed. "I imagine Higher Love provided guidance on the social engineering front?" Nolan asked.

Now it was Valeyriya's turn to look perplexed. Nolan looked Gregoriev, who shrugged. "If you're referring to the Facebook, Instagram and Twitter bots and trolls, the Russian Federation has more than enough resources to do this ourselves. Investigate the Internet Research Agency; you might be surprised how a lifetime of watching American pop videos, TV shows and movies informs the world about your dysfunctional country. Putin has used social media to poison public opinion and set neighbor against neighbor on every divisive issue in America. It's not to my taste, but it works. You Americans are laughably predictable."

"Fair enough." Turning back to Valeyriya, Nolan said, "Where did you come across Higher Love?"

"This next million goes to me, correct?" Valeyriya asked.

"Yes, if that's how you want it."

"But both of us remain unarrested?"

"Gregoriev has enough intel to trade for a free pass. It's really up to you."

"Higher Love has hacked the voter registration and tabulation systems for several states and fed the access codes to the FSB via the Farewell Group."

"How many states?" Nolan asked.

"Seven so far, with several more promised in the coming weeks and a total of twenty-one by end of October."

"Do you have the names?"

"Of the states, yes," Valeyriya said. "I name three when I board the flight out of this country, another seven when I arrive in Grand Cayman, and eleven more when I am in funds."

"We need more than just the states—the methods used to access the systems, the administrators' names, backdoors, passwords, and the entire approach."

"I have much of this information, but not on my person."

"Let me see if Obama will go for it. If he does, I will have a charter plane here to fly you both out tomorrow morning."

"Tell your president that World War III has started," Gregoriev said, "and the United States doesn't even comprehend it's under attack." He looked at Valeyriya. "I'm glad you're coming with me."

Valeyriya smiled. "Be certain you can access your funds. I have expensive tastes."

Nolan started typing. He already felt sorry for Gregoriev.

* * * * *

MANDALAY WINERY, OFF ZAX PEAK ROAD

Joanie and Mei Ling sat in the empty wine cellar. It was Mei Ling's turn to sleep, but her mother sobbed softly into her daughter's shoulder. "I killed a man. He probably had a family. He'll never see his wife and children again. I ran a car over another man last night at the storage lockers. So many people dead on the road earlier today. You're wounded and we're hunted like animals. Where does it end?"

"The man who killed Zaw would have shot Bert and maybe us as well," Mei Ling said. "Dad's to blame for all of this, and if Bruce dies, I will never say his name again. Here, take one of my pain pills and drink some water. I'll stay awake."

"I can't blame all this on him," Joanie said. "He sent Travis and Zaw to protect us. He wants us to be safe."

"If he'd cared about us, he would have stayed underground. Get some sleep. We're not out of this yet." Mei Ling's Vicodin had worn off. Ryder was right: sharp pain kept the mind alert, as did bitter anger.

Joanie palmed the pill and faked swallowing: her children needed her.

* * * * *

As per instructions, Bert sat behind the door of the manor house with the four Claymores joined in a daisy chain to the single clacker. An hour before, he'd heard gunshots in the distance. Two were loud: the Barrett, so Ryder had engaged. Then nothing for twenty minutes, and then another flurry of faint gunshots. Just waiting, nerve endings on fire, fidgeting, wanting to prowl and instead leaning against a stone wall, sweltering under a ballistic vest wrapped in a mylar blanket to reduce his heat signature.

With darkness came the night creatures. Every few minutes Bert heard a random noise from the young vines and stood to look through cracks in the drawn blinds into the absolute black. Ryder had told him not to do this, but if the stalkers were outside with infrared capability, then seated or standing he was a goner. In the distance, a snarl and then a yip reached his ears. The coyotes were about, bitching, whining and barking—good sounds indicating that no intruders were present.

Zaw. Those mongrels had smelled Zaw's corpse and were fighting over it. There was a crash as the coyotes knocked over the carport worktable. Bert grimaced. He wouldn't let a man who'd saved his life be eaten by wild animals. He opened the front door, flashlight in one hand and M-4 in the other and ran toward where animals fought over martyred Zaw's corpse.

* * * * *

UP ZAX PEAK ROAD

"Anaconda, this is Anaconda Red Three. We have infrared images at a location previously swept clean. It's well south of the team's location and within a few clicks of the turnoff road. All our other leads turned up empty. Do you copy?"

"I copy, Anaconda Red Three. Be advised that as of two minutes ago, by presidential order, all active duty servicemen have been recalled to base and all training exercises canceled. Eight of your twelve operators must head back to Ord, Beale and Travis pronto, including you. There won't be any birds up tonight, short of an emergency evac. Send the remaining four on foot down the spur road where Nolan's decoys are hiding and capture at least one of them. Interrogate using whatever methods necessary until he reveals the location of Nolan's family. Overnight we will replenish the search team and resume operations at first light."

"Requesting permission to remain with four-team, sir. They're still green."

"Negative. You can't miss roll call at 06:30."

"Roger that, sir. At least can I check out Mandalay Winery on our way down the mountain?"

"Yes, but don't take more than fifteen minutes. We're under suspicion and your trainees must be on base by 24:00. Ensure that all weaponry and ordnance go back into stores. Make do with what we've obtained from our own sources."

"Roger that, sir."

* * * * *

OFF ZAX PEAK ROAD

Ryder lay under the drug runners' flatbed near to the bridge and wondered what he would or could do if armed men approached from the main road. He had assumed they'd drive, but on reflection, they could just as easily infiltrate on foot. That meant he had to swing around to use the NVGs to scan both up and down the road. For the longest time, he didn't see anything in either direction. Then he picked out a tall man walking up the road from across the gulch. He couldn't discern detail even with the NVGs, but the man had a long gun and frequently turned to check his six. Ryder pegged him as the last gunman from Felipe's crew.

Ryder sighted down the barrel of one of the loudest rifles in existence. If he fired the Barrett, everyone within five kilometers would hear it. Coming on the back of the two previous discharges, cops in the area would zero in on his position. Ditto for HL thugs. Anyone wondering what was down this road would be alerted too. Ryder didn't have a knife, and even if he did, he wasn't certain he could slot anyone given how hard his hands were shaking. *The hell with it. Just let him escape.*

The man was almost across the bridge, just ten meters away. He stepped off the road and faded into shadows next to the vehicle. Ryder could see the glow of his phone. The call connected and a torrent of Spanish ensued. Ryder possessed a limited Spanish vocabulary, but he heard *muerto* several times. The word cut two ways: the narcotraficante's compadres were deceased, and, doubtlessly, so too would be the men who had killed them if this man had his way. Ryder hadn't factored in a second inbound wave of Don Randy's men, but after this call it was a certainty. Lying under a truck in the dark and the dirt became even less appealing.

The gunman stepped out of the shadows, unlocked the door and climbed into the cab. *What the hell?* The engine started and Ryder rolled out from under with only his NVGs in hand, the front wheels just missing him as the truck backed up to turn around. The narco paused to grapple with the gearshift while Ryder snatched the heavy Barrett away from of the oncoming rear wheels. The C-4 exploded with a roar. Debris rained down and Ryder gritted his teeth and waited for a buttress, sleeper or beam to end what had been an emphatically crappy day.

The driver accelerated up the decommissioned forest road. One hundred meters up, he turned on the headlights. Ryder split his attention between the getaway truck and the thirty-meter-wide void that the bridge had once spanned. Automatic weapons fire from up the road startled him and the truck's lights vanished as the engine stopped. *Holy hell, the driver had been ambushed.*

He fished out his walkie-talkie and powered up. "This is Ryder. Does anyone copy?"

"Yes, sir. What happened? We positioned the bodies and are on our way to you."

"The last narco drove the truck over the trigger and blew the bridge. You're trapped over there. Unless they use birds, you're safe. Rest tonight, then burn your vehicle tomorrow along with anything you can't carry. Cross the gulch and hide out for a day until things settle down. I'll work my way to Nolan's family and provide extra security tonight. Switch off your phones and walkie-talkies to save power. Check your walkie-talkies on this channel at ten and forty minutes after the hour."

An animated conversation ensued in Burmese. Ryder followed it not at all.

"No, sir," Arkar said. "I give cover fire. I have NVG spotting scope from car. Maung climb down and then up to you in one hour. Take cover and wait for Maung."

Ryder shook his head in admiration. There was no quit in Zaw's acolytes. "OK, bring the SAW to the edge of the gulch and set up behind cover. I'll be under the last truck facing up the road. I'll wait until Maung arrives, then we must exfil. If you hear the Barrett, cover me. If you see police, evacuate and do not engage. Do you understand?" Ryder heard two clicks in affirmation and powered down.

Ryder understood that he was trapped at the bottom of this road, but if he could lure his foes to the bridge's ruins, Arkar and the GPMG would tip the balance. If he waited too long, the police would arrive and he'd end up in San Quentin. Other than offering himself as human sacrifice, what did he have to tempt HL to venture this far down the road? *Of course, the van.* In five minutes, Ryder had moved it out of hiding and parked it in the open at the edge of the destroyed bridge.

* * * * *

MANDALAY WINERY

One of the laws of nature was that dead things felt twenty percent heavier than when alive. If Bert lived to be ninety-nine, he'd never rid his nostrils of the smell of death. He ignored the fluids leaking from the coyote tears in the plastic, hoisted the corpse in a fireman's carry, and hiked back to the main house. He laid Zaw on the floor of the rear downstairs bedroom and shut the door to block the stench. Bert resumed his vigil inside the front door, the right side of his chest searing with every breath. He breathed deeply to suppress a gag reflex.

* * * * *

OFF ZAX PEAK ROAD

The off-duty SWAT officer with the Walmart NVGs stood next to the steaming radiator of the stalled vehicle. He shined his penlight into the cab and declared, "We got a live one."

"Pull him out. Let's see what he knows," said the self-appointed leader, a younger man in a new camouflaged jumpsuit, worn paratrooper boots and an AR-15 loaded with Teflon-coated ammo. He shouldered his weapon and climbed up to peer into the cab from the passenger side. The driver sat upright, left hand covering his bloody face. "He's alone," said Jumpsuit. The SWAT officer yanked the door open and pulled the narco out by the shirt collar. The man landed hard on his back and cursed in Spanish. Two more guns joined the pair pointing at the blinded narco writhing on the ground.

"How many men are down that road?" Jumpsuit asked.

"Three across the bridge. It was boobytrapped and blew up after I crossed. No one is on this side."

"Where's Bob Nolan's family?"

"I know nothing. Those *hijos de putas* killed my friends."

"He's a fucking liar," one of the officers remarked.

"I don't think so. He's one of the drug pushers sent to kill Nolan's people. Sounds like they came out second best. How many were you to begin with, and is anyone else alive?" Jumpsuit asked.

"Six, and no."

"Put him down," Jumpsuit said. "He's a filthy Mexican drug animal."

"With pleasure," said a man in a plaid shirt and blue jeans. He drew his TOPS Black Eagle blade, bent over and dispatched the sightless man with a thrust to the heart.

"Let's hustle down to the end of the road and confirm the dirtbag's story about the bridge. Then we'll check in and see if Anaconda Red Three came up with anything at the winery."

* * * * *

OFF ZAX PEAK ROAD

The SWAT officer walked point because he had the only NVGs. He wasn't adept with his new acquisition, and Ryder remained undetected under the truck. At a range of only fifteen meters, Ryder steadied his trembling hands against the dirt and put a round through SWAT-man's goggles and out the back of his head. As Ryder's training kicked in, his hands steadied and his head cleared. He shot the second gunman through center mass, and the last two men dove into the woods. These men were no more competent than Randy's. He rolled out from under the truck and into the scrub. Out of habit, he moved after the second shot as *illuminate, shoot, move and take cover* were burned into his brain like the twenty-third psalm. From the manzanita on the right, a semiautomatic spewed bullets into the back of the flatbed and across the gulch. Arkar stood a better chance of catching a round than Ryder did.

Ryder fired again and saw a man crumple, then adjusted his NVGs to look for another target. Up the road, he heard the last man crashing through the brush. Ryder hustled to the road and not eighty meters away a hunched figure zig-zagged up the dirt road, green form distinct through the NVGs. It really was amateur night. Ryder put his shot into the man's lower back.

Nearby, the screams had subsided into moans. Ryder found the wounded man and resisted the urge to shut him up for good. He circled the prone figure until he located his weapon and nudged it out of reach. Standing out of sight above the man's head, Ryder removed his NVGs and flashed a light. No other arms were in view, but it was hard to be certain with the gore from a disintegrated shoulder. Shock and unconsciousness wouldn't be far behind.

"Help me! I'm bleeding to death."

"I can have a doctor here fast, but first, how many are out here?"

"Four, including me."

"I don't mean here," Ryder said, "I mean in your group."

"That's it. Only the four."

"You're lying and now you'll die."

"No! No! There were twelve in all. The others are active military and were recalled to base."

"I still don't believe you, and you'll bleed out before anyone finds you."

"OK, OK!" the man said. "They're checking out thermal images at a winery near here."

"Where are the keys to your vehicle?"

"On top of the gas cap."

Ryder sprinted up the road as the wounded man's weak pleas for a doctor faded to nothing.

* * * * *

MANDALAY WINERY

A door handle carelessly tested woke Mei Ling, though she wasn't conscious of the source. She nudged her mother and whispered, "Mom, there's someone outside. Wake up."

Joanie raised her head off the table and the bent forearms she'd used as a pillow. Mei Ling handed her a loaded shotgun. "I switched off the safety. If the door opens, shoot."

Bert leaned against the stone wall next to the front door, chin on his chest. A premonition prompted his eyes to open and a red dot danced on his Mylar blanket. *I'm dead* was his only conscious thought, but he managed to fling his body sideways and grapple for the clacker. In rapid sequence, four deafening explosions ripped the night as twenty-eight-hundred steel balls saturated the grounds around the main house. The red dot was nowhere in evidence as Bert reached for his M-4 and crawled away from the door.

The Claymores spewed .22 caliber-equivalent projectiles with a single-person hit probability of thirty percent out to fifty meters. The breach team fared better—and worse—than the averages as only a single pellet found flesh, but it tore out the carotid artery of the master sergeant. Back on their feet after confirming that the NCO was KIA, the two remaining men blew the lock and sought refuge inside the wine cellar. Simultaneous shotgun blasts killed one soldier and flattened the second. The wounded man lay on the landing at the top of the stairs, and there he died when Joanie shot him from halfway up the steps.

In the living room, Bert's walkie-talkie sat forgotten in the melee. M-4 in hand, he headed for the bedroom containing Zaw's body. He cleared the room, unlocked the window and slid it open. He couldn't see shit amid the smoke and dust. Another shotgun blast gave urgency to his mission and he popped his head outside. A gun butt to the face sent him reeling back into the room, spitting out a mouthful of broken molars and blood. He stitched both sides of the window frame with continuous fire until the injector rain dry. As he felt for a fresh mag, a voice behind him commanded. "Drop your weapon or die."

* * * * *

Ryder had the Barrett by his side as he pushed the Jeep Wrangler toward Mandalay Winery. Such was his fatigue and ill-ease from alcohol withdrawal that he couldn't remember the shape of the road as it wound among the new vines. The Claymores detonated and he responded by flooring the accelerator, ripping off his NVGs and switching on the headlights. Thirty seconds later, he heard two shotgun blasts meaning the women were under attack as well. A third report from a Remington rent the night. *Good! Give 'em hell, Nolans.*

He cut the lights and slammed the brakes just as he reached the entrance. He had to get a grip. If he drove in without lights, even with NVGs he couldn't go fast on that winding lane and he'd be in the gunsights of the rear guard in no time. Up ahead, someone expended a full mag on auto. It sounded like something Bert might do, so he was still in the fight. With all the shooting going on, they might be distracted enough for a sniper to go in on foot undetected. Anyone attempting to drive out would end up with a caste mark between his eyes.

He backed the Wrangler off the main road, fed the last of the .50 caliber ammunition into the Barrett's magazine, snugged up the NVGs and scanned for targets as he walked up the dirt road leading into the winery.

* * * * *

"If you don't come out, we'll execute Bert. You have ten seconds. Leave your weapons behind."

From below, Joanie spoke. "We have put down the shotguns. My daughter is in a wheelchair and can't climb stairs. You'll have to send someone down."

"You come up first, then we'll send someone down to carry your daughter up. Or else I'll drop a grenade down there and you can both stay." There were four unwounded men left with six dead and two wounded. The second-in-command had seen too much carnage to be in the mood to negotiate with a housewife who had killed his breaching team. "You have five seconds."

"I'll help her up the stairs, but we'll need light."

"Jenkins, put a light on them and kill anyone you see with a weapon."

"Not in our eyes, please. Just light the steps. They're slippery." Joanie had Mei Ling's arms around her neck and half her weight on her back. The three-legged mother-daughter team navigated around the blood and body parts one deliberate step at a time.

"Bring the vehicles up. Let's load our wounded and get the fuck out of here. Someone who knows how to work the radio, raise Anaconda. Tell him that we can't return to base as we've been ambushed and shot to hell. We'll need a safe house and surgeons. Our drone operators are dead, so we have no eyes up top. Also report that we captured three members of the target's family alive." Two men peeled and headed into the darkness with their NVGs showing the way.

* * * * *

Ryder lay flat among the immature vines. The absence of gunfire meant the fight was over. Two hundred meters away, two vehicles rumbled to life meaning his side had lost. He could kill one driver, but only at the cost of giving himself away. The kidnappers would then put guns to their hostages' heads, and he'd end up sacrificing his life for no permanent gain. He only had four rounds left in the Barrett, probably not enough to finish them off even if he had them in the open. He'd be lucky to be able to tell friend from foe once the shooting started. *Shit.* He thought some more, and the only sensible action was to pull back and follow the kidnappers down the mountain. Once he had reinforcements, he could mount a proper rescue but the first order of business was to walk the battlefield.

Ten minutes' search of two buildings made him feel like he was back in the Sandbox undertaking an after-action investigation. This time the people on the defensive were the good guys. Bert's post in the living room held only a Mylar blanket, a walkie-talkie and his phone. There was one bar of cell coverage and a new Signal message to Ryder, copied to Bert. Bob's text was three hours old and warned them that Don Randy's men should be considered hostile. Nolan was to arrive in San Antonio on Saturday to search for leads on Love. The last part of the text gave pause: *If one or more of my family is captured, safeguard any survivors, and in preference to attempting a long-odds rescue, Bert and/or you should join me in San Antonio. With you, we have a better chance of taking Love alive than if I'm on my own.* In addition to being the best codebreaker on the planet, Nolan was also clairvoyant. Ryder pecked out a reply, hit send and shut down the phone.

Why Zaw's body lay in the bedroom took a few seconds to divine. The missing chunks of plastic and bloody patches spoke to wild animals. There was blood on the rug and Bert's M-4 lay on the floor. Ryder climbed out through the shattered window frame and found half a man on the ground. The Higher Love operative and US Army lieutenant had underestimated Bert Nolan.

At the wine cellar, the two shredded bodies spoke to close range-encounters with double-ought buckshot. Up top, one man appeared to be unmarked until Ryder rolled him over—the side of his neck was torn out. Next to the man a phone lay crushed underfoot. With heart in mouth, Ryder ventured into the wine cellar expecting to find two dead women. He nearly teared up with relief when his flashlight turned up no blood beyond the foot of the stairs. *They were alive.*

Ryder beat feet to the entrance of the winery and heard an engine in the dark. He dropped to one knee and brought the Barrett up one more time. He recognized their rental van from the sound. One of the sniper rounds from the road fight at lunchtime had done a number on a cylinder head. He put the scope on the windscreen and dropped the rifle in disbelief. *WTF?* Maung was behind the wheel. The former commando had descended the arroyo and then climbed out the other side in record time. Ryder sprinted toward Maung until the Burmese saw him and pulled over. The SEAL flashed a penlight under his chin to keep his new teammates from shooting him. In two minutes, they'd agreed on the plan.

The Burmese had assembled a hodge-podge of law enforcement and Ramboesque weaponry laying on the backseat. Ryder didn't know the lay of the land, but for certain trouble awaited down the mountain. He took a look and salvaged two useful items, a Sig 226 that went into the center console and a Ruger 9mm hidden under the front passenger seat.

Hellfire and damnation if Maung's incessant channel surfing didn't eventually find the Sonoma County sheriff's radio frequency. Arkar made himself equally useful by pulling topo maps out of the glove box. Maung earned bonus points when he found a multi-port USB charger and cables. Ryder marked the roadblocks based on his eavesdropping on the round-robin radio traffic for twenty minutes, mapping a way up and then off Zax Peak on unguarded backroads.

They were cop-free and no worse for wear an hour later when the Jeep hit Route 128 and then two-lane tracks until 101 South. San Antonio was just down the road ... eighteen hundred miles away. Ryder knew they had to score a fresh ride before daylight as Higher Love would be in pursuit of their missing Jeep. For now, the three of them had half a tank and six hours until sunup.

Arkar looked the least-bad, so Ryder sent him into the gas station to buy water, ibuprofen, Red Bull and jerky. Ryder handed driving duties over to Maung and steeled himself for the most difficult phone call of his life. *What could he say to Bob?*

* * * * *

AFTER MIDNIGHT, SATURDAY MORNING AUGUST 20: RIO VISTA JUNCTION, CALIFORNIA

Hooded, gagged, earplugged and cuffed, the two Nolan women supported a dazed Bert after an hour-long drive.

"Play it anyway you want," the sergeant had said, "but we only need one of you alive."

Mei Ling and Bert were wounded but Joanie was grateful beyond words that they'd survived this horrible day. Her revulsion and regret for the murder of two more men at the wine cellar seemed ... well, naïve. They died as they had lived. Everyone was back in the vehicle and she could smell food. The SUV pulled out, hitting a curb and jostling one of her earplugs loose.

"I call first dibs on the half-and-half daughter," Andrews said.

"How you gonna fuck someone shot through the leg?"

"If she passes out, I'll just spit on my dick. Worked fine at Abu Ghraib."

The other man groaned. "Just pay attention and keep up with Sarge. He's getting too far ahead."

* * * * *

FOUR POINTS BY SHERATON, HUNTSVILLE INTERNATIONAL AIRPORT

Nolan emailed Walker a heads-up, showered and put back on the same clothes while Gregoriev and Valeyriya typed their auditions for amnesty into their phones. Despite his exhaustion, Nolan didn't sleep as he waited to learn the fate of his family. Finally, after two o'clock his burner lit up. He went into the bathroom.

"It's me," Ryder said. "Higher Love captured all three alive. They drove out of the winery seventy-five minutes ago in identical SUVs guarded by four or five Spec Ops–types. I couldn't engage without endangering your family. I'm sorry. Do you still want me to join you?"

"Do you have a vehicle? What about Zaw's men?"

"We're in a stolen Jeep and we'll need to swap vehicles before sunup. We're fine, just tired. You were right, Don Randy's men came at us and we killed all six of them. Between them and whoever the Nolans killed, there might have been a dozen casualties tonight."

"What condition is my family in?" Nolan asked.

"Impossible to say, but Bert's hurt. I didn't see fresh blood in the wine cellar where Joanie or Mei Ling were hiding, so I don't think they were wounded."

"If you're able, switch vehicles and drive to San Antonio. We have two days at most to capture Love before we hit the trade deadline. We need him sooner."

"We're en route. I have somebody in mind to add to our team: Tony Johnson. He's an ace marksman and interrogator, and fearless under fire."

"Sounds like a bad idea based on my previous meeting."

"No, you'll love this guy once you get to know him better."

"I doubt it but see if he's available."

"Sure," Ryder said. "One other thing. Yesterday morning at the hospital in Novato, Joanie received a call from Yu Kaili. She warned her that Higher Love was gunning for you and coming for them. That's why Mei Ling and Joanie agreed to go with Bert and me."

"I'll be damned."

"There's more. She told Joanie that you're the father of her son."

CHAPTER TWENTY-THREE

CONVERGENCE

SATURDAY AUGUST 20: PLACERVILLE

The two guards herded the three Nolans inside, Mei Ling supported on either side by her mother and brother. They shuffled from the SUV up the steps to the porch and into the front room of the rustic house.

"You'll remain here until you're released or buried out back," the sergeant said. "The guards will attach leg restraints and remove your handcuffs. You will remain in the interrogation room behind one-way glass. If you behave, there are books and magazines, meals, trips to the toilet and mattresses on the floor. If you don't, we'll drop you into the cellar and you can sit in the dark in your own piss and shit. Am I clear?" Sarge wasn't expecting an answer. He turned to his men. "I want your phones and fitness trackers, GPS watches, and anything else with wireless capability. And all weapons except your side arms. As of midnight, we're AWOL and by sunup the FBI will join the search. Stay indoors. Contact no one. I'll disable the internet before I leave. Don't injure the prisoners. This is a war and we will abide by the Geneva Convention.

"I have work to do elsewhere," Sarge continued. "Washington, bring up the *New York Times* home page on the PC. I need a proof-of-life photo of these three, and then the router leaves with me. In my absence, Sergeant Murtaugh is in charge. You three will share guard duty in four-hour shifts. Murtaugh's team is in the woods. Their orders are to shoot anyone who attempts to leave. *Anyone.* There's a microwave and frozen chow. Feed the prisoners twice a day. Washington, I'm putting you in charge of the internal security detail."

The skinny black NCO with the wounded forearm nodded and glowered at the two corporals, who returned his glare with equal malevolence.

One hundred-twenty miles away in Rio Vista, Arkar hotwired a Honda Accord parked off Highway 12. Ryder followed in the Jeep until they were under cover behind McPhail's Heavy Equipment where they transferred their weapons and gear. Next stop was Texas.

* * * * *

HUNTSVILLE INTERNATIONAL AIRPORT

That Bob Nolan had slept at all was a testament to his exhaustion. Pasan knocked on the door at six-thirty bearing coffee and crullers. Gregoriev and Valeyriya had shared the bed while Nolan had made do on the couch. From the change in chemistry, Nolan inferred that his roommates had conducted an undercover compatibility test in the pre-dawn hours.

Nolan logged onto Tor and saw that Payne had confirmed a deal, subject to the Russians delivering their reports to Nolan before they boarded. Gregoriev and Valeyriya held a short, animated conversation and replied, the Russian equivalent of "no fucking way" ringing in Nolan's ears.

After more back and forth, they came to a compromise. Nolan skimmed both files to confirm that there was sufficient substance. Gregoriev encrypted the documents with a passphrase and emailed them to Nolan. Once their plane landed in Grand Cayman, Gregoriev would text the decryption key to Nolan's burner. What Gregoriev didn't realize was Nolan's rapid skim had extracted more than one hundred valuable points from the combined twenty-plus pages of the Farewell Group's FSB's and SVR's anti-democracy operations in the US. Nolan no longer cared whether Gregoriev made good on his promise. When Nolan later had access to a recording device, he'd also tour the front hallway, living room, dining room, kitchen, upstairs three bedrooms, two bathrooms and the attic of his childhood home. It would take but a half hour to unpack the Russians' secrets, one light fixture, knickknack or furniture piece-per-nugget.

On the airport tarmac, Valeyriya reread POTUS's safe conduct letter and pro forma wire transfer instructions. She looked at Nolan and nodded.

Gregoriev handed back his Glock. "Thank you for your assistance. Please tell your Obama we aren't doubles or sources. If anyone blackmails or harasses us, I assure you I have a file on every politician in Washington irrespective of party affiliation. I release all of it to the public."

"I understand your position," Nolan said. "We call it a dead man's switch over here. If I can appeal to your sense of fairness, maybe you could leak something on Ginger once you're safe, since you've already torpedoed Crandall's campaign."

"I have a video of Ginger watching two prostitutes urinate on the same bed the Obamas slept in when they visited Moscow, plus copies of signed contracts for secret real estate deals in Moscow. Would that be sufficient?"

"Yes, something along those lines." The two men exchanged handshakes. "Enjoy your retirement, Vladimir."

"Try to stay alive, Robert."

Gregoriev and Valeyriya climbed the steps into an unmarked Citation. The gangway lifted and the door sealed. Nolan turned and followed Pasan to where the Baron sat. "How far to San Antonio?"

"It's almost eight hundred miles—just under four hours wheels-up to wheels-down."

"Let's get moving. I have until Sunday to capture the most dangerous man in the world and I don't know what he looks like."

* * * * *

THE WHITE HOUSE

Obama sat in the Oval Office after another sleep-deprived night. Surveillance footage and crime scene forensics had implicated Nolan in the deaths of Weill and Chumakov. Nolan may well be a patriot, but men facing consecutive life terms often reordered their priorities. With Nolan's family in Higher Love's hands, General Payne alerted the president to the obvious play: Nolan kidnaps Love and trades him for his loved ones. It was scarcely believable that no one in the US government knew where Nolan was. They had to find either Nolan or Love in a hurry.

Meanwhile, according to Nolan's sources, the leaked Democrat emails turned out to be a smokescreen for a two-pronged, multiyear assault on American democracy. From Russia, hackers, trolls and bots orchestrated chaos through social media, phantom causes and specious news organizations. Onshore, Higher Love had broken into the states' voter registration and tabulation systems to undermine the electorate's confidence in the fairness of any contest. All this with the presidential election less than three months away. What could the president do that wouldn't look partisan or like the ravings of a mental deficient?

* * * * *

BEECHCRAFT BARON OUTBOUND HUNTSVILLE INTERNATIONAL AIRPORT

Nolan put down the burner and took a slug of water. Via dictation he'd emptied his head of the reconstituted substance of Gregoriev and Valeyriya's testimonials. Though no expert on presidential politics, he felt comfortable that the specifics in the recording would be judged a good value for a million dollars and a free plane ride.

He considered the ramifications of Ryder's call. Higher Love was holding his family. If he turned himself over, there was no guarantee they'd release them. The only way out was to take Love alive. All Nolan knew was that the headman would be somewhere in San Antonio on Sunday, likely flying into Lackland AFB. Nolan would examine the scheduled flights and access passenger names. But Love remained a cipher: "an old white male formerly senior in government" wasn't a lot to go on. Higher Love had spent years building and arming a secret organization designed to protect its leadership and goals against the day they toppled America's democracy. He couldn't fight them because he didn't know who was in the command structure. Meanwhile, they hunted him. Nolan added fresh clothes, clippers and hair dye to his mental shopping list.

On the resources side, it was a thin roster: Ryder plus two driving east from California to arrive after midnight, and Hecker arriving from D.C. a few hours earlier. On the other hand, he might still have Obama's backing. When and if he secured the safety of his family, he'd pull the trigger and alert Payne. There wasn't any more to be done, and with ninety minutes until landing he shut his eyes and slept the sleep of the condemned, recriminations reverberating inside his head.

* * * * *

STATE ROUTE 247 OUTSIDE YUCCA VALLEY, CALIFORNIA

Arkar might have been a terrific driver on the streets of Rangoon, but that skillset hadn't survived a trans-Pacific relocation and the attendant lane discipline requirements. The late-thirties guardian of the junta's relatives drove with his hands frozen at ten-and-two o'clock, leaning forward so far his face almost touched the steering wheel. The Burmese liked his hip-hop loud. Maung compounded Ryder's woes by chain smoking a vile bargain brand of cancer stick.

Having been so close to death the last two days, Ryder reflected on his own mortality as the Accord emulated Brownian motion. In the backseat, he struggled to apply first-aid remedies to his litany of minor injuries. For the umpteenth time he admonished the driver. "Keep it under seventy-five miles per hour. We can't afford to get pulled over in a stolen car."

They'd had the good fortune to boost a car with a full tank, but now they were on vapors. Gas stations these days filmed everyone at the pumps. Once the Accord hit the priority hot sheets, it would be a few hours to a half-day before they were in custody or dead—if Arkar didn't do the cops' jobs for them first. Ryder saw a sign up ahead and called out. "Take the exit to Route 62. We need to visit Walmart. Arkar, slow down!"

Arkar and Maung in Walmart on Ryder's dime were like two elementary school kids in a Times Square candy store. Ryder was happy he'd pulled extra cash out of the hospital ATM in Novato. Was that just yesterday? It felt like a week ago. They loaded up on everything they would need to push on through to Texas with new phones, two ten-gallon gas cans and gun-cleaning kits. Ryder texted Nolan their new numbers before destroying their existing burners.

Ryder's hand shakes were down to tremors and he no longer had the urge to drink himself stupid, at least when he wasn't thinking about Bob's family at the mercy of those fascists. He cleaned, oiled and function-checked the salvaged weapons, loading and stacking them in the backseat. The arsenal was another good reason not to get pulled over.

Ryder rubbed the heels of his palms into his eyes and thought of his wife. Sally was a good mother to the twins and her own little girl, Louise. Ryder liked her most when he saw her feeding the twins in their highchairs—their chubby checks smeared with pumpkin puree—or joining them in a game on the floor with their toy trucks in front of an exasperating educational TV show. Sally, Sally, Sally ...

At the outset, their union had been a happy one, at least outwardly, but he hadn't understood Sally's true self on their wedding day any more than when he'd chatted with her on Facebook from Pakistan. Both of them wanted to be married, and each fixated on the idealized adolescents they had appeared to be two decades before. The thrill of the chase ended with the wedding ceremony. Sally was expecting and the fast money dried up after deducting the costs of the horse farm and gun shop. Then Ryder's father died of a stroke. Ryder spent three days on a bender and the IRS showed up three weeks later. Les and Paul arrived three months after that, the emergency C-section adding another forty grand to the debit side of the personal ledger about the time his commodities broker skipped town and left him with margin calls.

With seized properties, frozen assets, legal fees and tax evasion charges pending, Ryder didn't blame Sally for telling him to move out. Friends refused to take his calls, fearing he would ask for another handout. He was at the end of his rope when Dead Bob had called with the offer of adventure, funds and, maybe, the prospect of a good death.

What Ryder faced today wasn't what he'd reckoned on. Higher Love would either know who he was or would find out soon. If they were so keen to kill Bob, Ryder had to be climbing up their list with eleven KIA since yesterday, plus at least four more the Nolans had managed at the Mandalay Winery shootout.

Sally couldn't just disappear with three toddlers. Cutting hair was her only livelihood. The best he could do was to put a pair of Spec Ops veterans by her side: twelve-on and twelve-off for a grand a day each. Either Bob survived and made good, or Nolan went down and took Ryder with him, and USAA paid out on Ryder's life policy. Either way, funding wasn't a binding constraint.

He made the call to Sally. She wasn't pleased to learn that strange armed men would show up at the house, and that she and the kids should stay put. What about the beauty parlor? He had that handled, too.

He needed to reach out to Tony Johnson. The man was as good a warfighter as Ryder ever met—outside the SEAL fraternity, of course.

* * * * *

BEACHCRAFT BARON INBOUND AT SAN ANTONIO INTERNATIONAL AIRPORT

Nolan's phone picked up a signal before the landing gear locked. There was a Signal message from Joanie's burner. All it contained was a photograph of his family huddled around a computer screen showing the New York Times home page bearing today's date. That was followed by a voicemail from Joanie's phone. He had until noon Sunday to turn himself in. When he indicated his location, Higher Love would come to him. Once he was in custody, they would release one family member. Once he had identified his companions and ordered them to cease hostilities, a second family member would go free. Once they had completed their debriefing and were convinced that he had been completely forthcoming, they would release the final family member. Left unsaid was his death soon after. Did he have a preferred order of release? Could he acknowledge receipt?

The only thing unexpected was the length of time Nolan had to surrender. Why not noon today, or midnight tonight? It had to be a bottleneck on HL's side. *They won't be ready to interrogate me until noon on Sunday. Interesting.* He ignored their requests and made a mental note to change phones.

Ryder's Signal text arrived, alerting him of the new three burner numbers and estimating an arrival time after midnight on Sunday.

Someone unknown texted *Moneyfornothingandchixforfree.* Nolan forwarded the pass phrase and the files to Payne. Gregoriev was in the tropics rolling in dough … until his new gal pal split.

The Baron bounced to a stop and Pasan taxied to the corner of the airfield reserved for private clients of the High Flyers Club. It was just after eleven o'clock local time: Nolan had less than twenty-five hours to take Love alive.

* * * * *

THE WHITE HOUSE

Obama finished picking at a tasteless salad packed with high-protein pulses and quinoa. He really had to free the kitchen staff from Michelle's spell. This wasn't food—it was what food ate. General Payne's gofer popped in and handed the president a thin folder containing his unofficial national security adviser's latest work product.

There were two items, the first being printouts of the photographs of the seven men killed trying to kidnap Nolan's family earlier today in Northern California. The FBI had ID'ed five of them as either ex-military or law enforcement, with two unknowns. The two license plates were from Sonoma County unmarked police vehicles. Payne's conclusion was that Higher Love had deeply penetrated first responders at the local level. Perhaps this was only in Northern California, or maybe it was a broader phenomenon. The president could scarcely conceive of a United States where he couldn't rely on rank-and-file police officers to uphold the Constitution, but perhaps that was how far the rot had set in.

The second sheaf of documents made for equally grim reading. Payne had printed Nolan's Tor message and forwarded a hard copy for the president's immediate attention. Clipped on top was a photograph of the old spy's family—a battered young man, an exhausted model and a defiant wife—huddled around monitor showing today's headlines. Payne repeated Nolan's request that POTUS authorize Abyss staff to identify IP addresses that had accessed www.nytimes.com in the past six hours within three hundred miles of Healdsburg. Concentrate the search in depopulated areas: the rough planks featured in the photo suggested a cabin or similar. Payne's annotation said that he recommended POTUS rely on Q-Group out of San Francisco in addition to the Abyss team. They should involve local law enforcement as little as possible.

Meanwhile, the search for Bob Nolan narrowed by the hour. The FBI had tracked Special Agent in Charge Lonergan's family sedan from the Beltway south and west as Hecker made his way toward New Orleans. With luck, Hecker would lead them straight to their quarry. Payne had Q-Group out of Dallas on standby to collect the errant spy as soon as they confirmed a location.

CHAPTER TWENTY-FOUR

REUNION

SATURDAY AUGUST 20: I-59 OUTSIDE HATTIESBURG, MISSISSIPPI

Hecker had napped for two hours in the parking lot of Dreamland Bar-B-Que in Tuscaloosa. The rib restaurant hadn't been open in the middle of the night, but he'd always wanted to see it after watching a clip of Todd Blackledge chowing down there during a break in yet another rout by the Crimson Tide over Tennessee. Rejuvenated, Hecker had had the pedal to the floor for the last one hundred eighty miles when he saw flashing red and blue lights in his rearview mirror.

The young police officer was a humorless, rail-thin redhead. "Mr. Hecker, you were doin' ninety in a seventy and that requires a visit to the judge. Seein' as how it's Saturday, you'll spend the weekend in Hattiesburg's city jail if you can't post bail."

Hecker pulled his DEA identification card out of his wallet. "I'm working on a matter of national security."

"Show me your vehicle registration and proof of insurance, sir."

Hecker fumbled in the glove box, careful not to dislodge the 9-mil, and extracted the papers.

"This car doesn't belong to you."

"It belongs to Michael Lonergan, my friend and a special agent in charge with the FBI in Washington, D.C."

"An FBI officer loaned you this here car?" Officer Little's features contorted in a grimace.

"Yes. If you call him, he'll confirm this."

Hecker punched in Mick's number and handed his phone to the officer. Lonergan answered, convinced Richie Cunningham's unhappy twin he indeed was an FBI agent and vouched for Hecker. The cop looked up. "He wants to speak with you."

"Mick? Thanks for clearing me with the—"

"They're tracking—" And the line cut. Hecker frowned. What in the fuck had just happened? He forced himself to smile at Officer Little and said, "Rats, the call dropped."

"I don't want you goin' over sixty-five until you're out of Mississippi."

"Yes, sir."

Hecker started the vehicle and pulled back onto the freeway. *Son of a bitch, they're tracking me.* He was the unwitting pied piper leading the vermin to Nolan. But not for long.

* * * * *

I-10 OUTSIDE QUARTZITE, ARIZONA, AND SAN ANTONIO

"I had a helluva time getting a current number for you, Tony. Where are you? How are you?" Ryder was pleased to have the Spec Ops veteran on the line.

"I'm at the San Antonio airport waiting for someone."

"San Antonio? I'll be damned. I'm on the way there too."

"No shit? What's your ETA?"

"Sunday morning after midnight: about fifteen hours to go."

"I'm likely to be up. I landed new gig that will take a couple days."

"I was hoping I could add you to our team. We're providing security for someone you might remember from a few years back. It pays well, maybe twenty grand a day for a few days."

"Shit, sounds like trouble. But I'm interested in principle."

"You can count on fireworks with this guy. He's supposed to be dead and pisses a lot of people off."

"I don't know how long I'll be needed here but let me call you back when I have more. Maybe I can squeeze it in. I have to run—my subject just deplaned. Looks like she hasn't aged a day. That's about to change."

* * * * *

SAN ANTONIO INTERNATIONAL AIRPORT

"I completed the transfer of two hundred thousand dollars to your Sri Lanka account," Nolan said to Pasan. "Thanks for everything. I hope I won't need you but stick around for two more days. I may need you to fly a high-value target out in secret."

"I'll refuel the Baron and wait for your new phone number, but it's far too much money."

"Once you've been shot at, you can refund whatever you think is excessive."

Pasan chuckled and extended his hand. "I know you have an eye for the ladies. The one behind you is a stunner."

Nolan gave the pilot's palm a firm squeeze and turned around. "I'll be damned." Forty meters away, an Asian woman clad in designer clothes and sporting oversized fashionista sunglasses dragged a wheeled suitcase away from a private jet and toward the High Flyers terminal.

A new navy BMW X5 sped into view and stopped in front of the startled woman. The passenger door opened. Out popped a tall white man wearing wraparound sunglasses and a boonie hat that clashed with his Hawaiian shirt and khakis. The woman raised her arms in self-defense and struggled briefly, losing her shades in the scuffle. The man dragged her to the back of the SUV where the driver opened the rear hatch and another pair of arms bundled the captive inside. Nolan made for the vehicle at a fast walk, trying not to draw attention. The driver fetched Kaili's suitcase while the larger man slammed the hatch down and jumped back into the front seat. The BMW sped away, leaving Nolan with only a Texas license plate, a pair of scratched Prada sunglasses, and a confirmed sighting of the mother of his third child. *What on earth was Yu Kaili doing in San Antonio and who had just kidnapped her?*

Nolan looked around. The late Saturday morning foot traffic was minimal in the August sun. Nolan ducked into the air-conditioned High Flyers terminal. What personal or professional interest did she have in San Antonio? Was it a US government-sanctioned snatch? The situation had become curiouser and curiouser.

Fifteen minutes later, Nolan was in a rental car bound for Ingram Park Mall and from there to Lackland AFB when Tony Johnson's face popped into his head, displacing a mixed bag of memories involving Kaili. Johnson had been based in Afghanistan in 2014 before flying to Rangoon to help out Ryder, Hecker and Nolan. While at a DEA safehouse, Johnson demonstrated a flair for extracting information in a hurry. A few days later, Coulter's henchmen dragged Nolan into an interrogation hut on a deserted Australia beach. Who should greet Nolan but Agent Johnson, covered in gore and eating lunch?

Ryder had mentioned that Johnson had left Black Ice and was chilling out in Houston. Now Johnson was in San Antonio and Yu Kaili was first up. Nolan shuddered to think what would happen next, but as much as he'd like to help Kaili, he had to put his family's lives ahead of a former paramour until Love was in custody.

Nolan examined himself in the rearview mirror. His newly dyed brown crewcut and preppy clothes gave him a businessman-on-a-weekend-away look. He appeared calmer than he felt.

* * * * *

BOERNE, TEXAS, AND I-10 OUTSIDE PHOENIX

"Ryder, it's me," Johnson said. "I have a little time while the sodium thiopental percolates."

Ryder whistled. "That's not using a baseball bat to beat the shit out of biker tied to a chair. You said the target's a woman. Some *jihadi?*"

Johnson laughed. "She's more like a Vogue subscriber and a senior member of the opposition. From the list of questions, she's an expert on North Korea."

"Ooh, big time shiat. Smells like CIA or similar. Congratulations on the score. When do I find out if you can help us?"

"That's why I'm calling. I haven't even started on China Girl and I've learned there's a second subject coming in late on Sunday. I've been offered another hundred on top of the fifty they're already paying me. No word on who it is, but the big boss will personally supervise the sessions. I've worked for weird-ass clients in the past, but this group would make me laugh if they weren't deadly serious. So not this time, partner. What do you say we meet next weekend in the Quarter, eat dinner at K Paul's, take in some jazz and fuck a couple high-end whores? My treat."

"If I'm alive and upright in a week's time," Ryder said, "you have a deal on the dinner and jazz. Take care, Tony."

"Ride 'em hard, ride 'em fast and put 'em away wet, brother."

"Amen." Ryder disconnected the call and scrambled to find the number of Nolan's newest burner.

* * * * *

I-40 IN PHOENIX, ARIZONA AND OUTSIDE LACKLAND AIR FORCE BASE, SAN ANTONIO

"It's me," Ryder said. "Can you talk?'"

"Yes, I have you on speaker," Nolan said. "I'm sitting here watching car after car drive out of Lackland. I wouldn't be able to spot Love short of him wearing a Bigfoot costume. The passenger manifests show dozens of names. I'll have to kick it over to Obama's man in D.C. and hope the president can safeguard my family."

"Don't put your head in the oven just yet. Tony Johnson just called and he's in San Antonio on an assign—"

"I know. I watched him kidnap Yu Kaili two hours ago."

"You what? Look, he all but told me he's working for Higher Love. He said his questions were all about North Korea. Tony shot her up with truth serum and called me while he waited for it to take effect. He just received a new assignment from the same client. He's been hired to interrogate you for up to three days, and the top man in the client organization will be on hand to supervise."

"Very interesting," Nolan said. "I have the plate of the kidnap vehicle. Let me hack into the Texas DMV and find out where it's registered. Can you call Johnson back and ask him to just let Kaili walk away?"

"Tony's peculiar. Once he accepts an assignment, he never backs out. His word means a lot more to him than the Constitution."

"It means he's on the other side."

"I'm afraid so," Ryder said.

"Don't try to take him yourself. He's way too good. Wait for me."

"If I can find him, I'll stake out his location and wait for Hecker or you."

"Hecker? You didn't mention Hecker."

"Hecker's saved my life this week more times than you have," Nolan said. "He was undercover inside the Medellín Cartel, but ever since his senior contact decided to kill us both, he's been back to his old self."

"I don't want anything to do with him," Ryder said. "But back to Tony: the only way to handle him is via surprise. If he sees you first, you're dead."

"Thanks for the encouragement. I need to move. Just give me his phone number."

* * * * *

OUTSIDE PLACERVILLE, CALIFORNIA

Mei Ling lay flat on the table in the interrogation room while Joanie and Bert unwrapped her sodden bandages. She'd bled due to the exertions of the previous day, but the wound appeared clean.

Bert was encouraged on two counts. They still had their shoes. And on the personal front, his jaw had popped back into place—it wasn't broken after all, just dislocated. He'd lost four teeth and the left side of his face was swollen to hell, but his mind had cleared and the headache was bearable.

Bert helped his sister roll onto her back and raised her left leg behind the knee to create the space needed to apply a fresh bandage. Mei Ling winced but said nothing. In a conversational tone, Joanie spoke in Mandarin. "Those guards intend to rape you, darling."

"Over my dead body," said Bert in rusty Chinese.

"I saw those two leering at me. We can use this. If I can tease them into pulling their cocks out, I'll cripple them both."

"*Choi, choi, choi!* Don't even speak of it. We don't want you alone with those animals."

"Calm down, Mom. Mei Ling's right. If she ties up two of them, I'll take out the third. I just have to find how to exit this room at the same time they're trying to rape her."

"I'll tell them I need to pee," Mei Ling said in Mandarin. "Let's see how they handle it." Bert nodded. Ten minutes later, they'd established that the guards would allow Mei Ling to drape herself over Bert's shoulders and hop on one leg over to the only toilet. Bert waited for her outside the door and supported her on the return journey.

The two crackers ogled Mei Ling, only to wipe the smirks off their faces when Washington came out of the kitchen and looked at them.

"How did it go?" Joanie asked in Mandarin.

"We can take them," Bert said as he helped Mei Ling into a straight-backed chair.

From outside, Washington's voice came into the room over a speaker. "Speak English! The next person who speaks anything else gets thrown down the hole. Breakfast is in an hour if you behave. I left books and magazines on the table."

Bert gave a thumbs-up through the one-way glass and took a seat at the table. Vonnegut's *Breakfast of Champions* wasn't one he was familiar with. His mother came to him and leaned over to sort through the pile, settling on a one-year-old *Economist*. Before she returned to her chair, she left a huge safety pin in Bert's lap. She'd taken it off Mei Ling's bandage. Bert eased it into a trouser pocket.

* * * * *

RIVERWOOD ROAD, BOERNE, TEXAS

Riverwood Road boasted only two house designs: "very large" and "gargantuan." Mature Montezuma bald cypress, sun-beaten Esperanza and straggly cactus gave the landscaped yards an authentic if austere appearance. Nolan rolled by the two-story home situated forty meters off the main road. He spotted the blue X5, a black SUV and a red pickup that suggested the same three-man team from the airport was still involved.

He pulled over to consider his options. He could wait for the arrival of Ryder and the two Burmese. The four of them should be able to storm the house, but to what end? They'd be too late to save Kaili and too early to find Love. But one of the two men with Johnson—maybe Michael Kammerer, the registered owner of the X5 as well as the house—should be able to tell him more about Love and his movements.

The lower risk course would be to stay away from Johnson and Kaili, capture the first one of the two HL men who showed his face, make a run for it and question the prisoner somewhere far away. No, once Johnson realized he was a man down, he'd change locations and alert his clients. Try as he might, Nolan couldn't avoid the conclusion that he had to kill or capture all three men if he wanted to find Love before the deadline. Acting now omitted Ryder from the action, a strategy that carried many disadvantages and one benefit. Ryder wouldn't want to use lethal force against his friend Johnson, and his reticence could end up getting them all killed. Further prodding Nolan toward immediate action was the thought of Kaili strapped in the torturer's chair.

Nolan had a Glock with fifteen in the magazine, a bag full of cash and nothing else in his favor. Time for a deep think and a drive to the hardware store.

* * * * *

Two hours later, Nolan felt like a contestant on a giant scavenger hunt. Relying on the internet and poor network security, he'd made substantial progress identifying his quarry—Johnson plus two Texas Air National Guard reserves and the layout of the house—and perhaps most intriguingly, evidence of an advanced internet-of-things master hub. Hacking the home Wi-Fi network "Mike Hammer" was as easy as "Password123." Through Google Home, he watched one man in the family room staring at the TV. Johnson and the second man didn't show. A room-by-room video inventory revealed evidence of food and drink for three in the kitchen. No cameras in the basement indicated that the other two were down there with Kaili,

Prep work done, Nolan pulled up the driveway and parked the stolen van labeled "Keefer's Pest Control" next to the other vehicles. He shouldered a duffel bag containing his laptop and other tools, confirmed that the Glock was easily accessible and headed up the path with a silver canister of cockroach poison in his hand, an exterminator's breathing mask around his mouth and goggles perched on his forehead. He rang the bell.

* * * * *

OUTSIDE PLACERVILLE, CALIFORNIA

"Washington's asleep," Andrews whispered to Gomes as they observed the three Nolans through the one-way glass. "I say we go in and grab that piece of ass, drag her out at gunpoint, fuck her sideways and put her back before our friend is none the wiser."

"I think you're forgetting she's likely to tell 'em later," Gomes said, "and her brother is more'n likely to make us kill 'em before he lets us take his sister."

"As long as we kill Bert quiet, no one will give two shits. He jumped us, and you stabbed him in self-defense."

Gomes was indignant. "Me? Why me?"

"Because I'll have the Browning on them while you go in to collect the plates. We tell Bert to help his sister to the toilet: she don't get to decide, it's either go now or do without. Once he's out with her, we shut the door on Mom. You do Bert, we fuck her and stuff her full of Vicodin, then dump her back in the interrogation room. When Washington wakes up to go on duty in two hours, Bert's stone dead and the girl's in a coma. What's not to like?"

"That's a big boy in there," Gomes said. "Even with a busted jaw, he could raise a ruckus. I say you coldcock him with your gun butt as soon as he steps out."

Andrews smiled. "That'll work. I like the mom too. I have enough Vikes to turn them both into fuck-bots. If Washington wakes up, we'll offer him sloppy seconds or thirds."

Now Gomes was smiling too. "If Washington wakes up and gives us trouble, I'll cut his scrawny black neck and blame Bert. Bastard wrote me up twice this year so far. If we think he'll tell Sarge—"

"Then you kill the nigger to shut him up. Did I get it right?" A very much awake Washington backed his sarcasm with a pistol pointed at Andrews and Gomes. "Corporal Andrews, drop your sidearm and kick it toward me. Good. Put your hands behind your head and kneel. You next, Gomes. Move it! You're both a disgrace to Higher Love and the United States Army."

Washington walked to the side table where the Nolans' flex cuffs sat idle. "Andrews, cuff Gomes hands behind his back and then put a pair on yourself in front. Now use two fingers and pull Gomes' pig-sticker out of the sheath and toss it over there against the wall."

"Greg! Greg, relax bro," Andrews said. "We all be cool. How are we goin' to guard the prisoners if you have us in lockup?"

"Shut up. On your feet, then bend over and open the trap door."

Andrews made a half-hearted attempt to lift the hinged stone cover by the metal ring. "I can't budge it," he whined. "It's too heavy."

"Either open it, or I'll shoot you both where you stand."

Andrews found the strength to open the door on the second attempt. Wooden steps led down into darkness.

"Not so fast," Washington said. He frisked Gomes with one hand and turned up a lighter and cigs. Down the steps the frightened corporal went. A pat down of Andrews yielded a folding knife, a small bottle of pills, a can of snuff and three condoms. "You boys keep the rubbers. Have a gay old time."

Gomes plaintive voice rose up from the darkness. "I can't find the light switch down here. Can you give me that flashlight and spare us a little water? Come on, man. You know we weren't goin' to hurt you none."

"Get down there with your hillbilly rapist buddy and pray that Sarge is more forgiving than I am."

As soon as Andrews's head was below floor level, Washington heaved the trap door closed and latched it shut.

CHAPTER TWENTY-FIVE

THE EXTERMINATOR

SATURDAY AUGUST 20: LACKLAND AIR FORCE BASE

Two years under house arrest in his mountaintop retreat had given the bandy-legged rooster the energy of a bird dog on the first day of pheasant season. Though pushing eighty, Frank Coulter still had his ah-shucks smile and easygoing demeanor. Both were fronts, but coupled with a tan and a taut musculature, he could pass for a retired archeologist in his sixties. Coulter luxuriated in the feeling of freedom even if there were two FBI minders strolling ten feet behind him.

Tomorrow his boy Frank IV would witness his father receive an award and make a speech. Once Four Sticks departed, with a little scheming Coulter would shed his babysitters. He would remain at liberty long enough to stand over Nolan's corpse. With his life's work complete, he would accept whatever punishment the state meted out. But that was tomorrow. Tonight he was raising hell with Dick Burge, the crusty old bastard standing inside the terminal with a shit-eatin' grin on his face.

Colonel Burge, the commander of Camp Stanley and the Midwest Depot, was on the back end of a Special Forces career that included the ouster of Panama's dictator Manuel Noriega. Burge and Coulter had formed a fast friendship in Panama. The MWD was a top-secret repository of thousands of non-US issue heavy and light weapons, plus millions of rounds of ammunition and tons of explosives. Taking pride of place were the AK-47s of every vintage and manufacture, WWII era to the present. All untraceable back to Uncle Sam, and all available to liberation armies, proxies and puppets around the world provided they pledged to do the US's bidding.

Coulter implored the FBI babysitters to let the colonel and him ride back to Camp Stanley while they followed one car back. The Q-Group's acquiescence made Coulter suspect that Burge's vehicle was bugged. So be it.

"I'm glad they let you out to attend the ceremony," Burge said. "You did a helluva job in the Congo against Che, even if the recognition was fifty years in coming."

"Thanks," Coulter said. "The sad thing is half of the team has already passed. If the paper pushers had seen fit to honor the them even ten years ago, most everyone would still be around."

"Payne said that they'll fly in your boy for the awards session, but I'm thinking it might be better for him to miss the ceremony."

"Whoa. Why shouldn't I see Frank Junior? He's half the reason I petitioned to attend."

"Trouble's brewing and it might come to a head this weekend," Burge said.

"Stop speaking in riddles."

"Someone working on my staff tapped into the base security system last week. My men in the CCTV room were looking at static images while dozens of crates were moved out without authorization. The hack required expert coding skills."

"And how did you discover this?" Coulter asked.

"The old-fashioned way: we counted. Ten days ago, I was alerted that a Special Forces OD-A team would arrive at Camp Stanley with no explanation other than they were undergoing training. To date the detachment commander hasn't seen fit to drop by my office to introduce himself."

"They're prepping for a black op."

"Of course they are," Burge said, "but for the life of me I can't figure out what they're training for. I never see them outside for anything other than morning calisthenics. The rest of the day, they bash on keyboards in their quarters. I have a suspicious mind, and when one of the warehousemen reported the pallet stackers were out of place, I ordered a physical inventory of the facility. The computer inventory list and hard counts matched but the warehouseman swore that crates stacked two-high were three-high last week. We're still sorting out what's missing—several hundred AK-47s and thousands of rounds of ammo—but the most peculiar thing is that everything taken was manufactured in North Korea or shipped there from China. Why on earth would anyone steal the worst-quality weapons and most unreliable ammunition?"

"Either they're patriotic North Koreans, or something will happen that's pinned on North Korea."

"I'm worried that this may be related to tomorrow's ceremony. Now you know as much as I do. What do you want to do about Frank's visit?"

"Who are the VIPs attending?" Coulter asked.

"Other than you, former vice president Marmot is the only other dignitary." Burge grinned. "The dumbest man ever to chair the Senate."

Coulter smiled. "Remember when not being able to spell your vegetables was a scandal? We've devolved quite a bit since then."

"Yes, he's the one who forever changed the way school kids view tomatoes."

"I didn't realize he was still alive. He must be in his eighties."

"Yes, that would be about right. Maybe he discovered Scrabble late in life."

* * * * *

RIVERWOOD ROAD, BOERNE, TEXAS

"What do you want?" a man asked through the front door.

"Pest control. I'll be working outside. Are there are any pets or small children in the household?"

"No."

"Anyone planning on being outside in the next hour? I'm spraying a strong rodenticide. Best to remain indoors until it dries and avoid the white residue for a day."

"Can you come back another time?"

"This is the slot I'm scheduled for, so I'll make it fast."

Nolan knew that Weeks would be watching him through the peephole, but his only concern was that Johnson was on a torture break and would recognize his face on a CCTV feed. Nolan made a show of spritzing rat poison along the baseboards as he worked his way around to the back. He put down the sprayer and pulled out his phone with a freshly downloaded Google Home app. He switched off the CCTV coverage outside the house, as well as the motion detectors downstairs. Security system disarmed, he put on a pair of latex gloves and applied a sheet of sticky clear film on top of the bottom pane of the large window in the downstairs guest bedroom. Nolan made an inside-out loop of duct tape and stuck it to the middle of the plastic film. His glasscutter traced the inside edge of the clear film and he silently broke out the glass along the cut. Using his duct tape handle, he popped out the window glass without losing a sliver. He reached inside to flip open the window lock and climbed into an expensively furnished cowboy-themed bedroom.

Checking the home's CCTV feeds on his burner, Nolan saw William Weeks sitting on the couch watching the Astros next to a bowl of chips and a large pistol on the coffee table. Nolan didn't know anything about Weeks's training, but based on his reserve standing in the Texas Air National Guard, it was unlikely that he was more than a dilettante. Nolan needed to neutralize him without alerting the others, keeping him alive in case his principal target ended up deceased. He catfooted down the back hallway past a second guest room, a bathroom, a den and into the back of the living room. The Astros were getting hammered by the Indians at Progressive Field, a riveting contest judged by the empty Shiner Bock bottles.

Nolan reopened the app and popped the volume up five notches for two seconds before killing power to the TV. Weeks bounced out of his chair and worked the remote while Nolan countermanded his commands. From behind the back of the couch, Nolan saw that Weeks' weapon was still on the table.

"Put your hands up, turn around and kneel," Nolan said in the tone of a bored bank clerk.

"Damn it!" Weeks said as he complied. "I knew you weren't right."

"No, and you're far from all right. Say another word and I'll kill you and detonate the bomb in the basement."

Nolan turned the TV back on at normal volume. The Indians had a man on base. Nolan used heavy cable ties to bind Weeks's wrists and gagged him with a strip of dishtowel previously torn for the purpose. The former CIA cryptanalyst waved the pudgy fifty-plus-year-old to a substantial oak-and-leather armchair too heavy to tip over or rock. A roll of fiberglass-reinforced packing tape later, Weeks was immobilized in place. As Nolan left the room, Weeks starting yelling through his gag. Nolan returned and taped the dishrag in place with two full wraps around his head.

"If you try to shout again," Nolan said, "I'll tape your nostrils shut."

Nolan checked the CCTV feeds on his phone and disconnected the living room from the master array. Nolan crept down the back hallway to the kitchen. A closed door shielded the staircase leading down to the basement. A set of double doors opened onto an expansive deck with shaded tables, two barbecue grills and a beehive pizza oven. A large swimming pool sprawled at the base of the deck.

A cellphone on the kitchen counter caught Nolan's eye. The case was hand-tooled leather with a large MK embossed in the center and GOOD MOTHERFUCKER stamped along one end and HAPPY 50TH BIRTHDAY on the other.

Nolan went through his duffel bag and noted that he was down to the last roll of packing tape. He put on the respirator. Out came a spray can and off went the plastic safety clip. Nolan stood by the side of the basement door with a phone in one hand and the Glock the other. He dialed Kammerer's number and soon heard the theme song of *Rawhide*. The longer the phone rang, the louder the ring tone. Then the phone shut down and the call went to voicemail. Nolan killed his end before any noise emanated.

The basement door opened. In stepped a man wearing goggles, a butcher's apron, a long-sleeved shirt and rubber gloves. There were flecks and splotches of blood spotting the back of Kammerer's shirt. *Kaili's.*

"Don't move and don't make a sound," Nolan said while aiming the Glock at the center of Kammerer's back.

Kammerer swung his right forearm around, knocking the weapon aside but failing to dislodge it from Nolan's hand. Kammerer's left hook was on its way to Nolan's jaw when Nolan gave the Higher Love operator a spurt of bear spray. Kammerer's punch died before impact as the burning droplets saturated his nasal and oral cavities. Nolan took two steps back and eased the basement door shut before swinging the 9mm back up. "Get on your knees."

Kammerer was on his hands and knees almost before Nolan had said the words. Even through his airtight breezing apparatus Nolan's breaths had an acidic tang. Kammerer clawed at his face and rasped for breath.

"Lie flat on the floor with your hands behind you."

"Can't ... can't breathe," the afflicted man gasped.

Nolan wasn't buying it and reached down to freshen Kammerer's breath with a short burst into his nose and lips. Kammerer knocked his goggles askew and one eye instantly flushed red.

"Mike, lie still on the kitchen floor and cross your wrists behind you. If you don't do as you're told, I'll empty the rest of this can into both eyes and you'll go blind."

Kammerer retched and lay down in his own vomit, hands behind him. Nolan looped a zip tie around his captive's wrists and snugged the plastic strip. Another set went around the HL man's ankles. Nolan bent down and removed Kammerer's goggles, exposing the man's good eye to the awful fumes. Around the Air National Guardsman reservist's mouth went another half of a calico dishrag. Nolan applied two wraps of packing tape to secure the gag and tied Kammerer to the base of the kitchen island. The man's eyes streamed and his breathing still came in gasps.

"If you move or make a noise while I'm gone, I will bleed you like a hog."

Nolan fished a new can of bear mace out of his duffel. Glock in his right hand, Nolan prepared to imitate Kammerer's return with a casual bounce down the carpeted steps leading to the basement. He opened the door and received a shock: the lights were out. They were on when Kammerer came up. Nolan jerked back from the open door in time to avoid a single bullet that buried itself high in the kitchen's far wall, followed by two more through the plaster next to the door frame. The reports were muted: Johnson had a suppressor. Nolan backed away another step.

"Tony! It's Bob Nolan. I'm teamed up with Ryder. I don't want to fight. I need the woman and you're free to go. Just send her up." To Nolan's own ears, he sounded like an unconvincing Darth Vader through his breathing apparatus.

"She can't walk," Johnson said. "She's also in China's Ministry of State Security and possesses top secret information. I need to keep working on her."

"No, you don't. I work for POTUS and we're stopping Higher Love and arresting the leadership. You don't want to be mixed up in this. If you don't believe me, call Ryder and he'll confirm it. Higher Love is a treasonous organization. You're an American hero. Don't throw that away."

"The head of Black Ice recommended these people. He's an ultra-patriot."

"No, he's not," Nolan said. "He's part of a right-wing conspiracy to end democracy and replace it with a military dictatorship. Let's declare a truce: no guns and no violence while we talk. I'll show you some things online, and if you want to speak with General Payne, I can arrange that too."

"And what happens if I'm not convinced?" Johnson asked.

"I'll come back upstairs, we'll go back to our guns and may the best man win." Nolan texted Payne to call Johnson's cell ASAP.

The basement lights came on and there was Johnson at the bottom of the stairs, right arm still holding a fancy automatic with an infrared scope and a six-inch ventilated extension.

"You have fifteen minutes. Come on down." Johnson fiddled with his watch and three beeps sounded in succession.

"I have your two friends hogtied up here," Nolan said.

"Leave 'em be. We'll be done soon enough."

Nolan stepped onto the top step and shut the kitchen door behind him. "I'm stripping to my shorts. My clothes are covered in bear spray and I want to take off this mask."

"Oh, I thought you were channeling Reggie Ledoux down in the bayou."

"I'd love to talk *True Detective* with you over a scotch, but right now I need to see Kaili."

"I'm not starting from scratch. I've been persuading your girlfriend to cooperate. I found out that China supports Higher Love, but she's babbled nonstop—half of it in Chinese—and it's hard to make headway. There's a tie-in to North Korea based on her assignment in

Pyongyang. I also know that she wants to kill Mr. Love for kidnapping her. It seems she thought she'd be asking the questions today."

"Let me see her. Does she need medical attention?"

"If I stop, she'll be fine other than sore fingers. I don't like carving the pretty ones. It violates my sense of aesthetics."

"Let's go see how she is," Nolan said.

"Let's put a price tag on friendship," Johnson said. "How much is she worth to you? My being a patriot, I will honor our truce if General Payne calls to confirm your credentials."

"Let me understand. You'll stop interrogating Yu, upset your employers at Higher Love, and leave me alone because of patriotism, but you still want money for handing her over?"

"There's nothing unpatriotic about a finder's fee. I have a valuable commodity and I'm foregoing fifty thousand dollars by abandoning this assignment. I've also put a price on my head if Suzie Wong and you are right about Higher Love."

Nolan ground his teeth. "I'll pay you thirty thousand cash up front, and wire another seventy thousand into your account when we're away from this house."

Johnson's cell rang. His conversation with Payne was short, forceful and largely one-sided, with the former Ranger's contributions consisting of a rapid chain of "Yes, sirs" and "No, sirs."

Johnson shrugged and put the phone into his pocket. "He never was one for small talk, but he said you work for the executive branch on above-top-secret matters. He also confirmed that we're in Boerne. We'd best conclude our business and depart before all hell lands on our heads."

"Thirty thousand now, seventy thousand tonight for a healthy Yu, and you're out of the fight here. I don't want to end up facing you a second time."

"That sounds like an unreasonable prohibition on a man trying to earn a living. But another fifty would put me on the sidelines until at least the end of the month."

That was a lot of money to pay a man who wouldn't promise to not come back after him in ten short days. But Nolan shrugged and agreed, and they shook hands. Though they were both wearing latex gloves, Nolan had to resist the urge to wipe his palm on his boxers.

Johnson worked a keypad and a reinforced steel door opened. This was no basement workshop. Kammerer or his sponsors had paid for a soundproof medical facility with oscilloscopes, heart monitors, sensors, lights and all manner of medical equipment. Uninterruptible battery-driven power supplies lined the near wall, while overhead an HVAC filtered undesirable organisms out the air supply. There were four beds at one end with an operating station, a pharmacy and supplies section, and the admin and interrogation area up front.

Kaili sat strapped to a chair bolted to the floor, head down and either asleep, dead or exhausted. Her left hand was palm down on a table, leather constraints immobilizing her wrist and forearm. She lacked the nails on her first three fingers. The pliers holding the most recent prize lay on the blood-covered table.

Against all common sense, Nolan still had feelings for this dangerous and amazing woman. He ran to her side and touched her shoulder. "Kaili, it's Bob. Can you hear me? You're free. We're getting out of here."

Kaili shook her head and moaned in a low, hoarse voice full of pain. With shaking hands Nolan fumbled with her restraints. Johnson knelt and unlocked the shackles on her ankles.

"She'll be groggy for hours unless I give her an antidote that will have her up and around with barely a hangover. What about the thirty in cash?"

"It's upstairs in the kitchen. Circulated hundreds, rubber-banded and street-ready."

Kali celebrated her newly won mobility by vomiting on Nolan's bare leg. Naked save for his boxers, he felt particularly unclean. Johnson laughed and suggested that Nolan rinse off using the hose next to the abattoir's drain in the center of the room.

Johnson found a pill on the side table and gave it to Kaili with a cup of water. Nolan took extra care to spray the bile from between his toes. Dropping the hose and closing the spigot, he turned around to find Kaili on the floor with her back to him as she straddled the shoulders of an unmoving Johnson. What on earth?

Nolan sprinted over to find her right hand clenched around a syringe with her thumb on the depressed plunger and the needle up to the hilt in Johnson's neck. He was stopped cold by the combination of hatred and triumph in her glazed eyes. "What did you do?" he asked.

Her voice was slurred and hoarse. "I watched him. I saw him load five grams of sodium thiopental into this syringe. He said he would use it to kill me if I did not cooperate. Now he is the one who will die."

A tumult of thoughts and emotions poured over Nolan, relief occupying the top spot. "We have to go. Can you walk?"

"No. You must carry me. Take the camera." She made a broad wave with her unmaimed right hand. Nolan spotted the camera on a tripod, red light on and recording the last few minutes' activities. Nolan's mind shifted into flight mode, and he left Kaili's side to plunder the pharmacy in search of a mixture of medications and bandages to protect and repair her wounds. He confirmed that Johnson was unconscious and relieved him of keys, wallet, questions list and phone. He carried Kaili up the steps, told her to hold her breath and shut her eyes, and walked through the kitchen and onto the patio. He lowered the China spy down until she was in a shaded deck chair. Nolan gathered the rest of the contraband from downstairs and reaffixed the breathing apparatus before dealing with Kammerer.

Mike Kammerer found himself naked with his contaminated clothes cut off and left behind. Nolan used a wheelbarrow from the side yard and deposited him in the back of Johnson's black Ford Expedition. Kaili lay across the back seat, drinking water between groans. Nolan's enlarged collection of weapons joined Johnson's arsenal up front, with phones and wallets and anything of use from the pest control van. Out of his duffel, he pulled a set of clean clothes. Nolan left his fragrant boxers hanging from the antenna of the exterminators' van.

"We're leaving. Do you need anything?" Nolan asked.

"Shlutecave! Purff!" Kaili slurred.

"I don't understand."

"Shlutecave! Purff. BMMU in there."

Suitcase and purse in the BMW. *Of course.* He fetched the Tumi roller and Kate Spade bag and threw them in the back to keep their increasingly agitated prisoner company.

"We need to find a place where we can interrogate Kammerer. You rest if you can," he said to Kaili as he started the engine and dialed Ryder's number.

CHAPTER TWENTY-SIX

FAIR PLAY

OUTSIDE PLACERVILLE, CALIFORNIA

The voice over the intercom told the three Nolans to gather in the far corner of the interrogation room. After they complied, the sergeant came in with sidearm drawn and bottles of water cradled in his bandaged left arm. He scooped up the used paper plates and backed toward the door.

"So, it's down to just you," Bert said. He'd only discerned indistinguishable raised voices and two thuds, but that was enough to connect the dots now there was only one of them visible.

Washington slowed at the entrance. "Toilet break will be in one hour so long as there's no talking in Chinese."

"Our father is a multimillionaire," Mei Ling said. "He'll pay for our safe release if you drop us at a police station." She tried on a coy smile, but it didn't fit the mood.

"I can't do that," Washington said. "Each sentry group has different assignments. The guards outside won't recognize me, and we'd be dead before I started the engine."

"Just call the FBI or police. Help us and we'll pay you and put in a good word."

"I don't have any comms devices, and if I did, I still wouldn't do it. You don't understand, but this cause is way bigger than you or me. It's about saving the United States. America needs strong leadership from competent men more than it needs elections. Higher Love will bring that change, and Love will lead our country back to greatness as America's Caesar."

To Mei Ling's ear, it sounded like a kid reciting Sunday school catechism.

"My husband will pay you one hundred thousand dollars," Joanie said, "if you show me the bodies of those men who wanted to rape my daughter."

"They're not dead, just locked away."

"Kill them and the money's yours, and you don't even have to let us go. We'll never tell who did it either. We can pretend they were playing with a grenade and it went off, or whatever other idea you have."

At this statement, both Bert and Mei Ling checked to see if Mom was kidding. She was not.

"I'm a soldier," Washington said. "I heard what they said, and will advise our master sergeant. He has the authority to order them executed for such offenses."

The front door to the house opened and everyone jumped in surprise. It was Sergeant Murtagh. "We need to put them on a plane. Where are the other two?"

"In confinement for plotting the murder of one captive, and the rape of the two women. I put them downstairs in solitary."

"Leave 'em be. They'll starve in a week. All right you three, let's move it. We roll out in one."

* * * * *

MUSTANG CIRCLE, AMBER CREEK, TEXAS

Ryder and his Burma commandos were headed for San Antonio via El Paso with an ETA of one a.m. He had been pleased to hear Nolan's voice, and with a little rummaging through his de-fogged memory, came up with Will Tanner. The retired gunnery sergeant had recently returned from Afghanistan where he'd worked as a contractor after putting in his twenty. Nolan had said it was a grand idea, but could Ryder find him an address and call ahead? He was driving the deceased Tony Johnson's SUV with a tortured Yu Kaili in the backseat and a naked, bound and gagged Higher Love official in the rear. On balance, Ryder found it a reasonable request. As luck would have it, Tanner had planned a quiet night at home, and he recalled Bob Nolan from the DEA safehouse in Rangoon.

Once Nolan had Tanner's address tapped into Google Maps, he began to breathe again. Thirty miles was little more than a half-hour in light weekend freeway traffic. He had the windows down to blast away the bear spray that Kammerer had dragged into the vehicle. Kaili lay flat on her back, semiconscious and mumbling in Mandarin from time to time. Her tortured left hand lay flat against her stomach, fingers splayed. Kammerer was in the way back and occasionally flopped like a fish on a hot boat deck. Ryder hoped for Kammerer's sake that he wouldn't mar Kaili's suitcase or designer handbag as she had quite the temper.

Tanner had done well for himself, a two-story home on a quarter-acre plot with an attached garage. He'd had the foresight to move his pickup onto the street. The garage door clanked down as soon as Nolan cut the engine: someone was waiting.

Will Tanner was in his early fifties with a bronzed and wrinkled complexion from decades outdoors. His broad nose and broader shoulders hinted at large-bodied forebearers, a mixture of Native American, Mexican and European blood speaking to five generations in the Lone Star State. His smile split the gloom as he reached through the driver's window to engulf Nolan's hand. "I understand from Ryder your'n need of assistance. I'm pleased to help. Do you need a hand with the little lady?"

Kaili walked unassisted into the kitchen, where Tanner administered first aid from a giant trauma kit. The retired sergeant had a pot of chili simmering on the back burner, and once Kaili's fingers were bandaged, the new arrivals made short work of it. While they ate, Tanner led a gagged, bound and naked captive down into the basement.

Kaili painstakingly plinked at her phone with one hand.

"Can you talk?" Nolan asked. "Higher Love has my wife and children. I have to capture Love and make a trade. You came here to meet him. Where is he? Who is he?"

"I don't know his name," Kaili said. "I was to meet him tonight. I must send a message first, then I can speak."

"Do you have people in the area? We will need help. The FBI knows I'm in San Antonio and they'll be looking."

"I requested two men earlier this morning. Yes, I have a message. They're in San Antonio. What is this address?"

Nolan looked at her with fresh eyes: no makeup, both cheeks bruised, bloodied lip and still sporting curves to die for. He remembered the last time he'd seen her in Sri Lanka. She'd been his captive, but he had been surrounded by a posse of Ministry of State Security and PLA soldiers awaiting her order to kill him. As two foot soldiers laboring on different sides of the battlefield, he felt closer to her than he'd imagined he would. Against his better judgment, Nolan gave her Tanner's Mustang Circle street number and she punched it into her phone.

Tanner walked back. "I tied him to the pool table and told him if he pissed on the felt, he'd feel a cue up his ass." Tanner washed his hands and pulled two beers out of the fridge, twisted the caps off with his meathook fingers and pushed one across to Nolan as he took a seat.

Nolan savored the IPA after the chili, the stress and realization that he'd given Kaili maybe the last address he'd ever occupy. "I can't thank you enough for letting us use your home. At a minimum, it's kept me free long enough to try to capture the man who had my family kidnapped. The person strapped to your pool table is someone important in an organization called Higher Love. He may know the name of the leader, Mr. Love. Love's in San Antonio tomorrow, and probably right now."

"He arrived today, according to Kammerer," Kaili said. "I want my people to question him. We'll learn how much he knows." She appraised Nolan through clear eyes. "Why the brown hair?"

"It's a disguise, I guess."

"And just who might your people be, ma'am?" Tanner asked.

"I am a senior intelligence officer in China's Ministry of State Security. These men are MSS operatives sent to provide personal security. China opposes Higher Love and wishes to see Mr. Love captured and jailed. I assure you, our two countries' interests are aligned."

"How well do you know this woman?" Tanner asked Nolan. "Can she be trusted?"

"Bob is the father of my seventeen-month-old son, Ying Sheng," Kaili said.

Tanner winced.

"It's complicated," Nolan said. "We were closer once than we are now, but Kaili's an honorable person and wouldn't harm someone who's provided hospitality."

"Spare me the noble savage shit," Tanner said. "Why don't I just pick up the phone and call the police? Then everyone can hunt Love together."

"Kaili killed her torturer at the house we just fled," Nolan said. "I'm driving his vehicle and it's loaded with weapons. And there's Michael Kammerer, the man in your basement. By the time he's charged, lawyered up and questioned, Love will be long gone even if Kammerer cooperates. My family dies at noon tomorrow unless I have Love or turn myself over to his organization. We're playing for mortal stakes. I understand if you'd rather we went elsewhere." Nolan finished his beer and made to rise from the table.

Tanner's long arm reached out and grabbed Nolan by the elbow. "Sit back down. I won't pretend I'm comfortable having a spy from the People's Republic of China in my kitchen waitin' on two more spies to bleed a prisoner on a new pool table, but I'm good as long as Ryder tells me it's the right thing. If you'll excuse me, I'll make a call." Tanner's request sounded like an order, and Nolan stayed put as the big man left the room.

"I'm glad we are alone," Kaili said, fixing Nolan with those obsidian eyes. "There will soon be civil war in the United States. Once you free your family, come with me to China to meet Ying Sheng. He looks just like you. Then you can decide whether to raise your son with me or return to chaos."

Of all the things he didn't need, a paternity guilt trip conversation had to rank in the top three. Time to shift directions. "Tell me what business China has or had with North Korea and Higher Love."

* * * * *

THE WHITE HOUSE

"It's irresponsible that you lost an FBI car on the Louisiana border. It's unacceptable that the trace on the *New York Times* IP address bore fruit an hour after the kidnappers had abandoned their house, disappearing who knows where. It's—"

"Mr. President, if I could address these one at a time," General Payne said.

"Don't interrupt me! You come to my office on a Saturday evening to tell me there's no trace of anyone at the Higher Love compound north of San Antonio. Am I missing something?"

"It's immaterial where Samuel Hecker is, sir. He's headed to San Antonio."

"Yes, and if you'd maintained visual surveillance, he would have led us straight to Nolan."

"Mr. President, we are operating with the uncertain reliability of the local law enforcement personnel within these varied jurisdictions."

"General, that's doublespeak for you didn't have anyone you trusted to put on Hecker's tail, correct?"

"Yes, sir," Payne acknowledged. "As for the IP address search, the team did a commendable job in identifying the most likely targets— remote properties with two or more vehicles parked outside—but the Q-Group reached the Placerville location an hour late." He went on the brief the President on what they had found in the Boerne house and how they were flying forensics experts from Quantico to the site.

"It's peculiar," Payne continued, "because the door to the dungeon was armored, yet it was open. No bodies and no blood suggest that either Nolan had the passcode or the occupants voluntarily opened the door and left with him. We have to reconsider our prior assumption that Nolan isn't cooperating with HL. They have his family, so anything is possible. I suggest we consider him potentially hostile until proven otherwise, sir."

"And we have no idea what Nolan's driving, no ability to track his phone, and no idea of where he went?"

"No, sir," Payne acknowledged. "We're checking to see if Johnson's vehicle is at his home in Houston. If not, Nolan may be riding with him."

* * * * *

MUSTANG CIRCLE, AMBER CREEK

"I can tell you nothing about Higher Love until I receive instructions from President Liu," Kaili said.

"You've just confirmed that China either supports—or did support—Higher Love's planned military takeover in the US," Nolan replied. "From what Johnson said, it seems North Korea is also involved. Is Higher Love paying China to have North Korea attack the US as a pretext for launching the coup?"

Kaili examined her bandaged fingers. Her phone chirped and she used her right hand to unlock it and read.

The bounce in Tanner's step faltered when he walked back into the kitchen and saw the tense couple. As a divorcee, he knew the vibe.

"Ryder said you work for the President," Tanner said "and that whatever you do is in the best interests of the United States even if it seems like the exact opposite. He also said you CIA types couldn't tell a straight story to save your lives. Be that as it may, I have a bad feeling about you two. When the fireworks start, you're out and I'm off the team. But for the time being, USMC Gunnery Sergeant, retired, William Tanner at your service." He pulled two more IPAs out of the fridge. Nolan waved his off.

"I told Ryder that when I heard you were in town, I thought you were here for Coulter," Tanner added.

Coulter? "Frank Coulter's in San Antonio?"

"He will be at least tomorrow. I was planning on heading to Camp Stanley for the ceremony. I have the invitation on my phone." Tanner pulled up a battered cell phone with a cracked screen and used frankfurter-sized appendages to navigate. "Here we go. 'Sunday, August 21 at 11:00, Camp Stanley parade ground please join former Vice President David Marmot as he leads the commemoration of the fiftieth anniversary of the expulsion of Che Guevara–led Cuban soldiers from the Congo. A twenty-six-year-old SEAL, Frank Coulter, led anti-Castro CIA recruits and joined with 'Mad Mike' Hoare's 5 Commando battalion mercenaries in one of the world's most secretive and successful anticommunist insurgencies. Mr. Coulter went on to serve his country for more than forty more years, most recently in senior roles in the Central Intelligence Agency.

Refreshments and a light lunch will be served. Parking is limited, so please RSVP early.'"

Tanner spared a glance at Kaili. "Sorry, honey. That's why Africa didn't end up commie." Turning to Nolan, he added, "I received the invitation a few weeks back and dug a little online. Your buddy Coulter and his anti-communist Cubans led a ragtag group they'd recruited from Hoare for their navy and fought along the shores of Lake Tanganyika in 1965-1966. Che had over one hundred veteran Cuban soldiers, plenty of arms and hundreds of recruits. Outgunned and outnumbered, young Coulter and *los Cubanos* did a great job ridding the Congo of scum."

"Yes," Kaili countered, "which led to the reign of the murderous kleptocrat Mobutu Sese Seko, and decades of genocides that continue to this day."

"That may be so, ma'am, but he was no communist," Tanner said.

"Stop it," Nolan said. "Don't you see? Coulter is Mr. Love. It's the only explanation that fits."

"Let me call a couple people at Camp Stanley," Tanner said. "If Coulter's in town, chances are he'll be on base."

Nolan's burner vibrated. Hecker was close and wanted an address. Nolan complied.

The front doorbell rang. Kaili looked up. "Those will be my men."

* * * * *

OUTSIDE CAMP STANLEY, SAN ANTONIO

Coulter hadn't decided whether Frank Coulter IV should attend Sunday's ceremony. Assisted by a stiff glass of bourbon, he looked over Burge's stack of papers.

The colonel returned from the kitchen with a bowl of pretzels. "The Midwest Depot is understaffed; it's getting shut down at the end of September. Everything in those four warehouses is being moved to different locations. Too many investigative reporters wrote about the Midwest Depot being at Stanley, and the brass decided to spread the weapons elsewhere to keep the Nosy Neds at bay. The first move starts after Labor Day. In the meantime, I'm operating with a skeleton crew."

Coulter jotted down notes as he read through the inventory list. Ten minutes later, he adjusted his reading glasses. "Looks like one hunnerd forty-four AKs and thirty thousand rounds missing, forty-eight WY-91 hand grenades, and a dozen PLA night-vision goggles."

"Why only a dozen NVGs if they've stolen a gross of AKs and all that ammo?"

"My guess is only a dozen men are in on the action, and the rest is for show, or maybe another op. Do you have the names of the A-team in camp?"

"It's towards the bottom of the pile," Burge said. "I checked the DOBs and they're all too young for me to have commanded them."

Coulter flicked through the pages. "Dick, did you actually look at this?"

Burge glanced up from the sports section of *USA Today*. "Not really. I was in the warehouses until I went to the airport to pick you up. We'll be back at the inventory count tomorrow morning at 08:00, break for the ceremony and hit it again after lunch."

"Here are six surnames of your newest Green Berets on temporary, classified assignment to Camp Stanley: Park, Lee, Kim, Nam, Chan and Zu."

"Let me see that," Burge said. "My goodness, the biggest clue was right here. I'll call our head of HR and have her pull their personnel records."

"Don't bother," Coulter said. "I'll send it to Payne. Most of the time he's a sharp stick in my eye, but tonight he'll be happy to hear from me. He'll find out what's goin' on."

* * * * *

MUSTANG CIRCLE, AMBER CREEK

The two fit Asians in their late twenties introduced themselves as Eck and Meng and shook hands with Nolan and a wary Tanner. Kaili briefed them in their mother tongue, and they returned to the car to reenter two minutes later with cases not unlike Gunny's first-aid kit. Nolan would bet his eyeteeth that the contents erred on the side of trauma creation, not prevention.

Tanner led his guests downstairs to a sparsely furnished but functional game room with pool, darts, ping-pong and draft beer on offer. A turntable, Pioneer HPM 100 tower speakers, Marantz amp and a crate of classic rock vinyl albums rounded out the 1970s vibe. Farrah Fawcett and Cheryl Tiegs posters tacked to the veneer paneling on either side of the neon beer light completed the retro look.

One of Kammerer's restraints was a ratchet strap across his neck. He had another across his chest with his hands still tie-tied behind him. A nylon cord secured each ankle, pulling the feet wide apart and accentuating the vulnerability of his groin.

The men from China's Houston consulate unpacked a car battery and alligator clip-tipped cables. The gagged man whipped his head back and forth as he emptied his bladder.

Tanner walked up with a pair of scissors. "Before we came downstairs, this lady wanted to run twelve volts between your johnson and your nipples to put you in a talkative frame of mind. I think it's a marvelous idea, particularly since you helped pull out her fingernails earlier today. But this is a new pool table, so I talked her into giving you one chance to tell the truth. If you lie or resist, you'll never be able to use your cock or balls again. Nod if you promise to tell the truth."

Kammerer shook his head like it would fall off. Tanner handed the scissors to Kaili and stepped away. She cut the tape and dishrag, and ripped both off his face. Kammerer's eyes, nose, mouth and chin blazed red where the bear spray had burned.

"I don't know the details," Kammerer said. "All I did was build out the basement to Higher Love's specifications. They asked to use the house a week ago, so I took time off work. I'd never seen Johnson before, or the other person HL sent. I don't even know his name."

"Who's Love? Where is he?" Nolan asked.

Nolan's calm question didn't capture Kammerer's attention and he continued to babble. "I was asked to run the video session in the basement. I'm not a tor—EYEEEEE!"

Kaili stepped back to admire her handiwork. One alligator clip held Kammerer's penis sideways like an earthworm in a grackle's beak. With another graceful move, she'd affixed a second clip to the man's scrotum. She spoke in Mandarin and one of her colleagues spread the jaws of the last free clip over the battery's post.

"Nooo! Nooo! He's staying at the Mokara Hotel tonight. It's downtown near the Alamo. I don't know his name. That's all I know. I swear. I swear!"

"What does the name Frank Coulter mean to you?" Nolan asked.

Kammerer's eyes narrowed in concentration. He gritted his teeth and shook his head. "I don't recognize the name. I really, truly don't know the name." His body tensed in dread.

Nolan looked at Kaili. "I believe him. I'll head to the Mokara. Gunny, do you want to help me kidnap the world's most dangerous man?"

Tanner stood transfixed as Kaili's second assistant responded to her instructions by reinserting the gag and taping it in place. Kammerer's violent gyrations didn't make this an easy task. No sooner had Meng stepped back than Eck relaxed the spring-loaded jaws and closed the circuit for several seconds. Kammerer's body went rigid and he screamed silently with all his being. At Kaili's nod, Eck removed the clip and Kammerer went limp. The smell of roasted meat wafted up from the pool table.

"Let's go," Tanner said. "I've seen this movie before."

"Don't worry," Nolan said. "I'll buy you another pool table."

"I might need a new house after she's done with him. Did you catch the look in her eyes?"

"Oh, yes. I've seen it before." Nolan's phone thrummed in his pocket with a new text message. Hecker had arrived. *For fuck's sake, let me in.*

CHAPTER TWENTY-SEVEN

HOME SWEET HOME

SATURDAY AUGUST 20: MOKARA HOTEL, SAN ANTONIO

"More wine, Mr. Vice President?"

"Yes, the Opus One."

The sommelier obliged. Outside the picture window, tourists traipsed along the banks of the sparkling San Antonio River. In the private room, all was quiet.

The host clinked his dessert spoon against the rim of his wine glass. "Gentlemen, your attention please." He dismissed the waiters with a wave. "Give us the room."

Despite his eighty-six years, when the former veep rose to his full 6'3" height he made an imposing figure with white hair, an aquiline nose and deep blue eyes. "Thank you, Daryl, for arranging yet another wonderful evening with those committed to our cause. Tonight, we stand on the dawn of the new age, the next and best chapter in the history of this great country. The road has been long, but the outcome never in doubt, not with the staunch patriots in this room.

"In my address tonight, I want to lift the curtain on what you may expect in the future. Even those of long acquaintance may well be shocked, but we who seek to change the world must be bold. The great, misunderstood Thomas Jefferson wrote to James Madison, 'A little rebellion now and then is a good thing, and as necessary in the political world as storms in the physical.' Bismarck was less literary in 1862 when he addressed the Prussian parliament, observing, 'Not through speeches and majority decisions will the great questions of the day be decided ... but by iron and blood.' Accordingly, I shall be brief.

"Hitler should have won WWII and occupied the United States. That would have saved Americans another sixty years of corrupt democracy and ineffectual government. Two generations later, the true heirs to the Founding Fathers—dare I say it, white Americans— would rule. No American troops would be based abroad except in resource extraction zones. On the home front, there would be no violent crime or unemployment. Treasure squandered in the name of woolly-headed environmental causes instead would have fueled America's industrial rebirth. Those here who already accept the truth of my words, I beg you to remain patient, for our time will soon be at hand. Those of you who are disheartened, I bid you make haste and depart this gathering and this nation."

Two of the fourteen attendees filed out in silence, eyes down. The former vice president watched them with disdain.

"As in Rome, the state will seize the property of traitors, and family members not executed will toil in servitude. But the present is a worry, I must confess. In less than six months, a new president will be sworn in and send the current occupant of the White House back to Chicago to incite library sit-ins in keeping with his community organizer skillset.

"The forthcoming election provides us with an opportunity to further demonstrate the fatal flaw of our Constitutional system of government: anyone qualified to lead this country would be a fool to aspire to elected office. In 1776 there were two and one-half million free, white inhabitants of the thirteen colonies. Among them were Franklin, Jefferson, Adams, Hamilton, Jay, Hancock, Madison, Marshall, Monroe and Washington. That's just ten—I could name another dozen including Henry, Paine, Burr, Marion, the Lees of Virginia—and yet today the US population exceeds three hundred and twenty million, and we would be hard-pressed to name a half-dozen national politicians of high moral standing. That's a disturbing fact, yet universally accepted because our corrupt Electoral College and lobbyist-ridden system cannot be fixed. Instead, America requires a new model: empire."

A chorus of "Hear, hears!" rang out as plutocrats hoisted their glasses.

Encouraged, Marmot continued. "We cannot reverse overnight the unfortunate dilution of the Founding Father's bloodlines by social inferiors and unfathomably misguided immigration policies, but I promise you that the America at the end of the twenty-first century will be whiter, brighter and wealthier than the country we live in today. That is our pledge to our grandchildren and their grandchildren.

"Within the last forty-eight hours, under my orders, Higher Love moved to wartime footing. We are not at war, and, God willing, we may not need to fire a shot in anger. But make no mistake, it is war we wage to discredit the abomination who occupies the White House. The plan is well underway, and it will bring the secondary benefit of displaying China and its vassal North Korea as the perfidious states that they are. Second, we will ensure that Ginger is elected and then expose his treasonous actions and wholly compromised position via the blackmail we helped engineer. Our second great international rival, Russia, will suffer as a consequence of Ginger's humiliation. Third, we will birth the empire and return America to its rightful position as world leader, and purge the existing government of all elected and many appointed officials. May I live long enough to see the day, and with the support of you, the true believers, serve as your sovereign."

Marmot drew back his shoulders as he raised his wine glass. "To America's empire!" he said and basked in their rapturous applause.

* * * * *

OUTSIDE CAMP STANLEY AND WASHINGTON, D.C.

"General, Frank Coulter here. I'm at Camp Stanley ahead of tomorrow's ceremony. I'm grateful for the opportunity, and Colonel Burge tells me that I have you to thank for approving the flights to and from Dallas to permit my son to attend."

"Coulter, that's all well and good," Payne said, "but what does it have to do with the list of Special Forces operators you emailed me?"

"Someone in the Midwest Depot stole twelve dozen AK-47s of North Korea origin, plus thirty thousand rounds of ammo and nearly fifty PLA-issued hand grenades. They did it by manipulating security camera footage and altering the base's arms inventory database, and had insiders posted to security on the back gate. Those sentries are AWOL. A direct action team was posted to Camp Stanley for classified training ten days ago. Half the names are of Chinese or Korean ethnicity. Either this group works for North Korea or China, or someone tried hard to make it appear that way. Does any of this make sense, sir?"

"Yes, maybe it does. This is valuable information. I'll alert the president of your contribution."

"You can do more than that, sir," Coulter said. "I have two FBI agents outside the door. Allow me to leave Colonel Burge's home. He'll follow the next SF-operator who departs the base, and I can accompany him."

"Leave the fieldwork to younger men. The agents and you stay where you are. Neither Burge nor you is to share your suspicions with anyone on the base since we don't know how badly we've been penetrated. I also wonder if you're part of Higher Love and this revelation isn't misdirection."

Coulter drew an indignant breath. "I'm not part of Higher Love and have never been. I spent my career in service to our country and its institutions. Some may take issue with my methods, but never my motives."

Payne considered Coulter's mixture of outrage and sincerity. Coulter was an arch manipulator, the mastermind of the MH370 hijacking and the architect of DCI Perkins's 2014 murder. With Obama's backing, Nolan had uprooted most of Coulter's spook network, but like dandelions, no matter how weed killer was applied, there were always a few left behind. "Fair enough. I apologize for the insinuation. Let's start afresh. What's your impression of the depth of Higher Love's infiltration of the CIA, FBI and the rest of the intelligence community?"

"Maybe a few at the top, and more at the bottom, but I doubt it's nearly as many as you suspect. Most intel officers love this country and work to support the Constitution, flawed though it might be. Higher Love's contempt for the democratic principles sickens my ex-colleagues and me. The regular armed forces, including Special Operations, would be more fertile recruiting grounds for HL. Let me take the Camp Stanley SF men into custody. Allow me to interrogate them. Then you can judge my loyalty based on the results."

"Why haven't you mentioned Higher Love in our prior conversations?" Payne asked. "Q-Group would have handled it, and it could have earned you a pardon."

"Too many have people died for running afoul of Higher Love. Unlike former DCI William Colby, I never pissed in Mr. Love's soup, and unlike Bill, I'm still alive. The people who fancy themselves Higher Love–types compete to impress the top man with the purity of their beliefs and the brutality of their actions. You don't want to be on the wrong side of them folks unless you take all of them down at once. Let me ask a question. Where is Bob Nolan in all this?"

"Nolan? Bob Nolan has nothing to do with Higher Love's plot."

"Are you certain?" Coulter asked. "Unless my hunch is wrong, that kerfuffle in the desert earlier this week involved Nolan. If you weren't out to kill him, and I didn't send the team, that leaves Higher Love. If Nolan's still on the loose, either Love is after him, or Nolan's a mole and the attack was a smokescreen. No wonderin' you can't catch Love: your top spycatcher may be a double."

"Nolan hates Love more than you could imagine," Payne said. "Trust me on that count. The situation's too delicate to detain anyone from the SF direct action team. I'll send reinforcements to the base, and we'll deal with the Green Berets tomorrow when we have a better idea of what they're up to. I'll run the names on your email and brief you on the outcome. Good work, Frank. If things work out, this might be your ticket back to the big city."

"Yes, sir. Thank you, General Payne. Good night, sir." Coulter hung up and turned to Burge. "As you thought, I'm still not goin' anywhere."

"While you were chattin' with the general, the motor pool called to say Captain Park and Warrant Officer Lee have requested the use of a vehicle. I approved, but told them to record their destination and stall five minutes until I can position myself outside the main gate. I'll let you know what I find."

"Don't worry 'bout me. I'll manage to keep busy."

* * * * *

MUSTANG CIRCLE, AMBER CREEK

Nolan ushered Hecker indoors and Hecker handed him a license plate, screwdriver and four screws and quipped, "My luggage." The two men embraced despite each man's being overdue for a shower.

"Can I offer you somethun to eat or drink?" Tanner asked.

Nolan remembered his manners and made introductions. Tanner showed Hecker to the kitchen and gave him a tour of the fridge. Then he excused himself to conduct a weapons inventory of Johnson's SUV.

Exhausted from his drive, Hecker updated Nolan on Don Randy (warrants issued, but still at large), Sophie and C. J. (safe in London) and his trip across half the country (only a single grand theft auto charge pending).

Nolan didn't know where to start but gave his friend the latest on the family and Higher Love fronts. "We have intel that Love is staying in a hotel downtown. Tanner and I were about to start out when you arrived. Take an hour to eat and take a nap, and you can join us."

* * * * *

Up from the basement came a hopeless scream muffled by the closed door. Hecker started to his feet and Nolan made a calming gesture. "That's Kaili. She's downstairs with two heavies from the MSS. They're interrogating an HL official I snatched earlier today. He and Tony Johnson were pulling out her fingernails when I intervened."

"Tony Johnson? How is he mixed up in this?"

"Was. Kaili killed him. This other man, Kammerer, wasn't so lucky. Kaili's giving him her undivided attention."

From downstairs came pitiful weeping followed by sobs.

"You finish up," Nolan said. "I'll go down and see if she's learned anything else other than the amount of current required to broil a pecker."

The smell of burned flesh, shit and fear assaulted Nolan's nose as he descended the steps. He called out to alert the occupants of his approach.

"I'll come to you," Kaili said. "We're on break until he regains consciousness. May I have a cup of tea?"

"I'll see if he has any." Nolan looked into those furious eyes and didn't need to ask: Kammerer wasn't leaving the basement in anything bigger than gallon-sized freezer bags. "Hecker's here. We're headed to the Mokara. Much as we could use the manpower, it would complicate matters if MSS officers formed part of the kidnap team."

"I agree. We should not be involved. That man does not know Mr. Love's name, only that he is older and a former senior government officer. He knew nothing beforehand about the plan to torture and interrogate me."

"That helps somewhat and fits with what we previously understood."

"One other thing," Kaili said. "The original Mokara reservation was for one night, departing Sunday. Kammerer was told to extend the checkout to Wednesday, but he was not provided with a reason."

"It's because Coulter thinks he'll have me in custody on Sunday through whenever they finish questioning and execute me. I'm to be flown to San Antonio for interrogation when I surrender in return for the release of my family."

"Are you sure it's Coulter? He has been under house arrest. I am under the impression Mr. Love travels freely."

"Oh, it's Coulter all right. He's the one receiving tomorrow's award and the only plausible suspect. Maybe his guards are in cahoots and he travels without anyone being aware?"

Behind them, they heard a truncated scream and laughter. "Sounds like he has awakened," Kaili said. "Do you have any final questions for him?"

"Yes, I'd like the name and background of the man who was in his living room."

"Are you coming back here once you kidnap Coulter?"

"Yes, I think it's best that we stick together," Nolan said. "You have the China card to play even though you're not under diplomatic cover. At least they won't burn the house down if you're inside. I need to see my family freed, and those who helped me pardoned. Then I'll turn myself in."

"Why?"

"I've committed too many crimes to count. It has to end some time."

"Let it end in China as a free man," Kaili said. "Take care—I'm not finished with you yet, Bob Nolan." She turned around and barked something in Mandarin as she retreated.

Nolan climbed the steps with heavy legs and a reeling brain.

* * * * *

As Nolan walked back into the kitchen, Hecker was taking the last bite of a gargantuan sandwich. He found a box of Lipton in the cupboard and started filling the kettle.

"Tanner wants to see you," Hecker said. "He's out in the garage. Apparently the late Mr. Johnson's Expedition used to belong to the Counter Terrorism Center before Homeland swallowed it. His custom ride housed many useful items."

Arrayed on the garage floor was enough weaponry to give Travis Ryder goosebumps. Three Glock 17s, six spare magazines, one 9mm pistol suppressor, two M-4s, a sniper rifle with an enormous night-vision scope, boxes of hollow point ammunition, two pairs of night-vision goggles, figure-eight rappelling devices, climbing harnesses, heavy gloves, ballistic vests, Petzl climbing helmets, balaclavas, KA-BAR knives, tie-ties, riggers tape, dynamic climbing rope, a stun gun, flashlights, infrared beacons, a satphone ... the list went on.

Tanner let his guest take it all in. "I put the best on the hood. Take a look at these babies." He handed Nolan what appeared to be a cross between half a hockey puck mold and a sculpture of a miniature stereo speaker.

Nolan hefted the black device and put its weight at two pounds. "What is it?"

"It's an M2 SLAM, a selectable lightweight attack munition. They're normally only used by Special Ops. It's like hooking an Alexa speaker up to a Claymore. You can detonate a SLAM using a timer, IR motion sensor, magnetics, cellphone or trip wire. Instead of ball bearings like the Claymore, it throws a slug of metal through two centimeters of armor at ten meters. Short of a main battle tank, one of these takes out every armored vehicle in the world. I've never seen one in the US."

"Tony was resourceful, that's for certain. How many do we have?"

"Two. If you need more, you'd have to be going for Fort Knox. Best you try to find out what room Coulter's in. I'll pull up the hotel floorplan on my PC and we'll sketch out a plan, but first I want to charge the stun gun and satphone."

Nolan was liking Tanner more and more. He went back into the kitchen to quiet the whistling kettle.

* * * * *

MUSTANG CIRCLE, AMBER CREEK AND THE MOKARA HOTEL

"Good evening. I'd like to speak with a hotel guest, Mr. Coulter."

"One moment, sir," the receptionist said. "Uh, I'm afraid there's no one registered under that name."

"Could you try Richard Burge, please?" Nolan asked.

"Again, no one by that name."

"Never mind. I would like to book a suite for tonight through Wednesday night. Can you tell me what you have available?"

"Yes, sir. Our spa rooms come with deluxe king beds, five hundred-fifty square feet and in-room Jacuzzis. Our rate is $469 a night plus tax."

"I'm traveling with two companions, friends but not family. Do you have anything larger, more luxurious? A friend stayed with you several months ago and said they were housed in a large suite with great views."

"You must mean the Bowie Suite, sir. That has two bedrooms, a sitting room, living and dining rooms, and full kitchen. It's $1,450 a night, sir, plus tax."

"That's the one. I'll take it."

"I'm sorry, it's not available until … until your last night with us, Wednesday, August 24."

"Dang. OK, I'd like to reserve the Bowie Suite for Wednesday night, but for the next three nights, I'll need three rooms. Do you have three rooms on the same floor with the same views?"

"Do they need to be Spa Rooms, sir?" she asked.

"No, any non-smoking room will do," Nolan said.

"All our rooms are non-smoking, sir. I have three rooms on the seventh floor. I have two rooms with river views like the Bowie, and one city view room across the hall. Will that do?"

"Yes, let me give you our details. We'll arrive within an hour. Thank you." Nolan hung up after supplying false names and assuring the woman that he would be prepaying in cash for the first night, so there was no need for credit card numbers.

* * * * *

CAMP STANLEY TO THE MOKARA HOTEL

The guardhouse called the base commander's cell and told him the Special Forces 18A and 180A had left Camp Stanley and were signed out until 09:00 Sunday. Colonel Burge suffered from diminished night vision, and even at the best of times, he wasn't a first-rate driver.

He lost the Ford Taurus at the second stoplight. *Damnit!* He knew where the SF men were headed, or at least where they said they were headed, and made a beeline for the Mokara. He arrived less than a half hour later in light traffic. He thought he'd beat the Special Forces pair as he'd sped on US-90, but how would he know unless he sat and waited?

He waved off the valet. There was a rare parking space down the road that Burge was able to squeeze into on the third try. By turning around in the front seat, he could see the hotel's front entrance under the streetlamps.

Captain Park and Warrant Officer Lee pulled up minutes later. The driver pressed a bill into the valet's hand and the two men walked into the lobby. Five minutes later, the same valet was back. Burge scribbled on a card, pulled a portrait of Ulysses Grant from his money clip and strode to where the valets kept car keys in a cabinet.

Given to command, Burge lacked the common touch. How to attract the valet's attention? A couple of half-hearted throat clearings did nothing, so he erred on the side of forcefulness. "Hey, you! Not you, you." Burges' extended finger-pistol pointed out his addressee having a smoke with another car jockey. Burge motioned the man over.

"Here's fifty dollars. I need you to do something for me. That last car you parked, the red Taurus: when the driver comes back and asks for his car, whoever is on duty calls me on this number. It's worth another fifty if I'm here before they drive off, understood? If you go off duty, you inform whoever takes your place."

The valet nodded. *Another jealous boyfriend.*

Burge walked up to the hotel entrance and dialed to find out what was up with Coulter.

* * * * *

MUSTANG CIRCLE, AMBER CREEK

Tanner hung up. "Coulter's not booked into the guest quarters at Camp Stanley, but he's in the logbook for Sunday and they're expecting him."

Hecker looked less sanguine than he had minutes before. "A friend in the FBI emailed to report that El Patron and his crew are in the wind. We need to finish this Love business and rearrange our priorities, or I have to prepare for a lifetime in hiding. You're in the same boat too."

"We have fourteen hours before I need to turn myself over to Higher Love," Nolan said. "But if we can pull this off, we'll track down and kill Randy next week."

"I'm confused," Tanner said. "An hour ago, I signed up to kidnap the 'most dangerous man in the world,' Mr. Love. And now I learn Don Randy is the person you're really after."

"There's a difference between dangerous and deadly. Higher Love will overthrow the government unless it's stopped. His people will torture or kill on command, but he won't hunt down and kill everyone in your family as part of a vendetta. Randy Dozier defends his turf through bribery, intimidation and extreme violence, and he's after both of us."

Tanner shook his head and took a beer out of the refrigerator. "It's a half hour to the Mokara. Can you hack into the hotel computer system on the drive down?"

Nolan nodded. "It'll take no more than an hour. Anyone in today and out Wednesday is a prospect. If we link the military to any of the prospects, it's a suspect. As a fallback, I reserved three rooms on the same floor as the big suite. It's booked for the right number of days too. Could be Coulter's in there pulling the strings while a strawman fronts HL."

"Let me visit my gun cabinet and pick out a few odds and ends," Tanner said.

"I'll tell Kaili we'll be awhile. I think they'll stay the night."

"Wonderful, fucking wonderful. I'm the host for China's secret service when they vacation in San Antonio."

CHAPTER TWENTY-EIGHT

HOTEL HORROR

SATURDAY AUGUST 20: DOWNTOWN, SAN ANTONIO

Traces of capsaicin irritated their mucus membranes on the thirty-minute drive to downtown. At Nolan's request, Tanner turned onto a side street two blocks short of the hotel. On the darkened sidewalk, Hecker and the retired gunnery sergeant reviewed basic weapons fundamentals—grip, trigger squeeze, front sight alignment, etc.—while Nolan worked his laptop propped on the hood. It was a tossup whether the ninety-plus air temperature or the engine block was pumping out more heat.

Nolan's hacking arrived at an almost suspiciously obvious answer. Of the hotel's ninety-nine rooms, the only matching check-in and check-out dates were for the Bowie Suite. The hotel had given the former vice president a thirty percent discount. That didn't seem fair, but the hotel's favoritism was low on Nolan's list of grievances.

"Sam, Gunny, come over here." The two men tucked weapons into their holsters and joined him. "The only booking that matches Kammerer's confession is the big suite, but it's booked by Vice President Marmot. Coulter's nowhere to be seen. I can't even find Coulter's name on commercial or military flights into San Antonio."

"Maybe Dapper Dave Marmot is Mr. Love," Tanner said.

Hecker scoffed. "The man is so dense he couldn't spell cat if you spotted him the 'C' and the 'A.'"

"I used to think that," Nolan said. "He always seemed to be the dumbest person in any room he walked into. But maybe, just maybe, he's played the long game ... forty or fifty years of hiding his light under a bushel."

"It's a fine theory, but what's the plan?" Tanner asked.

"If Marmot is Mr. Love, he must be bursting with confidence. Otherwise, why would he turn on China and have Kaili tortured and questioned? He knew there would be repercussions and didn't care. Or deciding to be present at my interrogation tomorrow. This violates every principle that kept him off everyone's radar for so long. Maybe he's ready to step out of the shadows and show everyone how brilliant he really is."

The other two men looked doubtful.

"I agree that whoever is Mr. Love is, he must have a serious ego," Hecker said. "But it's a big jump to point the finger at the big beaver."

"What do you have in mind?" Tanner asked.

"We insult his pride and prompt an unscripted response," Nolan said. "He'll be well-guarded, and we'll suffer casualties in a frontal assault. Chances are he'll either be killed in the attempt, or we'll cause so much noise the local police will arrive before we can escape. Gunny, you case the lobby. When you're done, slip the concierge a twenty and ask him where the veep dined tonight. If the lobby's clean, go downstairs and wait for me with Sam.

"Sam, park in the basement close to the elevator. I'll check in and collect the keys. When I'm done, if Gunny's no longer in the lobby, I'll meet you two at the Expedition. We'll sketch out the final plan and take it from there."

* * * * *

MOKARA HOTEL

Colonel Burge was surprised to see Park and Lee loitering in the lobby. It was after 23:00 and he figured they'd be upstairs conspiring. He retreated outside into the stifling heat to call Coulter and ask what he should do next. Before he could dial, a large black SUV pulled up and a retired Comanche war chief exited and quickstepped into the lobby. Ah-hah! This would be the military man Park and Lee were waiting for. Burge reversed course and followed the retired middle linebacker inside.

Five minutes later, a middle-aged triathlete-type with dyed brown hair, black-rimmed glasses and a laptop under one arm passed Burge inside the main entrance and made a beeline for the reception. He looked vaguely familiar, but Burge couldn't place his face. Meanwhile, Quanah Parker ignored the two Asian American officers, reconnoitered the lobby and schmoozed the concierge. A minute later, he'd disappeared into a stairwell.

Coulter answered but was disappointed to find Burge on the line instead of General Payne. "Three military men in a hotel lobby doesn't prove anything. Order a drink and wait them out. Follow 'em when they leave."

"What about you?"

"It's only been an hour. Payne said he'd call when he had the files on the dirty dozen."

* * * * *

Despite the *eau de* bear spray, Tanner rolled up the Expedition's windows. Nolan had the architectural layout of the seventh floor on-screen. The other two peered over the front seat as the hacker pointed out the Bowie Suite, Room 700.

"I have keys for 701 and 702 next door, plus 714 directly across the hall with a door that opens onto the guard's rear. Our provocateur has to be Sam because either Marmot or his guards might recognize me. Gunny, we need you in 714 because you'll have the flank of anyone coming out of the suite."

"It's a great idea, but he'll have a man outside his door," Tanner said. "I won't be able to walk by unchallenged with a duffel bag full of arms."

"Good point," Nolan said. "The hotel tops out at seven floors. But there's a health club on the roof, a small pool and a sundeck. Let me pull up the schematic. The northeast corner is where 700 is, so 714 is the northwest corner beneath the sundeck. Is that good or bad?"

"It should be fine," Tanner said. "Let me explain how it all fits together."

* * * * *

It was 23:30 and Hecker and Nolan had visited their hotel rooms. At their end of the hall, a man in a dark suit sporting an earpiece paid them no heed. That detail was enough to tip the balance of probability away from Coulter and toward Marmot. Nolan was disappointed that there wasn't a connecting door joining 700 and 701, which would have simplified matters. From his overnight bag, he withdrew an M2 SLAM and set the timer for 01:00. If Plan A went to hell, Love would still die tonight when a molten metal tore through the plasterboard and insulation before the behind-armor effects converted the occupants of 700 into Hamburger Helper.

Nolan stepped out of his room, turned away from the guard and saw Hecker waiting for the elevator down the hallway. "I'm headed down for a nightcap before they close the bar," Hecker said in a loud voice. "Care to join me?"

"Let's not overdo it," Nolan grunted to the DEA man when he drew near. Nolan exited the elevator on the sixth floor, then took the stairs to the roof. Hecker continued to the lobby. He aimed to drink a double and spill a single down his shirt to complete the effect.

Nolan found Tanner in the far corner of the roof above 714. The old Marine was already in his rappelling harness and testing the locking mechanisms on the carabiners. He had an unlit headlamp on. Nolan used a penlight to locate the weapons bag. Tanner had tied himself off onto a wrought iron rail. Nolan used the post as a pulley and belayed the heavy bag down once Tanner had reached the balcony. The old codebreaker spent a few minutes tidying up on the rooftop. In fifteen minutes, Marmot would either be in their hands or they'd be dead, but the finality of this still didn't excuse sloppiness.

* * * * *

Tanner's application of filthy lucre into the concierge's palm had elicited that the vice president's party had dined in a private room within the Ostara restaurant. Tanner passed this nugget along to Hecker. John Barleycorn could be a cruel master, and Hecker's glancing blows off the wall hinted that he'd had too many distilled beverages. "I wanna talk to the vice president!" Hecker announced in a loud slur.

The ramrod security man ignored the tipsy guest, eyes straight ahead.

Hecker staggered to a stop. "I'm serious. I know he's in there because I just had dinner in the Oshhstarrah downstairs, and he took the elevator to this floor. I wanna shake the hand of a man who, despite zero qualifications, sat a heartbeat away from the real deal for four years."

"Sir, it's late and the vice president has gone to bed. Could you please lower your voice?"

"Lower my voice? I'm not talking loud. I just want to compare dictionaries with Mr. Potato Head. You think he'd like to play me for a hundred bucks a word in a spelling bee? You can be the judge." Raising his voice, Hecker said, "Hey, Davey, how many 'e's' are there in 'idiotic'?"

Nolan opened the door to his room and stuck his head out. "Bill? Is that you?"

Hecker and Nolan heard raised voices behind the suite's closed doors.

"Whatsa matter, can't find your thesaurus? You know what that makes you, Marmot? A chicken. An idiot chicken. I like the phrase. I'll print it on a t-shirt and—"

Both doors to the suite flung open with another man in a suit gently restraining a silver-haired, red-faced patrician in a blue silk bathrobe. "Let me go! I need to tell this fool off!" Dave Marmot was very much in charge, and his reluctant guard stopped impeding progress. The former vice president stepped into the hallway to face down his accuser.

Hecker brushed past Nolan and disappeared into the open door to collect his weapon. Nolan's Glock was pointed down in his right hand as he stepped into the corridor. Behind the two guards and the veep, the door to 714 opened and Tanner stepped out wearing a black balaclava and pointing a suppressed pistol. A plastic pistol grip stuck up in the air a foot over Tanner's head.

"No one move," Tanner said. "Hands remain in view. Drop to your knees."

The veep instinctively took a step toward sanctuary. Nolan had the Glock on him and said, "Freeze or I'll shoot."

"One at a time," Tanner commanded the guards in his barracks baritone. "Use your left hands, two fingers, to remove your weapons and toss them toward me. You first," he said to the sentry closest to the suite. Tanner swept across the hall and blocked the double doors. Nolan could see for the first time that Gunny had a sawed-off shotgun resting in a leather scabbard, barrel pointed down between his shoulders.

The guards obeyed and kneeled. Tanner extracted Johnson's stun gun and zapped each guard at the base of his neck. The men collapsed without a sound, the second convulsing on the carpet for several seconds. Tanner waved Nolan up to the veep, dragged each guard back into the suite and shut the doors.

Hecker left Nolan's hotel room and jogged toward the elevator lobby to head off possible reinforcements. The elevators chimed and he disappeared.

Nolan inserted a wadded pair of sweat socks into the veep's mouth and tie-tied his hands behind his back. A quick frisk didn't turn up a phone. "Gunny, take a look on the desk or nightstand and see if you can find his phone or a computer. We need one or the other."

Tanner went inside the suite. The elevator chimed again.

Nolan hauled his prisoner to his feet and stared into Mr. Love's baleful eyes. When he looked up seconds later there were two men with pistols pointed at him.

"Drop your weapon!" an Asian man said from maybe ten meters away.

Nolan thought about putting a gun to Marmot's head, but it was a stupid play. He couldn't make good on his threat and still retrieve his family. So close and yet so far. He dropped the Glock.

"Are you all right, sir?" the second Asian asked, holstering his side arm as he rushed to render assistance.

Love sputtered as he tried to spit out the gag. He gestured with his head toward the suite. Tanner walked through the door with a phone in his left hand and saw a disarmed Nolan with hands raised. Tanner lobbed the phone at Nolan's feet and shot Marmot's caregiver with a copper jacketed bullet through the heart. The other soldier responded with two rounds from his Glock 19. Both struck Tanner in the torso and the big man dropped. Nolan was on his hands and knees and bringing up the Glock when Love's bare foot cracked him in the ribs. Nolan collapsed but held onto his weapon.

Marmot saved Nolan's life by flinging himself onto the old CIA agent's back and sinking his teeth into his shoulder. The remaining man didn't have a clear target and held fire. Nolan put a bullet between his eyes.

Nolan elbowed the old man in the ribs, spun to his right, and threw his weight backward. Marmot gasped for breath, pinned to the rug. Nolan sat up, swung around and shoved the barrel of his weapon under Marmot's chin.

"You wouldn't dare, Nolan. Your family will die," Marmot said.

Well, that erased any lingering doubt.

Nolan shoved the balled socks back into that treasonous mouth. Tanner was dead as were the two soldiers. From inside the suite, he heard a guard stirring. Weapons littered the hallway.

Nolan checked Tanner's body. He didn't have any ID, but Nolan took Gunny's phone and stun gun, plus Marmot's phone. Grabbing the elderly biter above the right elbow, Nolan said, "We're taking the stairs fast all the way to the basement. If you resist, run, say a word or fall down I will execute you. The FBI rescued my family an hour ago, so I don't care if you live or die. Let's go."

They were in the stairwell when Nolan's phone buzzed. *What in the hell?* He yanked Love to a stop and checked the screen. It was Hecker: he was out front. Hotel security had locked down the underground garage and Johnson's SUV was the last vehicle out. *Wonderful.* Walking the former vice president of the US out at gunpoint through the lobby on a Saturday night. The two men resumed their descent.

Those two Asian soldiers flashed through Nolan's mind. They weren't MSS: one of them had been either Korean or Japanese, but definitely not Chinese. They were relieving the two men for midnight sentry duty. Speaking of which, those two zapped guards would be up soon, maybe looking for their employer and surely calling for backup. *Keep moving.*

Both men were winded when they hit the lobby. Marmot chose this time to collapse, calling Nolan's bluff. Nolan wasn't surprised and rewarded the subterfuge with two electrodes to the neck and three seconds of five thousand volts. Mercifully, the lobby featured only hotel staff, plus a gray-haired man who used his phone to click a photo.

The woman behind reception disappeared. *That's a 911 call.* The concierge ducked down behind the counter and popped with a handgun like a barkeep in a Western. Nolan shot him in the right shoulder more due to luck than aim. The sound of the 9mm discharge was muffled by heavy drapes and thick rugs. Nolan dragged his unconscious captive across the lobby without further challenge.

Nolan could see the Expedition on the street just outside. Hecker stood next to it, stair-side doors open and an M-4 in his hands. Nolan turned around and saw one of the bodyguards burst through the fire door, weapon raised. Nolan shot and missed. He heard Hecker shout. The guard fired twice. Nolan flattened out and both rounds sailed high. The lobby doors shattered behind him. Nolan sighted down the barrel with both eyes and pressed the trigger once, twice, three times. The assailant collapsed and lay still. Nolan turned, half-expecting a policeman to have a drawn weapon on him. Instead, it was a groggy Marmot just coming around and a thousand pieces of broken glass. Nolan didn't care. Outside the front door was a form ... no, a man ... no, *Sam.*

Nolan dropped Marmot onto the broken glass, yanked the sock out of his slack mouth and went to his friend. Hecker had bloody froth on his lips and blood over his neck and upper chest. He was conscious but unmoving. Nolan grabbed his friend's right hand and pressed the rolled-up socks into his palm. He placed the compress over the wound at the base of the neck above the clavicle. "Press here to control the bleeding. I'm taking you to a hospital."

Hecker spewed bloody foam, but no words sounded. Nolan lifted the DEA man under the armpits and dragged him into the backseat of the Expedition, propping him upright in the corner of the driver's side. For good measure, he belted him in place and urged his friend to keep pressing.

A blue-robed Love fumbled with Hecker's dropped M-4, trying to work the charging handle to clear a jam. Nolan was indignant. *Any normal hostage would have run away. This SOB stuck around and cut the cable ties with broken glass in order to shoot him.* Arrogance came at a cost, and Nolan's roundhouse kick caught Marmot on the side of his face. The former veep was unconscious before his head hit the sidewalk with the sound of a dropped squash. Nolan heard faint sirens as he tie-tied Marmot's hands for the second time, noting with satisfaction that the former veep had sliced his fingers cutting those tough plastic bands. Nolan threw the insensate traitor into the backseat next to a bleeding, burbling Hecker. He didn't bother with the seatbelt for his second passenger.

The engine was running and Nolan roared away, not noticing the white SUV that pulled out once he passed.

* * * * *

METROPOLITAN METHODIST HOSPITAL, DOWNTOWN SAN ANTONIO

Despite the flashing lights converging on the Mokara, no one had stopped Nolan and within a mile he'd calmed sufficiently to pull over and look up a hospital.

Hecker coughed blood. "I have to leave you at the ER," Nolan said. "They'll operate and you'll be fine. I'll take care of Don Randy. Your family is safe with me. Tell them nothing." Hecker grunted and spat more blood.

As Nolan skidded to a stop at the ER entrance, he let out a long blast on the horn. If there was a cop on duty, so be it. Two attendants pushing a gurney burst through the door as Nolan pulled open the driver's side rear door and said, "Help this man! He was shot once in the base of the neck less than ten minutes ago."

The attendants unbuckled a semiconscious Hecker and laid him on the gurney. A third man, this one in a lab coat, came outside. He looked at Hecker and gave the orderlies instructions to start IVs immediately and prep the patient for surgery. The attendants hurried off while the doctor walked over to Nolan. "What can you tell me about the wound?"

"It's from a 9mm pistol. No exit wound. He was shot maybe ten minutes ago. This happened as part of an undercover operation. There are bad cops and traffickers looking for this man. I'm needed in the field. Register him as a John Doe. I have to go. Notify the DEA here, but don't contact any local law enforcement. The sting targeted corrupt police officers, and they may try to kill him. Bring the DEA to the hospital and tell them to put two men on guard around the clock."

The doctor looked through the open door and saw an unconscious Marmot lying half on the floor of the backseat. "I'll call an attendant to take this man into the ER as well."

Nolan reached inside his backpack and pulled out a wrapped stack of bills. "Doctor, here's ten thousand dollars for the trouble I'm putting you through. I took it from drug dealers, so no one will miss it. The man in the backseat is central to an ongoing investigation. Hostages are involved and lives are at stake. I must transport him to a DEA facility where he'll be inspected by a physician prior to interrogation. I'd appreciate it if you didn't remember seeing this man if anyone asks. It will be safer for you as well. I must go." Nolan slammed the door, shielding the occupant from other curious eyes.

The doctor pushed the money back at Nolan. "I can't accept—"

"It's yours. Put it in a college fund or give it to charity." The doctor took the bundle and slipped it inside his lab coat, rebuttoning it as Nolan climbed behind the wheel and drove off. Before Nolan was out of the parking lot, he stopped at the realization that Marmot's security would be able to track the veep's phone and might already be doing so. Within seconds, the phone's battery, SIM card and back cover were scattered on the front passenger's seat.

* * * * *

On the other side of the ER parking lot, Colonel Burge watched the mime show with the unknown driver, the attendants and the wounded man. He forwarded to Coulter the picture of the armed man dragging the older man in the blue robe across the lobby by one arm of his cuffed hands. The photograph provided a pretty good likeness of each person's face considering it was a point-and-shoot before someone pointed-and-shot him. Less than ten seconds after the colonel had hit the send button, his phone rang. Burge answered while watching the driver conclude a transaction with a man in doctor's scrubs.

"Where did you take this picture?" Coulter asked.

"At the Mokara," Burge said. "I took the photo and ran out the front door before all hell broke loose. Six or seven shots were fired, and the driver of the getaway car took one in the throat. He's just been dropped at—"

"The man in the flowered shirt with glasses and brown hair is Bob Nolan. He's the one who is likely behind the arms thefts at the base and those mystery SF."

"What do you want me to do? He's parked thirty meters away ... no, wait, he's driving off."

"Don't let him see you but follow him. He's the key."

CHAPTER TWENTY-NINE

CRITICAL MASS

SUBURBAN SAN ANTONIO

With a start Nolan realized that he'd signed Hecker's death warrant by dismantling Love's phone in the hospital parking lot. He dialed Ryder and felt relief as the familiar voice answered. "What's your ETA?"

"Right on time: 01:00 in Gunny's driveway."

"Change of plans. Go to the Metropolitan Methodist Hospital downtown. Hecker's been shot in the neck and is in surgery. Men searching for Love will come to the hospital. We can't let them slaughter Sam in his bed."

"He's your friend, not mine."

"Hecker went on the Medellín Cartel payroll his last year in Asia. It was a top-secret DEA operation and it explains why he went weird. He couldn't tell you without risking his cover."

"Convenient. Bring in the police or the FBI."

"We've all committed jailable offenses in the last few days and need to keep the cops out of it," Nolan said, "but I did tell the hospital attendants to call the DEA and ask for guards. Let's compromise: you go to Methodist Hospital and leave once there are two DEA agents outside his room. I have Love and I'll make the exchange before first light. I'll need you for that."

"Now you're talking. I didn't drive two thousand miles to babysit Hecker."

"When I have the details, I'll use Signal and text you. Be careful. Higher Love has Special Forces in the area, and they'll be out for blood." Nolan hung up.

Next on Nolan's list was General Payne. He needed to make the call before he arrived at Tanner's house and Payne's techs pinpointed his location. Giving them his direction of travel was cutting it fine enough. He wanted them in the neighborhood but not crawling up his alimentary canal.

Despite the hour, the president's man answered on the first ring. "Payne."

"It's Nolan. I'm in San Antonio. I have Mr. Love. The one and only David Marmot."

"Marmot? Impossible."

"He had us all fooled. My family's still held by Higher Love."

"They're on a private jet from California that filed a false flight plan," Payne said. "We're using satellites to track their course. That's ongoing, but the initial course was south-by-southeast: they may be headed your way."

"They'll end up in San Antonio at the private passenger terminal because that's where I'm taking Marmot to trade for their release."

"Negative. You're not authorized to take that decision. Only the president can, and I'll advise him not to. Tell us where you are, hand Marmot across and let us take it from there."

"No deal. My family goes free or I don't produce Marmot."

"Nolan, listen to me. You've spent the last two years tracking this man down. It's always been your contention that rolling up HL requires a complete debrief of the top man. Letting him go ensures that he implements his succession plan and our efforts to eradicate his group will fail. Also, be aware there's a rogue Special Forces Operational Detachment A-team of twelve men bivouacked at Camp Stanley. They'll be coming for you. These are tier-two Special Ops and you're no match."

"Yeah, I just killed two of them at the hotel where I grabbed Marmot. We'll speak again soon." Nolan disconnected the call. That had gone as expected: badly.

He spared a glance into the backseat. Marmot was awake, though he feigned unconsciousness. The bloody wound in Nolan's back reminded him of the old man's viciousness. Nolan pulled over and hit the emergency lights. He checked the power meter on the stun gun and saw that it was depleted. Brandishing the Glock, he said, "Marmot, I know you're awake and heard the last call. I'm taking you to Yu Kaili. She's interrogating your man and he's giving us names as we speak. Sit up or I'll hit you with the stun gun again."

Marmot pulled himself off the floor.

"Raise your hands, palms facing me. Good. Lean back. Put your hands on your head and clasp your fingers. If you move from this position, I'll kill you."

"Only if you're more stupid than you appear to be," Marmot snarled.

"For your own sake, shut up." Nolan improvised a gag using riggers tape, wrapped the ex-veep's wrists together and re-taped the joined pair to the back of his head. Marmot's stylist would charge extra the next time he ducked into the salon. Five minutes later, the end result was a straitjacket fashioned from riggers tape and seat belts, with an emptied ammo pouch as a hood.

As Nolan climbed back into the driver's seat and started up the Expedition, he looked at his dashboard clock: 12:55. The fancy Spec Ops grenade was set to blow at one o'clock. He searched his phone for recent calls and redialed the Mokara's number.

* * * * *

Team Sergeant Suarez of OD-A team 1077 was sickened by the call that told him Detachment Commander Park and Deputy Detachment Commander Lee were dead. He'd mustered the other nine men of the A-team, and five of them had made it to the seventh floor of the Mokara in seventy-five minutes—damn near a record seeing as how they'd first had to gear up, requisition two base vehicles and drive fifteen miles. The four other OD-A team members headed for the arms cache.

The hotel swarmed with police, FBI and the former VP's people. Suarez and his men—identification produced confirming them as Marmot's bodyguards—looked at still images printed from the hotel security cameras. The principal kidnapper was in his fifties, clean-shaven with a brown crewcut and glasses with black frames. From his mannerisms, he wasn't ex-military, but from his shooting he might be a descendant of Wild Bill Hickock: Captain Park through the heart, WO1 Lee between the eyes, the concierge through the right shoulder, and a moving bodyguard in the lobby hit three times center mass for a clean kill. The lead kidnapper's wounded partner—either shot or hit by flying glass—was another white male in his forties with cherubic features and medium-length brown hair. Facial recognition scans were underway.

The late Captain Park's phone rang, and a homicide detective answered. He cupped the mouthpiece and called, "I need the most senior person from Talleyrand Security."

The operations sergeant took the call. "Suarez here."

"Marmot's phone went offline thirty minutes ago. Its last location was the Metropolitan Methodist Hospital just north of you. How many men do you have?"

"Five, including myself. The rest are collecting equipment."

"Good. You and two others head to the hospital and leave two behind to monitor developments. Give me the numbers of whoever's in charge of weapons collection. I need them to do something very important for our cause."

Suarez complied, wondering what this was about. The elevator bank was crowded with uniforms waiting for a ride. Suarez and his men took the stairs down to the lobby.

* * * * *

The phone rang in the Bowie Suite. An FBI agent sorting through the former occupant's private papers sat on the bed, picked up the handset and listened to Nolan's monotone warning.

"Bomb! Bomb! Bomb! Everyone out, out, out, now!" the special agent shouted as he ran. Mercifully, the hotel guests on the seventh floor had been evacuated an hour prior. Less than twenty seconds after the last person—a fingerprint technician dusting on the balcony of 714—had fled to safety, the M2 SLAM detonated in the closet of 701. The molten metal sprayed into the suite and outside hallway, shredding walls and piercing the bodies of the three dead men lying where they fell. The remains of the room burned for an instant before nine thousand gallons of water from the ruptured roof pool cascaded down, extinguishing the flames and washing corpses and evidence onto the street far below. A torrent of water poured down the length of the hallway and peaked at mid-thigh height. The special agent in charge pulled everyone back down to the lobby and altered the top priority to a search for more explosives.

Suarez thought it a waste to leave two direct action operators at the Mokara, but orders were orders. The streets were a nightmare around the hotel, with crime scene tape everywhere, barricades blocking access and a mixture of fire, police, FBI and bystanders milling about. Driving out of the muddle took thirty minutes, more time expended than if they'd jogged to the hospital.

* * * * *

MUSTANG CIRCLE, AMBER CREEK

"Honey, I'm home!" Nolan said with an ironic lilt.

"I'm in the kitchen making more of this disgusting tea."

He felt relief at the sound of Kaili's voice. Maybe because she was on his side and more than a match for America's would-be Caesar. Surely he was over his infatuation of two years ago that had led to near-fatal lapses in judgment in Sri Lanka. He put the pieces of Marmot's phone on the table along with the last M2 SLAM and accepted a cup even though he wasn't a tea drinker.

"Tanner's dead. Hecker's shot in the throat. I have Love locked in the car. People will be coming. Did you learn anything useful?" Nolan could scarcely believe that in a round trip of less than two hours he had traded at least one and maybe two lives for a man unworthy of anything more than contempt.

"Kammerer the stammerer? I am afraid the cat has got his tongue. He did provide the name of the man in the living room upstairs from my torture chamber, William Weeks. He is a marketing director at an investment firm in town." She pushed a scrap of bloody paper with a phone number across the table. "I am most interested in speaking with Mr. Love."

Eck and Meng came into the kitchen with blood-covered hands and forearms. They passed through the kitchen and Nolan heard the door to the SUV open. It would take them a while to cut Marmot out.

"I need him in good shape," Nolan said. "I have to trade him for my family before sunrise."

"President Liu also would want Love interrogated. But what if I gave your government someone who knows a dozen top Higher Love names and will confirm Mr. Love's identity? What would that be worth?"

"A waiver on whatever plot China and North Korea were hatching with Higher Love, and safe passage out of the US."

"So boring. I can leave any time."

Kaili was interrupted by her two men dragging Marmot through the kitchen and toward the stairs.

"Put him in the dining room," Nolan said. "Leave the lights off, draw the blinds and have one of your men watch the front and the other the back of the house. There are NVGs in the garage."

Kaili nodded and Love momentarily avoided a trip down to the basement butcher's shop. Meng went into the garage and came back with night-vision optics.

"How about a four-way trade?" Kaili asked. "Mr. Love for your family, and his top adviser in return for you coming to China with me. See our son. Decide what role, if any, you wish to play in his life. If you want to leave China, I won't object. If you wish to stay, you should know that I'll retire after this mission. I am tired of the intrigue and bored in Pyongyang. I'll start life anew with my little boy. Join us."

Again, the same angle. It rang false: Kaili was no empathizer. Nolan doubted that this praying mantis could avoid eating any former mate, particularly a disloyal one. He could imagine what poor Kammerer looked like. As if his voice came from another place, Nolan said, "I'll do it if you can obtain the release of my family."

"The man I met in New York City was Joseph Kleinwort. He is the architect of Higher Love's political philosophy and chief diplomat. He was the one who reached out to China last year."

Kleinwort? They'd had that crafty old bastard under surveillance for two years with nothing to show for it. Nolan looked into those unblinking eyes and thought he detected a human spark. Maybe she really did want him to meet their son. He'd been out of the Agency for so long that the only information he possessed which could be of interest to China was a copy of Watermen's original NSA files—which he didn't have with him—and details pertaining to Abyss, which would soon be irrelevant. "Let me speak with Payne and see what he says." Nolan excused himself and went out to the garage for privacy.

"Once you agree to the terms," Kaili called from behind him, "I must confirm the second half of our arrangement. Leave Payne on the line and bring the phone into the dining room."

* * * * *

AMBER CREEK AND CAMP STANLEY

Across the street from Tanner's house, Burge dialed his home phone.

"Burge residence," Coulter answered.

"I followed Nolan to 2236 Mustang Circle. He drove into the garage and closed the door behind him. This location is maybe an hour from Camp Stanley. I don't know how long they're planning to remain."

"Stay there and alert me if anyone leaves. I'll talk to the FBI and let Payne know. I'll figure out a way to come to the house. I'm dying to see Bob Nolan one last time."

"Wait, before you go," Burge said. "Did you learn anything about the OD-A team?"

"Yes, Payne called ten minutes ago. We were right about the languages: everyone but the team sergeant speaks either fluent Korean or Mandarin. It was assembled in the past six weeks. They've never been on a mission, and even Payne can't find out why they're in Camp Stanley other than it's part of a pending broken arrow drill."

"Why would anyone post a Special Forces A-team at a nearly defunct base to rehearse for a broken arrow, and the team members all speak Chinese or Korean?"

"Seems to me like someone might be planning to steal a weapon and they could be part of the snatch team," Coulter said. "I have their files, but my priority is to explain to the FBI that the man who killed three of their kind last week outside Camp Irwin is in San Antonio and ripe for a takedown."

"Good luck and keep me posted."

"One other thing, Colonel. The guard on the front gate called an hour ago to alert you that the ten ODA men stole two cars out of the motor pool and left the base."

"Dammit, we should have had someone follow them," Burge said. "Whatever they're up to is certain to be trouble."

"Yup."

* * * * *

METROPOLITAN METHODIST HOSPITAL

Suarez and two other NCOs burst through the swinging doors of the emergency room. The team sergeant sent one man to admissions while he canvassed the ER for a medical professional, the younger the better. He found a nervous resident with a clipboard speaking with a patient awaiting treatment. "Excuse me, I believe my colleague was brought in here about ninety minutes ago. He's eight-six years old with silver hair, about 6'3"? His name is Marmot, David Marmot.'"

"Sir, no one fitting that description has been in the ER," the young man said with a slight foreign accent.

"Any gunshot victims?" Suarez asked. "One of my friend's people may have been shot, or possibly wounded by flying glass."

"Oh, uh, not that I'm aware of. But the senior ER physician on duty is in surgery. You could speak with him when he's out."

"When will that be?"

"It's impossible to say. It was an automobile accident and a front-seat passenger was injured by an airbag: neck and spine trauma.

"I'll check with my colleague," Suarez said. "Can you tell me the minute the surgeon comes out of the OR?"

"If I'm still on duty, I'll try."

* * * * *

MUSTANG CIRCLE, AMBER CREEK

"All right, Bob, calm down, calm down," Payne said. "I realize it's your family we're talking about. If Kleinwort confesses to a Higher Love connection and if he independently identifies Marmot as Mr. Love, then I'll advise the president that he should lend support to your efforts to trade Marmot for your family. Is that acceptable?"

"Barely. Have your best men around the High Flyers building at San Antonio airport by four a.m. There's a second part of the bargain, and one you won't like. Yu Kaili was Higher Love's captive when I raided their safe house earlier this afternoon."

"I was wondering when you'd mention that detail. The Australians confirmed a DNA match from one of the fingernails recovered from the basement. Why was Tony Johnson interrogating her?"

"Something about North Korea's nuclear arsenal from the question list I took off Johnson's body," Nolan said.

"What did she tell him?"

"I don't know, and I don't think she has any idea either. They had her doped up. It was all recorded and I brought the videocam with me, but I forgot about it with everything else happening. Kaili took the chip."

"I imagine you'll want your old girlfriend to get away scot free," Payne said.

"That's right. And she's not in the MSS these days."

"I'll let her go provided she gives us the recording of her interrogation session."

"She may have already destroyed it," Nolan said.

"I don't think so. She'll want to watch it to see how well she held up under torture and find out what she told her questioners."

"I'm not so certain about the latter—she killed them both. I'm walking back into the house and I'll hand over the phone to confirm details. In the meantime, tell your men not to attack this house or interfere with our transfer of Marmot to the airport. I can't tell friend from foe, and my default action is to kill Marmot if anyone comes at us. Besides, I've committed a few felonies and POTUS and you will want space between us if I'm caught."

"The stakes are high," Payne said. "I hope you know what you're doing. Put Yu on the line, please, and when you have a chance mail me a photo of Johnson's question list."

"Just remember to call me the minute you find out where my family is."

Nolan passed his phone to Kaili. She walked out of the dining room and into the garage where her conversation with General Payne was inaudible. Nolan absently browsed through the M2 SLAM instruction manual. It seemed simple enough. Then he took the opportunity to address Marmot, who was shackled to a dining room chair. He had a red bald patch where the tape's removal had taken a clump of his plumage. Love appeared to be in good humor, all things considered.

"The trade is my family," Nolan said. "All three of them unharmed, for you. Are you in agreement?"

"And if I'm not?" Marmot asked.

"Well, we have one of your top lieutenants in custody. He won't name everyone, but he'll squeal enough to bring Higher Love down. That makes you redundant. Second, you've met Yu Kaili. She lost three fingernails earlier today and she's in a bad mood. If you want to see what she's capable of, we'll drag you downstairs to take a look at the burned and mutilated corpse of the man who gave up the Mokara. Third, I have nothing but my family to live for. If you renege on our agreement, I'll kill you via remote detonation of a bomb. If you kill me, you'll die anyway because the device will be on your body. It operates on a timer and is tamper proof. Your move."

"You leave me no choice but to agree." For someone whose life's work was being dismantled in front of his eyes, Love seemed almost cheerful.

"The location is at the private High Flyers terminal in the San Antonio airport. I assume my family is on the ground nearby. I'll give the pilot the coordinates where he is to park the plane once he lands. My family will transfer to a second aircraft. When it takes off and is out of range of shoulder-fired missiles, I will release you."

"That's unacceptable," Marmot said. "If I agree, there's nothing to stop you from handing me over to Obama or killing me."

"I won't leave until you're free," Nolan said. "When my family's plane takes off, I'll disarm the bomb strapped to you. We'll each have three armed aides. At that point, everyone takes his chances."

"It seems you've thought of everything. I'm in agreement. What do we do, call a taxi to the airport?"

"Not quite. At the risk of outraging your modesty, you'll lose the bathrobe and I'll tape the device to your back. I have preset the radio detonation frequency, and I'll set the timer as well."

Nolan went about his business, shielding the M2 SLAM from Marmot's eyesight as he affixed it to his lower back. He set the timer for 06:00, then devoted another ten minutes to a pair of flourishes, one cosmetic and one deadly.

"I didn't realize until today that you aren't America's dead hero, you are the biggest terrorist in history."

"Coming from you, I won't dignify that with a response," Nolan said. "You can lean back. I'll return in a minute."

Nolan passed Kaili in the kitchen. She was sipping tea and working her cell phone with one hand. His burner was on the table. He plugged it into a USB cable to charge.

"All good?" he asked

She looked up and gave him a smile. "Yes, General Payne is a pleasure to deal with. Dear, I had a fortune cookie with my tea. Do you want to see what my fortune reads?"

Dear? Uh oh. She pushed a sliver of paper across the table. TRAVEL BROADENS THE MIND, it read. SEE THE WORLD AND MAKE NEW FRIENDS. Nolan retreated to the dining room to pull up a news homepage so Love could read out the most current headline when he called Weeks.

CHAPTER THIRTY

PARANOID

DOWNTOWN SAN ANTONIO

"Wake up. Wake up!" William Weeks shook Tony Johnson's listless form.

Johnson moaned and massaged his temples. "I need water and more Advil. I wish I had something stronger. I feel like death."

"Barely five hundred milligrams and you're whining like this?"

"It's not lethal but it's still double the normal dosage for my weight."

"Maybe I should have left you in the basement," Weeks said. "You have three hours to pull your act together. There will be a prisoner exchange at five a.m. somewhere nearby. Bob Nolan has Love and he wants his family back in return. If Nolan's there, it's likely the Chinese woman will be there too."

At the hint of Kaili's name, Johnson checked his suppressed Sig with the Trijicon night sights. "Bring me more coffee. And Red Bull, lots of Red Bull."

* * * * *

AMBER CREEK TO SAN ANTONIO AIRPORT

"Pasan, it's me."

The pilot was slow to find his bearings. "Mmph. Bob? Is this Bob?"

"What's your maximum time aloft with a full tank and no passengers?"

"At least four hours."

"Is San Antonio a twenty-four-hour airport?"

"No, it closes from midnight to 3:45."

"I want you in the air before four o'clock this morning. You're a target on the ground. Take off as soon as you receive clearance. Land nearby if you can or circle if you must. I'll alert you to your destination, but it likely will be back at the airport at five o'clock. You'll pick up three of my family members, plus assorted others. What's your capacity?"

"Pilot plus six."

"Should be enough. Check your texts. An hour ago, I rented a refueling slot in Monterrey and bought your plane a one-time landing and takeoff voucher at Puerto Cabezas, Nicaragua. It's daytime only."

"Nicaragua? You want me to fly your family there?"

"They don't extradite and that trumps five-star hotel rooms. I'm on an encrypted satphone and my number is in the Signal text message. Be careful approaching your Beechcraft and leave your phone on."

* * * * *

MUSTANG CIRCLE, AMBER CREEK

Nolan put down the satphone and returned to the kitchen. Tanner had been in Nolan's life for what, two hours? Now he was dead. The collateral damage was too depressing to think about. Nolan cued up CNN.com, which led with the Mokara bombing and the anonymous evacuation warning just prior. The bomb squad was on site and the police had evacuated a two-block radius. Nolan wondered if they'd ID'ed Tanner's body before the explosion. Probably not, or law enforcement would already be here.

The just-ended phone conversation with Weeks perturbed him. Marmot had read the statement without inflection or deviation while Nolan pressed a Glock against the base of the traitor's skull. On the other end, HL's man had been cordial. It was as if both Marmot and Weeks supported his proposed actions. What did they have in their favor? *Ten Special Forces operators looking for payback.* Nolan's planned exchange location was too obvious. He needed to either pick a new location or tell Payne to flood the airport with even more men. No, if someone was disloyal, or the Special Forces detected their presence, his family would die. Nolan would have to leave POTUS and his man in the dark for as long as possible.

Nolan's brain continued to churn permutations and probabilities. If his family died, then Marmot would die unless the former veep thought the SF men could defuse the device. No, that was too risky. They'd take Nolan into custody and keep his family alive as leverage. Nolan needed a nap to clear his head. Just thirty minutes, but not at this house—it had passed its expiration date.

One of the MSS men rushed into the kitchen and spoke in Mandarin to Kaili, who woke with a start. "There is a man watching the house from a car parked down the street," she translated.

"Send your men out the back to check for others," Nolan said. "We may be surrounded. If he's operating solo, try to take him alive. If he picks up a phone or a radio, kill him."

She nodded and relayed the instructions. Both MSS men disappeared into the basement and emerged minutes later in black coveralls and holstered sidearms. Nolan shut off the remaining lights in the house and Kaili followed him into the dining room where Marmot struggled in vain against his restraints. There was enough moonlight for Nolan to see his outline.

"Mr. Vice President, there's a man outside. He might be your man, I don't know. I want you to understand that if anyone or anything enters this room, I will put a bullet into your head. I dismantled your phone, so no one's tracking it. If you were stupid enough to have an RFID chip embedded subcutaneously like someone's dog, it will be the death of you."

"Bob, I thought I heard a noise," Kaili said. "Check the house starting with the garage. I'll look after the prisoner."

Nolan hadn't heard anything, but the garage was a good place to visit, with its cavalcade of weapons to choose from. He handed Kaili his Glock.

Kaili knelt down next to Marmot. "I spoke with Weeks and told him to prepare the NEMP for transport. I gave him the code words, so he knows the orders are yours. If you double-cross me, you'll wish Nolan had shot you." Marmot turned and looked at her but made no effort to speak.

Nolan reentered the room sporting the sniper rifle with the Starlight scope. He'd replaced his Glock and handed Kaili an extra magazine. "I changed my mind about leaving the MSS out of the fight. Until Ryder gets here, you're all I've got."

All three heard the noise from the back of the house. Nolan padded out of the dining room and lay prone in the hallway with the scope to his eye. It was a bad black-and-white TV picture, but he could see into the kitchen. He heard the backdoor ease open.

Kaili walked past him and hissed something in Mandarin. A male voice answered in the same. "They captured the man in the car," Kaili said.

Nolan rose to his feet and Kaili turned on the lights. Eck and Meng bracketed a sixtyish Caucasian with a neat white mustache and cropped hair. "Bob Nolan, I was wrong about you," the man said.

"And who might you be?"

"Colonel Richard Burge, US Army, commander of Camp Stanley."

"Where's Coulter?"

Burge stared at Nolan.

"We don't have much time," Nolan said. "I have Love in the other room, and he has ten Special Forces operators looking for him. He had a dozen, but we killed two earlier tonight. We'll tie you up and leave you here. The FBI or the SF or the Girl Scouts will be along, and they'll either turn you loose, or kill you."

"Coulter said you worked for Higher Love," Burge said.

"Both of us were wrong. Earlier tonight I thought Coulter was Mr. Love. Turns out he's the ex-veep, Dave Marmot."

"Marmot? Preposterous!"

"Everyone reacts the same way," Nolan said. "He was second on my least-likely-suspects list, just above Mr. Rogers. But he fooled us all. Kaili, gag him, zip-tie his wrists and ankles to something solid and let's get going."

She nodded and her men went to work on Burge and a kitchen chair. Nolan motioned for Kaili to follow him into the garage. "Tell your men to make it possible for Burge to escape. He's a former Special Forces commander, so they don't have to make it too simple. Leave his keys with him too, but take his cellphone and cut the landline. Once we have Love in the Expedition, I'll reassemble his phone and put it in Burge's vehicle. Burge will drive off and Higher Love's men will track Marmot's phone. The diversion will buy us time."

She smiled and shook her head. "You are not a very nice man. I sense a kindred spirit."

"He's a friend of Coulter, proof enough he's an enemy." Nolan dismantled his cellphone and put the pieces into this shirt pocket. He partially reassembled Marmot's device, leaving it without the back cover and battery.

* * * * *

METROPOLITAN METHODIST HOSPITAL

Suarez's man in admissions faced the senior NCO with a smile. "There's a patient registered as John Doe just out of surgery for a lacerated trachea."

"Where is he?"

"There's more. The lady asked if we were from the DEA. I told her no, that we represented a sister agency."

"Any sign of our leader?" Suarez asked.

"No geriatric admissions in the last ninety minutes," the soldier said.

"Let's go upstairs and find out what John Doe knows before the DEA arrives."

Ryder stood to the side and feigned interest in a sheaf of registration papers on a clipboard. He drifted back into the ER where Arkar and Maung awaited instructions.

The three HL operators were on their way to the elevator bank when Suarez's phone buzzed. He answered it, listened for ten seconds and said, "Right away, sir," before disconnecting. Addressing his two men, he said, "Change of plans. Our leader's phone just came back up. It's moving and so are we. We'll return if we need to."

They jogged past the two Burmese and an East Texas peckerwood glancing sidelong at them as they made their way out into the night. "I'll tell the admissions lady we're from the DEA," Ryder said, "and we'll find out where they have Hecker. Walk over to the elevators and watch for anyone dressed like those three, particularly Asians."

* * * * *

Through the haze, Hecker recognized Ryder's voice. "Sam, it's Travis. There are men downstairs from Higher Love. They'll interrogate and kill you if you stay here. If you can hear me, move your right hand."

Hecker obliged with a thumbs-up and struggled to force open heavy eyelids.

"We'll find a wheelchair and take you out the side door. If you want, we'll drop you at a different hospital."

Ryder left Arkar and Maung and returned with a wheelchair after a five-minute delay. "I told the head nurse that Hecker's life was under threat and they must relocate him. She wasn't buying it. We have to move fast."

The two Burmese disconnected Hecker's IVs and heart monitor and lifted him into the wheelchair. Ryder glanced at Hecker's medical summary before dropping the clipboard into his lap. The former SEAL finished the deception with a blanket draped over his former mentor's shoulders and head.

Ryder pushed Hecker into the hallway and saw the path ahead blocked by a phalanx of nurses in purple scrubs. "Arkar, bring the car to the main entrance. Maung, clear a path—we're coming through."

* * * * *

AMBER CREEK AND THE WHITE HOUSE

Nolan had persuaded an obstreperous Kaili to ride with the MSS men, following Marmot and him as he drove away from ill-starred Mustang Circle. Nolan dialed and Payne answered straight away. "Have you found my family?" Nolan asked.

"At a private airstrip outside El Paso, less than two hours from San Antonio. They're heavily guarded and the plane is wired with explosives."

"Stand off. We have to do this my way. Did you extract anything out of Love's lieutenant?"

"Yes, he's terrified he'll be tried for treason and provided dozens of names. Some will be bullshit—he's mentioned yours for starters—but POTUS will still permit the swap to proceed."

"Listen carefully because there's been a change in plans. The exchange will take place at Lackland at 05:00. I will alert Higher Love at 04:20. Tell whoever's tracking me to drop back and look for other vehicles who may be following. I'll be at North Frank Luke Drive by 03:30 followed by a blue Volkswagen Passat. Neither vehicle is to be stopped. I need you to open up and clear out the GNR Avionics building where we'll wait prior to the exchange. No vehicles in the parking lot. Provide security only at a distance: no one inside or within sight of the building. Shut the airport, alert the tower to turn the airfield lights on at 04:45 and tell them a Beechcraft Baron registration N168TT will land and taxi to the Kelly Airfield Management Building at 05:00. Higher Love's aircraft is scheduled to land at five o'clock with my family aboard. They'll switch planes and the Baron will take off."

"That's contrary to our agreed location at SAT's private passenger terminal," Payne said. "Our men are already in place."

"The location was compromised. Higher Love's traitors in San Antonio are infiltrating the commercial airport and may tip the balance if the exchange takes place there."

"Have it your way. Be advised that the local constabulary identified Hecker and you, and issued a shoot-to-kill order on you an hour ago. Tell Yu that we'll reroute her jet from SAT to SKF but I'll need a video chip before she boards."

"I already have it along with the camera," Nolan said. "I'll leave it in reception at GNR."

"That's very trusting of her."

"Too trusting by half."

"Speaking of too trusting," Payne said, "don't you find it odd that Higher Love is willing to let your family fly off before Marmot is safely away?"

"I told them I'll accompany Marmot and defuse the IED once my family is safely in the air. So long as I'm not suicidal, he should be fine. As to how he makes his escape and avoids immediate recapture, I've not given it any thought since I don't care."

"The obvious play is to use you as a hostage."

"I don't think HL is stupid enough to think that POTUS won't trade my life for Marmot's if it comes to it."

"Enough speculation. I'll alert Q-Group to break visual contact with your vehicle and set up a loose cordon to Lackland. What route are you taking?"

"I'm on the 281 to the 410," Nolan said. "If anyone tries to stop me, I'll treat them as hostile."

* * * * *

DOWNTOWN SAN ANTONIO AND AMBER CREEK

"Bob," Ryder said, "we've got Hecker and will come to you, but we need your location."

"He was shot in the throat," Nolan said. "How can you move him?"

"I've seen his charts and he wasn't shot. Flying glass cut his trachea but missed major blood vessels. They've sewn him up and he's in the back seat, sedated but determined to help or die trying."

"Head for Lackland Air Force Base and take US-90 to Southwest 36th St followed by North Frank Luke Drive to GNR Avionics on the first right. I'll be there in a half-hour. Leave your vehicle description and license plate so Payne's men don't take you out. I've boobytrapped Love, and anyone nearby will die if I'm injured or slain in their attempt to rescue him."

"Fucking Nolan," Hecker whispered from the back seat, head finally clearing.

* * * * *

THE WHITE HOUSE

"General," Obama said, "I violated the Posse Comitatus Act of 1878 by deploying Delta operators to rescue Nolan's family. Now you tell them it's too risky. What went through your mind when you took it upon yourself to cancel the op?"

"If we free his family in El Paso, Nolan has no incentive to hand Love over," Payne said. "Nolan knows he faces life without parole if the locals don't shoot him first. He'll either deal Marmot to the Chinese in return for safe conduct out, or possibly trade him back to Higher Love in return for his life."

"A cynical view, Neil. I expect better from Nolan."

"Mr. President, ten minutes ago I looked at photos showing the tortured body of a Higher Love officer. Michael Kammerer's corpse was discovered in the basement of the home in north San Antonio where Nolan and Yu were holed up. The man had been emasculated, electroshocked, tongue torn out and killed by disembowelment.

Nolan committed these atrocities: he's cracked under the pressure and has gone insane."

"Every man has his breaking point, Neil." The president continued after a pause. "What if his family dies during the prisoner exchange?"

"I'll have a sniper take Nolan out. We can't leave him alive, not if there's a chance he'd find out that we had a Delta team stand down when they could have saved his wife and children. I don't want that man—even in a supermax facility—plotting my death."

"As you wish. Withdraw Delta and send them to Lackland against whatever contingencies may arise."

* * * * *

TWO MILES FROM CAMP STANLEY

"I'm telling you, Nolan said he originally had pegged you as Mr. Love, but later identified Dave Marmot as Higher Love's leader and took him captive."

"Well, as I live and breathe that man surprises me, as do you," Coulter said. "You managed to pop your tie-ties and escape, but you picked up a tail and the FBI uses you as a Judas goat."

"I'm just shy of the spot where the bureau told me to pull over, hit my hazards and keep my head down." Burge hung up and pulled over after the SLOW CHILDREN sign. He could feel the vehicles behind him.

A red Taurus cut in front and blocked him. Another car squealed to a stop behind him, but Burge only had eyes for the two men in the street with AK-47s aimed at him. Someone wrenched open the driver's door. "Put both hands on the steering wheel!"

Other hands opened the rear doors and lights played throughout the vehicle. "He's not here. There's no one but the driver in this vehicle ... will do." The same voice addressed Burge, "Where is he?"

"Where is who?" the colonel replied.

"Get out, old man, and think very hard. You either tell us where Mr. Love is, or we end you right here."

Burge climbed down from his SUV. "Bob Nolan has three Chinese working for him, and they drove off with David Marmot. He was headed to the San Antonio airport."

From fifty meters away, a spotlight picked out the three armed men and the old colonel with his hands clasped behind his head. "This is the FBI! Everyone freeze! You move and you're dead. With your left hands, take your weapons by the barrel, place them on the ground and lie face down in the street!"

In reply, two shots from the backseat of the Taurus shattered the light. Suarez's shouted commands died in this throat as a sniper's round felled him. A second shot dropped the SF man nearest to Burge. Burge leaned through the open door to hit the high beams and hid on the floor of his truck.

Again, the voice over the megaphone spoke. "Anyone who raises a weapon will be shot. We have three of you in our sights. Drop your weapons and lie down in the street."

A voice came over dead Sergeant Suarez's cell phone. "Surrender. We'll come collect you after it's all over."

Colonel Burge pulled himself back into the driver's seat and wondered, not for the first time, whether Frank Coulter was the joker in the deck. He made certain to keep both hands in view, palms out.

* * * * *

GNR AVIONICS, LACKLAND AIR FORCE BASE

Kaili and her two black-clad minions were deep in the building plotting against the Western democracies, possibly finding Nolan a seat on the next flight to China and definitely keeping an eye on Marmot. *Did I really agreed to fly with her to see my so-called son?* Nolan shook his head to erase the thought.

Arkar and Maung helped Hecker shuffle into GNR Avionics' reception area. Nolan checked on Hecker. His friend's combination of rasps, whispers and hand gestures gave Nolan sufficient comfort to leave him sitting on the couch.

A stranger entered the building, offered his hand and said, "Hello, Bob. Been awhile."

In front of Nolan stood someone who sounded like Travis Ryder, the man who had saved his children's and wife's lives a half-dozen times in the last three days. Except instead of the SEAL with the physique of a middleweight judo master, here was a puffy burnout with bloodshot eyes. "Jesus, you look like a roadie for Marilyn Manson."

"I'm not certain dogshit-brown hair and flowered shirts becomes you either, but here we are."

"Fair enough," Nolan said. "Follow me back into the work area." The men walked through reception and into a shadowy hangar littered with machine tools, and computer monitors and diagnostic arrays on carts. The fragrance went from artificial lilac to gasoline and lubricants. Nolan gave a wave to Eck and Meng, who had M-4s leveled at them.

"You see that man sitting in the middle of the floor tied up like a Thanksgiving turkey?" Nolan asked. "That's the famous Mr. Love. I taped an M2 SLAM to the small of his back and set the timer for six o'clock. One way or another, the SOB and his organization go down today. Oh, I also transferred a mill to your account earlier tonight. Pay taxes on it and settle up with the IRS."

"Fantastic," Ryder said. "Sounds like a happy day lies ahead. What could go wrong?"

"Everything. I suspected that Marmot had an ace and he's played it. When I called his man Weeks to tell him the exchange was at Lackland and not the commercial airport, he said that Higher Love had procured a nuclear EMP. If Marmot wasn't handed over in pristine condition, that weapon stayed in the wild."

"He's bluffing."

"I thought so too, until Weeks told me to check with Kaili. But she refused to say whether Higher Love has the arming codes. I'm guessing it doesn't, otherwise those bastards wouldn't be willing to trade the nuke for Mr. Love. It does, however, raise the necessity of keeping Kaili safe. President Liu is fond of her, and if HL takes her hostage, he might trade an NEMP explosion on US soil for one of his most trusted lieutenants."

"A win-win for China," Ryder said. "But why would you blow up Marmot if his people have a nuke?"

"A deal's a deal. If he doesn't deliver my family, he dies on the spot. I'm through with *realpolitik*. The entire system is rotten from all sides. I made certain that Weeks knew I had his boss on a timer backed by a dead man's switch."

"Jesus, you play in a rough neighborhood."

"I want you and the Burmese to take Johnson's Expedition down the runway to the Kelly Airfield Management Building," Nolan said. "I've instructed HL to release my family there. You confirm they're safe and escort them to the same Beechcraft and pilot who flew you last week. Join them for the flight. Pasan has the details, but I've purchased refueling, landing and temporary residency rights for you all in Nicaragua. I'll stay behind and take the heat. I'll also ensure that you all receive pardons."

"Come with us. There's room on the plane for—"

"The pilot plus six. Three Nolans and your team makes for a full bus. Just keep everyone safe and you should be back home with your family inside a month."

"It's a lot to process at 4:15 in the morning, but I got it," Ryder said. "What about Hecker?"

"I'll take care of Sam. We have to deal with baggage we picked up in D.C. that doesn't concern anyone else. You have forty-five minutes to conjure up Plan B in case you smell something rotten during the handover. Here's the keys. Johnson's SUV has an arsenal on the back deck. Pick out what you need. You don't know how relieved I am to have you out here."

"Your BS would bring a tear to a glass eye. I'll see you when it's all over. You have any spare cash?"

Nolan dug through his rucksack. "I have about thirty thousand. Here, take twenty."

Nolan walked over to a hooded and bound Dave Marmot. He prodded the man's shoulder with his foot. "In ten minutes, I'll call Weeks with final instructions. I need one more proof-of-life photo. If you say or do anything that upsets me, I'll start with your kneecaps and make it up from there as I go along."

CHAPTER THIRTY-ONE

BLACK SABBATH

GNR AVIONICS, LACKLAND AFB

Nolan walked Ryder out to reception wondering if the FBI had audio to go with the CCTV footage they'd be monitoring. He grabbed Ryder's shoulder in temporary farewell and then the former SEAL led Arkar and Maung outside to the purloined Expedition.

A call to air traffic control instructed that the runway lights go on in thirty minutes, and the man in the tower confirmed two aircraft holding twenty miles out. Nolan advised an amendment to the landing time for the Baron and asked that the HL jet be brought forward ten minutes as well to five o'clock sharp. Within two minutes, Pasan called his satphone and Nolan reiterated the updated instructions. Nolan added Pasan should obey only Ryder while on the ground.

Nolan turned his attention to Hecker, who had pulled himself upright on the reception sofa. The bandages around Hecker's neck gave him the appearance of half a mummy. Hecker's eyes followed him as Nolan took a seat and put on a Petzl headlamp liberated from the late, unlamented Agent Johnson's eclectic collection. "How do you feel?" Nolan asked.

"Fucking super. I'm dying of thirst, I can barely breathe and my throat's slit."

"Let me help you with your covers." Nolan cloaked both their heads with a Methodist Hospital–issue blue blanket and turned on his headlamp.

"If you touch my tits, I'll kill you," Hecker croaked.

"Listen up. The walls have eyes and ears, and anyone could walk into reception and kill us while we're under here. I rigged a small timebomb and taped it to Marmot's back. He's Mr. Love. We're trading him for my family. The handover's scheduled for five o'clock and the bomb's set to go off at six. I wired a detonator to it with a couple of wrinkles, so it's unlikely that anyone but me can disarm it. I read the manual earlier tonight, and this model also has a remote detonation override feature."

"Speak English."

"I programmed my cell to either detonate or disarm the bomb on command. Here's my phone. To unlock it, swipe a giant Z. There are four bookmarks in the Chrome folder labeled 'Author.' Inside the folder, one of the URLs says 'OOD' and looks like it leads to an online page for a book called *Ocean of Deceit*. The 'OOD' URL is the disarm trigger. The other three bookmarks look like they lead to other merchant pages for *Sloppy Lies*, *Piles of Lies* and *Endless Lies*, but they all detonate the bomb. The charge will blow the veep's spine out his naval and kill everyone downstream for thirty meters."

"What do you want me to do?" Hecker rasped.

"Hang onto it," Nolan said. "Wait for my signal to disarm unless they kill me, which I expect them to try to do. Even if they succeed, don't blow the bomb unless my family's killed too."

"What if I'm out of cell coverage?"

"How likely is that?"

"You shouldn't believe those phone company ads."

Nolan flipped the blanket off their heads and brought his Glock up to bear on the person owning the footsteps. "Oh, sorry," he said to Kaili. "You gave me a fright."

"Sorry to catch you unawares. Where did Ryder and his mercenaries go?"

"They'll effect the safe recovery of my family down the runway, far away from the cluster bombs, mortars or whatever else Payne will order dropped on Marmot. You should leave."

"That is why I need to speak with you. I too am concerned that Lackland will become a war zone. The jet back to China lands at 5:45 at the San Antonio airport. There is something there that I need to collect. I want you to come with me. We will depart here at 5:10, or whenever the shooting starts. Once you are with me, Payne will not touch you."

"You have that backward," Nolan said. "So long as you're with me, Payne or Higher Love may kill us both, though you're unlikely to be the target."

"I assure you, once you get into my vehicle, we will both be safe from the president's men."

"What deal with the devil did you make?"

"The first part you know," Kaili said. "Payne receives my torture tape. MSS officers receive training in resisting interrogation and I gave Johnson no useful information. The second was the promise to make you disappear. You are an embarrassment, Bob. A dead hero resurrected and tried for murder is a political nightmare in an election year. Come to China with me. If you do not like it, leave and reunite with your family. Just stay out of the US."

"Is this you talking, or Payne?"

"It is common sense. America and you are finished."

"I just want the lies to end," Nolan said.

"Nonsense, it is the lies that keep us going."

* * * * *

OUTSIDE CAMP STANLEY

Burge was back at home, drinking neat bourbon at a steady clip. Coulter matched him, thirst fueled by rage instead of relief. "I can't believe we're sidelined for the biggest thing since 9/11."

"Frank, unless you kill those FBI agents out front there's nothing to be done."

"Dammit!" Coulter pounded his fist on the tabletop and the bowl of pretzels bounced.

"Look at the bright side," Burge said. "With the ceremony canceled, Payne's given you permission to meet Frank IV at the airport when his plane lands. We'll have breakfast and he can catch an early afternoon flight back to summer camp."

"There has to be a way I can get to Nolan," Coulter said. "Give me the names of former SF men living in San Antonio who served under you."

"I'm not helping you hire an assassin. Let's finish our drinks, take a nap and get cleaned up. This early in the morning, it will be less than a half-hour to the airport."

* * * * *

LACKLAND AIR FORCE BASE

Pasan Wanigasekara landed in the predawn darkness and taxied to where Ryder's SUV sat with the hazards blinking. The former SEAL texted Nolan once he'd spoken with the pilot and confirmed that everything was a go. Despite prolonged time aloft, their plane had more than enough fuel to reach their refueling spot in Monterrey.

Ten minutes later, a Learjet 75 landed and rolled to a halt thirty meters away from the SUV. Ryder's Starlight scope picked out the first man down the gangway. He resisted the urge to shoot him and switched his focus to Joanie. She was followed by Mei Ling, who was supported by Bert. A sole guard brought up the flank. The two guards returned to the plane, the door closed and as per prior agreement, it taxied to the south end of the runway.

Ryder gave them each a hug and called Bob. "Everyone's here and no worse for wear."

"Put them on the plane and get airborne," Nolan said. "This has gone too smoothly so far."

"I'll text you when we're up."

"Enjoy your vacation and tell them I love them."

* * * * *

"Are we really free?" Mei Ling asked.

"Not until we're out of the country," Ryder growled. "We have one more plane ride, and we need to move it."

Bert and Ryder supported Mei Ling as she hopped along toward the twin-engine prop plane. Tears of relief flowed down Joanie's cheeks. Ahead and behind were the outlines of two trustworthy men, Arkar and Maung. The Learjet roared past them, leapt into the night and disappeared into the northern sky.

* * * * *

Three minutes later, the door shut and the Beech Baron taxied to the south end, turned and raced up the runway, engines thrumming in perfect synch as it lifted off.

Nolan stood outside GNR Avionics' front door, OPSEC be damned, and watched the plane gain altitude and bank to the west. At one thousand feet the Baron exploded, a macabre spectacle of fireballs and burning fragments of fuselage, tail and wings. Nolan stood speechless in horror until the debris hit the ground. He sank to his knees, unable to breathe. Sirens rent the predawn darkness. Horror gave way to anger and then grim resolve. He stood back up and reentered the building.

"What was that?" Hecker asked, still wrapped in a blanket. A look at Nolan's face told him the worst.

"The plane exploded. Either there was a bomb on board, or they shot it down. Use the phone. *Use the phone!*" Nolan kept walking, determined to see Marmot blown apart even if it cost him his life as well.

Kaili and Eck rushed into the reception from the hangar. "Bob, what happened? What's wrong?"

"They blew up the plane. My family's dead," Nolan said as he strode away.

Kaili said something to Eck in Mandarin and then spoke in English. "Put your hands where I can see them."

Nolan whirled around, hand already on the butt of his Glock. If Kaili wanted a gunfight, he'd give her one. But Kaili had her pistol pointed at Hecker. Hecker had shed the blanket and had a phone in his hand.

"Do it! *Do it!*" Nolan shouted.

Eck pointed an M-4 at Nolan's midsection. "Drop your weapon," he said in good English.

Nolan chambered the Glock, determined to kill Eck or die trying. Instead he fell to the floor, five thousand volts to the worse as Meng applied a stun gun to the back of his neck.

Kaili's weapon was in Hecker's face. "Drop the phone."

Hecker turned his upper body to shield the phone but Kaili was too quick for him. As he turned the device on, she drove her Glock into his throat. Hecker dropped the phone and clutched his wounded trachea as he spat blood from the reopened wound.

Kaili picked up his phone. "Talking under a blanket is a game for children," she said before turning around to check on Nolan and her prize. Nolan lay face-down and unmoving. She removed his weapon and satphone.

Eck and Meng followed their boss to where Marmot still sat bound and gagged in the middle of an empty span of oily concrete. She removed his hood and her men unlocked his restraints. The gag remained in place. "Nolan's family is dead. He's unconscious. The IED will explode at 6:00 unless Nolan deactivates it. We leave now for the San Antonio airport cargo warehouse where your people claim to have hidden the NEMP. When it is loaded on my plane, Nolan will turn your timer off. Do you have any questions?"

Marmot shook his head.

"There are two groups we need be concerned with," Kaili continued. "I will speak with the Americans. You will speak with Weeks and explain the necessity of us reaching the warehouse alive, otherwise you will be blown apart in fifty minutes. If you say anything out of the ordinary to Weeks, I will hand you over to the Americans. If anyone attempts to rescue you, my men will kill you. Are we clear?"

Marmot provided one slow nod.

* * * * *

GNR AVIONICS BUILDING AND THE WHITE HOUSE

Kaili spoke in low tones. "I held up my end of the bargain. Nolan left the recording of my interrogation in reception. Before the six o'clock deadline, I will persuade Nolan to disarm Mr. Love's explosive device and—"

"He just saw his family disintegrate before his eyes," Payne said. "If you think Bob Nolan will do that, then you know him less well than I'd hoped."

"That is my concern. We will drive to the civil airport. My charter jet lands at 5:45 a.m. We will load unspecified cargo onto the plane. I assure you the United States will be most happy to see it disappear."

"This is the nuclear device the North Koreans supplied to Higher Love, isn't it?"

"The details do not matter," Kaili said. "Simply focus on the realities of an election year. If anyone smuggled a weapon of mass destruction into the US heartland, the voters would abandon the party in power even if the weapon was discovered prior to use. I am providing a favor. What I require in return is your security detail remaining at arms' length. Minutes ago, Mr. Love conducted a similar conversation with his people, and Higher Love will not attack provided everyone behaves as I have described."

"I agree to your terms," Payne said. "We can provide a helicopter and have you at the San Antonio airport in fifteen minutes."

"That is a generous offer, but our preferred arrangement is via ground transportation. The critical path is not defined by minimizing travel time, but whether we can restore Nolan's cognitive functions."

"Oh, brother," Payne said. "Take note of the following phone number and dial it if you run out of options ..."

* * * * *

Kaili walked Marmot out to the consulate's Volkswagen and eased his naked body into the backseat. The two MSS officers dragged out a limp Nolan and shoved him in. Eck sat between the two antagonists and Meng drove. Kaili worked her phone, texting like a madwoman.

* * * * *

Hecker, able to breathe at last without spitting blood, sat exhausted on the same couch he'd occupied since arriving. The Q-Group found him there minutes after the China delegation had departed. After one look at his bloodied bandages and pale complexion they called for an ambulance. The EMTs found Hecker dehydrated and stuck a saline drip into one arm while they transfused another pint of blood into the other.

"You look like five miles of bad road," quipped one medical technician. "Don't you worry, there's a first-class hospital on the base. We'll be in Wilford Hall in a jiffy."

"No hospital!" Hecker wheezed. "Take me to airport. Bob Nolan. Call General Payne."

The Q-Group special agent in charge recognized Payne's name and approved the airport transfer. Well before the ambulance reached

SAT, he'd have tracked down the retired general's number and learned what to do with the bloody DEA man.

* * * * *

Nolan awoke with excruciating pain in his neck radiating up through the base of his skull. It hurt even to move his eyeballs. His vision came into focus and he saw a sign for the exit to San Antonio International Airport in two miles. Why was he headed there? Then the realization hit him: his family was dead. Nolan looked to his right and saw Eck staring back. Kaili was in the front passenger's seat. The third person in the backseat was Dave Marmot.

As Nolan's hearing returned, he could make out a few words. "What did you just say?" he asked Marmot.

"I said you disarm this bomb poking a hole in my back and I'll make you a wealthy man."

Nolan went for his throat, but the MSS officer easily held him at bay with one hand. With the other he displayed a weapon.

"What, you're going to stun me again?" Nolan asked. "You don't have time."

"No, but I'll shoot you in the testicles if you don't stop."

Nolan desisted and sat back. What was he worried about? Everyone would die in the next twenty minutes anyway.

Kaili gave instructions in Mandarin based on the map on her phone. The man at the cargo complex gate waved them through after checking the license plate. The Passat drove down a long row of airfreight forwarders as the stars faded with the arrival of the dawn.

Nolan wondered whether his dead family could sense his pain and if they knew how much he wanted to kill everyone who had harmed them. Maybe their souls would fuse in the afterlife and bright, comforting light would replace his anguish. Right now, he'd settle for nothingness, just an end to his torment and self-loathing.

They pulled into a warehouse and someone slid the door closed behind them. The overhead lights came on and they stopped next to a white pickup. Perched over it on the twin tongues of a large forklift was an olive-green case about three meters long and maybe one- and one-half meters high and two meters wide. Nolan was indifferent as to the contents.

What was much more interesting were a handful of East Asians with AK-47s and a tall white male in mirrored wraparounds standing next to pudgy William Weeks with the Brillo pad hair. Nolan smiled. *He would bring the walls of the temple down upon them all.*

Kaili walked around the Passat and opened the door for her former paramour while Weeks and a pair of the SF OD-A team fussed over

Marmot. Nolan looked at his watch: 5:50. He left the backseat without resistance while Love's handlers studied the duct tape holding the SLAM in place.

Kaili gently touched Nolan's elbow to pull his attention away from the men struggling to defuse the SLAM. "Bob, in the crate is a North Korean nuclear electromagnetic pulse bomb with a yield of thirty kilotons. If you don't disarm your bomb it will vaporize the NEMP. The blast will kill everyone in San Antonio and maybe much farther away. That is at least one and one half million people."

"I don't care," Nolan said.

"I see wires," someone called out. "Two ... no, three wires under the duct tape. Oh, hell, there's a timer here too, and a detonator. We've got less than eight minutes!"

Dave Marmot, American Caesar-in-waiting succumbed to a panic attack. "Get it off! Get it off me!" he shrieked, struggling in the grasp of his soldiers.

The gate rolled up, and Tony Johnson strolled in. "Good to see you again," he said to Kaili. "We never finished our conversation." He nonchalantly aimed his tricked-out pistol at her.

Nolan realized that Johnson didn't give a damn whether he lived or died either. He found it disquieting that his own nihilism mirrored that of this subhuman.

"We'll take the NEMP if you don't cooperate," Weeks said.

"You won't get very far," Nolan replied. "Every gun in the Southwest is outside this warehouse."

"Wait!" Kaili said. "Bob, look at my phone."

Nolan idly confirmed that his holster was empty. His head was clearer; at least he wouldn't die with a migraine. "What is it? A UFO video or a Bill Burr standup clip?"

"No, it's Ying Sheng. Your son. Look at your little boy." Her features softened as she implored him.

Nolan wanted to slap the look off her face, but instead he forced himself to glance at the screen. Damned if there wasn't a grinning Eurasian toddler, the spitting image of ole Bob. She swiped once, twice, three times and it was clear that even Photoshop couldn't have created these wonderful portraits. He had a child in the world. There was something good still out there.

"Shame he'll grow up an orphan," Johnson said. "It'll take more than one hundred fifty thousand to pull your ass out of the fire, Nolan."

Something snapped in Nolan. "I'll do it, but only if this man dies," he said. Weeks nodded.

Two subsonic rounds from an AK dropped Johnson with clean headshots. The torturer's sunglasses came off and Nolan reveled in his dead-fish eyes.

Kaili pulled out Hecker's confiscated phone. "Does this help? The phone you gave Hecker?"

"Oh, not really," Nolan said. "I'll need wire clippers, a small Phillips screwdriver and scissors, and Mr. Potato Head to lie on his stomach and remain still."

"Not so fast," Kaili said. "I want the NEMP in the back of the pickup and the keys to the vehicle. Mr. Love takes a ride with us and Bob disarms the device once the crate is loaded and I'm onboard the jet."

"We have less than five minutes," Weeks said.

"So, you'd better move."

CHAPTER THIRTY-TWO

MOURNING GLORY

SAN ANTONIO INTERNATIONAL AIRPORT

The sun was up and it would be another scorcher with blue skies and nary a breath of breeze. For those with nothing to live for, it was a great day to die.

Nolan sat across from Marmot, who had acquired a pair of pants and deck shoes. The silver duct tape around his middle was still his most appealing fashion accent. Kaili directed the white pickup out of the cargo complex and to a sizeable commercial aircraft. A pickup truck with a set of steps mounted from the bed up over the cab at a forty-five-degree angle offered cabin access. The belly of the aircraft lay open with a cargo conveyor angled upward into the bowels.

"What, the People's Republic of China uses MD-80s to fly its senior spies around?" Nolan asked.

"It is a COMAC ARJ21 prototype mid-range commercial jet, designed and built in China," Kaili huffed.

"It looks like a high-altitude delivery platform for an EMP that wipes out the US power grid, but maybe that's just me."

"I am not suicidal and you are delusional if you think that China would indulge in first use of nuclear weapons against any state, much less the US."

The forklift's arrival ended their repartee. Meng, Eck and two ground crew supervised the offloading of the crate and its placement on the belt up into the belly. Nolan told Marmot to climb onto the open tailgate and lie face down.

As Nolan began, the LED blinked 2:31 … 2:30 …. 2:29—the inexorable march of entropy and the end of the universe. He was tempted to stare at the flashing red light until they all died. Then he realized that he so hated the people who had ruined his world that he wanted Dave Marmot to live. He'd be a tyrant who killed millions and oppressed hundreds of millions more, but that was the wakeup call that America needed. *My gift to the people of America—the people who elected those who took it all from me—is to allow this psychopath to survive and perhaps rule.*

Nolan briskly clipped the wires, opened the back of the SLAM, disarmed the internal timer, removed the detonator and stopped the doomsday clock with thirty-two clicks to spare. He finished by ripping the duct tape off Marmot's back and holding the SLAM aloft like a newborn. "He's safe," was all Nolan said before handing the device to one of the humorless SF soldiers.

William Weeks and his Higher Love acolytes hustled their man to one of the two sedans that had pulled up while Nolan had worked. He looked at the five Special Forces operators bearing AK-47s and wondered if one would shoot him five times, or if each would take a single shot a la firing squad. Instead the men turned and climbed into the vehicles and raced away. *Probably had a plane to catch.*

Kaili stood beside him. She'd applied perfume— Opium, Joanie's old scent. That woman never missed a trick. "We're cleared for departure."

"I'm many things, but not a traitor. I'm staying."

"What about Ying Sheng?" she asked.

"I do want to see him, but not by flying on an airplane carrying a North Korean nuke intended for use on the US. Next month, let's find a safe place to meet in Asia. I very much look forward to playing with the little fellow." Nolan surprised himself with his sincerity.

"Just no numbers station tutorials, Bob."

"Well, not until he turns five."

She touched his chin and he looked down at her face. Kaili had applied concealer over the bruises from Johnson's slaps and cleaned up her bloodied lip. She was gorgeous and had her bedroom eyes on. He felt her press paper into his palm. "I wish you peace." Then she turned and climbed the steps without looking back.

Nolan looked down and saw a handwritten telephone number with a local 210 area code. His eyes filled and he heard, rather than saw, the pressure door lock closed. Tears poured down his cheeks as the repressed pain flooded over him. He was tired, oh so tired.

A sunburned man in coveralls approached. "Let me give you a ride to the terminal, buddy. You look like you've been through the ringer."

Nolan passively followed him into the airport services pickup supporting the staircase. Behind them, the big jet's engines increased in pitch and it rolled out onto the taxiway, number one for takeoff. Kaili stood over the pilot and copilot and said, "On authority of President Liu, amend your flight plan to Caracas. En route you will declare an emergency and divert to Havana."

If the Americans were weak enough to allow the NEMP to leave, then they were weak enough to tolerate it in its new home two hundred and thirty miles from Miami. Castro had a spare SS-20 intermediate-range ballistic missile and a launcher. China's technicians could marry the NEMP to the delivery vehicle and, should the day ever come, put it to use.

* * * * *

HIGH FLYERS CLUB, SAN ANTONIO INTERNATIONAL AIRPORT

Nolan had run out of tears by the time the truck stopped out front of the same private passenger terminal he'd stepped out of less than twenty-four hours ago. Somehow, he still had his wallet though Kaili had taken the satphone. His rucksack with his cash and laptop was back at GNR Avionics.

Hecker watched a broken man shuffle through the entrance into the artificially lit gloom of the lounge.

Nolan sensed a friendly presence and after his eyes adjusted, picked out Hecker and his rebandaged neck. Nolan walked over, cheeks and shirt still damp.

"I'm sorry," was all Hecker could whisper before he too started sobbing. Grief for Bob's loss intermingled with Hecker's fear for his wife and son, and a torn trachea made for uncomfortable tears.

"Why are you here?" Nolan asked.

"For some reason, the Feds didn't arrest me. There are two G-men behind me until my charter flight arrives. I get a free ride back to D.C. You fix this?"

"No, I didn't."

Hecker's face brightened. "Here's something you might like." He produced Nolan's burner. "Why don't you look up a good book online?"

Nolan shook his head in wonder at the recollection of Hecker's theatrics in GNR's reception. He didn't know how he felt about the US government or Love, but he knew he was through killing. He unlocked the screen and saw missed calls from Payne. But first he called the number that Kaili had given him.

* * * * *

HIGH FLYERS CLUB AND WILFORD HALL SURGICAL CENTER, LACKLAND AIRFORCE BASE

"Special Agent Denzel," said the voice on the other end.

"This is Bob Nolan. Is there a message for me?"

"Does anyone want to speak with Bob Nolan?" the FBI man asked.

Nolan heard a babble of familiar voices and a tussle for the phone. Ryder's voice came on. "Took you long enough. Your family was worried, but I kept reminding them that you're indestructible."

It took Nolan a moment to respond. "I saw the plane explode. I watched you die."

"We lost two good men, but no Nolans. Delta operators out of Fort Bragg grabbed us in the dark before we boarded. Sergeant First Class Earl Gerard volunteered to join Pasan, and paid with his life. You may remember Earl: he was one of the two who took Teller down in Shan State. Whoever did this will learn that SEALs have long memories."

"I'm sorry about your friend. Tell me about my family."

"A surgeon examined and cleaned Mei Ling's wound. She'll need a muscle graft, but she'll be fine. Bert has a cracked rib, busted teeth and a dislocated jaw but he's standing next to me and smiling to beat the band. Joanie, well, Joanie's crying again. She's probably thinking about the life insurance money she'll have to reimburse."

Nolan didn't think he had more tears, but these came from another source and trickled from the corners of his eyes. Hecker handed him a tissue.

"Walk me through the Delta rescue," Nolan said.

"The FBI had the private area of the airport staked out. Through their NVGs they saw someone sneak away from the Beech just before Pasan took off. They didn't know if the person was with you or against you and didn't want to spook the pilot and queer the deal. The Feds took infrared photos of the fuselage and undercarriage, both on the ground and in the air. They were fuzzy, but there appeared to be an anomaly near the tail. The information went up the chain and Payne greenlighted a Delta snatch team to act. I'm not as sharp as I should be, and six sneaky bastards got the drop on the Burmese and me."

"So why allow the plane to take off at all? Why not tell me my family was all right? I've gone through hell."

"I can't answer that," Ryder said. "When are you coming back to Lackland?"

"Right after I speak with Payne and find out what's up," Nolan said. "Tell everyone I'm fine and that I look forward to seeing them more than they can imagine."

"Oh, it'll be a hugfest for sure."

* * * * *

HIGH FLYERS CLUB

"El Patron?" Hecker asked.

"Possibly," Nolan said. "He has the motive and the expertise. But he would have had to work fast."

"Not really. He knew you were headed to San Antonio and the Cartel will have people here."

"What about our friends in government? Maybe not everyone was happy releasing Marmot and wanted to goad me into doing their dirty work."

"That's harsh, but believable. What about Miss China?"

"No, it's not her style," Nolan said. "She keeps family out of it." But he wondered if the dynamic was different now that Ying Sheng was on the scene. "Can you tell your minders that we need a car to Wilford Hall at Lackland AFB? I need to call Payne and square the circle."

"I'm on it."

* * * * *

HIGH FLYERS CLUB AND THE WHITE HOUSE

"What games are you playing?" Nolan asked. "Why didn't you tell me my family was safe?"

"You need to calm down," Payne said as gently as he could. "First, I didn't know if Delta had managed to stop your family from boarding. I only received confirmation during a phone call with Yu and I passed along the contact number you eventually dialed. Next, I tried your satphone and no one answered. Finally, I left a message on your cell. Did you expect me to paint the news on a water tower and hope you'd read it when you drove by?"

"All right, all right. I'll need to think through this, but it could have and should have taken less time. Who planted the bomb?"

"You tell us. Your MSS lady friend and Higher Love top my list. You have any other candidates?"

"A couple. Please let me see the reconstructed bomb once the crash site investigators are done. Every bombmaker leaves a signature, and I need to find out who he was."

"No, you need to cool off," Payne said. "I had the AG's office track your bloody path across the country. I reviewed their report and recommendations with POTUS. You're out of the woods unless you do something else stupid or violent."

"Out of the woods? There's a shoot-on-sight order out on me and I'm standing in a public place."

"We canceled it an hour ago. Now it's a simple BOLO, and no use of lethal force unless provoked."

"Thank heavens for small mercies," Nolan said. "But I'll still end up in jail."

"You'll get a free pass on Weill's murder. You didn't pull the trigger, Paolo Dozier had gunshot residue on his body and the slug didn't come from your gun. If asked, you were a hostage alongside Weill and were lucky to survive."

"OK."

"As for the Russian, you weren't present when Chumakov's girlfriend injected a lethal amount of Fentanyl. By the way, the Russians at the embassy seem to blame Gregoriev and Chumakov's secretary, so you're off the hook with Putin."

"Thank you."

"The shootings at the Mokara were all in self-defense," Payne continued. "We have it on CCTV. Insurance will cover the blast damage caused by the late William Tanner's placement of the IED. Did I miss anything?"

"Quite a bit, but no more murders spring to mind."

"On your side of the ledger, you need to keep your mouth shut, stay out of sight and spend your golden years tending to your family courtesy of the stolen bin Laden funds. Remember, keep a clean nose or the syringe that OD'ed Chumakov might be retested and your fingerprints discovered."

Nolan wanted to drop his phone in the trash bin and take a long shower, but the filth covering Payne reached all the way to Texas and was of the type that didn't wash off. "What about my family? Hecker? Ryder? The two Burmese security guards?"

"Same rules apply. We have something on everyone and no desire to use it on anyone."

"Tell me why Marmot was allowed to escape."

"First, we didn't have the means to arrest him without a nuclear holocaust. Second, we have footage of Kleinwort confessing to high treason and naming Marmot as HL's leader. We'll round up his one-downs all weekend and he'll be taken into custody after the Sunday morning talk shows finish."

"Where's the president on all this?"

"As far away as the spin merchants can take him," Payne said.

"I have to hand it to you. While I thought my family had died, instead of telling me otherwise you were busy orchestrating another perfect whitewash. Except I still face Randy Dozier, who's sworn to kill Sam Hecker's and my families. And Frank Coulter is on the loose in San Antonio. Can I expect assistance in either area?"

"We're hell-for-leather chasing the narcos. Coulter goes back to his mountaintop later today. What you do in your spare time is no concern of mine."

"Goodbye, General."

"So long, Bob."

Hecker shuffled up. "Car's out front," he whispered.

"We're getting away with it," Nolan said. "All of it. They're sweeping the whole thing under the rug."

"What about Don Randy?"

"We have to take care of him on our own."

* * * * *

HIGH FLYERS CLUB

Dick Burge held the door for his older, angrier and more hungover companion. "Looks like your son's flight is twenty minutes late. Come in, cool down and have some coffee while we wait." Their two FBI guards were deployed front and back.

Burge and Coulter headed to the barista's station when Coulter stopped in his tracks. "Do you have a weapon?" Coulter asked.

Burge saw where his friend stared. "We're under guard. If you pull a pistol, they'll shoot you."

"Do you have a weapon?" Coulter repeated.

"Yes, after last night with the Special Forces OD-A team still on the loose, I thought it prudent to—"

"Hand it over."

Burge complied. Nearby civilians made a hole and hurried from the geriatric racking the slide.

Oblivious to the incipient pandemonium, Nolan helped his injured friend shuffle toward the exit. They were less than ten meters away—a hipshot that Coulter could make in his sleep. Bystanders scrambled and a woman screamed. Instincts took over and Nolan grabbed Hecker by the shoulders and shielded his friend with his body.

"Federal officers! Drop your weapon or die!"

Either Coulter didn't hear or didn't care. The first round struck the hero of the counterinsurgency in the Congo in the left shoulder, staggering the old man. He still had Nolan—pathetic Bob Nolan—in his sights. *One shot, just one shot would be all—*

The second bullet entered Coulter's body under his left armpit, punctured his left lung, severed the aorta and pierced the right lung. He dropped his weapon, sank to his knees and pitched forward onto the floor. More people shouted and screamed, and the room filled with armed men, both uniformed and in plainclothes. One of their FBI minders hustled them outside until they were safely in the car and away.

* * * * *

WILFORD HALL, LACKLAND AIR FORCE BASE

Hecker felt like the best man with a nervous groom as they passed through security and were directed to Mei Ling's room. "Everyone will be happy to see you," he whispered to Nolan. "Don't worry about it."

As they were about to enter, Ryder exited alongside Arkar and Maung. A round of handshakes and thank-you's followed, and Ryder announced that they were headed out for Mexican food before crashing at a nearby hotel.

As Ryder's banter with the two Burmese heroes faded down the hallway, Nolan paused outside the room. "Go ahead, open it," Hecker said.

Nolan eased open the heavy door and slipped inside. He took a few steps and froze, relieved beyond words to see his loved ones all in one place. "I put you all through hell. I'm sorry," was all he could muster before Bert embraced him with a light touch.

"I'm glad you made it, Dad," he managed out of one side of his swollen mouth.

Nolan stepped back and beamed at his son. "Tomorrow we'll have an oral surgeon work on your teeth. Can you chew enough to eat dinner?"

"I've got a mouth full of dental wax. But earlier I managed sludge through a straw. It tasted like crap and I'm still hungry."

"There's a Wendy's down the road. I'll go buy a double order of chili and a Frosty. Would that work?"

"You bet, but I can do it myself," Bert said.

"No, you three stay indoors and out of sight. Just look after your sister and mother."

Joanie opened her arms and they hugged.

"I missed you," Nolan said.

"No, you didn't. When you're on an operation you don't think about anything but work."

"I miss being with you. Can I come back to Singapore with you?"

"Is this before or after you go to China to visit your new son and the spy-whore?"

Nolan winced.

"And any other surprises I should be aware of?" Joanie asked.

"I didn't know anything about this. I've had no contact with that woman in two years."

"I wish I could believe you, but you also said you didn't have sex with her."

"It was a crazy time," Nolan said. "But I lied to you. I didn't want to lose you and—"

"Listen to yourself." Joanie walked to the window and dabbed at the corners of her eyes with a tissue.

Nolan turned his attention to his daughter. "Hi, honey. How are you?".

"By some miracle, still pregnant," Mei Ling said. "Bruce regained consciousness and should survive now that the infection is under control. I'm flying back to San Francisco tomorrow."

"Don't you need a muscle graft?"

"I can do it there and rehab alongside Bruce."

"That sounds like a plan, honey. I can cover all your medical expense—"

"I have insurance and Bruce has money. I don't want or need anything from you."

Mei Ling's harsh words disheartened Nolan. She saw his distress and added, "I'm glad you're OK, and I understand why you do what you do. But you have to consider the impact your actions have on other people, starting with your family."

"You're right. I resigned earlier today. I'm through."

She looked away. "We'll see."

"I understand. Do you mind if I come out to California and spend some time with Bruce and you?"

"Don't you have somewhere you need to be, or someone to hide from?"

"I do have one last piece of business to take care of. You see the fellow standing over there with the bandaged neck? He's my good friend Sam Hecker. Sam's based in Washington and is still with the DEA. We have one loose end we need to tie up. It might take a week or a month. In the meantime, it probably makes more sense for you to stick together, and for Travis and his men to be nearby as well."

Joanie's voice dripped with incredulity. "You mean it's not over yet? There are still people out to kill us?"

"Maybe," Hecker whispered. "But this time the FBI and national law enforcement agencies are looking for these men as well, so we're not on our own."

* * * * *

"The administration won't publish the story of Russia's tampering," Nolan said. "It's too messy in an election year. They'll duck the partisan flak, kick the can down the road, and hope their woman wins."

"And what if Ginger wins?" Hecker asked. "With Russia's backing and our silence, it will be a near thing."

"That's if the Russians don't succeed in tampering with the vote counting machines. I heard about it on the flight down."

"Jesus. What will you do?"

"I'll leak all of it," Nolan said. "Let the press have it and see what happens. But before I do, I'll speak with Payne and ask him what the president plans to do. I'll offer them the chance to make things right, but don't hold your breath."

CHAPTER THIRTY-THREE

SOUL SURVIVOR

SUNDAY AUGUST 21: THE WHITE HOUSE TO LACKLAND AIRFORCE BASE

"Marmot gave us the slip," Payne said. "He's still at large."

"I thought you had the bust lined up for live TV?" Nolan asked.

"We were too clever for our own good. We arrested William Weeks in a silver wig and platform shoes as he stepped off a private jet in Santa Fe. Marmot was never onboard. POTUS specifically asked you to go online and find him."

"Satisfy my curiosity. What will the administration do about Russia's interference in the election?"

"Let's let the domestic policy experts handle it."

"That's a horse crap answer," Nolan said. "The people need to know."

"It's over your pay grade, soldier. Let it go and get back to work."

"I'm sorry, but I'm unavailable. I just saw my family for the first time in two years, and I look forward to catching up on lost time. Both of my children are recuperating from wounds suffered as a result of my actions. You can pull up someone else from the Abyss org chart to run your search."

"Let's see ..." Payne said. "Ah, here's the file. Joanie Nolan ... vehicular homicide in Novato at a self-storage unit ... second-degree murder on Zax Peak Road ... first-degree murder at Mandalay Winery. Bert Nolan ... second degree murder on Zax Peak Road ... three counts of first degree mur—"

"I'm done working for blackmailers with no moral compass."

"Moral compass? Who are you to lecture me on morality, and how dare you impugn the leadership of this country!"

"I'm through talking," Nolan said. "I've taped every phone conversation we've had. Leave us alone unless you want those recordings uploaded onto the internet." Nolan hung up, shaking with impotent anger. He hadn't had time to record everything or upload anything, but Payne couldn't know that.

* * * * *

LACKLAND AIR FORCE BASE TO THE WHITE HOUSE

Payne spent less than a minute fuming before his cell rang again. He answered with caution and listened to a subordinate.

"The FBI intercepted a phone call from Randy Dozier, the Medellín Cartel boss. He's in San Antonio. From his conversation, one of his people planted the bomb on Nolan's aircraft. We have him and two others under surveillance. Do you want them arrested?"

"No, ignore them and cease surveillance. Dozier is a confidential informant on a matter of national security."

"Do you want me to notify Nolan?"

"No, I'll do it. You can also withdraw security around the Nolans. There's no longer a credible threat."

"Yes, General."

* * * * *

WILFORD HALL

Nolan returned from his Wendy's run and handed Bert two chilis and a Frosty. In his absence, Hecker had collapsed and now occupied the hospital room next to Mei Ling's. Ryder sat outside, concern etched onto his tired features with his left hand clenching his right wrist to minimize the shakes.

"Do you realize there's no security?" Ryder asked by way of greeting. "I don't think there's even a cop in reception."

"When I left there were two men outside Mei Ling's room and another in the parking lot," Nolan said. "All FBI from the looks of them."

"Precisely. Then Hecker went down and we had a merry runaround until the medics determined he hadn't had a cardiac seizure. He's as out of shape as I am. I peeked outside and found the hallway abandoned."

"This isn't good. What about Delta?"

Ryder snorted. "They bugged out yesterday morning before sunrise on their Ghost Hawks. We're like Davey Crockett and Jim Bowie at the Alamo. I put Arkar and Maung in a cab to GNR Avionics. If we're lucky, they'll scavenge a pistol and maybe your ruck without getting arrested."

"For all we know, Wilford Hall is miked," Nolan said. "We need to be elsewhere to plan our next steps. We should go for dinner—I doubt Payne will send men to kill us so soon and in public. I warned him I had recordings of our phone conversations should something happen to my family. Randy knows that Hecker and I were at Lackland but not that my family survived. Tomorrow we'll work out a way to sneak my family out of town under cover."

"We can leave Arkar and Bert behind if they have weapons. Otherwise, we all stay put."

"That's it from me. I'm exhausted past the point of thought. I'll ask an orderly to put a cot in Mei Ling's room and I'll shower and crash. If you're wise, you'll do the same. At eight o'clock, let's meet for dinner and plan our next steps. Hecker and I have to kill Randy. That means I'll need you three on guard duty. After what you did to his men in California, Randy will be coming for you and your family as well."

"I'll wait for the Burmese and rack out in Hecker's room," Ryder said.

* * * * *

THE RIB HOUSE, NEAR LACKLAND AIR FORCE BASE

Maung drove the reclaimed stolen Accord. GNR Avionics was oddly vacant, with the only human activity at the north end of the airfield concentrated at the crash scene three-quarters of a mile away. Ryder sat next to Maung while Nolan occupied the backseat alongside the weapons and ammunition. Nolan found a Glock 19, a more compact version of the Glock 17 he'd used to good effect. He felt numb after six hours of sleep that a corpse would have envied, but he inspected the weapon nonetheless. Nolan loaded a round in the chamber: he wanted all sixteen chances if he had to draw.

"Take the next left and then another left," Ryder said. "See the neon sign with the pink pig? The Rib House has the best damned BBQ in San An-tone."

Maung parked in the farthest corner of the lot, the fading light rendering every object in shades of gray.

Three doors opened on the Accord and the men exited.

"Stop," Nolan hissed. "You see that man coming at us?"

Through the gloaming a Caucasian with big forearms, a melon-sized head and light hair hugged two giant bags of food. He paid them no heed and stopped next to a SUV with tinted windows. The driver's side door opened, and a man jumped out to run around and open the back door. Inside, Nolan saw movement and maybe a flash of gray before the carryout man dumped his bags and blocked the view.

"Everyone back in the car! Follow them, no lights. They're with Higher Love. I recognize the forklift driver from this morning at the airport. He's the one who loaded and unloaded the EMP."

Ryder took the driver's seat and Nolan sat up front while Maung sat in the back and loaded weapons.

Ryder eased out behind the blacked-out SUV, lights doused as well. "Who'd a thunk it—Mr. Love is a fan of the Rib House too."

"I'm not positive, but that may have been him in the backseat," Nolan said. "Maybe he hunkered down with someone who was tipped off ahead of a raid. If he's in between safe houses, picking up food en route makes sense."

At the junction of Old Highway 90 West, the SUV eased into traffic. Ryder gave it sixty meters and a two-car lead before turning on his headlights. "At night with only one vehicle, we have less than a fifty-fifty chance of maintaining contact and remaining undetected," Ryder said. "One missed stoplight and we're done, and if we come too close, he'll make us. I say we drive up to them, note the plate and phone Payne. I'm tired of getting shot at anyway."

Ryder jumped a stale yellow light to keep up, then mercifully the next light flipped red and the SUV stopped one car ahead of them.

Parked off the side of the road was a food truck with the service window area bathed in intense LED white light. A smattering of patrons waited, including a young man with a string tank top and a distinctive tattoo. "Pull over!" Nolan said. "That's Don Randy's boyfriend."

The light turned green. "I can't follow both," Ryder said. "Which one?"

"Turn right here, before he's out of sight."

Ryder jumped a lane, earned an angry blast, and turned right. Romero kept walking, oblivious to his pursuers.

"Pull over here," Nolan said. We can grab him."

"If we take him and he doesn't tell us where El Patron is, will you pull his fingernails out?" Ryder asked. "If not, stay calm and let's find out where he's headed. He has food for at least three, so Don Randy must be there too. Someone has to tail him on foot in case he ducks in between houses or makes a run for it. I'll follow in the Accord. If he gets into a vehicle, we may have to leave you. What do we do?"

Nolan was halfway out the door. "Use Signal to text. Big Brother is listening to our voice comms. If you find a medium-height, tanned rich Latino with a George Michael stubble and lots of bling, it's Don Randy. It's a kill mission." Nolan shut the door and hustled down the sidewalk.

"Use the Starlight scope to keep Nolan in view," Ryder said to Maung. "I'm more concerned about losing him than I am with finding Don Randy."

* * * * *

Nolan pursued Romero on foot for two hundred meters, turning off a broader avenue onto a residential road. The place was bereft of pedestrians, the daytime high of ninety-five Fahrenheit having pushed people indoors to stay.

As the younger man turned up a driveway, he heard Nolan's foot crunch a piece of discarded plastic. Romero dropped thirty dollars-worth of carne asada and clawed for the pistol stuffed into the front of his trousers. In his haste to draw, he yanked the trigger and the pistol discharged into his groin. He shrieked and collapsed onto the driveway, blood gouting from the dumdum round. "Randy! *¡Los coños gringos!*"

Nolan rushed to the wounded man and kicked the pistol away as Romero writhed in agony. A big man with a long weapon appeared in the front doorway. Nolan fired twice in rapid sequence to no visible effect. The assault weapon rose to the guard's shoulder and Nolan dove to the ground.

A spray of crimson mist behind the Hispanic gunman's head and the sound of a high-powered rifle signaled that Ryder was on the job. The man dropped straight down. Nolan stayed put, waiting for Romero's moans and calls for help to draw out his prey.

In the dark up the driveway, muzzle flashes and huge reports signified a new shooter. Nolan was grateful for the dark as the rounds whizzed overhead. He pivoted to face the new adversary, but still couldn't see the target until the muzzle flashed. The next shot ricocheted off the pavement and sent a rock chip into Nolan's cheek, just missing his right eye. He looked up to see Don Randy at the edge of the light spilling from the front door, splitting his attention between Romero and Nolan. A five-round M-4 burst from behind knocked the don onto his stomach. Nolan dropped to his knees and stared hard at the fallen Colombian. Maung sprinted low to the ground to the front door, kicked the AR-15 out of the dead gunman's arms and entered the house.

"What's the sitrep? Ryder yelled from the street.

"Romero shot himself in the balls and the don is down, condition unknown. I have him covered. Maung is inside now."

Ryder jogged to Romero and fished the weapon off the ground. "Romero's conscious. I'll check around the side and back of the house. If Randy moves, shoot him."

Nolan's eyes followed Ryder's progress up the driveway beyond the prone Colombian. When Nolan sought to reacquire the don's outline, something subtle had changed. The right arm was no longer splayed but pointed straight ahead on the ground. Nolan processed the danger signal and dropped flat. Randy inclined his head, saw his enemy and fired once. Three feet of flame and another boom accompanied the discharge of the Desert Eagle.

For a long minute Nolan lay still and would have stayed that way except he'd have drowned in his own blood. The bullet had blown out a chunk at the top of his shoulder where the veep had bit down previously. His left side was paralyzed but his right hand still held the Glock. He looked up the driveway and saw that same right arm move. When he thought he saw a head lift up to take aim, Nolan fired twice parallel to the driveway and skipped one off the tarmac. Over the ringing in his ears, he heard a heavy weapon thud and looked up to see the don's head drop face down.

Maung raced out of the house and aimed his M-4 aimed at the fallen trafficker.

"Don't shoot him!" Nolan rasped. "Grab his weapon and get Ryder. We must leave."

Dogs barked up and down the street as Prosperity Drive sprang to life. Nolan reckoned they were a minute away from vigilante justice. Ryder appeared next to Maung and took in the situation. "I heard you talking. Are you hit?"

"In the left shoulder. I'm bleeding bad. Randy?"

Ryder flashed a penlight on the don. "Shot four or five times and looks like he's dead or will be soon." He pulled a blowout kit out the right front pocket of his cargo trousers and applied an absorbable gauze battle dressing to Nolan's wound, then positioned Nolan's right hand on top. "Press hard."

"I'm likely to pass out. Romero?"

Ryder went over for a look. "Bleeding, but alert. Finish him?"

"Leave him. Help me to the car."

Sirens approached. Ryder sprinted to the Accord up the block.

"Nolan, I'll kill your wife and children the Medellín way," Romero said. "Everyone you love, dead."

Maung walked up and knelt beside Romero's head. He unsheathed the big knife and drew it across Romero's throat. Maung said several phrases in Burmese, wiped the blade on Romero's tank top and sheathed it. "You no threaten my friend," he said as he stood up.

Maung and Ryder dragged a semi-conscious Nolan into the back of the Accord. Wilford Hall was six miles away and Ryder drove the backstreets at the speed limit. Nolan appeared dead on arrival.

* * * * *

MONDAY AUGUST 22: WILFORD HALL

Joanie stood by the head of Nolan's bed. "I swear I don't know whether to smother you with a pillow or hug you for killing the men who threatened our children."

Nolan's bleary eyes struggled into focus as the post-surgery anesthesia wore off. Hecker and Mei Ling also there, both sitting in wheelchairs.

"Once you knuckleheads found out where they were," Hecker whispered, "why didn't you call the DEA?"

"We didn't want any survivors," Nolan said. Two years or even two weeks ago, he'd have told Ryder to follow the national security threat and track the Higher Love SUV. But Nolan had reprioritized.

Bert walked into the room. "I just got off the phone with the San Antonio police. Randall Dozier died at the hospital last night. Romero Calderon was dead at the scene. Since Dad's awake, they'll want a statement from him too. There are officers outside."

"Let 'em wait," Ryder said. "They already lined up a self-defense angle and the captain said they won't charge us for leaving the scene given Bob's life-threatening injury."

Hecker looked at his phone. "The local DEA just texted to say they recovered enough unencrypted information from the safe house to obtain dozens of warrants. The North American operation of the Medellín Cartel will be out of commission."

"That means I'm flying to San Francisco to see Bruce," Mei Ling said.

"Maybe I'll go out west and hang with you guys," Bert said. "And get my face fixed."

"I'd love nothing more than for the four of us to spend a week or two together," Joanie said.

Arkar and Maung stood quietly apart from the festivities.

"Our friends from Rangoon are flying out to San Francisco to see their families and look after Zaw's funeral arrangements," Ryder said. "Before they go, they'll ditch the weapons and burn the Accord. I have three little people and one big person to visit in Nacogdoches, and will be on my way as well."

"And I'm flying back to D.C. tomorrow," said Hecker. "Sophie and C. J. are sorting out flights."

"Thank you all so much," Nolan said. "Make certain I have your banking details. Also, Travis bought eight burners this morning. He'll install Signal and start a group chat. They may come in handy one day," said the wounded spy.

"We know, we know," Ryder said. "It's just a matter of timing. The difference between *Lord of the Rings* and the Bob Nolan Circus is at least Frodo knew when to quit."

"When I'm better, I'll climb Mauna Loa and throw a Glock into the caldera," Nolan said.

"Not your wedding ring?" Mei Ling asked.

"Anything but my wedding ring."

ACKNOWLEDGEMENTS

Wife Lai Fan continues to encourage my writing career, correctly calculating that I spend less money sitting behind a desk researching and writing than in the emergency room being attended to for various injuries incurred in athletic activities incompatible with an almost-sixty-year-old body.

For the second book in a row, bestselling author, corporate speaker and entrepreneur Don Mann contributed his SEAL Team Six knowhow to the close quarter combat scenes. Given how many action scenes there are, poor Don had to read almost every page.

In April I lunched with R. E. "Bob" McDermott. Over craft beer and barbecue, he offered several insightful suggestions about the future direction of the *Countless Lies* series.

Jim Hawes, the model for Frank Coulter's appearance (but not actions), published a hit book in 2018 called *Cold War Navy SEAL: My Story of Che Guevara, War in the Congo, and the Communist Threat in Africa.* Check it out online.

Aneirin Flynn once again designed the book covers and created the electronic and print formats. His father David helped out in 2020, too.

Geoff Smith (via Reedsy) provided expert editorial advice, paring twenty thousand words along the way in compliance with my instruction to make the pages turn themselves. Sèphera Giron did an excellent job as proofreader.

Mark Leslie Lefebvre supplied ongoing advice and expertise to branding, marketing and sales issues.

Another big thanks to the readers of the *True Lies* blog on www.bradleywest.net. This is where I get the inspiration to research and fictionalize contemporary conspiracies.

Bradley West
February,   2019

ABOUT THE AUTHOR

Explanations of conspiracies fascinate me, but only plausible ones. My fiction addresses various conspiracies or unsolved mysteries in what I hope is a believable fashion. With *End of Lies*, I moved on from MH370—with a brief detour to MH17—to address the election of 2016. I wrote the book in early 2017 before the most damning revelations came to light, but I'm leaving it as-is. Yet again, truth trumps fiction. *End of Lies* remains a work of fiction and isn't meant to be read literally.

* * * * *

I'm originally from Ohio but was always interested in living and working abroad, so I completed an undergraduate degree at Georgetown's School of Foreign Service. My first job after an MBA from London Business School lasted less than two months before my boss shipped me off to Singapore for a four-month project to keep me away from head office (rather than undertake anything momentous in the Far East). That short-term project is now in its thirty-sixth year. Along the way, I've been fortunate enough to live mostly in Singapore, but also logged many years in Hong Kong with stops in Kuala Lumpur, Bangalore and Colombo.

I live in Singapore, where I'm a keen mountain biker, former baseball coach and avid fisherman. I enjoy red wine, dark chocolate and raucous friends around the table. If you'd like to connect, I'm on Facebook under Bradley West, Author or visit www.BradleyWest.net for the *True Lies Blog*, information on other conspiracy thriller novels, more background on the author and an opportunity to own two eBooks plus a deep dive exclusive examination into the origins of Covid-19. (*Spoiler: It's not all China's fault.*)

Bradley West

A FAVOR TO ASK: PLEASE LEAVE A REVIEW

If you have a few spare minutes, please post an *End of Lies* review on Goodreads. Honest reviews help readers choose from millions of similar books. It's the principal way independent authors of eBooks differentiate themselves from the pack. Even reviews that aren't four or five stars establish credibility, particularly when the reviewer shares specific criticisms. Constructive suggestions also help new authors improve subsequent novels.

Amazon is the 800-pound gorilla in this space and their ranking algorithms weight reviews more heavily than actual sales (which are easily padded, especially for lower-priced eBooks). A review there would be welcomed and can be cut-and-pasted from Goodreads (plus add a title).

My Facebook author page is www.facebook.com/bradleywest.net, and I welcome your comments and contributions.

Thank you very much for reading *End of Lies*, and a double thank you if you find time to write a review or two.

Dark cure Chapters 1-4

Keep reading for an exciting excerpt from Bradley West's 2020 *Dark Cure: A Covid Thriller*, the first installment of the *Dark Plague* trilogy.

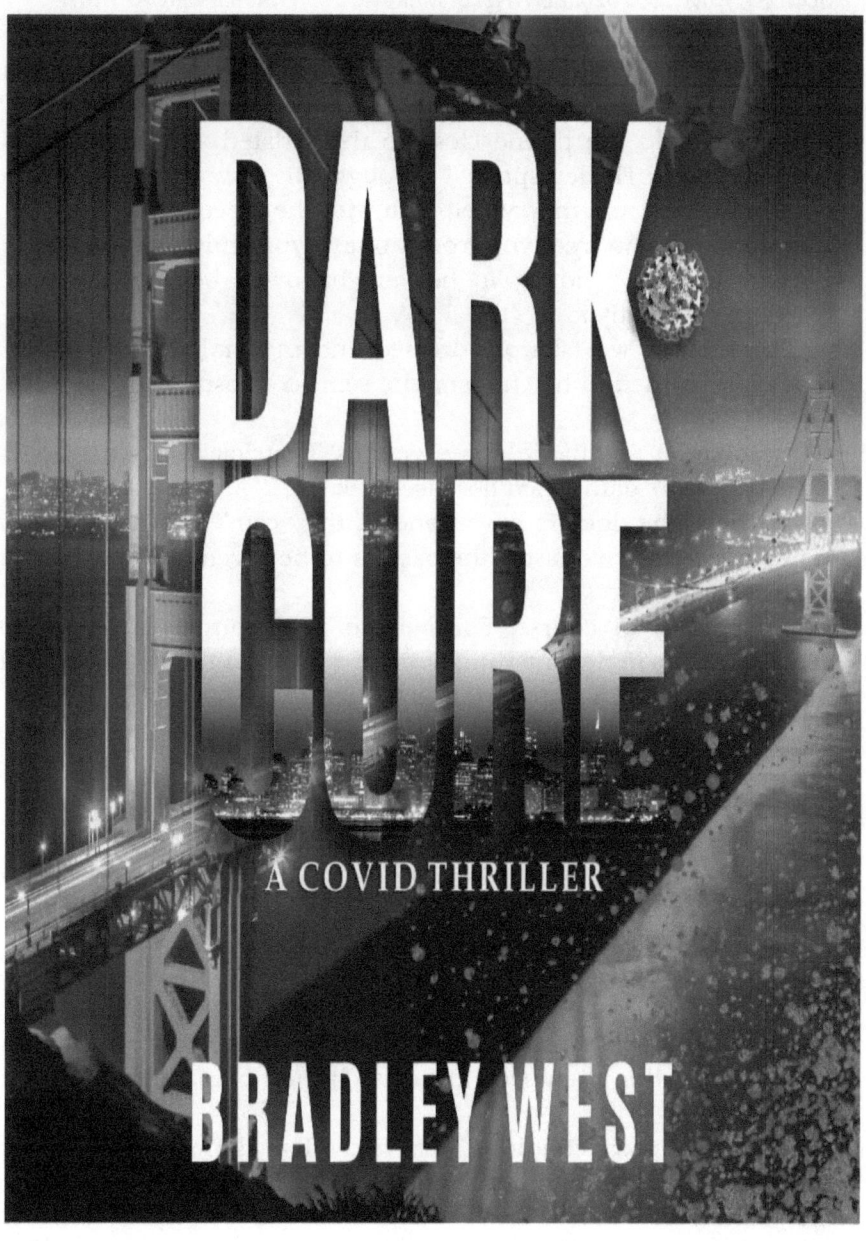

CHAPTER ONE

DEATH'S DOOR
MONDAY, JUNE 29, 2020: KENTFIELD, MARIN COUNTY, CALIFORNIA, NIGHT

The priest divided his gaze between the woman next to him and her intubated daughter behind the window. A masked and shielded ICU nurse held the phone close to the sedated woman's head and nodded. Father Healey spoke. "Through this holy anointing may the Lord in his love and mercy help you with the grace of the Holy Spirit. May the Lord who frees you from sin save you and raise you up.

"Our Father, Who art in heaven, hallowed be Thy name; Thy kingdom come, thy . . ."

The mother was sharply dressed and in her late forties. Rosary beads intertwined in her fingers, she semi-collapsed and clutched the priest.

"Stephanie! Stephanie! Stay with us!" Patricia Maggio gasped as rivulets of tears dampened her facemask.

"Patricia, the doctors have done all they can," Father Healey said. "They need to move fast if the baby is to be saved. Let me finish my prayers."

"Of course, of course. Forgive me." Pat composed herself as a hospital staffer in decontamination attire entered the ICU observation room and pressed a clipboard into her hands.

"Please sign or initial as indicated. This is for the emergency caesarian."

"Stephanie wanted to contribute her organs. Are those forms here?"

"No ma'am. Covid-19 damages the lungs, liver, kidneys and heart. We can't accept donated organs. I'm sorry."

Pat signed the papers unread and the orderly hustled away. The priest restarted the Lord's Prayer from behind his unported N-95 facemask. Two twenty-something adults, a woman and a man, dashed into the room and pressed their noses to the glass to view their sister and spouse. After a few seconds to catch their breaths, they looked to Patricia.

"She's in critical condition," Pat said. "They'll perform a caesarian. Sal's on his way with an experimental drug. We just don't know. Give me your hands and let's pray."

From inside Stephanie's room, an alarm sounded as the ECG flatlined. The nurse hadn't even dialed 3333 before the respiratory monitor triggered, too. Over the hospital intercom, a metallic voice announced the crisis. Within ten seconds, four nurses and orderlies rushed in and a nurse began CPR. Another med tech arrived with a backboard. The team worked with practiced efficiency: this was the third code they'd dealt with this shift.

To the shocked family members huddled on the other side of the window, it was a surreal experience.

The paddles came out and with the application of shock, Stephanie's body levitated off the backboard. Still no response. For the first time, those in the observation room could hear a raised voice from within her room. "Give me one milligram of Atropine." A nurse handed a syringe to the doctor.

Sal Maggio sprinted into the room rubbing sterilizing gel into his palms. "Pat, what's happening?"

"Her heart stopped! She's not breathing. Oh my God, my dear God, save my baby!"

Sal leaned into his wife so only she could hear him. "I have two dosages from Nancy." He turned to his daughter and son-in-law. "Keep the faith and comfort Mom. I've got something I have to do." He rushed out.

"You can't go in there or you'll get the virus!" Pat called after him. Sal didn't slow his pace as he headed for the ICU reception.

In a low voice, Father Healey recommenced reading Stephanie the last rites. He hoped he'd have enough time to make it through the Twenty-third Psalm before the code team gave up on the expectant women and her unborn child.

CHAPTER TWO

OUT OF BUSINESS
TEN DAYS EARLIER

FRIDAY, JUNE 19: SAN RAFAEL, MARIN COUNTY, CALIFORNIA, AFTERNOON

"Pulling the plug will be heart wrenching, but it's for the best." Chris Rogan, chairman of the board and senior partner at Bueno Capital, wore a big smile and a compulsory facemask that hung from one ear.

"We have enough money to fund at least two months' research," Sal protested. "That could lead to a breakthrough or buy us the time to attract a partner. Nafarm's worth a lot more with our team intact than in liquidation."

Rogan's smile faded as he stared at Sal with his dead eyes. "Nafarm exists only because Bueno Capital lent it three million dollars in April, secured against intellectual property and repayable on demand. We want our money. Have the wisdom to see things as they are, not as they were, or you wish them to be."

"Nafarm ran out of time," CEO Fraser Burns said to Sal. "At last count there are two hundred companies working on Covid vaccines, with four in clinical trials. We lost the race."

"We're adjourned." Rogan pushed back from the table and rocked in his chair to leverage his nearly three-hundred-pound bulk to his feet. "Fraser, you stay. I need to speak with you."

"I'll come to your office in a half hour," Burns said as chief operating officer Sal Maggio stormed out.

By the time Sal had climbed the two flights to his office, he had regained his self-control. He reminded himself that he'd never respected Bueno Capital in the first place. They'd bought their seat at the table because of the absurd valuation they'd placed on Nabokov Pharmaceuticals. In the crunch, "Boner Cap" behaved just as their Valley nickname suggested. Worsening his tachycardia by stewing over those assholes' decisions wouldn't help. He needed to move to damage control mode.

* * * * *

"I negotiated a three months' separation package." Burns had dialed up his friendly persona. "Rogan wanted to give you two weeks, but I reminded him that you held Nafarm together while I searched for a strategic investor. Everyone in the company owes you for the great effort."

Despite himself, Sal felt his blood pressure surge again. "Chris Rogan can stick his severance check up his ass. If he wants to pull the plug now, why did Boner Cap bother to lend us three mil six weeks ago? I haven't been home for dinner since and the research team sleeps in the break room. What do we tell Nancy and the others? We could be on the verge of something that Big Pharma would pay a fortune to see."

"None of that matters. We have ten days until the loan is due. Rogan read me the riot act: If we don't repay them in full, including default interest of ten percent, Bueno Cap owns all the company's IP."

A thought struck Sal and his demeanor brightened. "ChemFil is in expansion mode. Last week, one of their execs came in and said that they'd pay top dollar for our building and land."

Burns appeared to consider the idea, though it was always hard to tell what was going on in that undisciplined mind of his. With his swept-back chestnut hair, aquiline nose, strong chin and posh accent he looked like a CEO; he just didn't perform like one. Three years ago, Burns hadn't fooled Sal but the outsized salary and stock package had been too tempting to turn down even if it pushed Sal's retirement plans out a few more years.

"What? A specialty chems company wants to buy our building? What do they make, crystal meth?"

Sal managed a wry smile. "Yeah, that's what I thought. Seems they pivoted hard to supply hand sanitizer to Home Depot. They're scrambling for capacity."

"What kind of money are we talking about?"

"We bought the land and put up the building for two-point-three million. I floated that number and their COO said he could see paying a premium given the circumstances. Add that to the last of our cash and we can repay Boner Cap even with their loan shark's interest added on."

"Sounds promising. Maybe we should have been property developers instead of a biotech shop. Give the staff the lethal injection tomorrow." Burns stood and shouldered his tooled leather man-bag. "I have to dash to Minneapolis tonight for one last pitch tomorrow."

Sal nodded, but said nothing. He'd just fought the board for three hours only to see his boss fold the tent and delegate the dirty work. Two things were certain: That man had no pride, and Rogan and Burns had discussed more than employee severance packages.

* * * * *

As always, Nancy Jacobs was in her lab and dressed like a Liberian Ebola doctor. Sal waited ten minutes while she shed her hazmat garb and decontaminated. While he sat in the second-floor break room, his phone buzzed: It was Pat.

"Greg just called and he's at Mount Marin with Stephanie. They just admitted her with a 103° (*39.5C*) fever. They think it's the coronavirus, but it's Friday night so we'll have to wait until Monday for the definitive lab results. I'm worried for her and the baby. They made Greg leave. The earliest we can see her is nine o'clock tomorrow."

"Slow down, honey. Her immune system will fight it off, but I'm glad she finally got tested after feeling bad the last few days. Look, I have to go. Boner Cap did what I feared and shut us down and I think Burns was in on it. We can talk later. I'll be back late, so don't hold dinner." Sal disconnected as Nancy walked into the room.

Nancy wasn't much for small talk. Long hours and difficult working conditions had added years to a once-pretty face that no longer was on the youthful side of forty. "What is it, Sal? You look like your goldfish died."

He motioned her to join him at the table. "Stephanie's just been admitted to Mount Marin with Covid-19. She has a compromised immune system and we're worried."

"That's awful. I'm sorry."

"Thanks. He held the gaze of her brown eyes. "I wanted to meet because our investors decided to close us down by month's end. Given all the work your team put in, you deserve to be the first to know. Tell your people not to sign anything without speaking to me first. We may have a buyer for this building that could get everyone three-month packages, but I won't know for another week." He let out a ragged sigh. "I feel like I let everyone down."

"Sal, you put in more hours than anyone in the company. And this makes what I have to say easier. The protein cocktail failed the latest tests. Without human trials, we can't know for sure, but the vaccine could provoke a cytokine storm that overwhelms the immune system. My recommendation is to suspend the research."

Sal sat bolt upright. "Did you tell Burns?"

Nancy shook her head. "The last three monkeys died in the past three hours."

"So that's it? We're done?"

Nancy swiveled her head to confirm they were alone, then lowered her voice. "Not quite. I have a side project. Instead of a true vaccine, I developed an adjuvant, a drug amplifier that works with the general antivirals already in the market to treat a Covid infection by stimulating T-cells. I focused on remdesivir, a failed Ebola treatment."

Sal twirled his hand to urge her on.

"Well, I can't be sure—if we had another month and six more monkeys and I'd know for certain—but there's been a promising gain of function for one of the prototypes I synthesized. The only problem with this new drug—I've called it 896MX—is that the two main ingredients other than remdesivir are expensive and scarce. If you give me another week, I can produce a small sample batch."

Sal stood up, leaned over and kissed Nancy on the cheek through his mask. "You're a lifesaver. If you need anything, let me know."

CHAPTER THREE

PRESENT TENSE
TEN DAYS LATER

MONDAY, JUNE 29: KENTFIELD, CALIFORNIA, NIGHT

Barb Maggio embraced her mother in the observation room. In the adjacent room, the code team worked on Stephanie. A hand pulled blackout curtains across the picture window and blocked their view.

Pat broke free from Barb and pounded her fists against the tempered glass. "Stop! Wait! That's my daughter!" Father Healey and Barb rushed to Pat's side and helped her to a chair as her legs gave way. Pat's hunched shoulders heaved with wrenching sobs. After twenty seconds, she composed herself and pulled out her phone.

Stephanie's husband, Greg, made a couple of false starts to help his mother-in-law, but in the end did nothing except wear a pained expression. Like many people with Asperger's, strong displays of emotion unsettled him.

Father Healey was also out of sorts. In this time of sickness, he had many parishioners to comfort. Barb sensed his impatience and said, "Father, please go ahead. We'll let you know what happens." She pulled a granola bar out of her bag, pushed her mask down and took a bite either from nerves or the munchies.

The priest shook his head. "I'll stay until we hear from Sal."

Greg scrolled through his phone, standing a socially distanced six feet and an emotional lightyear away. Pat pulled out a compact to fix her tear-stained make-up, her mind elsewhere as her daughter lay next door, alive or dead she knew not.

Sal walked back in with beads of sweat on his forehead. He binned his latex gloves.

"They closed the curtains five minutes ago," Pat said. "You need to—"

"—It's okay," Sal interrupted. "I just saw her. She's stabilized and they've prepped her for surgery. At the least the baby should be all right as the doctors determined he was without a blood supply for less than a minute."

"Praise be to the Lord," Father Healey said.

"I gave the trial drug cocktails to Dr. Turney and he said he'd add one to the IV drip," Sal said. "If Steph survives the caesarian, maybe she has a chance."

Pat was back in tears, but this time with joy. She hugged her husband and he gestured for Barb to join their embrace. Greg stood to the side, uncertain whether this was a Maggio-only group hug or a more inclusive act. After a pause, he walked up behind Sal and put his awkward arms around the trio.

* * * * *

Tom Petty sang that the waiting was the hardest part. Barb's live-in boyfriend Jaime Gonzalez had joined the three Maggios and Greg for the longest two hours of their lives.

Folksy Dr. Turney poked his head into the room. "Stephanie is in the recovery room with weak but stable vitals. Her fever's broken, which is miraculous under the circumstances. You have a new family member as well. He weighed in at five-and-a-half pounds and we'll keep him in the neonatal ward for a couple of days while we wait for test results. Based on how well his lungs work, he should be fine. Is the father here?"

"That's me," Greg said. "Steph wanted to call him Tyson." He managed a nervous smile.

"Congratulations. Follow me downstairs for a mountain of paperwork."

"Sure," Greg said, now sandwiched in a non-CDC-authorized hug from his in-laws while Barb and Jaime shared one of their own.

The doctor surveyed the Maggio clan. "You all look like I feel. Everyone go home, have a belt of Buffalo Trace and get a good night's sleep."

Before the physician left with Greg, Sal managed an aside. "Did you give my grandson the second dose?"

"No, I didn't. He was born fever-free and breathes well. We swabbed him and will run a CAT scan tomorrow to check out his lungs, but it doesn't appear that he has the virus." The chubby doctor reached into his pocket and pressed a vial into Sal's hand. "If we need it, I'll call you. It's too early to tell, but it may have been a silver bullet." Dr. Turney gave Sal a close look. "You're a persuasive man, Mr. Maggio. I look forward to reading the results of the clinical trials when they're published next month."

* * * * *

The call had come at 4:57 a.m. Fearing the worst, Sal had answered wide-awake. Now it was 5:45 and Nafarm's parking lot was awash in rotating red and blue lights. The fire was out and the only structures standing were steel girders and the partially collapsed external walls. Two ambulances were parked with occupied twin gurneys behind the open doors. The EMTs minded their phones as they awaited instructions.

Sal shook his head as the sunrise illuminated the ghastly scene. How in the hell did their offices burn down the morning of the ChemFil closing? That was two-point-five million dollars down the Suwanee. And where was Nancy? Her cell was out of service and no one had picked up the landline. The cops were on their way to her house, but he knew that she hadn't made it out when he spotted her car in the parking lot. He stared at the two gurneys. *Nancy Jacobs, loyal to the end.*

A touch on his elbow startled him. It was Fraser Burns, hair wet from the shower. Sal was irritated that he wasn't wearing a facemask. "What in the hell happened?" Burns queried.

Sal flared at the accusatory tone and stifled an impulse to punch his ex-boss. "Let's find the fire chief and hear it from him. And put on a mask." At the very least, he'd have a witness to whatever Burns might say or do. Burns pulled out a used flimsy mask and struggled to get it to stay on in light of an elongated ear loop.

The chief didn't mince words. "The building went up too fast and burned too hot to be an accident. I've called in the arson investigators. With at least two dead, whoever lit the match faces a murder charge." He returned to confer with his firemen in their fluorescent-striped uniforms and grime-streaked faces behind full face shields.

"Who was in the building?" Burns asked. "It should have been empty."

"We had a contract with an outsourced security company that ended June 30," Sal said. "The night watchman's last shift was supposed to end at six o'clock this morning. And I hope to hell I'm wrong, but I suspect the second person was Nancy Jacobs. She worked a lot of late nights and often slept in the office. That's her car over there."

"Why on earth was she here?" Burns asked. "Didn't you fire her along with everyone else?"

"Nancy chose to work out her notice as long as the lab was intact. She was doing her best to find a cure even to the end."

"Whatever for? You told me the day after the board meeting that her team didn't have any saleable IP."

"She was working on a side-project that she thought showed promise. I gave her permission to keep at it until we handed over the keys later today."

"Did she produce samples or keep records? I want to see the details."

"All her lab notes and emails will be backed up in the cloud," Sal said. "I have no idea whether she had anything worthwhile. I'm still processing that it's her on that gurney over there. Can we discuss this later, please?"

"Mention that ChemFil is the lead arson suspect when you speak with the police."

"The CEO of ChemFil flew in last night from Vancouver to attend this morning's closing. They have decontamination cleaners coming in at noon. Why on earth would they burn it down?"

Burns gave him a look reserved for idiots and the senile. "So, they can buy the real estate for cheap and purpose-build whatever they want. Now we won't have the three-point-three million we needed to repay Bueno Cap." He clapped a firm hand on Sal's shoulder. "You wrap up here. I have to run."

"Run where? It's not even 7:15 and the fire chief told us to give the police statements."

"You can handle the bobbies. I have a tee time at 8:00 at Marin Golf Club. Potential new employer; don't want to disappoint. Let's speak early next week when we know whether the insurance will cover the loan shortfall."

"Our fire insurance lapsed at the end of June. If the fire started after midnight, we were uninsured."

"Ouch. Well, I'm sure you'll manage," Burns said before he ducked into his foreign sportscar. The dark blue Jag emitted a throaty growl as it sped off.

Sal was so upset by Nancy's death and Burns' possible complicity that on the drive home he rear-ended a garbage truck three blocks from home. The good news was the absence of damage to the City of Kentfield's sanitation wagon. The bad news was his Lexus required a tow truck and needed a new front end.

CHAPTER FOUR

MIRACLE CURE
MONDAY, JULY 6: KENTFIELD, CALIFORNIA, NIGHT

"A toast to Stephanie and Tyson!" Sal hoisted the champagne flute, his face flushed by the unaccustomed imbibing.

"To Stephanie and Tyson," the Maggio family and their partners intoned. They were seated at a long table on a deck with a stunning twilight view of Mt. Tamalpais State Park. The objects of their salute stayed seated as the newborn suckled at his mother's breast. From her chair, Stephanie beamed and lifted a glass of apple juice. Even that minimal movement left her sapped.

Patricia led the assembly in a brief, heartfelt prayer. She still couldn't believe Steph's miraculous recovery from the last rites a week ago to coronavirus-free and discharged earlier today and baby Tyson healthy as can be. They were truly blessed.

The smell of sizzling meat wafted from the grill while Sal eyeballed ribeyes. The Maggio clan passed plates up and down. When everyone had a steak, Sal presented his vision. "I worked on this plan for a long time and went into overdrive once the WHO declared a pandemic in March. Everyone at this table forms the core of what I'm calling the Manned Mission to Mars program, or 'the 3M' for short. I envisage thirty people settled in northern British Columbia on the 640 acres I closed on last week."

A masked Sal smiled at his audience's newfound attentiveness and took a seat at the head of the table. "I bought the land from absentee First Nations owners. There's a gravel road from the Alaska Highway to a dilapidated house, a barn, fallow fields, woods and two miles fronting the Kitsaw River. It's off the grid which means we'll use solar panels for electricity, and heat with wood. We can put up satellite dishes for internet and cable TV provided that those services continue. We'll need to clear the land and plant hay for horses and cattle and grow whatever foodstuffs the climate allows. The foraging should be fertile and the river's full of salmon every summer and fall. There are plenty of moose, deer and elk, too."

"Dad, what do you know about living off the land?" Barb asked.

"Nothing, but you have a degree in regenerative agriculture, and we'll follow your lead. We'll go one hundred percent organic at lower cost than if we relied on Big Ag for genetically altered seeds, fertilizers, and pesticides—substances which won't be available for very much longer in any event. The bonus is that we won't poison either the soil or our bodies."

"My work's centered on the Central Valley," Barb protested. "I know we won't be planting almonds or pistachios. How far north are we talking about?" Her partner Jaime filled her champagne flute.

"About fifty-eight-degrees north, three thousand kilometers from San Francisco. For the gringos, that's eighteen hundred miles. With global warming, it's the top end of North America's new temperate zone."

Greg had been watching his son struggle to coax milk from his wife's breast. The little fellow had fallen asleep, perhaps from exhaustion and not satiation. "Sal," he asked, "Is your plan to move once the travel restrictions ease? That might not be until next year."

"If you believe Pat's interpretation, we have witnessed the hand of the Lord and He doesn't like delays once He's made His will known. First the pandemic, my company burned to the ground, and now Steph's illness. We'll leave soon, before month-end in any event and I'll feed and house everyone through next spring."

"How will you get across the border?" lawyer Greg persisted.

"We'll cross somewhere remote at night. I already lined up a guide who operates east of the Rockies where Idaho and Montana meet Canada. He says that the security will tighten if people start to flee the U.S. as I predict. That's another reason why the 3M needs to get underway."

"I wouldn't trust a coyote," Jaime said. "In Mexico, they're crooks."

"With a former Marine sergeant by my side, I don't think he'll give us any trouble." Sal plucked at the Caesar salad.

Jaime exchanged a doubtful look with Barb who tonged another section of garlic bread onto her already crowded plate. Greg's expression was screwed in concentration as he considered the ramifications of illegal immigration, while Pat's eyes darted around the table as she silently beseeched everyone to just get along.

While her father processed a mouthful of lettuce, croutons and dressing, Steph offered her thoughts in a barely audible voice. "It sounds like you're serious, but I'm not sure you've thought things through. You want my husband to quit when he's one step below partner. Last week, Father Healey read me the last rites. I don't know when I'll be healthy enough to travel and Tyson arrived two weeks early. If Jaime's deported from Canada, he could lose his green card. Barb's NGO work requires high-speed internet which you said we might not have. This move is great for you, Dad, because you're rich and just retired, but not the rest of us." She slumped back in her chair.

Pat opened her mouth to speak, but Sal talked over her. "You're all grownups and you'll do what feels right," he said as his wife glared at him and topped up her Syrah. "You've heard me on this topic before, so I won't flog a dead horse, but this pandemic has shined a light on the fragility and unsustainability of the consumption-led, climate catastrophic pleasure dome that the U.S. created. Decades of underinvestment, too much debt and a dysfunctional political system have left our country—and the Western economic model—bankrupt. All it took was a single jump in hosts from animal to human to halt the world in its tracks—"

"Dad, you're beating that horse again," Steph said.

Sal carved out a piece of steak, charred on the outside and medium-rare within: It almost melted in his mouth. "After the next eco-catastrophe," he continued, "there will be no electricity or food once a solar flare takes out the power transmission and distribution grid, or Yellowstone erupts, or a tsuna—"

"Sal, enough already," Pat said. We've heard the doom-and-gloom story. We've read that dreadful *Deep Adaptation* article that upset Steph. It makes no sense to—"

"To what? Risk being deported from Canada if they catch us? It's not like we'd be dodging the Mounties all day. Where we're going is very lightly populated. Greg's the only one with a real career. The rest of you can get a job just like the one you left if you decide to come back. Greg, maybe you ask for an extended unpaid paternity leave, say for six months, to look after your convalescing wife and new child? By that time, you'll have a better idea whether Canada works for you."

Greg looked to Stephanie for support. She stared back, eyes pleading him to speak up. Instead, he said nothing and picked up an ear of roasted corn.

Sal continued his pitch. "I'm not asking for a lifetime commitment. I admit that my global outlook is pessimistic. But I'll take the financial risk and buy the motor homes, construction materials, tools and the first winter's food. You're responsible for your clothing and creature comforts. If I'm wrong about the state of the world, come back home in 2021 and view it as a long vacation. But if you sign on, you'll have to work like hell. We'll have limited time to become self-sustaining at the Thunderdome."

Jaime rolled his eyes. "The Thunderdome, huh? And I guess you've worked out a deal for Tina Turner to supply pig crap for our generators?"

"Yes, it's tongue-in-cheek, but I picked a cartoonish name for security. For my plan to work, you can't tell anyone. On this ark I'm Noah, and I approve all the animals. "

"Sal, your steak's getting cold and no one's eating," Pat said. "Please, can we talk about a weekend to schedule the baptism? If we'll be on the road soon, we'll need an early date with Father Healey."

* * * * *

Carla Maggio, the only child of Sal's older brother, greeted her uncle with an elbow bump. The masked duo placed their orders at the counter, then retreated outside to the shaded patio.

"You look a little haggard," Sal remarked. "These are busy times for a research biologist. Thanks for sneaking out on short notice. As I mentioned, it's important."

Uncle Sal was Carla's favorite out of her father's warring siblings. She had fond memories of his out-of-tune Springsteen singalongs with her and Steph as he drove them to-and-from their junior high soccer matches. That was more than fifteen years ago, and life these days was less joyful.

"How's Stephanie? Great news that she's out of the hospital. And little Tyson looks adorable."

"Her recovery's been miraculous. Those aren't my words, they're her doctor's. That's one of the reasons I came to see you." Sal stopped as their sandwiches arrived, bratwurst for him and a Mexican vegetarian wrap for her. In between bites, Sal briefed his niece and slid a padded envelope across the table.

"What's in here?" Carla asked.

"Twenty milliliters of the last of an adjuvant that Nancy Jacobs synthesized before she died. I hope you can reverse engineer what she called 896MX and make another batch. It could be a cure for Covid-19. You'll also find a thumb drive with all her emails, files and lab notes."

"Who owns the rights to this? Shouldn't they do the follow-up?"

"Normally, I'd agree with you, but last night I received an email from the CEO's law firm. He mismanaged the R&D budget and conspired with the VCs to pull the plug. In return, the board gifted him a million-dollar severance package that he bartered for Nafarm's intangible assets, among them drug formulations and research. The lawyer's letter directs me to hand over any drugs in my possession, plus papers and/or digital media. I wanted you to have this before I responded because Burns shouldn't have the sole right to these things."

Carla nodded. "Well, as it happens, I specialize in zoonotic coronaviruses. I'll just add what you have to the drug panel and run it."

"Don't put yourself at any risk. It's not worth it."

"As long as they can't trace it from you to me, you'll be fine. If it doesn't work, I'll keep it off the books."

"They may not be able to prove it, but they'll look hard at you." Sal looked over his shoulder in a survey of fellow diners' faces. He came up empty.

"Why? What did you do?"

"I hired one of Nafarm's IT people to wipe the cloud server after he downloaded Nancy's side project material. If he talks, I'm toast but he said he was headed to Mexico."

"Uncle Sal, you could end up in jail."

"I doubt it given today's world. That brings me to the second reason I wanted to see you. I bought a large property in British Columbia that should support at least thirty people. I'm recruiting a group to move up there maybe by month-end. I think Steph and Barb are in, along with their partners. We could use your skills."

"What skills? I'm a research scientist who studies viruses with the potential to jump from animals to humans."

"If what I gave you works, we'll need you to make more of it, maybe a lot more. We can't sit around waiting for herd immunity, not after Covid-19 almost killed Stephanie."

"I take your point." She leaned forward. "Don't tell anyone, but there's evidence that SARS-CoV-2 has mutated. The new strain is very virulent, maybe as high as seventy percent fatal unless detected within the first day or two of infection. Three days ago, we received lab samples from India and Bangladesh. Yesterday, we had a video call with the CDC, and they agree with our recommendation: The U.S. should enter a total lockdown with everyone confined indoors. As of this morning there are already confirmed Covid-20 deaths in Philadelphia, New Orleans and Oakland."

"Oakland? That's twenty miles away." Sal's voice was loud enough that other diners looked over.

"It was a shock to everyone. I have to get back to the lab. I'll give your trial cure top priority and let you know. I'll also mull over your offer to migrate to the Great White North. If it's to be self-sustainable, you'll need people who can farm, hunt, fish, log, build, fix things . . . it's a long list."

"I started out like that, but I had two problems. First, I don't know many specialists and even fewer I want to spend my life with. Short of taking out an ad for "Dentist wanted for Permanent North Woods Relocation," I don't know how to identify these specialists much less match up personalities. Second, I've been so busy trying to save my company, I spent my limited spare time working on things I could control, like buying the land and preparing the 3M's exit route."

Carla stood up and walked toward the parking lot. She turned back. "You realize that the idea of a sanctuary is flawed if you have the cure for Covid-20 or even Covid-19? People will come after you. To stay alive, you'll need a strong defensive plan and armed guards."

They walked to Carla's Tesla. "Email me when you finalize the people and their skillsets." She climbed behind the wheel of her bright red roadster.

"Does that mean you're interested?" Sal asked.

"I don't want to work with hazardous substances reporting to someone I don't trust. I expect my part of the lab to be loaded up with Covid-20 and we'll be locked down while we study it. That was the game plan with Marburg and Ebola, and lab staff died. I don't think anything's changed; if anything, it's worse since that woman became president."

"I'll see what I can do," Sal said. "We need you."

Carla nodded and pulled away.

As Sal merged onto I-580 West, he decided he would take a tougher look at his candidate longlist. His cell sounded and he took the call. "Hello, Fraser. I'm in the car."

Burns got straight to the point. "You must hand over the 896MX adjuvant as well as Dr. Jacob's emails and papers that you wiped from the cloud server and sign a new comprehensive non-competition agreement."

"I don't know what you're talking about. Where did you get that idea?"

"I'm at my attorneys' offices and recording this conversation. Earlier today I spoke with both Dr. Turney from Mount Marin and Father Healey from St. Agatha's parish. You need to consider what you say next, because I'll file a police report if you don't produce the stolen property by tomorrow morning."

"California is a two-party state, and you don't have my permission to tape this call so stop recording. Ask your lawyers to add a criminal defense litigator to your team. The arson inspector took my statement yesterday. His people were fascinated to learn that you purchased the company's research portfolio from Bueno Capital just days after headquarters burned down. Don't call me again." Sal hung up.

Sal's heart raced as he glanced at the speedometer and slowed down. It felt good to have told off that oily SOB. Nevertheless, his hands were clammy on the wheel and he wondered what unforeseeable events his actions might have triggered.

SEA OF LIES

For more *Countless Lies*, check out *Sea of Lies*, the 2016 best seller and first book in the series.

Flight MH370 disappears. Finding out what happened could ignite WWIII.

American, Russian and Chinese agents vie to discover the truth. Or bury it.

CIA cryptanalyst Bob Nolan finds the secret airstrip where MH370 landed. A beautiful Chinese spy joins Nolan on his quest, but will his new lover be his salvation or ruination?

The next eight days will see a war fought, a regime toppled, and lives upended as Nolan runs for his life, tries to protect his family, and unspools a dark web of murder and treason.

PACK OF LIES

For more *Countless Lies*, check out *Pack of Lies*,
successor of *Sea of Lies* and precursor to *End of Lies*.

Flight MH370 appears in Balochistan, Pakistan instead of on the seabed. A corrupt Malaysia Prime Minister, a devious CIA director and the secret forces behind Osama bin Laden's death conspire to thwart former CIA cryptanalyst Bob Nolan as he seeks the plane's fate.

Instead, he uncovers a devil's bargain with global terrorists, faces down the world's most dangerous hacker, and finds himself in the middle of the Taliban's attempted heist of nuclear weapons. In Sri Lanka, Nolan searches for proof of treason against a senior CIA officers while his ex-boss waits to kill him. Amidst the chaos, a sultry China spymaster entrances him while ruthlessly pursuing vengeance against his CIA colleagues.

Can Nolan discover the truth, or will it remain buried within the lies?

PRAISE FOR BRADLEY WEST'S NOVELS

Sea of Lies

"Crisp dialog drives non-stop realistic action across Burma, Singapore, Sri Lanka, China and Australia."

James Hawes, SEAL Team One
Cold War Navy SEAL: My Story of Che Guevara, War in the Congo, and the Communist Threat to Africa

* * * * *

"MH370's fate remains a mystery. This compelling and well-researched novel raises questions that require answers."

Dr. Dan Crosswell, Distinguished University Chair
in Military History, Columbus State University

Pack of Lies

"Starts off just weeks after the disappearance of MH370, with non-stop action torn from today's front pages."

John Carl Roat, SEAL Team One
The Terrorist: a SEAL Gone Bad

* * * * *

"Bob Nolan is the most unlikely and intriguing espionage hero I've ever encountered, equal parts uncanny intelligence, improbably sexual virtuosity and unlimited capacity for self-preservation."

DON D. MANN
New York Times Best Selling Author

Inside SEAL Team SIX: My Life and Missions with America's Elite Warriors

End of Lies

"West creates realistic characters and deploys them in an intriguingly complex plot. The result is an enjoyable, fast-paced thriller that I couldn't put down. "

RICHARD L. HOLM
Best Selling Author
The Craft We Chose: My Life in the CIA

* * * * *

"*End of Lies* provides compelling characters and meticulous research to deliver nonstop action. Just when you catch your breath, another showdown looms."

Howard Wasdin
New York Times Best Selling Author
SEAL Team Six: Memoirs of an Elite Navy SEAL

Dark Cure

"*Dark Cure* disturbingly imagines the near-future if Covid-19 mutates into a deadlier form. The writing is fast-paced and the plot fascinating."

DON D. MANN
New York Times Best Selling Author
Inside SEAL Team SIX: My Life and Missions with America's Elite Warriors